I0819173

The
FORTY-YEAR GRUDGE

BOOKS BY LIZA TULLY

The World's Greatest Detective and Her Just Okay Assistant

The FORTY-YEAR GRUDGE

LIZA TULLY

BERKLEY MYSTERY
NEW YORK

BERKLEY MYSTERY
Published by Berkley
An imprint of Penguin Random House LLC
1745 Broadway, New York, NY 10019
penguinrandomhouse.com

Library of Congress Cataloging-in-Publication Data

Names: Tully, Liza, 1956- author
Title: The forty-year grudge / Liza Tully.
Description: New York: Berkley Mystery, 2026. | Series: A Merritt & Blunt mystery; 2
Identifiers: LCCN 2025038657 (print) | LCCN 2025038658 (ebook) |
ISBN 9780593816806 hardcover | ISBN 9780593816813 ebook
Subjects: LCGFT: Detective and mystery fiction | Novels
Classification: LCC PS3602.R5318 F67 2026 (print) | LCC PS3602.R5318 (ebook)
LC record available at https://lccn.loc.gov/2025038657
LC ebook record available at https://lccn.loc.gov/2025038658

Printed in the United States of America
1st Printing

The authorized representative in the EU for product safety and compliance is Penguin Random House Ireland, Morrison Chambers, 32 Nassau Street, Dublin D02 YH68, Ireland, https://eu-contact.penguin.ie.

In memory of Esmond Harmsworth

The
FORTY-YEAR GRUDGE

CHAPTER ONE

No Thank You

When an invitation to attend a reunion of the Sarah Lawrence chapter of the Sigma Delta Tau sorority arrived in the mail, Aubrey Merritt, the nationally renowned private investigator, ran her eyes over it briefly and dropped it in the wastebasket.

"At least think about it," I urged.

She noticed me standing on the other side of her desk. "For god's sake, Blunt, what are you going on about now?"

"At least think about it," I repeated firmly. "You must have some old friends you'd enjoy seeing." I wasn't sure my boss *did* have any old friends. I hadn't met any of her friends, heard her talk about friends, or seen any sign of friends in the ten months I'd been working as her assistant. That was a problem, as I saw it. Her solitary life was likely one of the causes of her frequent crotchety moods, and as I reliably received the brunt of those moods, I was eager to find ways to ameliorate them.

She cocked her head at me quizzically. If I hadn't known her better, I would have thought the expression adorably puppylike. But she was never adorable. Her voice dripped with disdain when she said, "Are you seriously suggesting that I spend a weekend socializing with a gaggle of women I haven't seen in more than forty years? Who I didn't like much at the time and barely remember now? Why on earth would I do that? And why are you so eager to push it on me?"

"I'm worried about you," I said staunchly. "You've got circles under your eyes, and you're an absolute bear to be around, even more than usual. Gilby says you're not eating much—"

"Oh, so the two of you have been whispering about me, is that right?"

Gilbert Dixon was her cook, housekeeper, and occasional assistant sleuth. A big, fearsome-looking man with a big, fearsome-looking dog, he was as sweet a person as I'd ever met. We often hunkered together in the kitchen of the elegant Gramercy Park mansion where Merritt lived and we all worked, comparing notes on our employer. Both of us wanted to change her and knew we never could.

"Whispering, no. Talking, yes," I said. "You've spent the last week holed up in this office, getting surlier by the day. Gilby and I agree that you ought to be using this rare lull in our workflow as an opportunity to relax and unwind. Practice self-care. Get out and see people. Go to a play or the Met, take a yoga or Pilates class—anything to get your mind off crime and murder, and all the dark, depressing things you're usually thinking about."

Merritt drew herself up to her full height, and I reflexively drew back a step. She was only a few inches taller than I was, but she always seemed to tower over me.

"I'm surprised to hear you speak that way. You of all people ought to know that what I do isn't *work* to me. It's my vocation. I do it because I'm good at it and because it brings me a measure of satisfaction to impose a modicum of order on the moral chaos of our world. I don't want, have never wanted, to *get my mind off* it, as you so prosaically put it. In fact, I consider it a privilege to keep my mind *on* my work every minute of every day. And I expect the people I employ to do the same." A haughty, piercing look indicated that she meant Gilby and me. But mostly me.

"But, boss, when there's nothing to work *on* . . ."

"That's likely to change very soon!" she barked.

She was probably right. The Merritt Investigative Agency usually turned away many more potential clients than we had time to help. Our present inactivity was definitely unusual and therefore not particularly troubling. But that hadn't been my point.

"It's your spending so much time alone that Gilby and I are worried about," I said.

"Alone? I'm not alone. I often hear you and Gilby in the kitchen idly gossiping, and of course I have my drawings to keep my mind focused and sharp."

I glanced over at her easel, which stood beside a row of tall windows at the end of her long, book-lined office, a room I secretly loved, filled as it was with plush velvet chairs, her elegant Louis XIV desk, a scattering of Persian rugs, and numerous unusual artifacts, including carved masks and woven textiles from her travels to Africa and Southeast Asia, marble busts of Shakespeare, Freud, and Amelia Earhart, and (my favorite) the possibly four-million-year-old fossil of a primordial fish—a coelacanth—found off the coast of Madagascar and gifted to her by a man who signed himself *All my love, Harry.*

Scattered around the easel were about a dozen sketches she had ripped from the easel and tossed aside, only to start in on a new, presumably better, one. Her subjects were usually categories of some kind—human hands, for example. Or various species of frog.

Or different deciduous trees. Lately her passion had been New York City architecture, and the office floor was littered with charcoal sketches of the Empire State Building, the Guggenheim, Lincoln Center for the Performing Arts. One famous landmark after another rendered in clean, exact lines and precise detail. Her most recent subject, the New York Public Library, was sitting on her easel at the moment, every column and lintel accurately drawn, with one disturbing exception. Patience and Fortitude, the two magnificent marble lions that guarded the entrance, were completely out of proportion. They dominated the foreground, appearing to leer threateningly at the viewer. The slashing black marks with which she'd depicted them were positively frightening. It seemed the work of a disordered mind.

Your mind is already plenty sharp. It's your heart that needs attention, I might have said to her. But very few relationships can withstand that much honesty, and my relationship with Aubrey Merritt wasn't one of them.

"Observe, Blunt." Directing my attention to the drawing on her easel, she settled into an explanation. "We all think we know what we're looking at, but few people actually do. We see a building; we see four walls and a roof. If the building is famous and we've seen it enough times before, we might even be able to call it by its right name and say with confidence in what city it resides. But have we really noticed exactly what makes it so unique, identifiable? It's all the little details, their arrangements, their proportions, the emphasis the architect gave to one or another of them. A great building like this one has a character. It speaks to us about values, aesthetics, about its place in our lives, and it gives very clear signals about who its creator was."

She smiled slightly, pleased with herself, and I knew from that small, complacent smile that she was about to leap into her favorite subject. I wasn't wrong.

"Murder," she said, "is similar. Boringly similar in broad strokes but completely unique in others. The criminal can't help leaving his signature, however faint, just as an architect does. In the ways he attempts to hide what he's doing he paradoxically puts facets of his character on display. It's my job to discern those aspects of his personality he has unwittingly exposed."

She peered at me, not unkindly, but with a vexed expression, as if I were a problem she had yet to fully resolve. "Drawing is great practice for the investigative mind, Blunt. If you still seriously believe that you could be a successful investigator yourself someday, you would do well to hone your own observational skills. As we both know, there's room for improvement in that department. I know you have complained in the past about my being too critical of you, so let me add that I am speaking to you now with nothing but a kind desire for your betterment in mind."

I rued the day when I'd confessed that my dream was to eventually open my own investigative agency. Ever since then it had been a bad joke between us that all I wanted to do was steal my boss's trade secrets so I could run off and use what I'd learned from her to foolishly attempt to compete with her. That was not entirely untrue: I did, at one point at least, have that ambition. But my hopes in that regard were fading. Because for all my close observation of the famous detective at work, it was still unclear to me what exactly accounted for her success.

She freely admitted that she relied solely on "observation, logic, and psychology" to solve crimes. Which theoretically meant that any person in possession of eyes, a brain, and a heart ought to be able to do what she did. Yet so far I'd been unable to solve a single mystery either before or at the same time she did, even though I had access to the same information. I did suspect that on a few occasions she'd kept one or two critical details hidden from me on purpose, just to give herself an advantage. But that may have been my own sour grapes. In any case, she seemed to enjoy periodically reminding me that I was a rookie, implying that it would be a very long time, if such a time ever came at all, before I could be trusted to handle even the most basic little spousal-murder-to-collect-life-insurance case on my own.

I accepted the ribbing as the price I had to pay for working with a woman who, after three decades of consistently brilliant work, had assumed near-mythical dimensions in crime-fighting circles. In short, there was no better detective in all the United States to apprentice with. But increasingly it wasn't only personal ambition that kept me in her employ. Over the past year, there had been a fair number of truly magical moments when the two of us had got along famously, bantering like equals, our minds dancing together in true partnership—both of us, if I can be so bold, made a little better, a little smarter, by proximity to the other. At those times, and usually for several days after, I lived in a glow of happy fulfillment that I knew was more precious and affirming than anything I would be likely to experience as a sole practitioner.

Now I considered my options. The conversation about the reunion had not gone well. Yet I was unwilling to give up. Her stated reason for declining an opportunity that most people would find delightful seemed childish to me, nothing more than the thoughtless reflex of a woman who, for whatever reason, had made a needless, unhealthy habit of keeping to herself. (There had to be a reason, didn't there? I often speculated about what it might be.) As I'd already taken some heat for broaching the usually off-limits subject of her personal life, I decided to forge ahead and gain whatever progress might be possible. I pulled the invitation out of the wastebasket and read it out loud.

YOU ARE INVITED! PLEASE JOIN YOUR SISTERS AT THE FORTY-YEAR REUNION OF THE SARAH LAWRENCE CHAPTER OF THE SIGMA DELTA TAU SORORITY!

Where: The Muddy River Ranch, Pecos, New Mexico
When: Memorial Day weekend
Host: US Army Brigadier General Joan Battersea, ret.

Plus-Ones welcome. RSVP requested.

I placed the invitation flat on her desk, the words facing her, and made my voice very firm. "Absolutely no harm will come to your brilliant career or your charcoal drawings if you happened to spend a relaxing weekend catching up with your sorority sisters. And before you tell me you don't need a vacation, let me just point out that the stone lions at the entrance to the New York Public Library really do *not* look the way you've drawn them. They are not in proportion. They are horribly distorted. Since you pride yourself on accuracy, your mistake there ought to worry you."

Her eyes flickered to the easel.

Aha! I thought. *She's not sure. She needs to check the drawing to see if I'm right.*

I pressed my advantage. "With all due respect, boss, you would do well to take a few days off. You owe it to your clients to take care of yourself, if only so you can confidently maintain your own high standards. I may not know everything about the art of investigation, as you frequently point out, but I do know something about mental health." That was a brazen lie.

In the time it had taken me to speak those few sentences, Merritt had recovered her composure. With her usual cool complacency, she replied, "Good gracious, Blunt, just when I thought you were beginning to develop some professional dignity and rectitude, you descend to this insipid pseudo-counseling. As if, at the age of twenty-five—"

"Twenty-six," I muttered. I'd had a birthday last month.

"—you could possibly know what is best for *anyone*, let alone a person with almost four more decades of life experience than yourself. Let me reiterate, and I shall say it only one more time: I have absolutely no interest in sitting around among a bunch of aging women gabbing on and on about whatever nonsense occupies their minds. Their brilliant children, probably. Or, worse, their brilliant grandchildren."

Merritt herself had a grown son living in Los Angeles. He was her only living relative, as far as I knew. I wished she would talk about *him* a bit. Or talk *to* him once in a while.

I ought to have been deterred at this point, but I was not. I glimpsed another approach and decided to go for it. This would be my last attempt. "But wouldn't it be nice . . ." I said in a softer, more measured tone, "no, I mean, wouldn't it be *interesting*, from a strictly intellectual point of view, to observe how some of your sorority sisters grew and changed over four decades, and to what degree the arc of their adult lives does justice to the young women they once were? There are probably a lot of fascinating psychological insights you could glean from that experience to add to your store of wisdom."

"No, Blunt. It would be neither nice nor interesting. I'm sure it would be very dull. I would lose my mind from boredom. Now stop your shameless brown-nosing before you destroy whatever slim hope I have for your future. Go away. Leave me alone." She fluttered her fingertips in my direction, shooing me off.

I left her office in frustration. Aubrey Merritt was a truly impossible person to try to care about! It really wasn't worth the effort. Besides, she was right in one respect: Her mental health or lack thereof was none of my business. I was just there to do my assigned tasks (Monday through Friday, nine to five) while learning as much about the art and science of private investigation as I possibly could. Because someday I *would* start my own detective agency. And then we would see just how smart I, too, could be!

CHAPTER TWO

I'd Be Delighted

In early May, about a month after that fruitless conversation, I got married. Trevor and I, along with his mother, Zuzanna (mostly Zuzanna, actually), had been planning the event for almost a year. It was larger and more elaborate than I'd wanted, and I'd been a wreck leading up to it, worrying whether everything would go all right. But when the day finally came, it was gorgeous and perfect and everything we'd hoped for. Merritt and Gilby attended together. Merritt looked beautiful in a pale blue satin sheath, her blunt-cut silvery-white hair combed back smoothly from her forehead, little tinkling silver bracelets on her wrist, pale pink lipstick, and strappy silver sandals on her feet. Gilby, a six-foot-four-inch bodybuilder, wore a dove-gray suit that made him look even larger and more imposing than usual, though the lemon-yellow pocket square was a nice softening touch.

I assumed that Merritt hated being there and was attending only because it would have been the height of rudeness not to show up for my big day. I'd feared she would be sullen and miserable, but she made lively conversation with the other guests at her table, and even had a few dances with Trevor's great-uncle, who appeared to be delightedly entranced with her. I appreciated the effort she was making, even as I suspected she was counting the minutes until she could return to Gramercy Park, where, once again, we were very busy. Indeed, a few days after our contentious conversation, the cases had started flowing in again. I almost didn't want to take time out to get married. (Was I, too, a burgeoning workaholic?)

Trevor and I had a lovely two-week honeymoon at a little seaside hotel in Sicily, finding everything we needed to make us happy in the olive groves, the beaches, and each other. By the time I was back at work, I had completely forgotten about the Sigma Delta Tau reunion. Then, at lunchtime on the Thursday before the Memorial Day weekend, as I was bustling through the front door with Gilby's 150-pound bullmastiff, Sarge—a leash in one hand and a bag of take-out sandwiches in the other—I collided with a short, nearly bald, egg-shaped man in a mustard-colored blazer.

We both apologized profusely. Sarge sniffed the man's crotch. I pulled the mighty canine away with some difficulty and apologized to the man for that too.

When I looked up, Merritt was leaning against the open door of her office, watching the whole thing with a rare smile on her face. "Fitz, this is my assistant, Olivia Blunt. Olivia, this is John Fitzroy, husband to Joan Battersea, my oldest and dearest friend in the world."

Oldest and dearest friend in the world? Was this the Merritt I knew?

Mr. Fitzroy (aka Fitz) winked at me. "Joan and Aubrey were inseparable. You wouldn't see one without the other."

I almost blurted, *You've got to be kidding*, but thought better of it. The name Joan Battersea had rung a bell. I recalled that she was the host of the sorority reunion scheduled for the long holiday weekend that was about to begin.

"Joan will be delighted to hear that you've decided to come after all," Fitz said. He had the blustery, genial manner of a bon vivant. The windowpane pattern of his blazer and the big turquoise ring on his pinkie finger spoke of a refreshing panache.

"I'm looking forward to seeing her too," Merritt said with apparent sincerity.

"I don't suppose anyone but Joan and I ought to know why you're really there," Fitz said a bit uneasily.

"That would be best."

"Secrecy isn't my style, as you probably remember from all those years ago." He chuckled at his own garrulous nature. "But I suppose it's necessary in this situation."

"It's of paramount importance, Fitz."

"All right then. We'll keep it firmly under our hats," he said with a buoyant smile, his bonhomie easily restored.

When he was gone, I looked at Merritt blankly. "The sorority reunion? Really?"

She smiled sweetly.

"You insisted you didn't want to go! You said sitting around with a bunch of old ladies would be a waste of time!"

"What makes you think we'll be sitting around? This is a work trip. We've got a case to solve."

"We?"

"Naturally. There'll be a number of guests in attendance, and I'm going to need a second set of eyes and ears." She squinted at me critically, as if assessing my eyes and ears. Then she frowned, as if finding them unsatisfactory.

"But the reunion is this weekend," I pointed out.

"Correct. So we'll need to get a move on. Fitz is on his way to the airport now. He was in town briefly to oversee the sale of some fine art objects at Sotheby's. I need you to drop whatever you're working on and book us a flight to Santa Fe. Leaving tonight."

"This is so sudden!"

She gave me a flat look. "Try not to be obvious, Blunt."

CHAPTER THREE

Sweet Sorrow

When I got home, Trevor was in the living room yelling, "Oh no! Oh no! Oh my god!"

I stood in the doorway and waved my arms to get his attention. He stopped screaming and smiled.

"Nice day?" he asked in the sudden silence.

"It was okay, I guess. How about you?"

"Pretty good. I think I've got it finally. Want to hear it?"

"I think I just did," I said.

"So? What do you think?"

"Really good. You definitely had me convinced."

"Excellent!" He was clad in jeans and a Mets T-shirt, and his dark brown eyes glittered with excitement.

He limped into the kitchen, and I followed.

"Why are you limping?" I asked.

"I got shot in the leg. They added that to the script, so now when I chase the bad guy out of the house, no one expects me to catch him."

"Yeah, that makes sense. What's that on the side of your face?" I pointed to a red swelling on his cheekbone.

"Oh, that. No big deal. It'll fade."

"How did it get there?"

"Fight scene. A couple of punches connected. That's all. I'm fine."

"Aren't you supposed to have a body double for that?"

"Yeah, but . . . it's complicated," he said.

He obviously didn't want to tell me, and I didn't push. I faced my own hazards at work that I'd learned to downplay so as not to worry him, and I figured I owed him some space in that regard too.

Overall, I was very glad he had an acting gig. After his successful run as Bernard in *Death of a Salesman* last August had racked up a slew of favorable reviews, he'd been hoping to score a serious dramatic role on Broadway. For months he'd gone to one audition after another, but nothing had worked out. Then, just when he was ready to give up, he was offered a role in a limited series Netflix show filming in Manhattan. The role was bigger than anything he'd expected. He was playing the bookish adult son of a government official (actually a spy) who gets fatally shot by a supposedly random intruder (actually a hired assassin). Trevor's character witnesses the whole thing and is drawn into a dangerous plot that eventually uncovers not only the killer but also his father's shocking true identity. It was a really good role for him, and he was determined to succeed.

"Cheeseburger?" he asked, pulling the frying pan out of a cabinet.

"I don't have time."

He looked at me closely. "What do you mean?"

"I have to leave in an hour. I'm going to New Mexico."

"With her?"

Her was how he referred to my boss, Aubrey Merritt, arguably the most distinguished private investigator in America.

"We have a new case. We're flying out tonight and we'll probably be gone all weekend. I hope no longer than that."

"What about the showings?" he said.

I groaned. The lease on our tiny East Village apartment was up at the end of June, and for the last few weeks, we'd been scouring real estate websites, looking for a bigger place that we could afford. The opportunities were limited. Nevertheless, we had lined up three showings for tomorrow night, and we'd both been excited, hoping that one of the apartments would work out.

"Can you go and send me videos?" I asked.

"That won't give you a real feel for an apartment. What if the video looks great, but then we move in and you hate the place? No, I think we should reschedule. Both of us need to be there."

I shook my head. "We can't put this off. There are hardly any July apartments left. They're showing August and September now. You go and take videos. That will be good enough for me, I promise."

He shrugged, acting like he didn't care, but I could see that he was bothered. I'd gone on several work trips with Merritt since last summer, and each time I'd had to depart suddenly, leaving Trevor alone to either cancel plans or go places without me.

He opened the refrigerator door and stared glumly into its depths. "What about the party in Williamsburg Saturday night? And Sunday brunch with my mother at that new place on the Upper East Side? And the Memorial Day parade in Queens with your dad? Do you want videos of those things too?"

I drew back a step. It wasn't like him to be snarky. "Please don't be mad, Trevor. I don't have a choice."

"I know, I know." He closed the refrigerator door and turned to me sadly. "It's just . . . I was really looking forward to this weekend."

"So was I." I wasn't lying. I was truly disappointed to be missing the showings, the party, the brunch, and the parade. But I was also really excited about going on assignment with my boss. Whenever we traveled together, I performed actual investigative work, instead of the boring computer work that took up much of my day in the office. Sometimes Merritt even treated me like a partner: She would share her observations, ask my opinion, and bat around ideas with me. The truth was, solving mysteries side by side with Aubrey Merritt was just about the most exciting thing I'd ever done. But I didn't want to tell Trevor that, at least not at that moment. He was heading into a lonely weekend, during which he would have to explain my absence over and over to family and friends. Some of them would probably secretly wonder if our relationship was crumbling.

We looked at each other in silence for a few seconds, all these unspoken things hanging in the air between us.

"You're really excited about going, aren't you?" he finally said.

I nodded gently. "I am."

"Really, really excited?"

"You could say that."

He smiled a bit wistfully. "I'm glad you're excited, Olly. I'm glad you like your job." He wrapped me in a tight hug. "Don't worry. I'll miss you, but I'll be fine. Just make sure you look at the videos I send you so we can decide about an apartment."

"I definitely will, but if you don't hear from me right away, don't worry. I'm just busy with the investigation and I'll reply as soon as I can."

Wanting to demonstrate his complete support for my career, he checked the New Mexico weather report on his phone and made several terrible suggestions about what I ought to bring. Then he decided to help me pack, which meant that we spent about twenty minutes bumping into each other over and over in our tiny bedroom. Finally, to my secret relief, my duffel bag was zipped, and the Uber that would take me to the airport was waiting outside. With tender reluctance, we let each other go for our first weekend apart as a married couple. It was really very wrenching. Definite "sweet sorrow." But work was work, so I tore myself away, and the next thing I knew I was on a red-eye to Santa Fe with my duffel shoved into the overhead bin, that day's half-finished *New York Times* crossword puzzle on my laptop, and the austere Aubrey Merritt snoozing in the seat beside me, her silvery-white head grazing my shoulder with a casual intimacy that would have horrified her if she knew.

CHAPTER FOUR

False Advertising

Halfway through the flight, Merritt murmured, roused herself groggily, and sat up with a sudden jerk.

"Blunt. What are you doing?" she asked in irritated horror, as if it were my fault her head had been nestled on my shoulder.

I pointed to my laptop screen. "Learning stuff about the Muddy River Ranch."

Settling herself face forward in her seat, she straightened her silk shirt. "Well, what can you tell me?"

She was always asking me that. Whenever our work required facts, or any kind of general knowledge, it was up to me to provide it on the spot. I was always thinking ahead, trying to be ready for whatever question might be thrown at me. This was easier for me than it might have been for others, as I had been a fact-checker for an online media outlet in my previous job. I was used to doing research and could usually produce the desired nugget of information fairly quickly. Research was the one area in which Merritt afforded me a measure of respect, not all of which I actually deserved. At sixty-two years old, she resented technology as something that had sashayed into the world and impudently taken control of practically everything without asking her generation's permission. Having never taken the time to explore its benefits, she didn't fully grasp how quickly and easily Google, Siri, and ChatGPT brought knowledge to one's fingertips. I didn't see any reason to set her straight.

"I can tell you that the Muddy River Ranch covers twenty-three hundred acres of meadows, scrub brush, and forested hillside," I said.

The acreage astonished me. I simply couldn't get my head around it. I'd grown up in a little working-class 1930s house with a so-called yard about ten square feet, ringed for needed protection by a rusted chain-link fence, and I currently lived in an East Village apartment with a kitchen in which two people could not cook simultaneously. That one family could claim ownership of 2,300 acres sounded like a fairy tale to me.

"Go on," Merritt said.

"Let's see. How about this? Moving water is rare in New Mexico, which is why the ranch was named for the shallow, sluggish, rock-strewn Pecos River that meanders through the middle of it, twisting and turning for about three and a half miles." I was basically reading the screen now. "In this river live trout, rainbows, and browns." Knowing what trout were, I assumed the last two names also referred to fish. "The buildings consist of a ten-thousand-square-foot hacienda with seven bedrooms and nine bathrooms, a four-bedroom detached guesthouse, and a large stable with an office for the ranch manager. There is much to entice a guest—not only fishing, but also bridle paths, a shooting range, and a pool shaded by cottonwoods and willows. The lucky denizens of this enchanted corner of the world live in close spiritual harmony with the desert and its wildlife.

"I frankly doubt that," I ad-libbed with a snort.

"Just continue, please."

I kept reading. "Falcons and bald eagles soar overhead while coyotes, jackrabbits, and javelinas wander freely among the cacti and wildflowers."

"Javelinas?" Merritt interrupted.

I did a quick search. "A javelina, also known as collared peccary, is a medium-sized animal that looks like a wild boar." I turned my laptop to show Merritt a photo of four gray javelinas staring straight into the camera.

"Their eyes are very close together," she observed.

"They are not lovely creatures," I agreed.

I returned to the Wikipedia page and frowned at it thoughtfully.

"What's the matter?" Merritt said.

"This description is clearly biased. It mentions all those nice animals, but doesn't say a word about scorpions and snakes."

Merritt couldn't hide an amused smile. "Are you afraid you're going to be bitten by a diamondback rattler at my sorority reunion?"

"Of course not," I lied. "By the way, how do you know what . . . um, breed they are?"

"I visited Joan several times at her ranch when we were in college."

"And you saw an actual snake?"

"Oh yes. Many snakes. Diamondbacks. The most venomous kind. All between six and ten feet long and thick as a wrestler's forearm."

My stomach folded in on itself. "Really? Where did you see them?" I tried to remain calm.

"Well, one was coiled in the bottom of my bed. Between the sheets."

"Oh my god! That's awful!" I felt lightheaded and nauseated and wished I could turn the plane 180 degrees and fly straight home.

Merritt just laughed.

"Wait. Are you—?"

"Of course I'm kidding! Snakes don't sleep in beds! At least, not usually."

Relief flooded me even as a ball of anger clotted in my throat. "You shouldn't do that. It's not nice to scare someone like that."

"It's your own fault for being so gullible," she said a bit sharply, restating one of her persistent criticisms of me. Yawning, she leaned back in her seat. "How much longer?"

I checked the time. "About ninety minutes."

"If I fall asleep on your shoulder again, for god's sake give me a shove."

Maybe more than a shove, I thought. "By the way, when are you going to tell me what this case is about?"

"Patience. We'll be there soon enough. It will be better if you hear it first from the clients themselves. Less chance of distortion that way. By the way, Fitz and Joan are both lovely people. I sincerely hope you won't be so charmed that you believe everything they say." With that, she drifted off.

I leaned back, too, and tried to let the drone of the engines lull me to sleep. But when I closed my eyes, all I could see was a fat black rattlesnake coiled between the sheets at the bottom of my bed.

I was terrified of snakes. I'd had nightmares about snakes as a small child, long before I'd seen one in person, before the day my third-grade class was shepherded through the World of Reptiles at the Bronx Zoo. I remembered the incident only too well. Desperately needing to find an exit from the dimly lit maze of finger-smudged display cases, I'd allowed myself a tiny sliver of vision between the fingers of one of the hands clamped over my eyes. But I still managed to glimpse a long, oily body slithering along the bottom of cloudy plexiglass. I let out an earsplitting shriek and all but collapsed. It had been horribly embarrassing to be the only third grader in the school's entire history, so I was told, who had to be carried out of the World of Reptiles. This duty was performed by Mr. Driscoll, the nice science teacher. He sat me down on a bench outside and, as my anxiety waned, gently explained that I should not feel ashamed of my reaction. Evolution had apparently drilled the primordial fear of snakes into my *Homo sapiens* amygdala in an especially forceful and dramatic way, he said. This I should be grateful for, as it provided me with valuable added protection against one of mankind's most dangerous foes. He made me feel that the kindly deity called Evolution had given me, Olivia Blunt, a little something extra. I found myself drying my eyes and smiling. I even wondered if fear of snakes could be a secret superpower. Then, clearly satisfied with having fully exploited yet one more Teachable Moment in his students' lives, Mr. Driscoll took me to the snack bar and treated me to a soft-serve vanilla kiddie cone. (I would have preferred chocolate.)

Since that day I hadn't crossed paths with another snake, and had found solace in knowing that I lived in an environment rife with millions (literally) of disease-carrying rodents but mercifully devoid of snakes. I saw rats on the stairs, in the gutters, melting into walls, flattening their bodies to pancake width to slide under doors, disappearing like Houdini into cracks in the walls. New Yorkers were for the most part not terrified of rats. When one was caught on video dragging a pizza slice across subway stairs, and became a beloved internet sensation, I, too, smiled at the enterprising little critter. When another was caught standing on its back legs on a skateboard (as if it knew what a skateboard was for!), and was met with internet cheers, I added my own little clapping-hands emoji to the wave of New York City joy. The ease with which I coexisted with vermin was how I knew I was not a hysteric through and through. My phobia was specifically for snakes.

Now I had been spirited out of my comfort zone and set down in an alien territory in which my nemesis (Satan's emissary on earth) reigned supreme, and I mentally prepared myself for a personal challenge the likes of which I'd never before encountered. I was an adult now, I reminded myself, and I could handle the situation with aplomb. I would be brave and calm and would tell no one about my crippling phobia. I certainly would not admit it to Aubrey Merritt, who already thought of me as a lightweight. I would simply be very careful for the next few days, checking between the sheets each night before I climbed into bed, and always paying close attention to where I put my feet.

CHAPTER FIVE

The Muddy River Ranch

We drove through the gates of the Muddy River Ranch shortly before ten o'clock on Friday morning, a cloud of dry earth billowing behind our rented SUV.

The heavy carved door of the hacienda was opened by a forty-something woman with hay-blond, poufed-up hair. A wide-collared blouse strained across a big bust, tight jeans encased skinny hips, and pointy-toed ankle boots showed the smallness of her feet. The figure she cut was roughly that of an inverted triangle.

"Welcome to the Muddy River Ranch, Ms. Merritt. Aubrey, right? Can I call you that?" she said with a glossy, puffy-lipped smile.

"Actually, I'd rather you—"

But the woman had already turned her long-lashed eyes to me. "And you are?"

"Blunt. Olivia Blunt."

"Oh gosh. That's right. Aubrey's assistant. Fitz said you'd be coming too." She winked as if she knew a secret about me.

We were admitted to a grand foyer with adobe walls and a red-tile floor. There were several full-grown cacti in hefty earthenware pots scattered about and a chandelier that looked like an authentic wagon wheel hanging from the apex of a beamed and vaulted ceiling.

The woman introduced herself as Jenny-Lou McPhee, manager of the Fitzroy Fine Art Gallery in Santa Fe. "I've been with Fitz practically forever. I adore working for him. He's such a dear, sweet man."

I glanced at her left hand: no wedding ring.

"Who's at the gallery now? I mean, since you're here," I asked.

"We don't open until noon on weekdays. I usually come to the ranch a few mornings every week to help Fitz with paperwork."

Just then a long-haired, short-legged dog scampered into the room. It had white fur with black splotches, floppy ears, and a feathery tail. There was an orange ball in its mouth. It dropped the ball at Jenny-Lou's feet and looked up at her expectantly, tail wagging.

"I just played with you, Angel," she scolded with happy exasperation, scooping both the dog and the orange ball into her arms. Turning to us, she said, "This little cowpoke would play fetch all day long if he could."

Merritt wasn't listening. She was standing motionless, her gaze turned upward, her mouth agape. A painting of an enormous white lily was staring down at us like the blank eye of a heartless god.

Jenny-Lou saw what she was looking at and proudly explained. "An O'Keeffe, of course. There's another in Fitz's den. We have an amazing collection of twentieth-century fine art, thanks to Fitz. And if you look around, you'll see several contemporary regional artists who you better believe will be just as famous someday—that is, if Fitz has anything to do with it. He's very big on promoting our Southwestern art. There are some nice Native American artifacts, too, like that Hopi bowl over there from the prehistoric Anasazi period." Smiling with arch pleasure, enjoying our surprise, she pointed to a side table, where sat a squat clay bowl I wouldn't have looked at twice.

Merritt and I exchanged incredulous glances. We were clearly thinking the same thing. It would be so easy to break into this big airy hacienda (you knew simply by looking at it that there were bound to be unsecured doors and windows) and steal any number of priceless paintings and artifacts. At least the ranch was fairly isolated—about fifteen miles southwest of the sleepy town of Pecos and the highway into Santa Fe.

"Now, don't go worrying about people stealing things," Jenny-Lou scolded amiably. "We've got cameras over the front gate and all the entrances to the main house. No one can break in here without our knowing."

Merritt and I remained silent. Neither of us wanted to contradict her outright, but of course we knew that the security measures she'd described were anemic at best and, furthermore, that no place on earth was safe from a skilled and determined thief.

"Come on, you two, follow me," she said in a high-pitched lilt, as if coaxing a couple of recalcitrant children. "You can gawk all you want after you say hello to Fitz and the General."

With the little dog tucked under her arm, she set off down a long red-tile corridor. The walls were covered by faux medieval sconces and beautiful oil landscapes of desert hills, crags, and mesas, along with one painting of a lonely-looking cowboy on horseback. There was a grand stairway with iron balustrades and an antique grandfather clock that began to chime as we passed—long, slow, ponderous gongs. I looked at my phone; it was exactly ten a.m. The sound followed us into a room at the end of the corridor. It had white stucco walls and dark wooden beams. French doors along one wall let in bleached Southwestern sunlight. I had just enough time to notice these details before my attention was claimed by a big-boned, ungainly woman bearing down on us with ferocious eagerness.

CHAPTER SIX

The Threat

Aubrey Merritt! How wonderful to see you after all this time!" she exclaimed.

Tight curls of wiry gray hair framed a square face, presently broken into a wide smile. She wore baggy linen pants, a shapeless T-shirt, and a sleeveless cotton cardigan with big patch pockets that bulged out from all the times she'd stuck her fists in them. She was over six feet and bulky, and her movements were a bit clumsy. I worried that she might trip over the furniture in her haste to greet her old friend.

"It's good to see you too, Joan," Merritt said with a smile.

Was she acting? Given her previous opinion about reuniting with her sorority sisters, what else was I to think? It wasn't out of the question. She performed as well as a trained actor when she wanted to disarm a witness or gain their trust. At the moment, though, I could have sworn she was truly pleased. There were even little pink blushes of happiness in her cheeks.

The women briefly embraced and stepped away from each other quickly. The show of affection seemed to have embarrassed them both. It even embarrassed me a little, as I'd never seen Merritt hug anyone before. She introduced me as her assistant, and I received a tight, vigorous handshake from the woman who'd been identified as Joan Battersea. Eye contact was steady and direct, almost more than I wanted. I immediately felt certain, rightly or not, that Joan Battersea was one of the most forthright persons I would ever meet, and that every word coming out of her mouth would be the truth, the whole truth, and nothing but the truth. This knee-jerk reaction was exactly what Merritt had warned me against, so I tried to repress my natural impulse to trust other humans and adopt a cold, suspicious attitude. She told me I could call her Joan, but I knew right away I wouldn't cross that line. I would address her the way Jenny-Lou McPhee had, as General Battersea or General.

"I was so disappointed when you declined the invitation, Aubrey. Then Fitz texted that you'd changed your mind and were on your way. And here you are! Looking wonderful, I might add. Not a day older!"

They both laughed at the absurdity of this.

Fitz had been standing by, looking on beneficently. Now he came forward, and more greetings circulated. We took seats in deep leather chairs with padded armrests that were clustered around a big round coffee table with a burnished copper top. He asked if we wanted some refreshment. When Merritt requested ice water and I followed suit, he circled behind a rustic pine bar. Mounted on the wall behind it was a very long, heavy-looking musket with a metal bayonet. On another wall, mounted on a plaque, were a bunch of old pistols that looked like they might have been used in gentlemen's duels of the eighteenth century. There were other guns too; the room was full of them, I realized. Handguns displayed on side tables, shotguns leaning in corners. Most of them looked old, possibly antique. Apparently, Fitz was a collector.

He returned bearing ice water in heavy glass mugs as large as beer steins. As he put one down in front of me, he said, "You like guns, Ms. Blunt?" He had seen me looking.

"Ah, not especially." I didn't want to admit that the sight of a gun, any gun, even a very old one, sent me into a tailspin. Forget hunting; where I came from, guns were used for one thing only, and that was to kill people. Maybe out here in the desert, things were different. Maybe. I would try to keep an open mind.

"Have you ever fired one?" he asked.

"No."

He pointed to the musket. "That gun was used by the colonists in the Battle of Lexington, Massachusetts, in 1775. For all we know, that gun right there might have been the one that fired 'the shot heard round the world' that kicked off the Revolutionary War."

"Interesting," I said dryly.

"It still fires, you know."

"Does it?"

"I was thinking of giving a demonstration this weekend, if people are interested."

I smiled vaguely and sipped my drink.

General Battersea was saying, "Can you believe how young we were, Aubrey? My god, we were just babes in the woods! Not a clue about the world, about love, about anything! And now look at us. We're old and wise, and I'm not kidding either. There's been a lot of water under these ancient bridges."

Merritt chuckled in agreement.

"Fitz and I have been following your career, by the way," the General went on. "It's been exciting to see how your reputation has grown. I would never have predicted it—but don't take that the wrong way. It's nothing to do with your abilities. It's just that, when we left school, you were so excited to have been given a job at the Metropolitan Museum of Art. I was sure you'd be running the place in no time."

"That didn't work out too well," Merritt admitted without regret. "I was too . . . let's say *female*, for them. You remember those days, don't you? When women couldn't do anything?"

"Oh, I sure do." The General emitted a hearty, rumbling laugh. "I was in the armed forces, don't forget. One battle on the battlefield, another in the ranks."

"But you stuck with it, and made your mark. Congratulations, Joan. Brigadier general is quite an accomplishment."

"And you—a famous detective! That's a lot better than working at a stuffy old museum, if you ask me. We've done all right for ourselves, haven't we? And to think we were the least popular girls in Sigma Delta Tau!"

This amused them both greatly. The General threw back her head and guffawed, and Merritt grinned with delight.

When they'd recovered, the General said, "By the way, I know full well that Fitz dragged you here against your will."

"I'm always willing to go where I'm needed, especially when an old friend is involved," Merritt said diplomatically.

"Come now, Aubrey. I know you better than that. I doubt that friendship had anything to do with it. I suspect that my dear husband lured you here by offering you a mystery to solve. Well, he's wrong. There is no mystery. But I'm not sorry he tricked you, as that was probably the only way I'd get to see you again!"

"I was tricked?" The frown Merritt allowed to pass across her face indicated that, if deceit was afoot, she would not find it funny.

"Not in the least!" Fitz said in gruff good humor. "I would never do such a thing. But I admit that you're owed an explanation. You see, Joan and I are having a stubborn difference of opinion about an issue I consider quite serious, which she insists is trivial."

"And what is that?" asked Merritt.

"Here, let me show you." Fitz walked over to a big rolltop desk filled with cubbies and little drawers. He picked up a five-by-seven-inch card on stiff paper. Even from a distance I could see that it was the invitation to the reunion, sibling to the one I had laid on Merritt's desk weeks ago, when I'd tried to persuade her to attend. He handed it to Merritt.

She studied it with her characteristic deep focus—silent, fierce, almost palpable. For a long time the only sound was an ice cube popping in a glass. It never failed that whenever Merritt examined a piece of evidence, the room went quiet.

Finally she handed the note to me. My fingers tingled when I touched the stiff cardboard; excitement trilled in my chest. This was the moment I loved, the first clue, the official beginning of the case. Some of my boss must have rubbed off on me, because I felt my own mind gathering focus, preparing to work.

The invitation was exactly as I remembered it: the same Greek letters at the top and all the same details. There was nothing to warrant the prompt summoning of a private investigator. It wasn't until I turned it over that I saw what the problem was. On the back someone had scrawled in thick red Sharpie, in fiery, sharp-angled letters: **She who lives by the sword shall die . . .**

My blood ran cold. How ugly. How disturbing. Who would write such a thing? And why on this particular missive, this generous, kindhearted invitation, which was only meant to bring old friends together in harmony and peace?

It was my job as Merritt's assistant to keep a record of the details of each case, so I laid the invitation on my lap and snapped pictures of it with my phone. Then I did a quick Google search. As I'd suspected, the words were an incomplete paraphrase of a Bible verse. Specifically Matthew 26:52.

Fitz was leaning back, one leg crossed over the other. "Now do you see what I mean?"

Merritt was sunk in thought. Fitz struck a wooden match on the sole of his leather shoe and lit a cigar dangling from his mouth. His cheeks sucked in as he drew on it. Soon he had it going, and the smoke wreathed around his head, creating a blurry stink.

Merritt looked from him to the General. "This doesn't worry you, Joan?"

"Not in the least," she said defiantly. "You see, dear friend, this is not the first threat I've received in my life, and I guarantee it won't be the last."

"It's true," Fitz said. "Joan has been getting these things for years. Ever since she spearheaded the Army's sexual harassment initiative and angered a lot of people who apparently liked it better when women were fair game. I can't begin to tell you how disturbing it's been. The vile, disgusting things people say. It's shocking to think that anyone would ever speak that way to another human being, much less to a brigadier general of the United States Army. I thought when Joan retired we'd finally see an end to it, but it appears that isn't to be the case."

"Fitz is very protective of me," said the General, making a show of fond gratitude, but I could sense marital irritation bubbling underneath. "What he ought to have added is that nothing has ever come of the many threats I've received over the years. Not one thing. Which is why I consider myself well within my rights to ignore this one."

Her husband dismissed her with a snort. "This is a very different situation from the ones we're used to, my dear. You should be able to acknowledge that much at least!" His frustration was breaking through. I feared we were about to witness a marital spat.

"The people who write these things don't even have the courage to sign their names. I haven't been intimidated by these cowards in the past, and I don't intend to start now," the General retorted with heat.

Fitz leaned forward, the glowing cigar pinched between thumb and forefinger. "For god's sake, sweetheart. Be reasonable. Whoever left this in the mailbox obviously knows where we live, knows you'll be home this weekend, knows there will be people milling around. This is a perfect opportunity for a stranger to get close to you without creating suspicion."

The General stared into the middle distance, apparently unwilling to confront her husband directly in front of company. Yet there was a sharp edge in her voice when she said, "Really, dear heart, I do wish you weren't making such a crisis out of it."

"Sweet love of my life! Please! You're not thinking clearly!" Fitz sputtered at her. "You've become numb to these things, and don't appreciate the danger you're in. If there was ever a threat to take seriously, it's this one."

The General turned her attention to me for some reason. A gentle smirk indicated that she thought the discussion was absurd and wanted me to think so too. I returned a tiny smile of support, having no idea what else to do.

"Let's ask Aubrey what *she* thinks," Fitz urged. "If she agrees with you, I'll stand down and not mention it again. If she agrees with me, you must promise that you'll listen to her and follow her advice."

"All right, all right. I promise," the General huffed.

Fitz turned to Merritt. "What do you say, Detective?"

CHAPTER SEVEN

Merritt Takes the Case

Merritt sidestepped the marital fray and got down to business. "Tell me about this invitation. Exactly where and when was it found?"

Fitz replied, "It was in the mailbox at the gate to the ranch. Jenny-Lou brought it in with the rest of the mail Tuesday morning."

"Does she always bring in the mail?"

"Sometimes. She comes here one or two mornings a week to help out in my office, and on those occasions she usually checks the mailbox on her way through the gate."

"I see. I assume you informed the police?"

The General muttered under her breath, "Completely unnecessary."

Fitz ignored her. "I certainly did. Two officers came from Pecos. They said they couldn't do anything because no crime had been committed. They promised to have a squad car drive by the house every few hours, but I haven't seen any. The fools need an incident, it seems, before they'll take any action."

"You didn't think of canceling the reunion?" Merritt asked the General mildly.

"Absolutely not. You can't give in to these people, Aubrey," she insisted, pressing her original argument. "That's rule number one. You never show fear, and you don't retreat unless absolutely necessary. Whoever wrote that silly thing won't push me an inch, I assure you."

Merritt moved on. "Who had access to the invitations?"

"I invited all the sisters from our year. Twelve altogether, five of whom accepted. A few brought their partners and one brought her son. A total of nine guests. With you and your assistant, we have eleven total. Which is lucky, as we can accommodate that number right here on the ranch and don't need to rent rooms at the bed-and-breakfast in Pecos."

"I suppose your staff had access to the invitations before they were mailed?"

"I guess so. They were sitting on that desk right there for a few days. Someone could have taken one off the top."

"The printer had access to them also, of course."

"The printer? Huh. I hadn't thought of him. He has a shop at the industrial park south of Santa Fe. A nice enough fellow; Fitz knows him well. I can't imagine why he would want to threaten me."

"There's no conceivable reason why Larry would want to harm Joan," Fitz concurred, huffing at the absurdity of it.

Merritt smiled enigmatically. I knew what she was thinking. We all believe we know more about other people than we really do.

"I hear you have a sophisticated security system, Fitz. Is there a camera covering the mailbox?" she asked.

"Unfortunately, no. There's one at the front gate, but it points toward the driveway, to record cars entering and leaving the ranch. It doesn't pick up the mailbox or cars passing on the road."

Merritt turned to the General. "Think, Joan. Imagine a Venn diagram. In one circle, anyone who might want to harm you. In the other, people who had access to the invitations. We'll find our suspect in the overlap."

The General wagged her gray head. "I can't think of anyone."

"You, Fitz? Anyone come to mind?"

"No. But we wouldn't necessarily know the culprit. You see, Aubrey, that's just the problem. Joan has enemies all across this country and all over the world. Fanatics. People who wrap their vile words and deeds in the banner of patriotism."

Merritt nodded thoughtfully. "Which makes it impossible to define the first group in its entirety. But the second group can still be narrowed down."

"Are you saying you intend to take this seriously?" The General seemed doubtful but not close-minded.

"Of course I do. Your life has been threatened." She frowned disapprovingly at her old friend and let her voice become hard. "I'll leave it to you to reflect on why you chose to put your head in the sand."

At first the General appeared stumped by Merritt's criticism. Then her broad shoulders slumped. "Did I? Oh, I don't know. Maybe you're right; maybe I did. I suppose I thought I could just wish it away. I'm usually not naive about these things—really, I'm not. It's just that I'm so *tired* of them. I'm tired of being the butt of jokes and the object of people's hate. I'm retired now, finally living full-time on my ranch—after so many years spent in dusty, dirty, often dangerous places, with people always watching to see how I, a woman, could succeed in commanding so many men. All I want now is to enjoy some peace and quiet with my family and friends. I think I've earned that right, haven't I? After everything I've done?" Her voice broke ever so slightly—a tiny crack in the facade.

"Darling . . ." Fitz said tenderly.

I too was moved by the strong woman's display of vulnerability. Part of me wanted to jump to her defense and declare, *You definitely have that right, General Battersea! You deserve all the peace and quiet you can get!*

Merritt, however, was not one to commiserate. "Come now, Joan, I don't think I need to remind you that wanting something doesn't mean you're going to get it. The unavoidable fact of your situation is this: You rose quite high in the military, and you became a lightning rod. The worst among us might have a handful of enemies, but you, my friend, have legions of enemies, known and unknown, all over the world. The fight isn't over for you, and it may never be. Now, today, for your own safety and that of your family, you need to accept that reality and act accordingly."

The General pursed her lips and twisted her features into a grimace. But she didn't object.

"Fitz happens to be right," Merritt continued. "This threat is different from the ones I assume you're used to. Whoever wrote those words knows where you live and what you're doing this weekend. A few days ago, that same person or an accomplice stood at the gate of your private residence with the express purpose of instilling terror. Whether they intend to follow that up with physical harm is something we won't know for sure until and unless it happens. But it's a possibility that must be taken seriously."

The room fell heavily silent.

Fitz puffed quietly on his cigar, having the good sense to let Merritt finish the work for him.

Finally the General sighed. "All right, Aubrey. But what would you have us do?"

"There's no easy answer. The danger could come at any moment, from any direction. I would insist that you remain locked in your bedroom all weekend with an armed guard outside your door, but I know you won't agree to that. And even if you did, you still might not be safe. Closed rooms have windows, and criminals are often remarkably resourceful individuals." Merritt shook her head dejectedly. "Honestly, I'm not sure how I can help. I'm usually asked to solve crimes, not prevent them. I fear that keeping you safe this weekend is beyond my abilities."

"My dear Aubrey, you mustn't think you're responsible for my safety! Not in any way, shape, or form. Don't you agree, Fitz?"

"Oh, absolutely. I didn't drag you out here to put an outsize burden on your shoulders. Joan and I are your friends; we ask only for your insight and guidance."

Merritt sighed. "To start, I have one simple rule for you, Joan: Do not be alone at any time this weekend. Keep either Fitz, me, or someone you trust with you every minute. No, wait. We can't be sure who is trustworthy. So it has to be one of us—either Fitz or me." She cast a troubled gaze at me. "Blunt, too, I suppose. The three of us will split the bodyguard function while the reunion is going on."

I wished I could shrink into the woodwork. I didn't want to be anyone's bodyguard. I had zero faith in my ability to ward off an attack, and Merritt ought to have had zero faith in me also. My professional goal was merely to spring into action after the victim was well killed and thoroughly deceased. And the killer had slipped far, far away.

The General seemed about to comment, but Merritt barreled on. "Now, we ought to start trying to identify, to the extent that we are able, who the culprit might be. We can begin with one obvious and rather striking fact: Whoever scrawled that message wanted to direct our attention to this weekend's festivities. Why? That's our first question."

"You don't really think one of our sorority sisters could be involved?" the General asked in astonishment.

"That is clearly the inference the perpetrator wishes us to draw. It's a bold and provocative opening gambit—a gauntlet cast at our feet, if you will. I think we should humor our enemy by picking it up and wielding it as clumsily as we no doubt will. Frankly, we have no other move at this point. So let's start by considering which of our sisters might be capable of such a cruel trick. You said that nine guests are here this weekend, not including Blunt and myself. Who exactly are they?"

"Well, let's see. There's Eve Exeter and her husband, Conrad Zander, from Boston and . . ."

"Blunt, will you kindly write down these names?"

I pulled up my Notes app and started typing.

"The Korns, Barbara and Jacob. They're from Boston also. Nova Olsen is coming alone from Santa Cruz. Kathy and Dave Lafferty drove all the way from upstate New York. They're combining the reunion with a road trip across the United States. And, let's see . . . the memory isn't what it used to be . . . oh, right . . . Bree Jumper is here with her son, Peter."

"When did they arrive?"

"The Laffertys came on Wednesday and have been sightseeing in the area, and the others flew in yesterday. Nova Olsen ought to be arriving soon. I put the three married couples and Nova in the guesthouse. Bree and her son have bedrooms in this house. I suppose people are exploring the ranch or enjoying the pool before they go to the shooting range. Fitz has arranged a skeet shooting activity this afternoon for whoever is interested. He wants you coastal folks to get a true taste of the West."

Skeet shooting? I had no idea what that was. I wrote it down in Notes.

"I don't plan to participate myself," the General continued. "The sound of gunfire is associated in my mind with . . . well, with other times and places."

"Understood. I'm not a fan of recreational shooting myself. So let's you and I skip the gun sports and spend the time together, just the two of us. We have a lot of catching up to do," said Merritt.

The General smiled fondly at her guest. "Yes, indeed. It feels like only yesterday that we were strolling across the quad together." She paused and grew more serious. "I'm very glad you came, Aubrey. It means a lot to me, more than you may realize. I was such an odd, clumsy girl, with my sunburned skin and dusty cowboy boots. Straight from the desert, I was. Not exactly the Sarah Lawrence type. When the girls made me the butt of jokes, you always came to my rescue and made me feel safe. It's funny, isn't it? I can function in a war zone but I barely survived our sorority. Now here we are again, forty years later, and nothing has changed. I'm still asking you to keep me safe."

"You helped me too, Joan. I wasn't a social butterfly myself."

"But you were never as awkward as I was. There was something about you, a confidence—the girls wouldn't have dared make fun of you, even with those enormous black glasses you always wore. No, you were a righteous and uncompromising young lady, Aubrey—not someone to be trifled with. And you were very quick to tell the professors where their logic was faulty, as I recall."

Fitz chuckled as Merritt replied with a smile, "You're too kind, old friend."

CHAPTER EIGHT

The Therapist Arrives

At Fitz's request, the ranch manager, Barry, accompanied me to the parking lot to help bring in our luggage. He was fortyish, with stringy, shoulder-length blond hair and a ruddy, weathered face. His dirty jeans were held up by a leather belt with a hand-tooled silver buckle, and his cowboy boots were worn down at the heel and curled up at the toe.

He barely greeted me and insisted on walking a few paces behind me on our journey out to the gravel lot. A couple of times I tried to initiate a friendly conversation with no luck.

As he was hauling Merritt's Louis Vuitton behemoth out of the back of the SUV, a red Toyota Camry with Texas plates pulled up beside us, and a tall older woman with long gray hair got out. She was wearing a loose linen sleeveless dress, almost down to her ankles, in a dull olive color, set off by a saucer-sized seashell on a leather strap. Her feet were encased in brown suede Birkenstocks; her toes were unpolished, the toenails slightly yellowed; and her wrists were stacked with multicolored friendship bracelets and an Apple Watch.

She beeped open the trunk of the Camry with her key fob and turned to Barry. "Would you?"

Indicating with a nod that he would return for her luggage, the ranch manager staggered back to the house laden with ours.

The woman offered me a guarded smile, unsure of what my role might be. "I'm Nova Olsen. Sigma Delta Tau."

"Olivia Blunt, assistant to Aubrey Merritt, also Sigma Delta Tau."

She looked toward the sky with a gentle frown. "Aubrey Merritt. My, my. That does bring me back. I haven't seen Aubrey in . . . well, since graduation. She must have become very important to be traveling with an assistant."

I wasn't sure how to respond, so I changed the subject. "Where are you coming from?"

"I flew in from San Francisco this morning."

"We came in this morning from New York. We must have been at the airport the same time as you," I said with more enthusiasm than the subject really warranted.

"I'm afraid I wouldn't have recognized Aubrey if I'd been standing next to her. We were never close at school, and forty years is a long time. I imagine we've all changed quite a bit since then. For better and for worse." She gave a sly, abstracted smile. "I expect this weekend will be quite an interesting experience."

CHAPTER NINE

The Detectives Confer

If I were going to murder someone, I wouldn't advertise my intention beforehand by sending a death threat," I said.

"Certainly not," agreed Merritt. "The point of a death threat is simply to terrorize. The sender likes to imagine the victim living in constant fear for his or her life. If the victim were to actually die, the fun would be over."

"So maybe General Battersea is right. It's just words. The sender isn't likely to follow through."

"Except . . ." Merritt said thoughtfully. "Why did she scribble the message *on the invitation*? That's what I keep turning over in my mind. It points directly to this weekend and suggests a personal connection. Why drop such an obvious clue into our laps?"

"Maybe because she—assuming it's a woman—actually *wants* to be discovered, so she intentionally reduced the suspect pool to make it easier for us to find her. That's a thing, right? Criminals wanting to be caught?"

"In all my years, I never met a criminal who wanted to be caught. But it's not out of the question, I suppose."

"Maybe the whole thing is just a very mean prank. The sender simply wants to ruin the weekend. She knows the General will spend the next few days worrying that one of her old friends intends to do her harm, and trying to guess who it might be. Maybe the sender figures that word of the threat will get out, and then everyone will be on edge. She intends to just sit back and enjoy watching the reunion implode."

"A petty social sadist? Out to ruin another girl's party? Is that what you're suggesting?"

"Yeah, sort of."

Merritt considered. "Hmm. I like it."

Pleased with my contribution, I pressed forward. "Do you remember any of your sorority sisters being very sadistic?"

"Oh yes. I think we all were to some extent."

I had another idea. "Or maybe one of the sisters has an old score to settle, and this is how she's choosing to do it. Sub rosa, if you will."

"An old grudge . . . I suppose that's possible too. Although Joan was hardly the sort to inspire that degree of resentment. But she might have damaged a sister without knowing it. And now that girl—that *woman,* I should say—is enjoying her revenge without having to out herself." Merritt shrugged with disappointment. "I sincerely hope that's not what's going on. I dislike dealing with such petty stuff."

We were in a big corner bedroom on the second floor of the hacienda. There was a high white four-poster bed, a richly colored Navajo blanket folded neatly at the end. A knotty pine dresser, a small desk with a straight-backed chair, and a large soft armchair in the corner between the windows. Barry had left Merritt's gigantic suitcase inside the door, and now Merritt asked me to lift it onto the upholstered bench at the end of the bed. It weighed a ton. She opened it and proceeded to hang up all the beautiful clothes she'd brought, shaking each item out lovingly beforehand.

I sat in the armchair, feeling a bit chagrined. I'd whittled my clothing choices down to the absolute basics and forced myself to stuff it all into a carry-on so we wouldn't have to hang idly around a sluggish baggage carousel on my account when we landed in Santa Fe. I obviously needn't have bothered. I could have brought along a camper's trunk if I'd wanted to, if I had the clothes to fill it. Which I didn't.

Merritt flicked a speck of something off the lapel of an elegant white jacket. "By the way, Blunt, you forgot one of the most obvious possibilities."

"What?"

"Can you really not think of it?"

My mind was blank. "No."

"Don't you see what just happened? What you just did?"

"No."

She sighed with gentle exasperation. "The sender pointed you toward a certain path, and you obligingly walked down it."

I frowned as her meaning slowly dawned. "You mean the sender wants us to *think* she's connected to the reunion when actually she isn't?"

"Exactly. A simple trick of misdirection. Very basic."

I wanted to say something smart to redeem myself, but there was really no point. I'd clearly fumbled (so early in the investigation!) and I had to live with it.

Merritt regarded me with sad pity before hanging her jacket in the closet.

"If that's the case, we're back where we started. The sender could be anyone," I said.

"Not *anyone.* We do possess three concrete facts about our girl, if woman she is. One: She had access to the invitations. Two: She or an accomplice was at the ranch gate sometime between Monday morning when that day's mail was collected and Tuesday morning, when Jenny-Lou brought that day's mail to the house. And three: She either owns or borrowed a red Sharpie."

"That's not a lot to go on."

"Correct. You and I will have to work very hard to spin that straw into gold."

"I think we can say a few other things about our girl as well," I said, eager to make up for my earlier lapse. "She's a Bible reader. And she doesn't like war."

Merritt shook her head. "Those are not reliable facts. They could be red herrings, part of her disguise, like the invitation itself. The only thing we can conclude about our girl's character—and this only if the invitation is indeed a ruse—is that she has a devious mind, that she enjoys coming up with little tricks like this one. In which case, she would probably want to stay nearby, close to the festivities, for the pleasure of observing how her game was working out."

Having unpacked her suitcase, she closed it and said, "Put that somewhere, would you?"

I naturally resented being given all the menial tasks, but what could I do? I couldn't very well say, *Put it away yourself, why don't you,* without risking my job. So I raised myself reluctantly out of the armchair, lifted the empty suitcase off the luggage rack, looked around for a good spot, and ended up sliding it under the bed.

Merritt, meanwhile, settled herself in the armchair I'd vacated.

"Enough theorizing," she said. "It's time to get down to business. While it's possible that the sender has nothing to do with the reunion, the reunion is nevertheless where we have to start. I want you to look at that guest list and do some research on each sorority sister in attendance and their respective plus-ones. I need to know what each sister has been doing generally for the last forty years and, specifically, for the last five. Get that information to me as quickly as you can, as I want to have some background on my sisters when we meet. Meanwhile, I'm going to spend the afternoon catching up with Joan. I find that I do have some residual affection for her, and I'm loath to let her out of my sight if she's in danger. Also, I wouldn't be surprised if she knows more about what's going on than she's admitting."

"Really? You think she's hiding something?" This was another possibility I hadn't considered.

"It would explain her nonchalance." Merritt pointed to the door. "Get going now. You've got work to do. By the way, I want you at the skeet shooting this afternoon. Keep your eyes and ears open. And please don't try to be smart, Blunt. You get yourself in trouble when you do that. Just observe. Carefully, discreetly. As the great novelist Henry James advised, try to be a person 'on whom nothing is lost.'"

CHAPTER TEN

Olivia Does Her Homework

I'd been given a place on the otherwise deserted third floor. It was a funny little room, if you could call it that, as it was actually a doorless alcove at the end of a hall that was open to the floor below. The room was monastically furnished with a twin bed, a rickety night table, and an antique chest of drawers. The only window was small and shut tight. As the air on the third floor felt close and humid—the central air-conditioning was not as efficient up here—I tried to open it and, when it didn't budge, squatted down and got my shoulder into it, until I'd pushed it up enough to feel fresh air streaming in.

The view from this north-facing window was of hazy red hills undulating across the horizon under a vast and dazzling cerulean sky. It was a foreign landscape to me, almost otherworldly. I felt a gentle sense of dislocation and experienced that slight inner tremble that comes from sensing that you're in a place you know nothing about, where you can take nothing for granted, where your ignorance of the terrain, perhaps even of the customs, puts you at a disadvantage. Dry dirt, randomly punctuated by scrub brush and cacti, covered a long, descending slope to what I assumed was the Pecos River, presently hidden from view by vegetation and strangely shaped rock formations. Closer to the house, off to one side, glinted the turquoise water of the pool. It was noon by now, almost 80 degrees, and several people were sitting out there—I could hear the murmur of male and female voices, and I spied someone's straw hat through the feathery branches of the cottonwood trees that surrounded the pool area. Under my window but off to one side was the roof of the veranda. Directly beneath me was a three-story drop to hard ground.

I pulled my laptop out of my backpack and was about to sit on the narrow bed, which someone had made up with fresh white sheets and another folded Navajo blanket, when I thought better of it. Feeling a little foolish, but needing to do it, I swept back the covers to check for rattlesnakes. There weren't any. So I proceeded to sit cross-legged on the bed and opened my laptop. I worked quickly and steadily, and seventy minutes later I had compiled the information Merritt wanted, or at least most of it. I did not go back the forty years she'd requested; that was asking way too much for the deadline (ASAP) she had given me. (Not to mention that, in my opinion, such a large amount of data probably wasn't necessary anyway.) I concentrated instead on each person's current situation and recent past.

Sigma Delta Tau Sorority Sisters & Their Plus-Ones:

1. Eve Exeter, PhD. Professor of biology at MIT. Famous for her pioneering work on sirtuins. Cofounder of Cambridge-based biomedical company Lifespan, Inc.

   She was not on Facebook, Instagram, or even LinkedIn. But there were loads of photos of her at biomedical conferences, standing in various lineups of dour-looking scientists, as well as a YouTube video with thirty-six views of her giving a lecture on the role of the protein SIR2 in cellular regulation in yeast. I made it through approximately two minutes of the video, until her droning monotone and long, flaccid, expressionless face brought me to a point of such excruciating boredom that, if I'd been an attendee, I would have shot myself in the foot so as to be carried out on a stretcher.

Dr. Exeter lived with her husband in a quaint Victorian house on a shady Cambridge street. The couple had no children. She went to her lab at MIT seven days a week, riding her single-gear Schwinn bicycle down Mass Ave each morning to get there. She had recently sued a motorist, unsuccessfully, for allegedly causing what she claimed was a life-threatening accident that had left her with a bruised rib.

Sirtuins? I had no idea what they were. I turned to ChatGPT.

ChatGPT: Sirtuins are a family of proteins that play important roles in cellular processes such as DNA repair, gene expression, and metabolism. Some studies have suggested that activation of sirtuins may have anti-aging effects, including the potential to extend life span.

In particular, one sirtuin protein called SIRT1 has been linked to life span extension in several studies of yeast, flies, and mice. These studies have shown that increasing the activity of SIRT1 can lead to improvements in a variety of age-related conditions, such as metabolic disorders, neurodegenerative diseases, and cancer. However, it's important to note that while these findings are promising, more research is needed to fully understand the relationship between sirtuins and life span extension in humans.

Research on the sirtuin protein was started in 1991 by Dr. Eve Exeter of MIT after her groundbreaking discovery that sirtuins are NAD+-dependent protein deacetylases.

2. Conrad Zander, PhD. Eve Exeter's husband, professor of entrepreneurship at the MIT Sloan School of Management. Cofounder with his wife of Lifespan, Inc.

   Photos showed a handsome older man, well-dressed and fit, with sharply defined features and a full head of wavy salt-and-pepper hair. Even in photos he exuded an unmistakable, if muted by age, charisma. The term *silver fox* danced across my mind. Most of his ratings on Rate My Professors were negative, with students grousing about his inadequate office hours and general aloofness. The few who liked him gushed with fawning adjectives such as *brilliant*, *pioneering*, and *life-changing*.

3. Barbara Korn. Senior headhunter at Darby Summers, a Boston-based national recruiting company with snazzy offices in a newish Seaport skyscraper. The company website featured a long list of all the Fortune 500 corporations that relied exclusively on Darby Summers for all their hiring needs. The page dedicated to job seekers began with these rather ominous words: *We know who's who. And who's looking for who. Could it be you?*

When I checked Facebook to get a sense of Barbara's personal life, I found myself scrolling through endless photos of a pocketbook-sized West Highland terrier named Sweetie-Pie, usually either cuddled in the crook of Barbara's arm or staring blankly into the camera, a sprout of white fur sticking up from her forehead, decorated with a pink bow. Sweetie-Pie dressed cutely for various occasions. Last Christmas, she had donned the costume of an elf, her usual pink hair bow switched out for a red one. Meanwhile, Barbara's grown daughter, Hannah, and two granddaughters, Zoe and Amelia, looked sullen and miserable in the few posts that featured them.

4. Jacob Korn. Barbara's husband, manager of Cross-Platform Integration Systems Research and Development (CPISRD) at Google.

   Korn was a pudgy fellow with a patchy beard and smudged eyeglasses that perched unevenly on his nose. It looked as if the greasy, unkempt appearance that plagues some adolescent boys had not only never left him but also had become more pronounced over the decades. A video game aficionado who regularly posted his *Fortnite* scores, he had achieved some renown in the gamer world. When I studied his picture more closely, I noticed that his eyes were slightly crossed.

5. Kathy Lafferty. General science teacher (biology, chemistry, environmental science), newly retired from the McDowell-Benson Middle School in Syracuse, NY. Awarded the coveted Science Teachers of America

Plaque of Meritorious Service for her years as a New York State Science Fair senior judge. Nominated four times for the Syracuse Star Teacher Award but never won. Currently, she was a local organizer for the annual Walk for Alzheimer's and the annual March for Breast Cancer.

Kathy had full pink cheeks, a happy smile, and soft blue eyes. She enjoyed reading, cooking, gardening, and spending time with family.

6. Dave Lafferty. Kathy's husband, newly retired Syracuse cop.

   There was surprisingly little information online about Officer Lafferty. Was that police policy, or had data been scrubbed? Without the time I needed to dig deep, I had to be satisfied with a dribble of personal information: Dave and Kathy had four children—Kayleigh, Kevin, Bruce, and Maddie—and eight grandchildren. The Laffertys and their extended family were all active parishioners in the Holy Spirit Church in downtown Syracuse.

7. Bree Jumper. Author of the bestselling Owensaug Trilogy. The marketing copy on the richly illustrated boxed set was not about Bree Jumper per se, yet it told me everything I cared to know about her:

   The Owensaug Trilogy features twelve-year-old heroine Ferguntress Philliter, a human child stolen as a baby from her parents and raised by woodland fairies in the fairy city of East Thock. With the help of her loyal wolfhound, Hollanheart, Ferguntress roams far and wide, seeking her true identity. Will she find her way back to the faraway Land of Sapiens? If she does, will she want to live there? Will the sapien boy, Jay Cortez, who appears to her nightly in the form of a quivering hologram, play any part in her final decision? Is he real? Or just a lost and lonely fairy girl's strangely compelling fantasy?

Bree Jumper had penned several quickly forgotten YA novels before she'd hit on this wildly successful venture. She'd just come off a whirlwind cross-country promotional tour, speaking at conferences, bookshops, schools, and libraries, often to sold-out crowds of, among others, tween girls dressed in flowing robes and flowery headdresses.

Bree was a Florida native, divorced, a bartender before she took up fantasy writing, and the mother of Peter Jumper.

8. Peter Jumper. Bree's eighteen-year-old son, a licensed welder and 2024 graduate of Fort Pierce High School, where he was voted Most Likely to Engage in Violent Crime. (*Not cute, not funny,* I thought.) His Instagram posts featured him in a metal helmet and wraparound goggles and thick fire-retardant gloves, wielding a 400-degree blowtorch, sparks flying out like bursting fireworks. A video clip showed him pounding molten metal with a heavy mallet. You could hear the brilliant brassy clang of metal on metal and the hiss and sizzle of the sparks emanating from the point of contact. His Instagram died abruptly back in December, so, following a hunch, I tried Telegram, and in a stroke of luck, and because he used his Instagram handle

@imeltmetal, I tracked him to a weapons-loving chat room where users spouted insane conspiracy theories and bizarre political beliefs.

Peter Jumper worried me.

9. Nova Olsen. Therapist from Santa Cruz specializing in grief work and PTSD. She had a thriving clinical practice and authored a blog called *Life After Death* that boasted over eighteen thousand grieving subscribers. In her blog she wrote openly about all aspects of her personal life—money, dating, senior sex, and her beauty and skin-care rituals. (She made her own aloe vera lotion by pressing the leaves of the aloe vera plant in her backyard.) And, of course, her own tragic losses. First her parents in a car accident when she was twenty, then her closest friend to cancer, then her son to suicide ten years ago, an event that precipitated the end of her thirty-year marriage to the boy's father, the formerly nationally ranked tennis pro Adam Olsen.

That was it. Nine guests. Nine suspects. All but one over sixty years old.

I closed my laptop, kneaded my forehead, and pressed my fingers gently against my eyes. I suspected that my blink rate dropped to near zero when I was doing research, which explained the headache, dry eyes, and photosensitivity that inevitably accompanied intense computer work for me. When I felt a little better, I read over the document I'd created.

Had one of the nine individuals on my list left the death threat in General Battersea's mailbox? If so, which one? And why?

I thought back to my recent discussion with Merritt about possible motivations. The one I considered most likely was an old grudge. Maybe General Battersea had stolen someone's boyfriend all those years ago, and now the jilted woman was hell-bent on time-delayed revenge. But I simply couldn't picture the General stealing anyone's boyfriend. And even an expert grudge holder wouldn't terrorize her sorority sister forty years later for that offense. Or would she?

Of course the sorority sisters and their plus-ones were not the only people who might wish General Battersea harm. There was also perky Jenny-Lou, whose gushing praise of Fitz had struck me as suspicious. And what about surly, no-eye-contact Barry, whose heart was probably uncharted territory to his employers? Both had access to the invitations as they sat on Fitz's desk waiting to be mailed.

I leaned back against the pillow, overwhelmed by the difficulty of the case. I was also physically tired. Keeping my fingers clicking across the keyboard for the last seventy minutes had been an act of will, especially as I hadn't slept since we left New York. I decided to scooch down and rest my head on the pillow for just a minute or two . . .

I woke in a panic and immediately reached for my phone. It was two fifteen! I'd been asleep for over an hour. Where was Merritt? Was she waiting for me? What had I missed? I ran to the bathroom in the hall, brushed my teeth and tangled hair, splashed cold water on my face, then quickly changed into cargo shorts and a fresh T-shirt and hurried downstairs.

The hacienda was quiet. I wandered around, looking for anyone. The grand foyer was cool and empty, the huge O'Keeffe silently presiding. My footfalls echoed on the tiled corridor that led to what I had dubbed Fitz's Den of Guns. No one was there, either, just our uncollected water glasses sweating on the coffee table. Mounted over the stone fireplace, the second masterful O'Keeffe showed the skull of a poor, innocent cow who had died, decayed, and had its bones bleached into brittle, blinding whiteness by a merciless burning sun. Who would want to paint such a thing? Why would anyone hang it on their wall? The empty eye sockets. The tongueless mouth. The nasal passages that snakes could crawl through and probably had.

The thought of snakes made me break out in a sweat. I hurried out of the room with a terrible nursery rhyme singsonging in my head: *The snakes crawl in, the snakes crawl out, the snakes crawl up and down your snout. One little snake who's not too shy crawls in your ear and out your eye.*

CHAPTER ELEVEN

The Past Is Never Past

A caterer in black pants and a white shirt was in the process of dismantling a lunch buffet on the veranda. She let me grab a chicken salad sandwich and some fruit cup before she took the serving dishes away.

Two stragglers were still planted at a round table covered with empty plates and glasses. They waved me over and introduced themselves as Kathy and Bree, though of course I already knew their names—and much more than that—from having just stalked them on the internet.

When they learned I was Aubrey Merritt's assistant, they were delighted. Not with me so much as with the idea that Merritt was at the reunion. They couldn't wait to catch up with her.

"That one's made a name for herself, that's for sure," Bree Jumper said. She had short gray hair that spiked at odd angles, chunky red cat's-eye glasses, and a generally disheveled appearance. Her T-shirt announced OLD IS THE NEW BLACK, and the glass she was sipping from had traces of salt around the rim. "Aubrey was always so serious and intense—didn't you think so, Kathy? Like she just couldn't stop trying to figure things out. Didn't matter what it was: people, life, appliances. If the house blew a circuit, she'd be the one to fix it. She was so analytical, she made me feel like I had straw for brains."

Me too, I might have said.

"Well, your train of thought *was* a bit hard to follow at times," Kathy said gently. "I think your imagination just went into overdrive once in a while and left us all in the dust. But you definitely *didn't* have straw for brains."

Bree half closed her eyes as her inner clock wound back to the early eighties and the goings-on inside the Sigma Delta Tau sorority house. "I can't say I *liked* Aubrey, but I didn't hate her either. She had a certain . . . how should I say it? . . . Penetrating presence."

Kathy nodded. "Aubrey scared a lot of us, but I don't think anyone hated her. At least not the way we all hated . . ." Seeing me sitting there, she didn't finish the sentence. "Oh, I shouldn't—"

"Go ahead," Bree scoffed. "It's not gossip if it's the truth."

"I don't think Olivia wants to hear it," Kathy said.

"Oh, but I do!" I said. Who hated whom in the Sarah Lawrence chapter of the Sigma Delta Tau sorority forty years ago was *exactly* what I wanted to hear.

"No, I'm sorry. I promised myself I wouldn't spread any negativity this weekend," Kathy said, making a show of high-mindedness that I hoped wouldn't stick.

Bree downed the last of her margarita, plunked the glass on the table. "You do realize, don't you, that by *not* telling Olivia, you're just making her more curious and blowing the whole thing up even bigger."

"Even so, I'm not going to engage in hurtful gossip."

Bree pulled a vape pen out of a small velvet pouch with a beaded lizard design. She saw me looking. "You like this little purse? I got it yesterday in a touristy shop on Canyon Road. Near Fitz's gallery. You really ought to visit his gallery before you leave. The artwork on display is absolutely stunning. I'd buy something if I had an inch of wall space to hang anything on. My house in Florida is all windows, you see." She started vaping and turned back to Kathy. "You have to promise me one thing, my dear, and I *mean* it. I'm *serious*." She gave a little hiccup.

Kathy rolled her eyes at me.

"Promise me you'll confront that bitch before this weekend is out. I will be *very disappointed* with you if you just scamper around like you always did, like a sweet little chipmunk, pretending nothing's wrong. That woman ruined your life! She's your *archnemesis*! Like Moriarty was for Sherlock. Lex Luthor was for Superman. That's got to deserve a word or two of acknowledgment at the very least. You don't want her thinking she got away with it, do you? I promise, none of the girls will blame you if you let off a little steam this weekend. Honestly, I think we'd all love to see some fireworks."

Shrugging in my direction, Kathy answered a question I hadn't asked. "I had no idea she'd be here. She wasn't on the guest list when I checked. If I'd known, Dave and I would have driven right through Santa Fe and gone straight to Phoenix. I have a cousin there."

"I'd really like to know which girl you're talking about," I said.

Kathy waved her hand in front of her face. "No, no. Never mind. Forget you ever heard this."

Bree exhaled and gave me a level gaze. "We're talking about Eve Exeter. Always was and always will be a capital *B* bitch."

"Wait a minute, Bree. That's not fair. She was only a bitch to me,"

Kathy protested, claiming whatever high ground was left. "Not to you. When was she ever a bitch to you?"

"She was a bitch to everyone."

"Okay. But what did she *do*?" I said impatiently.

"Don't tell her, Bree!" Kathy insisted. "I don't want this story circulating. Let's please just leave the past alone."

Bree inhaled deeply and, holding the smoke in her lungs, croaked, "The past is never dead. It's not even past." She exhaled fully. "Who said that? Hmm. Faulkner, I think." Turning to me she asked, "Does my vaping bother you?"

"No."

"Thank god. I'd rather have a cigarette, but these days . . ." She sighed. "In novels you always have to give the characters something to do with their hands. Whittling is my standby. Fairies are always whittling. Or weaving flower garlands. That works better for the girls."

"It sounds very traditionally gendered," I couldn't help pointing out.

"Oh, it is! God, yes. Fantasy is horribly traditional. That's what people want, you see. The archetypes. The warrior, the princess, the dying king, and so on. An evil other is absolutely necessary, preferably an army of them. If I had to cast Eve Exeter in a fantasy tale, she'd be a witch who lives alone in a distant ice castle. She'd be the uninvited godmother who curses the newborn princess at her christening, thereby totally ruining the poor child's life."

"Not totally," I said with more passion than I'd expected myself to muster on this topic. "Because the brave knight would save her, am I right?"

Bree smirked. "Sure. If you want to believe that sort of thing. But don't come crying to me when it all goes to hell."

Kathy redirected the discussion to the subject she didn't want to talk about. "You've got to stop bad-mouthing Eve. You're going to poison Olivia's mind against her."

"Olivia knows I'm just kidding. Don't you, Olivia?" Bree gave me a wink.

I didn't know what to say. *Was* she just kidding? Or exaggerating for the sake of the drama she clearly loved? I couldn't tell. All I knew for sure was that there was plenty of animus in Bree Jumper, enough to fill many more fantasy trilogies with murder, mayhem, and severed heads. And what of Kathy Lafferty? Was she as saintly as she seemed, or was she sitting on a buried powder keg of resentment? And what exactly had happened between Kathy and Eve forty years ago?

The lull in the conversation allowed us to hear a distant *pop-pop-pop*. It sounded like fireworks.

"Listen, they started shooting. Let's go down and join them." Kathy rose from the table and led the way in her commodious floral skirt, sleeveless top, and espadrilles. Her fleshy arms were pink with sunburn. Bree and I followed at a slower pace.

"Have you ever been skeet shooting?" the novelist asked me, linking her leather-skinned Florida arm in mine as we strolled into what I sincerely hoped would not be a hail of bullets.

I admitted that I hadn't, and went on to rather nervously explain that I was morally opposed to hunting and, while I would gladly observe the group activity, would not personally be shooting a skeet.

Bree gave me a funny look, then laughed. "The skeet aren't alive, you know. They're just silly little clay discs as big as your palm that get slung out of a mechanical arm and then fly across the sky. You don't actually kill anything."

"Oh, in that case . . ." I said, feeling foolish.

Bree pulled me back suddenly. Pressing my entire arm into her bony rib cage, she held me firmly where she wanted me. Her tequila breath wafted across my face. "Just so you know: Eve was *horrible* to Kathy when we were at school. Utterly, tragically horrible. I swear, if Kathy doesn't grow a pair and shoot an arrow straight into that woman's arse this weekend, I may have to do it myself."

CHAPTER TWELVE

Skeet Shooting

The scene we came upon made a nice tableau. Renoir might have painted it, if Renoir had been a cowboy. Three women and two men were seated off to one side, in a little grove of feathery pinion pines, while two men (Dave Lafferty and Peter Jumper) were lined up at the shooting range, wearing puffy earmuffs and holding long-barreled shotguns, waiting for their turn to take aim at one of the fluorescent orange discs (aka skeet) that flew across the clear blue sky at regular intervals. Sporting a ten-gallon white cowboy hat and a denim shirt with mother-of-pearl snaps instead of buttons, and looking as delighted as a ten-year-old boy, Fitz was working a handheld device that controlled the release of the discs.

I didn't see Merritt or the General anywhere, but the alleged wicked witch, Eve Exeter, was prominently seated at a picnic table, flanked by Barbara Korn and Nova Olsen. A short distance away, Jacob Korn and Conrad Zander lounged in folding chairs, deep in conversation.

Kathy's footsteps slowed, then stopped, when she saw who was there. "On second thought, I think I'd rather go to the pool," she said.

"Oh, for god's sake, she's not going to bite you," Bree scolded.

Kathy considered this statement for a moment and came to a decision. "I'm going to the pool." Without explanation, though none was needed, she headed back the way we'd come.

"Isn't that the most foolish thing you can imagine?" Bree said. "Forty years! Yet here we are, acting like silly little girls." She sighed. "I suppose I ought to keep the poor thing company for a little while at least, until she drives me completely batty." Then Bree, too, headed back to the house.

I went on by myself to the shooting range. Just as I arrived, there was a blast of gunfire, and an orange disc burst open in the sky. Its many shards rained down heavily on the desert floor, and Fitz let out an enthusiastic cheer.

"Nice shot, Dave!" he said to the retired cop. "Your turn, Peter. Ready?"

Looking tense and a little scared, Peter slipped a cartridge into the chamber, closed the gun, and raised it to his skinny shoulder. When the disc flew out and arced across the sky, he shot.

"Whoa! You got a little ahead of it!" Fitz called out. "Remember, Pete: Point, don't aim!"

Peter scowled, and when he saw me watching, he scowled even more.

The women at the picnic table made no motion to invite me to join them. Unwilling to break into what appeared to be a private conversation, I stood a little apart and continued watching the men shoot. I was disappointed once again by the strictly aligned gender roles. I supposed I'd be seeing a lot of that over the next few days.

Eventually Dave and Peter took a break, and Fitz called me over. "Come on, Olivia! Your turn!"

"Not really my thing," I called back.

"Oh, come on. Give it a try! I insist!"

I sighed. He was so keen on it, it felt awkward to refuse.

He handed me the earmuffs and a shotgun, explaining, "This big boy is an old-style single-barrel shotgun with an open choke, and this little baby here"—he held up a red cartridge with a brass cap—"is number nine birdshot, which will give you a good spread and enough punch to break the clays reliably."

"Okay." I had no idea what he was talking about.

He showed me how to insert the cartridge, close the barrel, and put the gun up against my shoulder. "Hold it firm right there," he said. "There's a hollow curve in your shoulder. Can you feel it? It ought to feel natural."

"I don't think this is ever going to feel natural," I said nervously. It didn't help that the earmuffs made my own voice sound far away. "I can't believe I'm actually doing this. Are you sure it's safe?"

"Safe as can be. Now, when the target flies out, keep your eye on it, focus, and relax. There's no rush. You have more time than you think. Keep the barrel slightly ahead of the target, and when it feels right, pull the trigger. You'll probably miss the first few, but you'll get a feel for it. Now go ahead and put your finger on the trigger. Yes, right there. Very good."

"Oh my god. I can't believe I'm doing this."

"When you're ready, say *pull*, and I'll press this little button here on the remote control, and the target will fly out of that low shed over there. It's going to be traveling away from you, so you don't need to worry about it falling on anyone after you shoot it."

"You mean I'm supposed to shoot it?" That may have been the stupidest thing I'd ever said.

"Well, you're going to try. Are you ready?"

"Oh my god. I can't believe I'm doing this," I said again.

"Here goes. Keep the barrel pointed up, don't let it drop."

"It's heavy."

"Yes, I know. But you really need to control where the barrel of the gun is pointing. You want it to be pointing up, toward the sky. That's where the clay pigeon will be. No, no, not that high. Just . . . medium high. Yeah, that's it. Keep it there. Very good. Okay, are you ready? Here we go. One . . . two . . . three!"

The orange disc flew out of the little house where I guess they all lived, and seconds later a great blast filled the air. I staggered back several paces, somehow managing to keep hold of the shotgun, which nevertheless swung wildly. "Oh my god. That hurt!"

"There's a bit of kickback with these old shotguns," Fitz said. I noticed he was quick to take the weapon out of my hands.

"A bit? That was like a hard punch in my shoulder!" I looked around, dazed, checking to see whether the world was the same. I had no memory of having pulled the trigger, but who else could have done it? Finally I looked up at the sky, as if the orange disc might still be there. "Did I get it?"

"Ah, no. Not that time," Fitz said. "You were a little late on the trigger, and I think you may have been pointing the barrel in . . . let's just say, the wrong direction. Want to try again?"

"No, thank you. I don't ever want to do that again."

"Well, you certainly don't have to. But I'm proud of you, Olivia. At least you tried. And maybe you'll change your mind later. I'm always ready to help if you're interested."

"I don't think so, Fitz. But I do appreciate the opportunity."

"Here, let me show you how it's supposed to be done." He wasn't bragging; he just wanted to demonstrate. I handed him the earmuffs, and he put them on. Then he handed me the remote control and told me which button to push when he said *pull.* I did as I was told and watched in awe as he blasted one pigeon after another at three-second intervals—*bang, bang, bang, bang*—clean as could be—the pigeons exploding like bursting stars against the bluer-than-blue sky. It was a surprisingly gratifying sight.

"You're really good at that," I said.

He smiled proudly. "Practice." He nodded in the direction of Eve, Barbara, and Nova. "You think I can get those gals over there to give it a try?"

"You can always ask."

He turned to them. "Ladies! Come on over now. It's your turn!"

To my surprise, they acquiesced. I watched their lesson for a while, observing their different personalities with interest. Eve Exeter, the scientist, was grim, determined; she blamed Fitz for giving poor instructions when her first shots missed, as they all eventually did, despite his tutoring. Barbara Korn, the headhunter, was so inept I wondered if she even knew which end of the gun the bullet came out of. After several failed attempts to hold the shotgun properly against her shoulder, followed by a patient explanation and a series of careful demonstrations by Fitz, she looked miserably overwhelmed, and simply handed the shotgun back to him without having fired it once. Nova Olsen, the therapist from Santa Cruz, was a very different story. She raised the shotgun and assumed the correct stance with the hard, aggressive confidence of a dominatrix with a whip. She learned quickly, and in no time she was blasting one clay pigeon after another out of the sky. *Pull! Pull! Pull!* she shouted with increasing urgency as bursts of orange disc fell in quick succession onto the desert floor. We were all a little thunderstruck by her energy and skill, I think. Even Fitz started to look a bit frazzled. After a while he said his supply of pigeons was exhausted, but I think he just wanted her to stop.

"You're a natural, Nova," he told her with sincere respect when she handed him the gun. She returned a rather indifferent smile, her chill California vibe magically restored, and we all strolled back to the hacienda together.

It occurred to me that John Fitzroy had gone to great lengths to teach his wife's guests to shoot.

CHAPTER THIRTEEN

The Barbecue

The Sigma Delta Tau Fortieth Reunion Barbecue was in full swing poolside. The guests were standing in small groups or sitting at one of four round, linen-covered tables, each adorned with a centerpiece of desert succulents with tiny American flags on toothpicks stuck into the soil. Platters of grilled street corn, bowls of bean salad, and various salsas covered the buffet table. There was also a huge sheet cake in the shape of a torch, the sorority's symbol, the appropriate Greek letters and border florets drawn in icings of blue and brown, the sorority's colors. The sound system was playing an early eighties favorite: "Don't Stop Believin'."

The air was cooler now that evening was coming on, the sunlight more mellow and forgiving. People were dressed in their best casual clothes, some of the women with light sweaters tossed over their shoulders. Smells of vinegar and fire starter emanated from a massive propane grill at which a well-muscled man in a cowboy hat, American flag apron, denim shorts, and tall cowboy boots was flipping rib-eye steaks. A bar offering beer, wine, and mixed drinks was manned by a leathery middle-aged woman with a full neck tattoo.

It felt classic—a good ol' American barbecue with a Southwestern flair to usher in the beginning of summer. All the guests except Merritt looked happy. They had got used to each other over the course of the day and now they were at ease and enjoying themselves—smiling, laughing, and talking a little louder than usual with bright brassy voices.

Merritt and I decamped to a table in a far corner. As always, the great detective was appropriately attired, today in white jeans and a denim shirt, both miraculously crisp despite our travel, with a red bandana knotted stylishly at her neck. Her enormous black Guccis shielded not only her eyes but the entire upper half of her face, but that didn't prevent me from accurately reading her mood. I knew her so well at this point that I could gauge her level of tension from the set of her jaw.

"I don't like this case," she said. "Joan needs a bodyguard, not a detective. If she wasn't a friend, I would have refused to get involved." She sighed resignedly. "But we're here now, and we need to do what we can. So tell me what you learned since I saw you last. And please, make it good."

I described my lunch with Bree and Kathy, and what I'd observed at the skeet shooting. I concluded with this: "Kathy Lafferty really hates Eve Exeter."

Merritt grimaced. "Some things never change."

"Do you know what that's about?"

"I'm afraid so. It's a long story and irrelevant for our purposes. Suffice it to say that Kathy has every right to be angry. *If* what she accused Eve of all those years ago is true."

"Is it?"

"At the time I believed her. Now I'm not so sure. Even good, decent people like Kathy can get lost in the difference between their perceptions and reality. But if she was lying, it wasn't out of spite. I think I can say that with some degree of certainty. Kathy was never a hateful person, only insecure, which is more forgivable but can be just as dangerous. She was very needy; mostly, she needed permission to be as smart as she actually was. She'd had to fight for many things in her life, even for her place at Sarah Lawrence, which she could attend only on full scholarship. The rest of us had wealthy parents, summerhouses, etcetera. We knew the difference between a Bordeaux and Pinot Noir, knew how to dress, what to say at social gatherings, how to handle boys. She didn't fit in, and she knew it. It must have been painful for her. I'm sure we were insensitive to her in many ways we didn't realize. It's possible that envy and repressed anger distorted her perceptions and caused her to make wild accusations against Eve. But, again, if I had to bet, I'd say she was telling the truth."

"Bree said Eve was 'utterly, tragically horrible' to Kathy. Those were her exact words."

"'Utterly, tragically horrible' is a typical Bree phrase. It's no surprise that she rose to prominence in a profession that rewards fantasy and exaggeration."

I was naturally curious to know what kind of grudge would last forty years. But I wasn't going to press my boss again lest she think I was a lowly gossip hound. Which I absolutely was. Just like everyone else. After all, a good story is a good story. On that point at least, I agreed with Bree. But Aubrey Merritt was made of sterner stuff.

"What about you? What did you do this afternoon?" I asked her.

"I spent the time with Joan. It was a pleasant experience."

"Uh-huh," I said, taking note of her stiff tone. Sterner stuff indeed. "Did you find out who might have been threatening her?"

"She's unusually quiet on that point, dodged my questions expertly. She's quite a brilliant woman, Blunt. Very shrewd. Remember that."

"Are you suggesting that she may have sent *herself* a death threat?"

"Let's just say that there are a number of open questions."

We gazed out at the celebration. It was lovely to see people enjoying themselves in the golden light of sunset. The sound system was playing Eurythmics's "Sweet Dreams," and a roaming caterer with a pitcher of sangria was stopping to top off glasses. Eve Exeter and Barbara Korn, along with their husbands, were sitting at a table together, enthralled by a story General Battersea was telling in her booming, good-natured voice. There was a burst of shrill laughter at its end. I noticed that neither Fitz nor Jenny-Lou was present at the gathering. Dave Lafferty was also missing.

Merritt left me to join the General's table. People immediately welcomed her, made room for her. She wore a pleasant smile, seemed to fit in perfectly, but I knew the whole thing was an act. She was waiting, watching, as she always was. She was busy being a person upon whom nothing was lost.

I was about to sample some of the dishes on the buffet table, when someone clinked their fork against a glass to get people's attention, and the General stood up to address her guests.

With a warm smile, she said how delighted and thankful she was to each and every one of her cherished sisters who had come all the way to the Muddy River Ranch and made the first day of the Sigma Delta Tau reunion so wonderfully memorable. She promised another stellar day tomorrow, starting with a seven a.m. lap swim for those who cared to join her here at the pool.

Some people laughed; some groaned. No one, it seemed, wanted to get up that early. But one voice rose above the others. Eve Exeter said that she would be delighted to meet the General bright and early tomorrow morning. She explained that she swam every morning without fail at the MIT pool, and she hated missing even one day, adding that she began her workouts at six a.m., not seven. From across the pool, I saw Bree Jumper roll her eyes.

Barbara Korn tentatively waved her arm. "I'll go too," she said.

Eve seemed surprised. "Really, Barbara? I don't think of you as an early riser. As I recall, you used to sleep half the day back at school."

"People change," Barbara replied defensively. "Anyway, I had a lot of anxiety back then. College was a really hard time in my life. I had to go on Xanax."

There was a beat of silence. If she was waiting for a word of sympathy from Eve or anyone else, she didn't get it. The party had been so festive, so much what everyone had wanted and hoped for, that her confession was like a flat note ruining the music. I imagined people muttering to themselves, *Debbie Downer.*

Barbara attempted to rectify her mistake. It started out well, then took a turn. "I'm different now. I actually like getting up early and I enjoy working out. I take exercise classes twice a week at a gym, so I can do my usual routine while you two high achievers put me to shame as usual."

"Wonderful! Anyone else want to join us?" the General asked brightly.

"Don't look at me," Bree Jumper said. "I'm in bed until the crack of noon. Writers need a lot of REM sleep. It helps the creative process."

"Aubrey?" The General looked hopeful.

"I'm afraid not. But thank you for the invitation."

"You, Olivia?"

I glanced at Merritt, whose stern gaze and single raised eyebrow were as good as a spoken order.

"I'll be there," I said. Of course I would. I was expected to babysit and, if necessary, throw my body between General Battersea and a bullet.

Just then, there was a shattering of glass followed by a scream. The caterer had dropped the sangria pitcher and stood frozen with her hands clamped over her mouth. I jumped to my feet, ready to protect the General if need be, but she was unharmed, just aghast like everyone else. Now the caterer was running away, leaving the broken pitcher where it was. Something had obviously startled her, and several of us went to look. There on the concrete, dripping with spilled sangria, was a scorpion. Eight legs, lobster-shaped, with pincer claws, and a spiny tail curled over its back. Kind of a purplish-brown color. Puce. An ugly word for an ugly creature's ugly color.

"Whoa. Awesome," murmured the person next to me.

I turned to see Peter Jumper staring intently at the scorpion. The corner of his mouth twitched with a flickering smile of delight.

The bartender with the neck tattoo elbowed her way into the circle. When she saw the scorpion, she gave a snort of disapproval, which I think was intended more for the squeamish caterer than the party-crashing arachnid.

"Relax, everyone. I'll take care of it," the bartender said in a loud, no-nonsense voice. "Will someone please get me a jar?"

"I'll do it," Peter said in a weirdly soft whisper. I thought he was volunteering to get the jar, but instead he bent over and picked up the scorpion by its curled tail. Wearing a disturbing rictus grin, he stood tall and held it aloft like a trophy. Everyone took a step back as the thing dangled helplessly under his pinched fingers. Then for no discernible reason he lurched toward me and waved the creature in my face.

I nearly passed out.

"Peter, put that scorpion down right now!" It was Bree Jumper scolding her son as if he were a naughty nine-year-old, which was frightening in its own way.

Peter shrugged unconcernedly, swung the thing like a lasso around his head, and hurled it into a hedge of manicured juniper bushes.

Shaking her head at the whole sorry business, the bartender returned to her post. Peter stomped off somewhere, with no one urging him to stay. I sat down at the closest table and tried to collect my wits, and the squeamish caterer came back with a broom to sweep up the remnants of the broken pitcher.

"Sorry about that, folks," General Battersea said. "It's getting near sunset, and that's when they come out. That one probably crawled out of the pool filter. In any case, there's nothing to worry about. They only sting if they feel threatened, so if you see one, just leave it alone. And be sure to shake out any articles of clothing you leave on the ground. As I said, there's nothing to worry about."

CHAPTER FOURTEEN

Make It Right

"You poor thing," Nova Olsen whispered to me. "What was he thinking to wave that horrible thing in your face? I've been telling Bree for years he needs to get into therapy. Here, I brought you cake."

She slid a plate in front of me. It was chocolate cake with blue frosting and blue and brown florets. It looked good. I thanked her.

She and Kathy Lafferty sat down at the table, one on each side of me, both with slices of cake, their dinner plates pushed off to the side.

"Kathy and I were just discussing old grudges and what to do about them," Nova told me confidentially.

I perked up. Here was an opportunity to solve the mystery of the forty-year grudge! I smiled at the two women, noting that Kathy looked even more upset than she'd been that afternoon.

"It was all such a long time ago," Kathy said, resuming her conversation with Nova. "It's silly to be thinking of it now. I have no idea what I would say, or what she would do. What if she denies it all? What if I just end up making the whole thing worse?"

Nova replied, "I've been a therapist for thirty years, and I can tell you that it's *always* healthier to confront the situation. In my experience these things turn out to be not nearly as bad as you think they'll be. The outcome can be very positive: Fences are mended, relationships are healed, and everyone involved is better off. It takes courage to be truthful, but it's almost always worth it in the end. Isn't that right, Olivia?"

I nodded and leaned in a little closer.

"It's the *almost* I worry about," Kathy fretted. "*Almost* always worth it. But what if it's not?"

"Dear, sweet Kathy. You were always such a good person—so considerate and helpful to everyone—and I can see that hasn't changed. But I also see how much you're suffering right now, and that is *not* okay with me. Please. Face the situation and do what you need to do."

"I guess you're right. I *am* suffering. When I saw her this morning, it all came rushing back, and now I can't get it out of my head. I feel like I can't breathe, like a huge weight is pressing on my chest. I don't dare tell Dave she's here. He hasn't figured out who she is yet. He'd be livid if he knew. He takes what happened more seriously than I do."

"Yes," Nova said knowingly, "that's just what we do, as women. We hide in our relationships, putting others' needs ahead of our own. And so we justify not standing up for ourselves. But Dave is *not* the important person right now, my dear. He'll be fine. We'll all be fine. It's *you* you should be thinking of."

Kathy looked around nervously at the other guests chatting and enjoying the evening. "It's such a lovely reunion. Trust Joan to make a success of it. She was always the one who held us together."

"Joan is a remarkable woman. But so are you! Look at everything you've done over the years! Now it's time to show how strong you've become. To prove to yourself that you're not afraid to face your adversary, to fight for yourself. It doesn't matter if it happened yesterday or forty years ago or a hundred. You were wronged, deeply, and you never received the apology due to you. It's *not* too late to ask for it. Young Kathy is still inside you, and she's hurting. Do it now for Young Kathy. Take her part, protect her, show her you're strong and brave enough to take care of her today, even if you couldn't long ago."

Kathy bit her nails. "I don't know. I don't want to ruin the weekend for everyone."

"There you go again. Putting your own needs last. If I had a dollar for every woman who came into my office and worried about the *other* people in her life! Try to think about it this way: Everything happens for a reason. We're all here together for a reason. *This may be your reason.* Fate is handing you a golden opportunity that may never come again—a chance to make things right at last, not just with Eve, but with yourself. Don't miss this chance. Get out there and fight for yourself!"

"Okay, okay. I'm going to do it." Kathy started to rise and was almost erect, when she suddenly plopped back down. "Are you sure, Nova? Really sure?"

"I'm completely sure."

"Okay. I'm going. Wish me luck."

"You don't need it, my friend. You have all the strength you need inside," replied the therapist.

CHAPTER FIFTEEN

A Confrontation

Kathy Lafferty, former middle school science teacher, dressed in a loose, flowery linen shirt over yellow capris, padded along the side of the pool in rubber flip-flops decorated with pink plastic flowers. She approached the table where Barbara, the General, and Merritt were sitting. She hesitated when she realized Eve wasn't sitting among them, as she had been just a minute before. Looking disoriented and uncertain, her plan foiled already, she cast an anxious glance back to Nova, who pointed to the buffet table, where Eve was spooning bean salad onto a paper plate. Kathy reoriented herself and marched toward the new location. She planted herself directly behind her nemesis, which was a mistake, because when Eve turned away from the buffet, plate in hand, she nearly spilled the bean salad on Kathy's shirt. Eve was almost six feet tall, lean and imposing. She was used to being seen, heard, and obeyed, and she glared in surprise at the little obstacle in her path. Kathy was a plump five feet two inches, her round face puffy from sunburn.

Everything told me this would not be a fair fight. I cringed in anticipation but couldn't look away.

Kathy's voice was too quiet for me to hear, but I could tell from the ramrod stiffness in her spine that she was indeed saying her piece, standing up for herself. Eve's expression was first puzzled, then quietly amused, and finally annoyed. The conversations among the other guests quieted as people turned to look at what they instinctively sensed was not a friendly encounter. Even the caterers paused in their work, and the cowboy chef, who'd been scraping the grill, held his spatula aloft as if asking for silence from his workers. Actually, I think that's exactly what he was doing. Literally everyone was trying to hear what was being said.

Just when, by my estimation, Kathy should have been concluding her speech, Eve said something low that I couldn't hear, but the smirk on her face made her hostility plain. Kathy's cheeks bloomed red, and she started to sputter. Then anger rose and took hold of her, and she started bellowing loudly enough for everyone to hear every word: "How dare you deny it! You know it's true! You know what you did to me!"

Eve Exeter, unruffled, spoke again, keeping her voice low. Whatever she said was obviously not conciliatory. Instead, it pushed Kathy over the edge into full-blown hysteria. She began shrieking. "You owe me an apology. More than an apology. You owe me the career you stole from me! I hate you! You ruined my life! You're a fraud and a bully and you always were!"

Kathy's voice was strangled with wrath, pain, and a certain hopelessness, as if she knew she had no chance of being understood and respected. She had been bottled up for decades, stoppered by the custom of self-control, by her own caring, unselfish nature, and now the volcano was erupting, the lava sweeping everything in front of it, setting the world ablaze.

Eve looked up, saw the many eyes upon her, and realized that the thing most dreaded at social gatherings—a scene—was happening. And she was in the middle of it. Perhaps, in some people's estimation, the proximate cause of it.

She gave a simpering little smile at us rubberneckers and started to make her escape back to the table where her group (I couldn't help thinking of them as "the cool girls") was seated. She hadn't gone very far, still carrying the plate of bean salad, when Kathy, following closely, snatched at her arm.

"Don't you walk away from me!"

Eve swung around, angry now, "How dare you put your hands on—"

Before she could finish the sentence, Kathy grabbed a full glass of sangria off a table and threw the liquid into Eve's face.

Eve sputtered, raised a hand to her stinging eyes. "What on earth? You crazy bitch! You're out of your mind!"

Kathy looked startled. Maybe she was amazed at what she'd done.

This was the moment, in my opinion, when Kathy ought to have followed through decisively. If only she had delivered the perfect one-line coup de grâce that would have left no doubt in anyone's mind that she stood firmly behind the hurled drink, that she absolutely did not regret it, that Eve Exeter had truly deserved that insult and many more—then she might have emerged victorious and rallied people to her cause, whatever it was.

Instead, she faltered, let the now-empty glass fall and shatter on the flagstone, and, with a strangled cry of rage and humiliation, darted around the pool and through the gate with her silly sandals flapping like too-big clown shoes.

There was silence until the brilliant colors of her shirt were no longer visible through the trees. We all just sat there, wondering what would happen next.

Nova Olsen spoke first. "I'll go to her," she said, and hurried off after the distraught woman.

Barbara slid to Eve's side, offering a paper napkin printed with the colors of the American flag. She reached out to support Eve by the elbow, ready to lead her back to her place at the table. But Eve jerked away. Her straight spine seemed to have become even straighter. In a stern, unflinching voice—a voice that had informed decades of hapless students that the failing grade they'd earned in her class was well deserved—she addressed her onlookers.

"I can't imagine what got into her to be so . . ." She searched for the right word. "So very rude. But she always was unstable, and it appears that hasn't changed. Sad, really. To think that, at this age, one could be so at the mercy of one's emotions and . . . well, I'll be kind and say one's *infantile, pathetic delusions.*"

Bree spoke up quite clearly. "You're not going to pretend you don't know what that was about, are you? We all know what that was about." She brought a hand to her mouth to camouflage a hiccup.

Barbara piped up, squaring off against Bree. "You stay out of this, Bree. It's between Eve and Kathy. It has nothing to do with you."

I recalled the phrase *generals talk to generals, lieutenants to lieutenants.* Barbara was appointing herself Eve's lieutenant and, by facing off against Bree, implying that Bree was a mere lieutenant too.

Bree was having none of that. She was a general in her own mind. "No, *you* stay out of it, Barbara. You were kissing Eve's ass all through college, and now you're doing it again. When are you going to admit you're a closeted lesbian and you really want to fuck her?"

Barbara sputtered and choked out a few incoherent words before Joan Battersea, the real general, hastily cut in. "Ladies, please. Enough bickering. Listen to me. If there's one thing I learned from war, it's that in the end there's one winner and one loser. It may seem unfair, but it's nature's way. The winner takes all."

"Sounds like my divorce," muttered Bree. She raised her glass and called to the bartender, "Another dark 'n' stormy, dear."

The General continued as if she hadn't heard. "As I'm sure we all know, the dispute between Eve and Kathy went up the chain of command, and the finding came down that Eve was in the right. She was completely cleared of wrongdoing. I understand that Kathy was devastated and, no doubt, felt betrayed and humiliated, and obviously it still stings. Now we all have to do what we can to help her through it. That's what friends are for."

Eve hurried to agree. "That's right. The matter was put before the biology professor, the chairman of the biology department, and the academic dean of the university. They all found in my favor and against Kathy."

"But Kathy wasn't there to tell her side of it!" protested Bree. "She'd gone home to take care of her sick mother. And the next thing she knew, she was expelled! The issue was decided without her evidence!"

"That wasn't my fault. She could have been there if she'd wanted to be," Eve said.

"You obviously don't know anything about sick mothers," Bree said.

The gate creaked, and we all watched in dread as Nova circled the pool at a dignified pace, so different from Kathy's clumsy departure.

"How's she doing?" Merritt asked.

"She's okay. She's in her room with her husband. She's pretty upset. I think, you know, she'd been carrying this for quite some time. Dave's not too happy about it. He says they're leaving in the morning."

"Oh my goodness. That's completely unnecessary," said the General in consternation. "Of course she should have aired her grievance if she felt it was necessary. I support any person's right to speak from the heart, no matter how difficult the subject is. But there's no point in running off now that it's done. We're her friends. We're here to help and support her. I'm sure every one of us can sympathize with her pain, whether it's justified or not, and Eve will certainly forgive her. Won't you, Eve?"

Eve's face was stony. She said nothing.

The General carried on, oblivious. "I'll go and talk to her, poor thing. We can work this out—all of us, together. That's the SDT way! We're too old, my friends—and we ought to be too wise—to let a silly kerfuffle ruin our reunion!"

"*Kerfuffle* is your term, Joan. I doubt it would be Kathy's," Bree said dryly, and tipped back her glass to get the last drops.

I was liking Bree more and more. She was the only one stepping up to defend Kathy. Even Nova, who'd pushed Kathy into the disastrous confrontation, seemed to be distancing herself from its result. But I did wish Bree hadn't laid in to the dark 'n' stormies the way she had, because when every pronouncement is accompanied by a burp, a hiccup, or a slurring of words, it does undermine a speaker's gravitas.

Except for her one expression of concern, Merritt had been silent. I had noticed her keen gaze shifting to each member of the group in turn. What was she thinking? What motives was she sussing out? I couldn't fathom how this so-called kerfuffle had anything to do with our remit to protect General Battersea from an anonymous death threat. It seemed to have nothing to do with our client at all.

I would soon discover how wrong I was about that.

CHAPTER SIXTEEN

Death Threat #2

The General was about to march off to the guesthouse to convince the Laffertys to stay at the reunion, when the gate creaked again and we all turned to see Dave Lafferty storming toward us, red in the face, fury sparking in his eyes. A leather shoulder holster over his T-shirt cradled a handgun.

A gun? Really? How's that supposed to help anything? I thought with mounting panic.

Barbara let out a startled yelp, Nova turned white, and I was ready to duck for cover. Merritt was silent, alert, leaning slightly forward, ready to move quickly to neutralize the danger if need be, in whatever way possible, though I couldn't imagine how she or anyone could stop the retired cop from doing his worst. Bree was the only one who spoke. She held up her glass once more—a favorite gesture, apparently—and cried out, "Hail! He has come! Welcome the Great Avenger!"

Despite the damp pink stain on the front of her blouse from the hurled sangria, and the rude banter from the fantasy writer, Eve stood tall, in full professorial mode, pumped up with the righteousness of her recent condescending speech. But now Dave Lafferty had arrived on the scene with a handgun strapped to his chest, and even Eve's facade wobbled. Dave was a far different creature than his wife—a man for whom confrontation and violence was all in a day's work. We all knew that what Kathy couldn't or wouldn't do, her husband could and possibly would.

A stream of invective flowed from his mouth—a hodgepodge of words not usually heard in polite company, much less at sorority soirees. I caught some pieces of it: "You smug, selfish old bitch . . . a total fraud, a cheater . . . have no right . . . think you're such a genius . . . using other people . . ." His voice rose, and we all heard this part loud and clear: "I could kill you right now!" He reached for the gun.

Eve shrank back—we all did. Only Merritt and the General rose out of their chairs.

Then, with a lingering smirk, a smirk meant to be observed, Dave let his hand fall to his side. From where I was sitting, it looked as though he hadn't actually touched his weapon, only waved his hand across the air in front of it to give dramatic weight to his threat.

We all exhaled, though not entirely, because as long as Dave Lafferty was angry and armed, none of us was safe. It was a shocking turn of events, most likely unprecedented in the sorority's long history. No doubt boyfriends had caused ruckuses at dances many times in the past, and a few had probably screamed sexually frustrated obscenities on the street outside the Sigma Delta Tau house, but I was willing to bet that nothing quite like this had happened at a sorority event before.

General Battersea was not amused.

A retired cop might have been expected to intimidate a tenured professor, but he was no match for a former brigadier general. In a flash, moving faster than one would have thought possible, Joan Battersea inserted her bulky self between the two adversaries.

"Stand down!" she bellowed at the cop. And when he didn't instantly comply: "I say, soldier, stand down immediately!"

Dave Lafferty was clearly not a soldier, but as a police officer he had worn a uniform, taken orders, and conducted himself in a manner befitting his station in an iron hierarchy of power, so there was enough of the regimental reflex in him that he responded automatically, if unwillingly, to the General's order.

You could see his fury draining away—see the starch leave his shoulders, and his puffed-out chest deflate—to be replaced by a more tractable demeanor. He slowly scanned the worried faces around him, and seemed to perceive what was happening, what he himself had done. Then he gave a grunt that conveyed grudging acquiescence, but not submission. A grunt that said, *I'll do what you say, but I take back nothing. Count yourselves lucky that I'm agreeing to go away peaceably.*

In silence we watched the second Lafferty retreat, and breathed a collective sigh when he was gone. It had been a second ugly scene to add to the first. A sad finale to an otherwise stellar day.

Eve Exeter was stiffly submitting to a sloppy hug from Barbara Korn. Bree Jumper was smiling artfully, no doubt intending to steal the material for a clash of Viking-like tribes in her next book. Nova Olsen had assumed her unruffled therapist mask. I wondered how she felt about the advice she'd given Kathy now.

Merritt caught my eye. One eyebrow rose a millimeter, just enough for me and no one else to notice. She seemed to be telegraphing a message, but I had no idea what it was. She did a lot of things with her eyebrows; they were her most expressive feature. Yet I rarely understood what they were saying.

The General, on the other hand, was easy to read. She was vexed and disgruntled. Pacing in a circle, she muttered to no one in particular, "This is ridiculous, just ridiculous. All this over a silly . . ." She hesitated, choosing the next word carefully. "Misunderstanding." Her frown deepening, she huffed, "I simply cannot let this tomfoolery ruin the weekend. They *must* understand they are among friends. There is absolutely no reason for retreat. I'll go and talk to them immediately." She set off with a sturdy, decisive gait.

Now from my distance of about twelve feet, I saw Merritt's eyebrows, both of them, shoot up, and her dark blue eyes stare at me with considerable force. In case there was any doubt about her meaning, her index finger pointed. This time I got the message.

Springing out of my seat, I called after the General, "Wait! I'll come with you!"

The General didn't seem to hear me and didn't slow down. She was on a mission.

As I trotted after her to the guesthouse, I wondered what my boss expected me to do. Was I supposed to act as a bodyguard, somehow preventing our host from being shot to death by the angry ex-cop? If so, I was vastly underqualified on a skills level. And, psychologically speaking, I was just an average nonheroic human being, unequal to, and completely uninterested in, the task of endangering, possibly losing, my own life to protect the life of a clearly rash individual who, knowingly and by her own choice, may have been marching straight into enemy fire. The best I could do was hope that Dave Lafferty had come to his senses and tucked his service revolver into whatever locked box it was supposed to be stored in.

CHAPTER SEVENTEEN

Olivia and the General Bond

The ex-cop did not answer the General's forceful knock. It was Kathy who cracked the door of the Laffertys' room just enough to see who was there. When she recognized her visitor, she squeezed out of the room without letting the door swing open, thus depriving both her riled-up host and her angry husband of any visual contact that might further incite either one. She was clearly an experienced peacekeeper—unsurprising given her long career in middle school education.

Though there wasn't any obvious reason for secrecy, I stepped back a bit, so as to be partly hidden by a juniper bush at the corner of the guesthouse. From this hidden spot, I watched furtively as urgent explanation, anger, understanding, and kind commiseration passed in quick succession between the sorority sisters, each emotion expressed in body language and the interplay of harsh and gentle tones that reached my ears. The conversation ended in a hug that looked comically lopsided, given the great difference in the women's heights. I took this to mean that the General had agreed to forgo direct communication with the offending party, and that the situation overall was on its way to being resolved. The reunion would continue as planned, with everyone making a good-faith effort to restore the festive atmosphere.

As the General made her way back to the barbecue, I looked for an avenue of escape. If she realized that she'd been followed and spied on, she would probably be annoyed. But I was too late. She was bearing down on my position with her usual purposeful stride, made a little quicker and crisper by heightened emotion, and there was really no dignified way, short of throwing myself on the ground and hoping for the best, of remaining unseen.

The General stopped and peered at me quizzically. "Olivia? Is that you? Why are you hiding behind that bush?"

I stepped out, offered a sheepish smile. "Just making sure you're okay."

She gave a dubious grimace. "And what would you do if I weren't? If, let's say, I was suddenly attacked by an enemy combatant? You're obviously not armed. Have you been trained in hand-to-hand combat?"

I shook my head. I couldn't do knuckle push-ups either. Or jog fifteen miles carrying a heavy pack on my back. I couldn't squirm under coils of barbed wire, or wade through a murky swamp without crying. I lollygagged in bed every morning, daydreaming pointlessly as chunks of my precious life that I would never get back flew by. The police, the military, the Secret Service, and the FBI would probably all stamp REJECT on my application. Yet here I was. I decided to change the subject.

"May I accompany you back to the barbecue?" I asked politely.

She shrugged her big lumpy shoulders. "No harm in that, I suppose."

Let's hope there won't be harm, I thought as I trotted beside her, matching my steps to her own.

"Tell me about yourself, Olivia," she said in her brusque but friendly manner.

I was pleased that she'd asked. I'd been feeling a bit invisible at the reunion so far. Everyone seemed to be wondering what on earth I was doing there, but had been too polite to inquire. So I obliged the General with a summary. Born in Queens, mother died when I was ten, father a handyman. Childhood spent reading detective stories. High school GPA: average. Queens College, English major. College GPA: average. Postgrad jobs included barista, bicycle courier, assistant to a roof gardener, reader of slush-pile manuscripts, fact-checker for an online news agency. Then, a year ago, my big break: the job as Aubrey Merritt's assistant. My ultimate goal: to open my own detective agency.

"Oh, and I'm married," I added. "I got married May second." I felt a little guilty for having almost forgotten about Trevor. To make up for it, I enthused at length about our Sicilian honeymoon, his brilliant, budding acting career, and the fact that we were presently seriously scoping the market for a bigger apartment in New York City. That made our marriage seem weightier. We weren't just two aimless grads shacking up in a tiny East Village walk-up anymore. We were an adult-ish couple intent on moving up life's ladder—hopefully to an apartment with an elevator and windows that actually opened. Maybe even (I dreamed of this daily) an in-unit washer/dryer.

"You seem like a very solid young woman, Olivia. Aubrey is lucky to have you," the General said warmly. "And congratulations on your marriage. Trevor sounds like a wonderful young man."

I flushed with pleasure. I had no idea what she meant by *solid*. I didn't feel solid at all, more like a cloud of random gases. And I knew full well that I had said nothing to suggest that Trevor was wonderful or that my boss was lucky to have me. But I appreciated the General's kindness. In a stroke of courage, I replied, "Now tell me something about yourself, General Battersea."

She was silent for a few paces, and I worried that I had overstepped my bounds. Then, wistfully, she said, "My great-great-great-grandfather, Wilson F. Battersea, came to this country from England in 1861, just after the start of the Civil War. The petroleum industry was in its infancy then, and he found work on an oil rig in Pennsylvania, of all places . . . He met my great-great-great-grandmother, Ilvira P. Goodfellow, at a church dance in . . . The band was playing . . . Ilvira said . . . and Wilson replied . . ."

After reciting a snippet of her forebears' utterly banal alleged courtship conversation, the General shared a hodgepodge of ultra-specific names, dates, and places that I didn't really care about and couldn't have followed if I'd tried. So I didn't bother trying. I simply put an interested look on my face as I dreamed about finding an amazing apartment, and when she was finally, at long last, finished with her meandering ancestral tale, I piped up with "Wow. That's really interesting."

"You're a good listener, Olivia," the General said with a smile.

It made me happy to think she liked me. I liked her, too, and fervently hoped she would come to no harm during the reunion. This innocent thought boomeranged immediately. I suddenly remembered that I wasn't there to idly *hope* for her safety. I was supposed to be actively *ensuring* it.

My eyes darted in several directions, seeking out places where a sniper might hide. But the light had been fading rapidly for the last hour, and the landscape—what I could see of it—was drenched in shadow. This was my first dusk in the desert, and it felt a little frightening, vaguely hostile. Without the sun's burning rays to warm the atmosphere, the temperature had dropped rapidly and significantly. The insect noises were louder and more shrill—

different insects from the ones I'd been hearing like white noise all afternoon. It felt like everything was changing, not just the light, but the plants and animals too. The desert was becoming a different place. I'd just been getting used to one of its faces, and now I was being introduced to the other.

Ahead in the gloom, the pool area was silent. The pool lights were on, and the turquoise water emitted an eerie glow. One lonely caterer was all that was left of the party, gliding like a ghost, packing up the dishes and trash. Soon the place would be completely deserted, the placid water quietly inviting nocturnal creatures for an off-the-record sip and dip.

"We ought to be getting back to the house now," I said, trying not to sound fearful.

The General closed her eyes and, turning her old, weathered face to the bruise-colored sky, slowly inhaled the dry air. "I've always felt safe here," she said after a long exhale. "The desert is a peaceful place for an old soldier to come home to."

I made a gentle empathizing noise as my mind filled with images of scorpions, snakes, and assassins.

CHAPTER EIGHTEEN

Real Estate

The party had migrated to the big air-conditioned living room, where General Battersea announced to the group that the Laffertys were reconsidering their decision to depart the next morning. She made it sound innocuous, as if they had merely adjusted their travel plans. "Oh, and they decided to retire early this evening," she added lightly, as if they were simply tuckered out from having had such a big, fun day.

Everyone rolled along with that version of events, no one daring to make a comment or ask a question, lest it raise the whole ugly business again. And so the memory of the recent "kerfuffle" was communally pushed into the fog of the almost forgotten. Such were the ways of polite society.

My eye slid over to Eve Exeter, whose face registered no joy at the thought that the Laffertys would be among the group again the next day.

A silly game of charades ensued. Apparently the sisters had enjoyed playing charades on those long-ago 1980s weekend nights when there was nothing else to do—no chaperoned dances with select fraternities or mandatory fundraisers for approved worthy causes. Now they gleefully resurrected their old pastime, acting out their parts with youthful abandon.

After about an hour of juvenile hilarity, I noticed that Peter Jumper, who had been sitting by himself in a corner wearing headphones, had slipped away. Shortly after that, Nova Olsen bade the group good night, claiming weariness after her long day of travel, and the men—Fitz, Conrad, and Jacob—drifted out to the veranda, where I saw them talking over drinks in the wavering yellow glow of tiki torches. Fitz smoked one of his fat cigars in a way that involved a lot of rather lascivious licking and sucking.

Since the General was safely in Merritt's company, and the overall situation seemed stable, I slipped into the deserted kitchen to check my messages. The caterers had parked some of their stuff on the table—big silver trays, linen napkins, glassware. There was a box of wine on the tiled floor and what was left of the SDT sheet cake on the marble counter. I opened my phone. As promised, Trevor had sent videos of the three apartments he'd visited with the broker earlier that evening.

He had written, I like the last one. It's only four blocks from Central Park. The broker says we have to move fast. I'll hand deliver a deposit first thing tomorrow if you agree.

I viewed each video once, twice, and a third time, just to be sure. Then I wrote: I get that #3 has a great location but there are only three small windows, and the hallway is really narrow and cramped. The whole place seems kind of dark and claustrophobic. Not much closet space either. Where's the laundry?

His reply came a minute later. It's in the building.

Where in the building?

The basement.

Did you take a video?

No, Olly. I did not see any point in filming washing machines and dryers.

Oh. Okay. I was actually more interested in, like, the ambience.

It's a laundry room. The ambience sucks.

Did you go down and actually look?

No. Why would I do that? Why would anyone do that?

It could smell like mold. There could be cockroaches. People could have left half-eaten sandwiches in the trash.

I didn't get a reply for a long time. Not even pulsing blue dots. I was starting to wonder if the Mets had just scored a run, thus blowing out his mental circuitry, when this happened:

Which apartment do you like?

Well, #2 is not bigger in terms of square feet, but it's an airier space with much better windows and a southern exposure (more light). Also higher up (less street noise). And the foyer isn't nearly as ugly and depressing as the other one. And from what I could see in the video, in that closet you didn't open, but the door was ajar when you walked by, I think there was a stacking washer/dryer unit in there.

Yeah, I think I remember the broker saying there was a laundry closet or something. What did you think of the first apartment?

I wanted to say something positive to show I had an open mind, and hadn't already settled passionately and irrevocably on Apartment #2 after the washer/dryer confirmation, so I wrote, It has a nice fire escape where we could grow tomatoes in the summer. The vines could twist around the railings.

The fire escape? Is that all?

That's all I can think of. You? Thoughts about #1?

So it's between 2 and 3.

Yup. Location versus Light (and Laundry).

At this point in the negotiation, I was almost sure I would prevail. Because there is simply no contest between Location and Light that Light won't win. Light is joy, pleasure, and illumination. Nothing compares to it. *Location* is just another word for *I'm a lazy cretin who won't walk a few extra blocks.*

Trevor probably sensed that somehow, in a slippery, roundabout way, the issue had been decided, but he fought on a little longer.

It's a longer commute for you. You'd have to take the 6 from 86th to 23rd and then walk to Gramercy Park.

My choice, freely made.

Again, a delay. As the seconds ticked by, my confidence wobbled. Was I making a mistake? Not in my choice of apartment (#2 was clearly the best) but in not requesting more information about Trevor's needs and preferences, and giving them equal weight to my own? After all, a nice apartment was nice, but a happy marriage was priceless. Maybe Trevor really loved Apartment #3 for its proximity to the park, and would never be happy in airy, out-of-the-way Apartment #2. Maybe he would agree with me just to get along, but would secretly harbor a resentment, and our new apartment would always be a subtle sore point between us, a little nub of discontent, and by slow degrees our relationship would sour, and the man I loved would lose his happy smile. I was just about to text back, *Actually Apartment #3 looks really nice too!* when this came in:

I just looked and there's a Trader Joe's on the corner and a pizza place a few blocks away. Their specialty is ham and anchovy. The reviews are great.

Ham and anchovy? I nearly gagged.

Awesome! I can't wait to try it! Hey, did you notice that big wall in the living room where we could put a really big TV to watch the Mets and Rangers?

Oh, yeah. Now that you mention it. Good idea.
So I guess we'll take it, right?

I think so.

Okay. I'll drop off the deposit check in the morning. Good talk, Olly. Sweet dreams.

Good night, Trevor. 🩶🩶🩶

CHAPTER NINETEEN

The General Goes to Bed

The grandfather clock was plodding through ten ponderous gongs when the General announced that she was heading off to bed.

Merritt and I followed her up the stairs and into her bedroom. Her bed was as well made as any I'd seen: There wasn't a bump, lump, or wrinkle in its taut, tucked, Navajo-themed bedspread. The old girl was a soldier all the way.

I checked the closet and behind the door. No one.

"Fitz's bedroom is at the other end of the house," the General told Merritt. She didn't seem at all troubled that she and her husband had separate bedrooms. I got the feeling that, whatever degree of romance might have existed between them in the past, it had mellowed into a comfortable friendship made possible in part by their living totally separate lives.

I made my way around the perimeter of the large room, closing and locking the four windows—two at the front of the house, two at the side.

"Is that really necessary?" the General asked.

"It is until we know you're out of danger," I said.

"Have I no say in the matter?"

Merritt cut in. "None whatsoever. You promised Fitz you would abide by my wishes, and that's what you must do."

"It's a shame. I love the night air and the sound of the cicadas."

"You'll survive," Merritt said dryly.

An ill-advised remark in my opinion, as our client's survival was far from assured.

"Check the bathroom, Blunt," Merritt said.

Switching on the light, I entered the tiled room. Bright, white, unadorned. A single toothbrush in a silver cup. A shower curtain pulled tight across the bathtub made me catch my breath. I swept it back with a sudden, vigorous jerk, to catch whoever might be lurking behind it by surprise. (The shower scene from *Psycho* was never far from my mind.) The shower was unoccupied.

The medicine cabinet over the sink was whispering to me. I itched to see what was inside. Merritt and the General were talking in the other room, paying me no mind. I weighed the risks. The General was a neat and tidy person, not one to hoard gels and creams, nor was she a hypochondriac likely to have a dozen prescriptions crammed onto the thin shelves. It was a good bet that, if I opened the door, an avalanche of products would not rain down and clatter into the porcelain sink, letting everyone know I was snooping.

I was right. The shelves were sparsely populated with antibacterial ointment, Tylenol, a cheap drugstore moisturizing cream, Band-Aids, manicure scissors, and dental floss. The whole kit and caboodle could have fit inside an Army ditty bag.

I returned to the bedroom in time to hear the General say, "This is a late night for me. I'm usually in bed by ten, up at six thirty on the dot. Then it's straight to the pool for my morning swim, followed by coffee, shower, breakfast, and I'm ready to tackle the day by nine a.m. I credit my good health with keeping a strict routine."

"Good for you, Joan," Merritt said perfunctorily. "Now, remember what I told you. Blunt and I are leaving now, and I need you to lock this door behind us. Good night."

Together, my boss and I left our client's room and waited in the hallway until we heard her lock the door.

My odd sleeping quarters on the third floor happened to be directly over the General's bedroom. As I was getting ready for bed, I heard some movement on the floor below: a squeak, a thump, a woody grind, and a gruff *humph.* The General was opening one of the windows I had just closed. The cool night air, the sound of crickets—these things she would not be denied.

What on earth was I going to do about that? If I went down and scolded the General, told her to shut and lock her window, she might oblige me and then open it again the moment I'd left. She was a sixty-something former brigadier general, not a toddler to be controlled by a hired nanny-sleuth. But if I did nothing, and someone crawled in the window to do her harm? That would be my fault for knowing the room was unsecured and doing nothing about it.

I sighed. Merritt was in the guest room on the second floor, at the other end of the house, somewhere in the vicinity of Fitz's. What if she were sleeping? Should I wake her up? I decided to text her.

> Sorry to disturb. The General opened her window. Please advise.

I waited for ten seconds, then twenty, then thirty. It was like Merritt not to read her messages, much less respond to them in a timely manner. She was a stickler in so many other areas, but when it came to texting, she was as lax as every other boomer I knew. She seemed to think that the ridiculously long communication delays that had hampered and hobbled her generation were somehow better and more virtuous than the instant communication most of the world now enjoyed.

Just when I was about to march down to her bedroom and bang on her door, my phone pinged. Her reply: Thank you. I'll take care of it.

Out of curiosity, I listened at the top of the stairs. I heard my boss walk down the hall and knock sharply on the General's door. The door opened and a muffled conversation took place. It was short, things were decided, and Merritt went back to bed.

I returned to my bedroom and listened carefully. The window didn't close.

Whoa. The old broad was a tough nut to crack. What on earth was I supposed to do now? I stuck my head out my window, trying to check on hers, when the General stuck her head out *her* window and craned her neck to look up at me.

"What are you doing up there, Blunt?"

"I'm waiting for you to close and lock your window, General."

"I see. You and Aubrey make quite the team, don't you?"

"We do our best."

"All right. Since it means so much to you. Good night, Blunt."

"Good night, General."

She disappeared; the window closed. I waited until I heard it lock, and then I waited a little longer until the square of illumination that fell on the ground below her window disappeared. At last our client was tucked safely in her bed—or so I allowed myself to presume—and I was free to crawl into mine.

But not before flinging back the covers to make sure that no reptile had slithered in since the last time I'd looked. Merritt had said she was joking about the diamondback, but with her I could never be sure. Unsurprisingly, the bed was unoccupied. The sheets were crisp and clean and welcoming.

I slipped between them gratefully. I was extremely tired. Between the red-eye from New York, the rented car, and the drive to the ranch, followed by skeet shooting and barbecuing, not to mention the constant stress of living in a rattlesnake-infested environment and of waiting for our client to be murdered—it had been a long day. You would expect that after such a day a person would fall asleep in minutes, but I had no such luck.

I couldn't get it out of my head that General Battersea was sleeping in the room below mine. I knew that every precaution had been taken. Objectively, there was no reason why I shouldn't shut my eyes. But I also knew that her life was in danger at every moment until the culprit was identified and neutralized—it was *in my hands*—and the responsibility for protecting her weighed on me like nothing ever had. First thing tomorrow I would urge Merritt to swear off death threat cases forever. Because no crime could possibly be as stressful as a murder that hadn't happened yet.

I lay awake, listening to the sounds of the night—crickets, odd animal cries. The house was probably quite safe, I told myself. Fitz had assured Merritt that he would lock up tight. He could do this, he said, remotely, from his phone. And hadn't Jenny-Lou made a point of telling us just how secure the property was?

As my eyes closed, the old grandfather clock on the first floor began to emit faint, dignified chimes. I counted up to eleven, matching their cadence to a mantra: *Nothing to worry about . . . nothing to worry about . . .*

CHAPTER TWENTY

An Accident?

I was halfway to dreamland when I heard a sound that was definitely something to worry about. General Battersea's door had made a soft *whoosh*, and now a pair of slippered feet were padding across the wooden planks of the hallway. *The woman is incorrigible,* I thought as I listened to her quietly descend the stairs.

I then heard a series of bumps and thumps, followed by a burst of swear words.

I went out to the landing in the T-shirt, sports bra, and athletic shorts I always slept in, and flicked on the light switch in the hall. There was General Battersea, sitting in a disgruntled and untidy heap at the bottom of the staircase, rubbing her ankle above the edge of a boiled-wool slipper.

"Are you all right?" I called down to her.

"My ankle," she replied. "I think it's sprained. Darn it. Just what I need."

I went down the stairs in bare feet. The light in the first-floor hallway was dim—just the glow of a few wall sconces—but it was enough to see by. "Can I help you up?"

"No, no, no. I can get up myself." She rolled onto her hands and knees, but when she put her weight on the ankle, she winced again. "Oh damn, damn, damn. The damn thing hurts. I suppose it really *is* sprained."

"Stay there. I'll get some ice." I ran off to the kitchen and made an ice pack by folding some cubes in a dish towel.

When I returned she was sitting on the bottom step, rubbing her ankle. She took the ice pack and applied it, then looked up at me with an expression of glum frustration. "Of all the silly things that could happen. This is just what I don't need right now."

She was rather brazenly making no excuse for her escape attempt.

"Were you going somewhere?" I asked innocently.

"I was just coming down to get some warm milk to help me sleep. I suppose all the excitement has got to me a bit."

"Next time, text me, and I'll get whatever you need."

"You are a relentlessly helpful young woman, Olivia."

"Thank you."

"For now, you can just help me back to my room, and then bring up some warm milk, if you don't mind." She paused. "And a small slice of that chocolate cake, if there's any left. I'm supposed to be watching my weight, so you should probably make it a *very* small slice."

"Of course," I promised devoutly. "It will be tiny."

We smiled at each other like mischievous schoolgirls. We both knew it wouldn't be.

"Honestly, I think it was the thought of that chocolate cake that was keeping me up. Not that I'm not also concerned about that other thing."

"The threat on your life, you mean."

"Yes, that thing. The threat."

"By the way, General, how did you fall? Did you catch your slipper on something? Or step on the hem of your robe?"

"No. There was something on the stairs, midway down, something small. A ball or something. I didn't see where it went. It must have rolled."

I looked around and didn't see anything on the stairs or in the hall.

"I'll try to find it later. For now, let's get you back upstairs." With her arm over my shoulder, we limped together, step by step, up the stairs. I helped her into bed.

"You should probably have some Tylenol for the pain and swelling," I said.

She frowned. "I'm not sure I have any."

"You do. There's some in your—"

"Actually, there may be some in the medicine cabinet," she said, interrupting me before I could incriminate myself.

"I'll look there. And you'll want to keep that ankle iced for as long as you can stand it." My stint as a mediocre high school soccer player had taught me a few things at least.

I brought out water and two Tylenol from the bathroom. Then I went to the kitchen, microwaved a mug of 1 percent, and carved a nice big slice of chocolate cake with two blue icing florets. I put it all on a tray with a fork and nicely folded linen napkin, and carried it up to her. She was sitting up in bed, and, as I placed the tray on her lap, she said dejectedly, "I won't be able to swim in the morning, not with this ankle. Would you hand me my phone? It's there on the dresser. I need to text Eve that I won't be joining her. Oh, and didn't Barbara say she was coming too? I don't think I have her contact info. Oh, well, Eve can let her know and they can decide between the two of them what they want to do."

I handed her her phone. She frowned. "Oh, frustration. My glasses are somewhere. Will you be a dear and send the message for me?"

I found Eve Exeter among her contacts, and the General dictated the following message: I sprained my darn ankle and won't be able to swim in the morning. You and Barbara should go ahead without me. There are bathing caps and fresh towels in the cabana. Enjoy! I sent it off.

The General was sipping from the mug when I realized we had a logistical problem.

"General, I'm sorry. If you don't mind . . ."

"What is it?"

"I'm sorry I have to ask you this but . . ."

"Out with it, Olivia."

"Would you mind getting up and locking the door behind me when I go out? It's important, you know, that the door is kept . . ."

"Yes, yes, yes. The door must be kept locked at all times, says my good friend Aubrey." She set the tray aside, threw back the covers, and rolled off the mattress in her unexpectedly pink nightgown. "It's fine. I don't mind. I gave her my promise. So there we go. Go ahead of me, Olivia. Go, go, go."

She limped along behind me and shooed me into the hall.

I waited until I heard the lock turn, then sighed with relief as I imagined her hobbling painfully back to her bed. She had made that little logistical problem easy for me. *She's really a very sweet person,* I thought.

"Good night again, General," I said rather tenderly. "Please don't go out by yourself again."

"Go to bed, Olivia," I heard her say.

CHAPTER TWENTY-ONE

Failure

My alarm woke me at 6:40 a.m. I had set it when I thought I'd be accompanying General Battersea to the pool, and had forgotten to turn it off. Hoping to catch a few more minutes of rest before the workday began, I silenced it and rolled over in bed.

I was in the liminal state of almost sleep when I heard the grandfather clock's distant musical chimes. I counted seven. I was drifting once again in gray semiconsciousness when a faint *pop* reached my ears. The sound was soft and brief and not particularly worrisome. Then I remembered that the previous day's shooting had sounded just like that.

I jumped out of bed and ran to the window. There was nothing out of the ordinary near the house, on the red dirt slope behind the house, or in front of the stables. My position didn't allow me a look at the entire pool area, only the roof of the cabana and one side of the flagstone patio. A quick motion happened there—a shadowy figure dashed across my narrow field of vision and was gone.

I shoved my feet into sneakers and raced down the stairs. I didn't think about what I might find at the pool. I just ran. As I passed the grandfather clock, I noticed that the time was 7:16.

At first I thought someone had dropped dye in the water—a dark maroon color was spreading across the shallow end of the pool. Then I realized it wasn't dye; it was blood from a body floating face down. It was a large body, a woman's body, in an olive-green camo bathing cap with the word ARMY printed in black letters on the back.

The General's been shot! I thought frantically. She must have changed her mind during the night, decided that a sprained ankle wasn't enough of a disability to interfere with her precious routine, and slipped out of the house without telling me. After getting her text last night, Eve and Barbara must have decided not to show up. So the General had gone swimming by herself. And somehow the shooter had managed to discover that slim window of vulnerability and had turned the biblical threat into a prophecy.

I needed to call 911 immediately, but my phone was in my room, and I couldn't lose precious time running back to get it. The General might be dead already, but if she wasn't, I needed to get her face out of the water before she drowned.

I jumped into the pool, half ran and half swam over to her in water about four feet deep, and saw a big bloody wound in her shoulder, chips of bone exposed. I tried to flip her over, to get her face out of the water, but her body kept rolling away from me. So I pulled her over to the stairs and, with several great yanks, dragged her up them until her head and torso were out of the water. Then I rolled her over.

That's when I saw it wasn't General Battersea. It was Eve Exeter.

CHAPTER TWENTY-TWO

Help!

In movies people always seem to know what to do when they find a possibly dead body. They act swiftly and decisively. Help is called for. Tourniquets are tied. I desperately wanted to function with the same skill and efficiency, but right away things started to go wrong. My jittery fingers slipped right off the slick wet flesh of Eve Exeter's neck when I tried to find a pulse. CPR was made impossible by the fact that her upper and lower jawbones were clenched together as tightly as a sprung bear trap. I tried squeezing her cheeks together to get the jaw hinge to unlock, but her mouth still refused to open. Chest compressions were next on my list. Dimly recalling instructions I had read once in the distant past, I curled my hand into a fist and placed it in what I thought was the correct position, just under the breastbone. I pushed down as hard as I could, but she wasn't lying flat, so her body just bent like a soft inflatable doll's under the pressure, and at the same time it occurred to me that I might have just confused a chest compression with the Heimlich maneuver. Then I noticed that blood was spreading through the shallow water surrounding her body. So I ripped off my T-shirt and hastily threaded it under her back and over her shoulder to cover the wound. Since the sleeves were too short to tie together, I had to use both hands to clasp the cotton shirt tightly against her upper chest. My make-shift bandage made no difference: The blood continued to spread.

The situation was clearly above my pay-grade. *I'm definitely signing up for a first aid course when this is over,* I thought. I was almost certain that Dr. Exeter was dead. But if that was true, why was blood still flowing? Didn't that mean something was pumping—i.e., her heart?

I desperately needed professional help, but how could I get it without a phone? My anxiety surged to a new height. I'd already squandered an excessive amount of time with my half-assed lifesaving attempts, and the situation was only going to get more dire from here. Finally I started doing what I should have done from the beginning. I yelled for help. And yelled. And yelled. And when help didn't instantly appear, I screamed. Once I started screaming, I couldn't seem to stop. My stomach was doing somersaults and seemed to have levitated into my throat. I screamed so loudly I thought my esophagus might pop out of my mouth.

It was Fitz who came running first, followed by Merritt. As soon as he realized what was happening, he whipped out his phone and punched in numbers. Merritt was by my side seconds later. I was by this time babbling incoherently but still clenching the truncated arms of the T-shirt around the scientist's chest. When Merritt touched my shoulder, it felt gentle and consoling, like an angel's touch. She tried to pull me away.

"You can let go now, Blunt. She's gone." When I didn't move, she pried my fingers from the wet wad of bloody T-shirt. "You did your best. She's gone. Let her go, Blunt. You did your best."

I staggered to my feet and lurched around like a drunk person, not knowing whether to sit or stand or what to do. My face felt frozen in a silent scream, and my gut was heaving.

"Here. Sit down." Merritt led me to a chair, and the instant my butt touched the seat, I started to cry.

Merritt paced in front of me, moaning. The last time I'd seen her so upset was when I'd almost gotten myself shot in pursuit of a criminal. Ever since then I'd tried to practice better situational awareness, but I feared that I might have just screwed up again very badly—not that that was the most important issue at the moment.

Nearby, Fitz was yelling our location to the 911 dispatcher, as if extra volume would make the first responders arrive faster.

In the silence after he hung up, I heard Merritt's muttering voice. "I *told* you not to go anywhere alone. Why didn't you listen, you stubborn, stubborn woman? Why didn't you listen to me?"

It took me a moment to realize (with relief) that she was addressing the corpse, not me.

"It's not her, boss," I said quickly. "It's not General Battersea. It's Eve Exeter."

Merritt looked at me as if I had three heads, then bent over and peered at the dead woman's face, tightly framed by the Army swim cap. "Oh my god. Fitz! Fitz, come here!" She frantically waved him over, and to my wonderment and quiet satisfaction, I noticed that she, Aubrey Merritt, the nationally renowned PI famous for her icy logic, was getting a wee bit hysterical, just as I had.

She clasped his arm desperately. "Fitz, did you see Joan this morning?"

"What?" he said, confused.

"We need to find Joan. Right away!"

"She's right there!" He gestured helplessly at the corpse.

"No! That isn't her. Look again." She pulled him closer to the body and pointed. "See? That's not Joan. It's Eve."

Bending over the corpse, he let out a strangled cry. "Oh, thank God. It's a miracle! Thank you, God!"

"Fitz. Listen. We need to find Joan, quickly. There's no time to waste."

He stood straight. His large hazel eyes were bright with shock, but he pulled himself together. "She's usually here at this time. Something must have happened. I'll go and find her."

"She sprained her ankle," I offered from the sidelines. Without context, it sounded asinine.

Fitz and Merritt barely heard me. Their minds were in sync, leaping ahead together.

"When you find her, stay with her. Don't let her out of your sight, not for any reason!" Merritt cried after him as he hurried away.

With Fitz dispatched, Merritt turned to me. "Tell me exactly what happened."

I made a garbled noise. I couldn't remember anything that had happened before I discovered the body, or anything after that either. There was a hole in my short-term memory, like the hole in Eve Exeter's back. If you asked me what day it was, I couldn't have told you.

"Look at me, Blunt." She snapped her fingers in my face. "Over here, right here. Look at me."

We locked eyes.

"Think. What did you see and hear?"

I shook my head. It was hopeless. All I could see was a woman's body floating in a circle of bloody water. The image was hovering before my eyes, blotting out everything else.

She clasped my shoulders and shook me gently. "Get a hold of yourself, for god's sake. Look at me. Think, Blunt, think."

I concentrated on my boss's familiar face—normal, two eyes, pale, tense.

"You heard the gunshot," she prompted. "You followed the sound to the pool. Did you see anyone?"

"Just her . . . floating . . ."

"Anyone else? Go back to the beginning. Take your time."

I wiped my tearstained cheeks and put myself back in my bedroom. "There *was* someone. I saw from my window."

"Very good. Man or woman?"

"I couldn't tell."

"Clothing?"

I felt terrible, knowing I was going to disappoint her. "I can't, boss. It was just a shadow, or a movement. It lasted a second at most."

"Okay. Did you hear anything?"

Closing my eyes, I replayed running down the slope to the pool. Silence. When I got to the gate, there was a sound. "The gate scraped across the flagstone when I pushed it open."

"Good. The gate was closed when you got here, and you opened it. Carry on."

My heart had been beating so fast. I'd been puzzled by the color of the water, then . . . my world shrank to nothing but me and the body.

Merritt must have realized how useless I was, because she stopped trying to get information out of me. "Okay. We've got to move quickly now. This is a crime scene. When the police arrive, they're going to tell us to leave, and they won't let us back until they've processed the scene and removed whatever evidence there might be. I need you to videotape this entire area before they get here. Everything. As fast as you can."

"My phone's back at the house," I said weakly. I didn't even bother asking if she had hers. She often forgot to take her phone with her. (She routinely neglected to charge it too.)

"Go and get it. Quickly."

As I ran back to the house, I had the weird sensation that I wasn't quite inside my body. My legs seemed farther away than usual, and the objects I passed appeared slanted, off-kilter. It felt like the earth had tilted on its axis and I was in danger of slipping off. My world was literally rocked. *Trauma*, I thought. *That's what this is.*

I raced through the back door, pounded down the hall, and was about to run up the stairs, when I spied a bright spot of color peeking out from under the table in the hallway. Angel's orange ball. Of course. That was probably what the General had tripped on. It must have bounced down the stairs after her fall and rolled almost out of sight. I didn't have time to grab it and, as it was not at present a hazard to anyone, I left it where it was.

CHAPTER TWENTY-THREE

The Crime Scene

Merritt was hunched over the lip of the pool, peering down at something in the water, when I got back with my phone. She gestured for me to come over.

The water had been darkened by blood minutes ago; now the blood had dissipated and the water was merely pink tinged—clear enough for us to see what was resting on the bottom of the pool, quivering like a hologram under the weight of water. Unmistakably, it was one of the old-style single-barreled shotguns that many of the guests, including me, had been firing at the shooting range yesterday.

"Smart," Merritt said approvingly. "No fingerprints, no DNA."

Our eyes met. I could see how pleased she was, and I was glad we were alone. Someone who didn't know her might have thought she was complimenting the murderer. She wasn't, not exactly. She was simply glad that his brain might be bigger than a pea. I had often heard her complain about how stupid most criminals were. She loved to point out their mistakes and frequently scoffed that they made her job too easy. If they'd done this *one little thing* differently, she would explain, they might have gotten away with it. The fact that Eve Exeter's murderer had obligingly provided us with what was very likely the murder weapon, while at the same time cagily denying us any of the information we might have hoped to glean from it, meant that he probably possessed some degree of intelligence. Thus, the case might be more stimulating for her, and she would feel more satisfaction when it was solved.

I might have pointed out another possibility: that the killer was a clumsy idiot who'd dropped the gun in the pool by accident. But I didn't want to squash her joy.

"That's one of the skeet shooting guns," I told her, knowing that she hadn't attended yesterday's shooting activity. "They're kept in the ranch manager's office. In a wooden case with glass doors—to show them off, I suppose. There were three or four in use yesterday, all exactly alike, as far as I could tell. Even if they'd all been put back where they belonged and the doors had been locked, anyone could have broken the glass and taken one."

"Fitz was teaching the guests how to use them, is that right?" she asked mildly.

"Correct. He seemed eager to get everyone up to speed. Peter Jumper got a lesson. Dave Lafferty didn't need one, as he already knows everything about guns. Eve, Barbara, and Nova tried their hands." I mentally ran down the list. "Kathy and Bree didn't participate. Oh, and Conrad Zander and Jacob Korn were there when I arrived, but I didn't see them shoot."

Merritt nodded. "We'll talk more about this later. Right now we have work to do." She pointed to a large puddle on the flagstone. "Eve must have thrashed about quite a bit to send this much water onto the ground. She must have seen the shooter coming and was trying to pull herself out of the pool to escape from him when she was shot."

"Or she didn't see him coming at all, just felt the bullet rip into her. It was a shoulder wound, so she might not have died right away. She might have sent all that water onto the flagstone as she was trying to climb out of the pool, bleeding profusely the whole time," I added.

Merritt nodded. "If we can find the spent cartridge, we'll know where the killer was standing when he pulled the trigger."

"Wait a minute. Why do we keep saying *him*? The shooter could easily have been a woman. In fact, it probably *was* a woman."

Merritt gave me a bald stare. This was no time to quibble over pronouns.

I proceeded to document the crime scene, paying attention first to the perimeter of the pool area: the decorative bushes, the earthenware pots filled with flowers, and the empty clay pots that were cracked and chipped. There was a lizard in one of the pots—a green horny thing with protruding yellow eyes and long, wrinkled toes. I let out a startled yelp when I saw it, then glanced over quickly to see if Merritt had heard. She had. But she just shook her head at me in hopeless exasperation and continued with her own inspection.

Throughout this process, I was aware that my efforts were, if not fruitless, then at least unlikely to be helpful. My earlier attempt to save the scientist's life had managed to thoroughly contaminate the scene. Not only had I splashed water on the flagstones as I dragged the victim's body up the steps, but I had then tramped around practically everywhere in sopping wet sneakers, leaving confused trails of damp footprints behind.

The guilty sneakers were still on my feet, still squishing when I walked, my heels chafing against damp canvas. The rest of my clothes—my sports bra and athletic shorts—were wet as well, and my hair was dripping. Rivulets of chlorinated water kept coursing down my back, making me shiver.

A white terry cloth robe was folded across the back of a chair, a pair of aqua flip-flops on the ground nearby. There was a cell phone on the patio table, next to a pair of sunglasses. I grabbed it and, kneeling by the body, held the screen over the corpse's face. The phone recognized its owner, the home screen opened, and I navigated to Dr. Exeter's text messages.

The message I'd sent from the General's phone had gone out at 12:04 a.m.: I sprained my darn ankle and won't be able to swim in the morning. You and Barbara should go ahead without me. There are bathing caps and fresh towels in the cabana. Enjoy!

12:06 a.m. Eve replies: Sorry to hear that. Ice it and rest. Talk soon.

12:08 a.m. Eve texts Barbara: Joan sprained her ankle and won't make it to the pool tomorrow morning, but I'm still planning on it. See you there at 7 a.m. No excuses!

12:16 a.m. Barbara replies to Eve: Too bad Joan can't make it. I'll be there. Wouldn't miss it for the world. 🙂

I photographed the series of messages, but before I could dig deeper into Dr. Exeter's digital communications, I spied a small red object nearly hidden in the shrubbery. It was an empty plastic cylinder about two inches long, a little fatter than my thumb, one end capped with brass, the other torn apart.

"I found the cartridge!" I called to Merritt as I snapped a few pictures.

She came over. "Very good. It looks like the killer was about fifteen feet from the target when the shot was fired. Not point-blank range but close enough that an amateur could have done it."

"Should I pick it up?"

"No, we'll leave it for the police to find. Now come with me."

She led me to the cabana. "Is that yours?" she asked, pointing to a shoe print just inside the door. She was obviously aware that I'd been leaving trails everywhere.

I denied responsibility. The cabana was one area I hadn't trespassed on. It was a long, rectangular room, its windows covered with closed venetian blinds.

"Get some pictures." She switched on the overhead light, and the room sprang to life, revealing a stack of plastic chairs, a pool vacuum, foam kickboards, and noodles in neon colors. Fresh towels were stacked on a counter next to a full-size refrigerator.

I knelt and took a couple of close-ups of the shoe print. The fact that the inside of the cabana was cool and dark had kept the damp print from drying out completely, but there was still barely anything left to see. The outline was indeterminate. The toe and heel were missing, so I couldn't measure the size of the shoe against my own foot. The most discernible part was the tread under the ball of the foot, but even that was faint.

I searched for more footprints. Sure enough, there were others—half prints, outlines, the barest smudge of a tread mark—indicating a person's progress from the front of the cabana to a door at the back.

"Something doesn't make sense," I said to Merritt. "If the killer was on dry ground when he took the shot, how did his shoes get wet?"

"The gun was found near the victim's body, so we know he was on that side of the pool at some point. He may have wanted a closer look at his target after he took his shot, perhaps to satisfy himself that she was dead. If, as you suggested, she didn't die immediately but was trying to escape as she was losing blood, he may have needed to push her back into the pool and hold her underwater until she drowned. Then he dropped the gun in the pool, and exited through the cabana."

The wail of approaching sirens ended our conversation. It sounded like the first responders were speeding up the long drive to the hacienda. They'd taken longer than I'd expected, which probably had something to do with the remoteness of the ranch. Merritt and I exchanged glances. We'd worked with cops before. It was a toss-up between the ones who welcomed the famous detective's involvement and the ones who wanted to protect their turf from outsiders. We'd soon know which kind we'd be dealing with.

"Go out the back," Merritt instructed. "Get yourself to the stable and check the gun cabinet. See if one of the guns is missing, and if the others match the one in the pool. I'll run interference here, and we'll catch up back at the house." She paused, then said sternly, "Be careful, Blunt; don't get any heroic ideas in your head."

CHAPTER TWENTY-FOUR

Everyone Is a Suspect

I went out the back door of the cabana and down two rickety steps to an area of dry grass. Trash barrels, broken kickboards, and empty cardboard boxes were littered about. A dirt path wound through scrub brush and cacti toward the stables some distance away. Part of the paddock fence was visible from where I stood.

I won't deny that I was scared. From the footprints in the cabana, it was clear that this was the murderer's escape route. What if I found him or her? But that was unlikely. They would have scuttled out of sight by now.

I arrived at the stables without incident. A rear door was ajar. I pushed it open and walked down the line of stalls. The horses were huffing and shuffling around. Was it my imagination, or were they restless? Had they heard the gunshot? Were they upset by the approaching sirens? I emerged into the open area where the horses were watered, brushed, and harnessed. Barry, the ranch manager, wasn't there, which suited me fine, as I didn't want to have to explain what I was doing. I slipped into his office and crossed immediately to the gun cabinet. The glass wasn't smashed, as I'd expected. Instead, the doors were wide open. A colorful beaded strap dangled from a key that was still in the lock. Sure enough, one of the shotguns was missing. Whoever had removed the shotgun hadn't smashed the glass at all. They'd unlocked the case with a key.

"What are you doing here?" said a gravelly voice behind me.

I whirled around. I'd thought I was alone, but there was Barry in the doorway. He was chewing something. From the bulge in his cheek, I guessed it was a plug of dipping tobacco. A wave of fear passed through me. The way he'd appeared in the doorway so stealthily . . . and his gaze was weird . . .

"Do you know there's a gun missing from this case?" I asked with more bravado than I felt.

His eyes shifted to the gun case, checking to see if I was right. "What of it?"

"Do you know who took it?"

"Could have been anyone. Maybe someone's doing target practice in the desert."

"Wouldn't they have to sign it out or something first?"

"Sign it out?" He made it sound stupid. "No."

"Who knows where the key is kept?"

He pointed to a small ceramic dish on his desk. "That's where it's kept."

"Out in the open," I said, more to myself than him. "Where do you keep the ammunition?"

"Right there." He pointed over my shoulder to a shelf beside the gun case.

"Not much security, I see."

"What's this about?" There was a hard edge to his voice now.

At that moment a uniformed police officer strode through the wide-open doors of the stable.

I pointed to the gun case. "There. See the empty space? That's where the murder weapon came from."

"Murder?" Barry said. "What the hell are you talking about?"

The cop wasn't interested in the gun case. I'm not sure my words registered at all. He was staring fixedly at Barry. "You, sir. I'd like you to come with me." He turned to me as an afterthought. "And you."

Barry objected. "Wait a minute. I work here. I just got here a few minutes ago."

The cop placed his hand on his holstered revolver. "No problem if you do as you're told, sir."

"I don't know what you want with me. I didn't do anything."

"Just a few questions up at the house."

There was a momentary standoff in which Barry seemed to realize it was pointless to argue. Without another word, he and I left the stable side by side and trudged grimly toward the hacienda with the officer following us. His revolver was holstered, not pointed at our backs, but I'd had a gun pointed at my head less than a year ago, and the memory of that trauma was never far away. It returned now. Not for the first time, I wondered if this job was worth the constant risks to my life.

CHAPTER TWENTY-FIVE

Chaos and Confusion

There was chaos and confusion in the hacienda. The guests were being rounded up, some roused from their beds, and brought to a central location in the living room. The cop told Barry and me that we were not to leave the house until we'd given our statements to the detective sergeant. Then he left us alone. I looked around but didn't see anyone who looked like a detective sergeant, and no one was taking statements. Barry disappeared into the kitchen, and I wandered through the rooms, observing people and listening in on conversations.

Not all the guests had arrived. The ones who were there were trying to figure out what was happening. They apparently hadn't been told about the murder. There was a rumor that the caterers had been barred from entering the compound, and there was universal dismay and incredulity over the lack of coffee. A housekeeper named Alma who had arrived for work before the lockdown was receiving the brunt of the outrage. I heard Jacob Korn haughtily inquire of her when breakfast would be served. Alma was barely five feet tall, with thick ankles, strong arms, and sharp black eyes. If looks could kill, Jacob Korn would have been the morning's second corpse.

I ran upstairs and stripped off my wet clothes. They smelled bad in a way I didn't recognize, and my once-white sneakers had acquired a disturbing pinkish tint from the bloody pool water. My hair was damp, and when I came downstairs in dry clothes, I still felt clammy and chilled, even though the temperature was now in the seventies, having climbed steadily as the morning wore on.

After a bit of searching, I found Merritt on the far end of the veranda. She was seated next to a planter brimming with yellow wildflowers, speaking quietly to Fitz and General Battersea. Fitz was red-faced and agitated, while the General was pale and subdued. Merritt waved me over.

I sat down in time to hear Fitz sputter, "Who would have thought he'd actually do it? It's unbelievable! Simply unbelievable! He's a madman, a maniac. Poor Kathy. Poor, poor Kathy. She'll never recover from this."

"Has anyone told Conrad yet?" the General said in quiet anguish. "Someone needs to tell him. He shouldn't find out from the police. It should be one of us. Will you tell him, Fitz? No, that's not right. I'll tell him. It should be me."

Merritt leaned across the table. With one hand on her friend's arm, the other on Fitz's, she pulled them close. In a low voice she said, "Listen, you two. Dave Lafferty may have had nothing to do with this murder. That bullet might have been meant for Joan."

"Nonsense! We all heard what Dave said last night! He very clearly threatened Eve's life. You heard him yourself. You were there!" Fitz protested.

"So I was. As of now, Dave is the main suspect, and I have no doubt that the police will apprehend him quickly. But the fact remains that Joan received a death threat a few days ago, that her morning routine was no secret to anyone. The killer might well have expected to find Joan alone at the pool this morning. And now the woman who *was* alone at the pool has been fatally shot. A woman, I might add, of similar stature and build, whose hair was hidden by one of Joan's Army bathing caps."

Fitz and the General exchanged confused glances, as if in their horror and shock over the murder, they'd forgotten the reason Merritt was with them in the first place. What Merritt was suggesting ought to have terrified the General. Who wouldn't be terrified to know they'd just literally dodged a bullet? But she reacted in a whole different way.

She turned to her husband, wild-eyed. "My god, Fitz, if that's the case, then this murder is our fault! We knew there was potential danger, and yet we did nothing to warn our guests. Now Eve is dead. How could we have let this happen?"

"My darling, I tried to tell you that. You wouldn't listen."

The General stared into the middle distance with eyes made briefly sightless by sudden guilt. "Then it's my fault. It's because of me that Eve is dead. How selfish and stupid I was!"

Merritt wasn't one to tolerate histrionics. "Stop it, Joan. You're not helping anything. Responsibility for a murder lies with the murderer. No one else. End of story."

"Wise words," Fitz interjected.

Merritt continued speaking sharply to the General. "And I didn't say you *were* the intended victim, only that you *could* have been. For that reason we need to redouble our efforts to keep you safe. Because once the murderer learns he made a mistake—if that's what happened—he may try again."

The General blanched but was unable to summon any words. Her hands were trembling. She curled them around each other, as if needing to hang on to something. This was the first time I'd seen her scared, and I wasn't sorry about that if it meant she finally understood the grave danger she was in. Maybe now she'd start doing what she was told.

Just then, Alma bustled over to complain to her employers that the guests were hungry, there wasn't enough food to feed everyone, they were out of coffee beans, and cooking wasn't her job.

"Where the hell are the damn caterers?" Fitz roared to no one in particular.

Alma's face was firmly blank. The caterers were not her responsibility either.

Fitz turned to his wife and repeated the question at a lower volume. "Where the hell are the damn caterers?"

The General started to get up. "I'll go see what I can do."

Merritt put a hand on her arm. "No, Joan. You stay here. I have some questions for you."

Merritt, the General, and I joined Alma in staring silently at Fitz. With no way out, he grumbled and followed Alma back toward the kitchen, where I assumed he would just add to the tumult until Jenny-Lou arrived.

"Who knows your morning routine?" Merritt asked her friend.

The General looked pained. She'd barely caught up to the fact that one of her guests had been murdered, barely accepted the idea that she might have been the shooter's real target. Now Merritt was putting forward a third unpalatable idea: that the shooter was someone she knew.

Looking defeated, she complied. "Jenny-Lou. Barry. Alma. Most people who work here know I'm usually at the pool in the mornings."

"That covers staff. Who among the guests knew your morning routine?"

"I talked about it a few times yesterday. I can't remember exactly who I spoke to."

"So we can't rule anyone out. Except maybe the caterers."

The General blushed. "I did mention it to one of them. Steve. He was that very good-looking young man at the grill. He asked if anyone actually swam in our pool—I think he was teasing me a little—and I bragged that I did, every morning, seven a.m."

I said to Merritt, "The General spoke about it again last night at the barbecue. Remember? She asked if anyone wanted to join her, and Eve and Barbara said they would."

Merritt was silent for a moment, processing. Finally she turned to the General. "Tell me what happened last night. Why weren't you at the pool?"

"I had a little mishap. Olivia can tell you about it. There was something on the stairs. My legs came out from under me, and I made a very undignified landing on my rump." Her voice rose on the last word, as if she were reenacting the surprise she'd felt at the time.

"I think it was one of Angel's balls," I said. "I saw it this morning. It rolled under the hall table, which is why we didn't see it last night."

The General let out an irritated sigh. "I keep telling Jenny-Lou to pick them up. Why that dog needs so many toys, I'll never know. He can only fit one in his mouth at a time." With another sigh, she continued. "Anyway, I ended up twisting my ankle. Olivia was kind enough to get me some ice and Tylenol. We texted Eve to let her know I'd had a little fall, nothing serious, but I thought it would be better to rest my ankle for a day or two. I told her there were towels and everything she might need in the cabana."

"Did you text Barbara as well?"

"No, I figured Eve would do that if she decided not to go."

"Eve did text Barbara," I said. "Barbara replied that she still intended to go. 'Wouldn't miss it for the world,' she said. Here, I'll show you." I pulled up my photos of the women's text messages and passed my phone to Merritt, who read each screen carefully.

When I offered the phone to the General, she waved it away. "I believe you. I don't need to see it."

"Listen carefully, Joan," Merritt said. "The police will start taking statements soon. Immediately after you give them yours, I want you to go to your room and stay there with the door closed and locked. You will open the door only to me or Blunt. No one else, Joan. *No one else!*"

This time General Battersea didn't argue.

I noticed that Merritt's list of the people the General could admit into her room did not include her husband, John Fitzroy.

CHAPTER TWENTY-SIX

Sheriff Casey Takes Control

The sheriff was a heavyset, bull-necked man from Pecos named Dutch Casey. He had a taut, protruding belly that looked more like muscle than fat. Everything about him seemed both hard and soft at the same time. His face, though cherubic in shape and rosy in complexion, managed to have a merciless, severe aspect. His hair was sparse, showing a pink scalp, but it stood up straight from his forehead in sharp spikes like a porcupine's quills. His hands were small and pudgy, but I had no doubt that, curled into fists, they could be deadly if he wanted them to be.

Having positioned himself in the center of the room, he was making a slow revolution as he addressed the ring of confused and frightened people sitting and standing on its perimeter. The ranch was on lockdown: No one was allowed to leave. We would all remain inside the hacienda until he and his deputy had spoken to each of us in turn. Meanwhile, more officers would be arriving soon to search the grounds, rounding up whatever stragglers they could find. A helicopter pilot had been engaged to scour the ranch's 2,300 acres from the air.

His deputy, Nathan Roundtree, was a slender Native American man who hung back, observing the group with careful eyes. He was nowhere near as imposing as Casey, but he looked smarter, if only because he didn't appear to be hobbled by a giant ego and its bottomless needs.

Everyone was in some form of slack-jawed disbelief. A murder! Eve Exeter fatally shot! It was as shocking as if a deadly lightning bolt had struck from a clear blue sky.

General Battersea raised her hand like a schoolgirl. "Excuse me, Sheriff Casey—"

He silenced her with a curt "You'll get your turn to speak." If he knew he was addressing a retired US Army brigadier general, he didn't show it. He treated her—he treated us all, actually—as if we were silly, stupid people who *of course* had been prancing around the desert getting ourselves killed like the clueless coastal elites we were. As if we were all guilty—if not of murder, then of *something*—and he was going to turn us upside down and shake the truth out of each and every one of us.

"No one gets away with murder in Pecos County. Not as long as I'm in charge," he actually said. Merritt and I exchanged troubled glances. The more he talked, the more our hope of establishing a fruitful partnership with him faded.

Barbara Korn was wearing a loosely belted bathrobe and scuff slippers, and her husband, Jacob, looked grungy and irritable in a baggy mesh muscle shirt that showed how hairy his arms were. Barbara was smearing tears off her cheeks with a balled-up tissue. Jacob looked annoyed and aggrieved, as if he were being forced to participate in a meaningless bureaucratic process that was wasting his time.

A quite different demeanor was evidenced by Peter Jumper, who was lounging against a back wall, one dirty boot sole marring the white paint. He appeared more attentive, more keenly interested, than I had known he could be in anything other than his phone. It was as if actual spilled blood had finally been newsworthy enough to pry his attention away from a screen. Or perhaps it had stirred a dormant predatory instinct in him. Or fed his violent fantasies. I found myself studying him surreptitiously. Every once in a while a sly, inappropriate smile twitched at a corner of his mouth.

Bree and Nova were sitting next to each other on a couch across the room. I saw them exchange startled glances as it dawned on them that they were going to be treated as suspects. Of course they were suspects. We all were. How many times had Merritt told me that a murder investigation is the opposite of a trial? Everyone who'd been in the vicinity of a murder, even the pizza delivery guy, was *guilty until proven innocent.*

There was a low buzz of conversation. Nova straightened her long neck and swiveled her head, scanning the room. Bree elbowed her. Nova shook her head. I could guess what they were doing. They were looking for Dave and Kathy, just as I'd been doing. But the Laffertys weren't there.

It was around that point, I think, that almost everyone—or at least those of us who'd witnessed last night's scene—began to wonder if the Laffertys' absence was significant. Meaningful glances were exchanged, but no one seemed in a hurry to shout out what we all knew: that Dave had threatened the dead woman's life less than twelve hours ago.

Our hesitation could be explained in part by the fact that Sheriff Casey's demeanor did not encourage audience participation. But it wasn't just that. What friend or acquaintance wants to point a finger at a fellow partygoer in a murder case? What if you were wrong, and that person went to prison for life? Best for us all to wait a little longer and see if the Laffertys strolled in late, grumpy from having been woken up, and just as shocked by the murder as everyone else.

Casey announced that he was ready to begin taking witness statements. "I'll start with whoever found the body," he said.

I stood up and dutifully followed him and Deputy Roundtree down the long tiled hallway, past the ancient iron sconces, into Fitz's Den of Guns.

"So you're the one who found the body." Sheriff Casey looked me up and down with vague disappointment.

He, Roundtree, and I were ensconced—perhaps too comfortably, given the purpose of our meeting—in the deep leather chairs that circled the copper-topped coffee table. O'Keeffe's cow skull horrified me from one side of the room; the Revolutionary War musket terrified me from the other. Directly in front of me, the French doors admitted a gentle wash of brown hills and heavenly blue sky. The scenery looked fake for some reason, like a painted mural, and that depressed me. It was about ten thirty a.m., three hours since I'd discovered the body, but I felt like I hadn't reached the nadir of the experience until right now.

Wanting to spare the lawman the trouble of having to coax information out of me one morsel at a time, I launched into a fulsome answer of every question he would be likely to ask, a few questions he ought to ask and probably wouldn't, and several questions he didn't know he definitely needed to ask.

Most importantly, I reported that there had been two separate death threats. The first: an anonymous written threat to General Battersea, which had arrived at the ranch a few days ago. The second: a spoken threat to the victim herself, which had been uttered publicly by one of the guests at the reunion—a retired cop named

Dave Lafferty, who for whatever reason had not been present at the group meeting.

Skipping over the threat to the General, Casey landed heavily on Dave Lafferty.

"If he's trying to flee, he won't get far. We'll put out an APB," he said with cold satisfaction.

I then explained who I was and who I worked for. When I dropped the name Aubrey Merritt, I didn't get one glimmer of interest or nod of recognition. The sheriff appeared not to have heard of her, if that was possible, so I provided a short professional bio, including some of the famous cases she had solved, and her NALPI (National Association of Licensed Private Investigators) Lifetime Achievement Award. The more I said, the more Nathan Roundtree perked up and showed interest, but Dutch Casey seemed to be making his face extra lax, his expression extra flat. The more credentials I piled on, the less impressed he became. Before he could cut me off, I put the matter to him bluntly: Collaborating with a private investigator of Aubrey Merritt's caliber would help him solve the crime faster and more efficiently.

"Look, sweetheart," Casey drawled. "I don't know how you do things back East; maybe you've got a lot of fancy detectives who went to Ivy League schools and all, but here in San Miguel County, we don't have much use for special consultants. We do things the old-fashioned way, and we catch the bad guys just fine. So I suggest you and your friend just sit back, rest yourselves, and watch how it's done."

Nathan Roundtree's face arranged itself into a crooked frown. I got the impression that he was disappointed by his boss's dismissive attitude, that he would have enjoyed joining forces with a celebrated PI from NYC. Our eyes met, then he looked away. *Come on, Nathan. Say something!* I wanted to whisper. But he didn't speak up.

CHAPTER TWENTY-SEVEN

Logic Is Our Friend

I had just left the lawmen and was on my way back to the living room when I heard something.

"Psst, Blunt."

I glanced up and down the hallway, didn't see anyone.

"Here. Look up."

At the top of the stairs was Merritt. "Come up. I need to talk to you."

I quietly ascended the stairs and followed Merritt into her bedroom at the far end of the hall. She closed the door softly behind us.

"We're supposed to wait downstairs until they've taken all the witness statements," I reminded her nervously.

"Nonsense. Sit down. We have work to do."

I sat. "What kind of work?"

She tapped her forehead. "Mind work. *Thinking.* Something I doubt we're going to see a lot of from our friend Dutch Casey."

"I just spoke with him and Roundtree. I tried to convince him to work with us, but he wasn't interested. To put it mildly."

"I'm not surprised."

"I told him about the threats, both of them, and he got really interested in Dave Lafferty. He's putting out an APB on the Laffertys' RV. When he thinks of it, which I'm sure he will soon, he'll check the CCTV footage to see exactly what time Dave and Kathy left the ranch."

"Of course. Those are the correct and obvious things to do. I expect he'll have the Laffertys in custody in a couple of hours at most."

"But . . . you don't think Dave did it, do you?"

"It would be foolish to exclude him. But there are other possibilities to consider."

"Right. Such as the possibility that Eve Exeter was shot by mistake, and the intended victim was actually General Battersea."

Merritt waited expectantly for several seconds, her eyebrows elevated. "And? What else?"

I had the awful feeling I'd had too many times on the soccer field: that I was for some reason way out of position and the game was happening about a mile away.

"Is that really all you can think of?" she persisted.

I searched my brain for whatever I'd missed. "I suppose it's also possible that . . ." I began optimistically, but the sentence refused to finish itself.

"Cast your thoughts back to yesterday morning. To the invitation. You held it in your hand. What do you remember?"

I could picture it clearly in my mind. The Greek letters, the SDT torch, and the colorful lettering. But that wasn't the important part. I turned it over in my mind and looked at the back. "I remember the scrawl in red Sharpie: 'She who lives by the sword shall die . . . '"

"Yes, yes. We know that. To whom was the invitation addressed?"

I concentrated again, turned the invitation front and back. “Why, no one,” I said with some surprise. “It was addressed to no one.”

“Exactly. We *assumed*, Blunt. Oh, how we assumed! We assumed it was intended for Joan because it was delivered to her ranch and because the Bible quote suggested a military connection. In fact, *anyone attending the reunion could have been the target*!”

It was so obvious now. We’d just assumed! That was a bush-league detection mistake.

“This is why doctors don’t treat family members, lawyers don’t represent friends,” Merritt fumed. “They don’t want emotion to cloud their judgment. This is why I usually refuse to call my clients by their first names. I need to keep them at arm’s length to protect my objectivity. But here I went against my own strict protocols. I accepted a friend as a client! Because I cared about her, because the possibility that she was in danger deeply concerned me, and I had a strong urge to protect her. Wrapped in my worry and affection, I neglected to notice that Joan was not the only person at the reunion who might be at risk. Joan understood this herself just now, and I am ashamed to admit that the possibility had not even occurred to me until she mentioned it!”

“So we have three scenarios,” I said slowly, putting the list together as I spoke. “One, Dave Lafferty did it. No connection to the threat. Two, the threatener did it but got the wrong person. Three, the threatener accomplished exactly what he set out to do. Eve Exeter was his intended target. General Battersea was never at risk.”

I waited for Merritt to agree, but all I got was a look of sour impatience.

“What?” I said defensively. “Did I miss something?”

“What about the fourth scenario?”

“There’s another one?”

She groaned with exasperation. "Oh, for goodness' sake. It's staring you right in the face! What if the person who killed Eve Exeter was neither Dave Lafferty *nor* the threatener?"

Thorny implications sprang up in my mind. It would be bad, if the fourth scenario was the right one. Very bad. "In that case, we could have *two* murderers on our hands—the one who just killed Dr. Exeter and another completely different person who might kill General Battersea at any moment."

"Correct," she said grimly. Her dark blue eyes gleamed with grim intensity and something I'd never seen in them before—fear.

I was scared too. The case was sprouting heads like an angry hydra. "What do we do now? Where do we even start?" I asked a bit desperately.

"Logic, Blunt." She began to pace. "When you feel overwhelmed, when you're lost in a maze of possibilities, always return to logic. Logic will always be there for you; it is your steady, reliable friend. As long as you treat it with respect, feed it nothing but verifiable facts, give it time to do its work, and are willing to abide by its results, it won't steer you wrong. If logic tells you something, don't barter, don't second-guess, no matter how unlikely its conclusions seem. So, how shall we begin?"

She didn't wait for my answer, which was just as well, as I didn't have one.

"I'll tell you how we'll begin," she said. "We'll consider our four scenarios carefully, one by one, and identify the line of inquiry that affords the best possibility for progress. Are you with me?"

"Yes."

"We can dispense with Scenario number one—Dave Lafferty killed Eve—for now. Sheriff Casey is on that trail, and he's made it clear that he doesn't want us around, so let's step aside and let him follow his single-minded pursuit of Dave Lafferty. We'll eventually learn whatever he does or doesn't uncover, and, in the meantime, we'll make use of the relatively free rein we'll have to follow other lines of inquiry.

"Scenario number two—Eve's murder was a case of mistaken identity—poses a difficult challenge at the moment. There are too many suspects, not enough leads. I suggest we leave it alone until something breaks our way—which it will, fear not, and probably soon. Scenario number four—the threat against Joan and the murder of Eve are separate, unrelated crimes—only doubles our workload. Which leaves us with what?"

"Scenario number three," I said promptly, glad for the softball.

"Exactly. So we'll start with the following question: Who would want Eve Exeter dead?"

"Other than Dave Lafferty."

"Obviously."

"Let's see." I frowned, my mind a blank.

She sighed resignedly. "Statistics show that nine times out of ten . . ." She paused, offering me an opening to complete her thought.

"The husband did it!" I crowed triumphantly, finally getting something right.

CHAPTER TWENTY-EIGHT

The Ostensibly Grieving Widower

The blood in the pool had dissipated, leaving wispy tendrils of a muddy tan color suspended just below the surface of the water. The forensic team was packing up its gear, while a uniformed cop stood by, guarding a large area cordoned off with yellow police tape. Everyone else was back at the hacienda, except for one lonely onlooker.

"I'm so sorry, Conrad," Merritt said gently as we approached the new widower.

Conrad Zander stood close against the tape, gazing at the pool. Yesterday, he'd looked confident, self-satisfied, a man of the world; today he seemed broken and very much alone. I wondered what he was thinking. Maybe he was wishing that he could rewind the tape, back to the moments before his wife was shot, when she was healthy and alive and there was still a chance he could do something to alter her fate. Or was he glad she was dead? Was he, in fact, gloating over a successful kill?

He turned slowly to greet us. "Thank you, Aubrey. I honestly don't know what to say or do or even think. I don't really believe it yet."

"Would you like to go back to the house so we can sit and talk?"

"I'd rather not. I don't want to be around any of those people right now. I know they mean well, but I don't want their sympathy. I need to deal with this on my own for a while."

"Do you want us to leave?"

"You can stay, Aubrey. You're not like the others. You look at things clearly and see them for what they are. I know you're not going to try to comfort me with platitudes."

I wasn't sure where that left me, so I just stayed quiet and continued standing at my boss's side.

"Thank you, Conrad. I appreciate that. You and I . . . we both use reason as our guide. Like Eve did."

There she goes again, I thought. Merritt was really good at using subtle flattery to get people to drop their guard. I always held my breath, thinking for sure that her prey would cotton on to her strategy, but few ever did. Most opened up like flowers in the sunshine and played right into her hand.

"My wife was a superlative biochemist. The best of the best," Conrad said.

"You were very proud of her."

"We were proud of each other and of what we built together."

"Your company, Lifespan, Inc."

He grimaced, as if the name pained him. "I don't know what will happen to the company now. I suppose we'll muddle through. But why bother? What difference does any of it make without Eve by my side? Maybe I'll just sell the bloody thing and go back to teaching."

Merritt made a commiserating noise. "Conrad, I know this is a very difficult time, so soon after Eve's death. But you're aware, I'm sure, that the sooner we start looking, the better chance we'll have of finding her killer. So I hope you won't mind if I ask you a few questions."

"I thought Sheriff Casey was in charge of the investigation."

"You talked to him?"

"Him and his deputy. I told them what I knew, which isn't much. This crime is senseless, ridiculous, unbelievable. Dave Lafferty is clearly criminally insane. I'm no supporter of the death penalty, but the way I feel right now, life behind bars is too good for him."

"It's true that Dave is the primary suspect at this point. But I'm wondering if there is anyone else who might have wanted to harm your wife. Did Eve have any enemies that you know of?"

"Enemies?" The word seemed to surprise him. "It depends on what you call enemies. I'm sure there were plenty of students who didn't like her. Young people at schools like MIT can be very arrogant. They've been told all their lives they're geniuses, and it can be hard for them to countenance any evidence to the contrary. But I hardly think they would murder a professor in revenge for a poor grade—unless of course doing so would have a positive impact on their careers. But I don't see how that would ever be the case. Usually the MIT degree itself is enough to open doors. Potential employers aren't that interested in GPA.

"As for colleagues? I don't think so. Lifespan is built on Eve's groundbreaking accomplishments. She put her heart and soul into her work, and her passing will be a terrible blow to the company."

"What about competitors, people who might want to cripple Lifespan?"

"As far as competitors go, there are none. Our product is unique and patented. No other company in the world right now is doing what we do."

Taking a step back from the police tape, he faced Merritt directly. "I sincerely hope you don't intend to waste time hunting for a hypothetical killer. Remember Occam's razor: The simplest solution is usually the right one. And the simplest solution is Dave Lafferty."

Ignoring his condescension, Merritt replied evenly, "Dave is without doubt a prime suspect. But I think you'll agree that there are a few problems with that theory. First, why would he have murdered Eve less than twelve hours after a number of bystanders heard him threaten her life? Would he have been that stupid?"

"Of course he would. Lafferty is clearly a very stupid man. Only an idiot would threaten someone publicly in the first place, carrying a gun, no less."

"I suspect that Dave's behavior at the barbecue was not as rash as it looked to us. He's a former police officer, remember. He likely knew there would be no penalty for his threat, and he kept his gun holstered to show he was in control. His intention was merely to intimidate Eve, and you could argue that he succeeded. Murder is an entirely different act. It is orders of magnitude more consequential than a public threat. Dave would have been keenly aware that, given his public threat, he would be the primary suspect if she was murdered. He could end up being tried in a court of law and, if convicted, he could spend the rest of his life behind bars. Would he really have taken such a huge risk?"

"You're giving him too much credit, Aubrey. People like him don't think things through. They act on impulse, especially when they're angry, and we all saw how angry he was last night."

"If it had been a truly impulsive act, I think he would have used his own gun. But whoever shot Eve made a carefully considered decision: They chose a weapon that many people had access to and that a number of guests had been taught to use. Then he dropped it in the pool after he fired it—another intelligent choice. This was not a crime of passion. It was planned."

"So? I'm sure Lafferty worked enough murder investigations in his career that he knows all the tricks and was confident he could get away with it."

"In that case, he would have been at the meeting this morning, pretending to be as shocked and horrified as everyone else. Instead, he drew unnecessary attention and suspicion to himself by not showing up. I still don't know where he is, though I suppose we'll find out soon."

Conrad shrugged. "You can't expect people like him to act rationally."

"There's another issue that troubles me," Merritt said. "How would Dave have known where Eve would be?"

"Everyone heard the plans she made with Joan."

"Dave wasn't there when that conversation occurred."

"His wife was there. She could have told him. And by the way, what an awful woman *she* is," Conrad said, veering off the subject. "What could have got into her to bring up an old grievance that had been put to bed decades ago? What could she have hoped to gain? It makes no sense."

Merritt stayed on track. "Were you aware that Joan had an accident last night and wouldn't be at the pool this morning?"

"This is the first I've heard of it."

"Barbara was also supposed to meet Eve this morning. Were you aware of any communication between them?"

"I didn't keep tabs on my wife's conversations with her friends. Especially Barbara. That woman was always hanging around, nosing her way into our lives. It seems to be an occupational hazard of people in her profession—headhunters, they're aptly called—to stalk people of status. They can't help themselves; they're like moths drawn to the flame of other people's success."

"You're saying Barbara was a stalker?" Merritt asked mildly.

"Oh, not a real stalker. Just a . . . a pest, I guess you could say. Eve tolerated her for old times' sake and because Barbara and Jacob were early, and generous, investors in Lifespan. It was a smart move for them to get in on the ground floor. They stand to make a decent profit when the company goes public."

"When will that be?" I asked.

"October first. It's been in the works for a while." He sighed wearily. "I'm sorry, ladies. Let's continue this conversation another time. I'm getting tired now. I'd like to be alone."

"I understand," Merritt said. "This tragedy is . . . beyond words. Let me know if you think of anything that could be useful to the investigation. I want to do everything I can to help find Eve's killer."

"Please, Aubrey. Lafferty is the man. Don't draw the process out longer than necessary. The only thing that affords me any comfort is believing that Sheriff Casey will find him and put him behind bars as quickly as possible."

Merritt paused, studied the widower carefully with a particularly penetrating look in her eye. Finally, she said, "In fact, I have evidence that points in a different direction."

You do? News to me, I thought.

"What evidence? What are you talking about?" he replied almost angrily.

"I can't say any more."

"The forensic team told me they found nothing but a spent cartridge. They're going to dust it for prints. If you've got something else, you need to tell me. I have a right to know."

"I'm sorry, Conrad. I can't disclose my information now. Soon, maybe. I have more digging to do."

"I can't accept that, Aubrey. This is my wife's murder we're talking about. If you have a suspect in mind, I want to know who it is."

"I wish I could tell you, but as you can imagine, this is a sensitive time in the investigation. It's better if I stay quiet for now. Please don't worry; I'm confident I'll find your wife's killer fairly soon. I've never failed to solve a murder case, and I don't intend to start now."

I looked at her in surprise. It wasn't like Merritt to brag, so she must have had a different motive for citing her extraordinary record of success. As I pondered her enigmatic little smile, it dawned on me that she wasn't trying to reassure Conrad Zander. She was trying to scare him.

A snarl crossed his face as he turned away. For several long moments he gazed at the pool until, in a thoughtful, almost mournful tone, he said, "All these guns, Aubrey. Four hundred million of them—more than one for every man, woman, and child in America. It escapes me, this penchant for gun violence. It makes me very grateful for my Quaker heritage."

"I didn't know you were a Quaker."

"I'm not, really; my mother was. She used to take me when I was a child to a little Quaker meetinghouse in Cambridge, on the green there. In my memory it's a peaceful sanctuary, always bathed in sunshine. I'm an atheist now, of course. But something of the Quaker spirit must have rubbed off on me, because I find that in my adulthood I'm a committed pacifist, won't touch a gun."

"If only more people were like you," Merritt gushed.

Neither one was being honest. They were merely reciting lines from a script they'd created together on the spot. They then proceeded to smile at each other with fake affection, and I got the weird impression that they were both enjoying their little dance of mutual deceit.

CHAPTER TWENTY-NINE

Film, Food, and Nerves

General Battersea was not happy about being confined to her bedroom, but she was complying with Merritt's orders for now, according to Fitz. He was pale, jittery, talking fast, but he was keeping himself together as best he could, cognizant that he needed to be a stabilizing influence on his anxious guests.

At Merritt's request, he took us into a basement control room, where a bank of five video screens monitored the ranch's main gate and four entrances to the hacienda.

"I showed this to Sheriff Casey already, and I'll show you as well. I've got it right here." He brought up a piece of film. "See there? That's the Laffertys' RV leaving the ranch at seven twenty-four."

We looked down on the vehicle as it approached the gate and disappeared under us, leaving a small, dirty cloud in its wake.

"Did any other vehicles enter or leave the ranch?"

"Nada. I went back to five a.m., two hours before the murder, and there was nothing."

"What about the other cameras?"

"Nothing. The only person up at that hour was Jacob Korn. He entered the side door at about . . . oh, I can't remember. Here, I'll show you."

He futzed around at a different screen and soon brought up some footage showing about a couple of feet of paved walkway, a few steps leading to the side door, and the edge of a bush. Merritt and I were patiently waiting for something to happen when—out of the blue, it seemed—Jacob Korn appeared, walking with a quick, determined stride, a laptop computer under his arm. When he was at the door, about to open it, the camera was directly above him, and all we could see was the thinning hair on the crown of his head. I thought that would be the end of it, when for some reason he looked up and stared straight into the camera lens for several seconds. Then he went inside.

"Play that again," Merritt said.

Fitz complied, and again we watched Jacob Korn come into view, pause at the door, look up at the camera lens, and stare at us fixedly through his smudged glasses, as if he knew we were watching him.

"Four seconds. That's how long he looked at the camera," Merritt said.

"What do you make of that?" Fitz asked.

"Nothing. Yet."

We went back upstairs. It was lunchtime. Merritt said she wasn't hungry, and went to talk to the General, while Fitz and I proceeded to the dining room.

Alma had plunked platters of random foods on the table for guests to pick at: cold cuts, limp lettuce, white bread, Hellmann's mustard, bruised bananas, uncut strawberries, and a family-sized box of Wheat Thins. Fitz confided that the housekeeper was very upset, that after the unpleasantness at breakfast, when she had been treated rudely for not supplying coffee, she had hung up her apron and attempted to leave the ranch, but an officer had barred her way, explaining that she had to remain on the premises like everyone else. Ever since then she had been slamming cabinet doors and scrubbing things with excessive force. At one point she announced that she had just mopped the floor, and no one was allowed to enter the kitchen until she said so. Hours later, the floor still wasn't dry.

"Any chance the caterer will show up?" I asked Fitz as the two of us stared despondently at the unappetizing dishes arrayed before us.

"I'm afraid not. Apparently he draws the line at murder gigs. *Murder gig* is not my term, I assure you. 'Violence ruins food,' he told me. 'The taste buds become so dull you might as well serve franks and beans.' I told him I didn't care what got served; I just needed to feed about a dozen hungry mouths. That didn't go over too well with our local culinary diva. 'Try Frosted Flakes,' he said huffily and hung up. A few seconds later he called back and barked, '*Do I* look *like disaster relief?*'"

Fitz shook his head in disbelief. "I've dealt with artists all my life, Olivia, and I can tell you they're among the most neurotic people you're ever going to meet. But they're nothing compared to a celebrity chef."

"I'm sorry, Fitz. I'd help if I could."

"Don't worry about it. Jenny-Lou is on her way. She's saved my hide so many times I'll never be able to repay her. She's going to stop at the supermarket in Pecos, and she'll work with Alma to get us all fixed up. Three meals will get us through until tomorrow afternoon, and by then I sincerely hope Sheriff Casey will let you all go home. If he doesn't, I'll call my congressman. There's no reason why you all need to be here. I suppose Casey just wants to get his hands on Dave Lafferty first."

By now everyone had been questioned by the police. The guests were scattered around haphazardly, some at the dining table, eating limp sandwiches and trying to make sense of what was happening. Some folks had gone back to their rooms to shower and change. Others believed that they had been prohibited from leaving not only the ranch but the house itself, and they were complaining to each other about the miscreants who had taken a more liberal view of the sheriff's orders. Everyone was on edge.

The only being unaffected by the morning's tragedy was Jenny-Lou's little spaniel, Angel. With an orange ball clamped in his jaw, he trotted around the room, dropped it at someone's feet, sat back on his haunches, and stared hopefully at his mark. When the person didn't respond—as no one did, because who wants to play fetch when there's been a murder?—he picked up the ball and went on to the next potential playmate. Eventually he came to me, and I took pity on him. I rolled the ball down the length of the hallway. He chased it at breakneck speed, pounced on it zestfully, and returned it to me with a sense of proud accomplishment.

We played this way for several minutes until a stern voice broke the rhythm of the game. "Blunt. What on earth are you doing?"

"Oh, nothing much," I said nonchalantly.

"Yes. I can see that," she replied. "Well, come along. There's work to do."

CHAPTER THIRTY

Conjugal Misery

Barbara and Jacob Korn were at a table on the veranda, slumped and solemn, amid empty glasses and a plate of broken crackers. Barbara appeared emotionally cratered, as if a meteor had hit her straight on. Jacob looked sour and restless.

"May we join you?" Merritt asked.

"If you want," Jacob replied indifferently. He shoved the only empty chair at the table around in a clumsy effort to make it more accessible. I dragged a chair from an adjoining table, and Merritt and I sat down.

"You've both spoken to Sheriff Casey, I assume?" Merritt asked.

They nodded.

This time Merritt didn't bother with condolences. Looking straight at Barbara, she said, "Tell me what happened last night. You got a text from Eve saying that Joan had sprained her ankle. What time was that?"

"The text came in at about twelve fifteen, I think. Is that about the right time, Jacob?"

"About that," he said.

"We were still awake, both of us reading in bed. I said, 'Oh, Joan won't be there but Eve's still going, so I'll go too.' I was sorry to hear about Joan's accident, but it didn't change my plans. I was looking forward to spending time with Eve. I set my alarm, but I didn't notice at the time that my phone was on silent, and I ended up sleeping right through until about eight a.m. I hardly ever do that."

"That's not true," said Jacob. "You oversleep all the time. I should know. I'm the one who has to drag you out of bed in the morning so you don't miss work."

"It must have been the sangria," Barbara went on, ignoring her husband. "I usually don't drink that much."

"That's not true either. I've seen you drink a lot more than that."

Barbara appeared not to have heard him. "Anyway, I was dead to the world until the police knocked on our door with the news about Eve. I still can't believe it. I feel terrible. If I'd been there as I intended, she might still be alive." Barbara dabbed at her eyes with a balled-up paper napkin. "I never thought . . . when Dave made that threat . . . it just didn't seem possible that he would actually do it. If I'd known he was that unstable, I would never have let Eve be there alone."

Before Jacob had a chance to contradict his wife, Merritt turned her attention to him. "What about you, Jacob? When did you wake up this morning?"

"Early. Sixish."

"Did you hear the gunshot?"

"I did. I was here at the hacienda when I heard a single shot. Not loud enough to wake anyone. Just loud enough that I knew what it was."

"What time was that?"

"Sometime after seven? Can't say exactly. Seven thirty, maybe. I didn't think too much about it. I figured someone was at the shooting range."

"So early in the morning?"

"Why not? Shooting is a big sport around here. There was all that skeet shooting yesterday; then last night that kid, Peter, was blasting a shotgun out in the desert."

"How did you know it was Peter?"

"I saw him and Fitz walking back together, past the barn, carrying guns. Fitz told me he'd been giving Peter some pointers on target shooting. The kid was sullen as a rock, but Fitz was cheerful. It crossed my mind that the poor guy had probably always wanted a son."

"Why didn't you wake Barbara when she overslept? You knew she was looking forward to meeting her friend. And, as you say, you've gotten her out of bed plenty of times in the past."

Jacob gave Merritt a piteous look, as if her question could not have been more ignorant. "Because my darling wife would have just cussed me out like she always does and gone right back to sleep."

"I wouldn't have. I *wanted* to go swimming," Barbara said with quiet dignity. She turned toward Merritt. "Don't listen to him, Aubrey. He thinks he knows everything about me, but he doesn't. I'm not nearly as lazy as he makes out. I've had a very successful career, and you can't do that if you're always sleeping in." Sighing, she turned over the phone that had been lying on the table and proceeded to gaze longingly at the picture that popped up on her screen. Her face visibly softened.

Curious to see what had caused the transformation, I leaned toward her, hoping to peek over her shoulder. Noticing my movement, she obligingly turned the screen to face me.

"That's Sweetie-Pie," she said. "Isn't she beautiful? She's boarding right now at the Puppy Palace back in Cambridge. I miss her so much whenever I'm away. She misses me too; I just know it. They say she won't play with anyone when she's there; all she wants to do is sleep."

"Damn dog has a better life than most humans on this planet," Jacob groused.

As I looked more closely at the photo of Sweetie-Pie, this time through Barbara's adoring eyes, I felt ashamed of my previous uncharitable reaction to the scrawny pup's vapid gaze and stupid hair bow.

"She's lovely," I said almost sincerely.

"Thank you. She's my precious girl," Barbara said with a transcendent smile.

Leaving Barbara and me to our soppy puppy-gazing, Merritt turned once again to Jacob Korn. "Why did you come to the hacienda so early this morning?"

"I had work to do."

"What kind of work?"

"You wouldn't be interested."

"I'm very interested."

"It's technical. You wouldn't understand it."

"Try me. I might surprise you."

He looked annoyed by Merritt's persistence.

When he didn't say anything, Barbara jumped in. "Jacob does IT consulting for Conrad in addition to his regular job at Google."

"Really? Conrad didn't mention that you're an employee."

"I'm a consultant, not an employee," Jacob corrected stiffly.

"I see. How long have you been doing that?"

"Couple of years, I guess."

"You're interested in the supplement industry?"

"I couldn't care less about supplements. People want to waste their money on that snake oil, that's their business. The only reason

I agreed to consult for Conrad is because my wife sank practically all our money into his company, so I feel motivated to do what I can to help it succeed."

"It was *my* money, not *ours*," Barbara retorted. "I discussed it with you at the time, and you said you thought it was a good idea. On the other hand, when you sank *your* money into that video game company, you didn't bother mentioning it to me." She offered us a smirk of petty triumph, proud but not happy to have landed one in the marital boxing match.

Jacob stared at the distant red hills and pretended he hadn't heard.

Merritt turned to Barbara. "You believed that Lifespan would be a good investment."

"Oh yes. I always supported Eve—I believed in her completely. And I was right to. She was a brilliant woman, and her company is on the verge of becoming a huge success."

"I assume you're referring to the IPO on October first? Conrad mentioned it."

"That date's been pushed back indefinitely," Barbara asserted.

Jacob grimaced. "No it hasn't. Conrad's sticking with October first."

"That's not what Eve told me."

"Why would she bother telling you? You don't work there. You're not in the loop."

Barbara shrugged off the remark. "Eve confided in me a *lot*, Jacob. About everything—work, her personal life, everything. She cared deeply about her product."

"It wasn't *her* product. Conrad did most of the work."

"It was definitely her product. She discovered that thing . . . I don't remember what it's called . . . and then she created Sirt-X so her work would benefit humanity. She oversaw all the safety and manufacturing processes—stuff Conrad doesn't know a thing about—so her product would be the very best it could be. Her legacy was very important to her."

"Her *legacy* . . ." Jacob repeated with a wince of disgust.

Merritt and I soon left the troubled couple. I was glad to get away, as the conversation had given me that sad, hollow feeling you get when you spend time with unhappy people.

"They seem to actually hate each other. Why don't they just get a divorce?" I said.

"Sherlock Holmes couldn't solve that mystery," Merritt replied. "But it doesn't surprise me that Barbara married a man like Jacob. I remember, back in college, that if you set Barbara loose in a roomful of fraternity boys, a few of them possibly decent, she'd home in on the very worst of the bunch and immediately embark on the fruitless task of trying to please him."

I was reminded that all these women had been young once, even younger than I was now. They'd already lived whole lives of success and failure, happiness and suffering.

Who did you *fall in love with?* I wanted to ask my boss. But I kept my mouth shut. Oddly, the more time I spent with Aubrey Merritt, the less likely it seemed that I would ever have the nerve to ask her about her past.

CHAPTER THIRTY-ONE

It's the Frog's Fault

After the enervating meeting with the Korns, I had an overwhelming urge to speak to my husband. I went straight to my room and called him.

"What's the matter?" Trevor asked after I'd said nothing more than *hello.*

"Are you aware that between forty and fifty percent of marriages end in divorce?"

"I've heard that, yeah. Why are you asking?"

"Merritt and I just spoke with this couple. They were awful. Everything she said, he said wasn't true, and everything he said, she disagreed with. When they weren't contradicting each other, they were ignoring each other. They obviously can't stand each other but for some reason they stay together. They've been married for over thirty years!"

"Mmm. Terrible."

From his indifferent tone, it was obvious that the significance of the topic hadn't come home to him yet.

"That's not the only bad marriage in this crowd either," I continued. "The woman who was murdered . . ."

"Wait. Someone was murdered?"

"I didn't tell you?"

"This is the first I've heard of it."

"Yeah, this woman was shot. In the pool. I tried to save her, but she was already dead."

"You tried to save her? How?"

"I jumped in the water and pulled her body over to the stairs and tried to give her mouth-to-mouth, but her jaw was locked shut. Like a bear trap. Not that I know anything about bear traps, but I can guess. It didn't really matter, though. Like I said, she was deceased."

"So that death threat you told me about . . . it was real." He seemed pensive.

"It looked that way at first, but it turned out the wrong woman was killed. So either the death-threat sender made a mistake, or there are two bad guys around. We're still trying to figure it out."

"And this woman was shot right in front of you? At the pool?"

"No. I was sleeping but I heard the gunshot so I went running down . . ."

"Wait. You ran to the place where there was a shooter?"

"Well, yeah. Where else would I go?"

"Was that smart, Olly? I mean, shouldn't you have run in the opposite direction?"

I sighed with exasperation. Not for the first time, I wondered whether Trevor truly understood what I did for a living. He seemed to think that when I used words like *killing* and *murder*, I was talking about a TV show or some kind of weird spectator sport. He didn't seem to grasp that my job was, among other things, catching killers. Real, actual killers. And that if there was any chance I could clock one of the bastards in flagrante delicto, with the gun still smoking in his hand, I was sure as hell going to try.

With a touch of impatience, I said, "I must have told you twenty times by now that the Merritt Investigative Agency, where I work, investigates crimes, murder being one of the big ones. When people get murdered, my boss and I try to figure out who did it. We're not out here baking cookies, Trev."

"But, Olly, detectives are supposed to show up *after* the killing, when the killer *isn't there anymore.*"

"That's just what happened! The killer was gone by the time I got there."

"I don't mean that. I mean, the murder is supposed to have happened in the past—like, a day or two or at least a few hours before the detectives are called in to investigate. That's how it's supposed to work."

I groaned silently. I loved my husband madly, deeply, truly, but he could be a real stickler about the weirdest, most petty things, like where salt and pepper shakers belong (on the counter, not in the cabinet) and how tomatoes should never be refrigerated. Now a woman was dead, and instead of saying, *Oh no, how tragic,* he was getting caught up in chronology.

"Does the timing really matter that much?" I asked.

"Yeah, it matters! What if the guy saw you seeing him, and decided to eliminate an eyewitness? You could have been murdered too!"

"I don't think so. Killers tend not to stick around. Once they make the kill, they're out of there. And if for some strange reason he *had* remained at the scene, it's not like I would have waved and introduced myself. I'm not that stupid. Now can we please get back to the reason I called?"

He sighed. "Sure. You wanted to tell me about the awful married couple."

"Not just them. All the married couples here are some version of disturbing. Not just the two who hate each other, but also the dead woman and her husband. They were, like, a power couple kind of thing, where it looks like they got married mostly to start a company so they could both be successful."

"That happens, I guess."

"I think it's weird, don't you?"

"I don't think about things like that very much."

"Well, I do. And it gives me a bad feeling. Should you marry someone if you don't love them?"

"Who's to say they didn't love each other? Maybe they did, and their company was like a child to them. And they were very happy."

"Then there's Fitz and the General," I continued. "I can't figure them out. They seem to really love each other, but they've spent a lot of time apart over the years, and Fitz is very close to his secretary, and she apparently adores him—like, a *lot.* And he and the General sleep in separate rooms. What's that about, do you think?"

"I have no idea, Olly. And I really don't care."

He was obviously losing interest in the conversation, but I needed to think it all the way through, so I kept going. "The last couple, the Laffertys, are the only ones who seem happily married. They're on a road trip together and they act like they really love each other. Which is nice. But the husband might have murdered the victim to avenge his wife's honor, so maybe they love each other a little *too* much, if you know what I mean."

"I honestly don't see what any of this has to do with us."

"Because . . ." I needed to say this carefully. "Because there appears to be a lot of ways to really screw up a marriage and, if possible, I would like to avoid them."

"Good. So would I."

"So now that we're married, maybe we should start paying attention to all the possible pitfalls, and discuss them and try to understand them, just so we're cognizant and don't walk into them unawares."

"Nope. No way. Absolutely not. I am not going to imagine every last thing that could go wrong in our relationship so that we can start obsessing over them. Nothing good will come of that. The more we start thinking about problems, the more likely they are to happen. We'll start reading into things too much, finding warning signs in stupid things that we ought to just get over. I intend to stay positive, to always think the best of both of us, even on the bad days. So if you want to make me miserable enough to get a divorce, you're going to have to try really hard. Because I intend to *totally ignore* the so-called warning signs and always think the best of both of us. If it turns out I was wrong all along, and our marriage really is miserable, I'll probably be the last to know."

I didn't appreciate the way he'd turned my simple suggestion upside down and inside out, but what he was saying did make a weird kind of sense. In any case, there was no point in continuing the discussion, because I could tell from his tone of voice that stubbornness had set in.

"Fine. In that case, can you just promise me one thing?"

"Depends what it is," he said warily.

"If we end up hating each other, promise me we'll get a divorce."

"Olly, we just got married."

"I know! But things happen. People change. And they have all kinds of problems. And, even though I agree with you that we don't appear to be assholes at this precise moment, one or both of us could turn into an asshole as time goes on. All I'm saying is, if that happens, let's promise each other that we won't stay married and let our marriage drag on and on, year after year, until we're both like . . . like . . . I don't know, like moldering fleshpots of misery!"

"*Moldering?* Are you sure?"

"Yes, *moldering*. It's exactly the right word in this context. Look it up."

"No, that's fine. I believe you. But . . . *fleshpots*?"

"Yeah, like pots of flesh. What else?"

"Hmm, no. I don't think so. *Fleshpot* means something else, something very specific. I can't remember what it is right now. It's not a word I think about very often."

With unearned conviction, I explained, "A *fleshpot*, obviously, is a person with no heart or brain, just lots of formless, Jell-O-like flesh that you could stuff in a pot, I suppose. If you wanted to."

"And then it would molder. Apparently."

"Not always. But it could molder. Anything can molder."

"Well, we're not going to do that. Or be that. That's not going to be our future."

"Sure. We believe that now, but who can say what the future holds? No one gets married thinking they're going to get all broken-down and hopeless, but it happens. Quite a lot apparently. And if it happens to us, then we have to be strong and look squarely at that reality and promise each other that we won't just passively sink into a life of petty retributions and cutting remarks."

"I appreciate where you're going with this, but, honestly, I just don't see that happening."

"Who does? It creeps up on you, apparently. Like that thing with the frog. The water keeps getting hotter and the frog keeps trying to ignore it, and before you know it, the frog is completely cooked. And dead. And we're supposed to think it was a perfectly natural phenomenon and not the frog's fault. But that's wrong. It was *totally* the frog's fault! That frog was living in la-la land and didn't have the sense to see what was happening and jump out of the pot while it still had some energy in its muscles and hope in its heart that it could have a better life in water that was not continuing to heat up long after it should have stopped. If that frog had been a little smarter, a little braver, it would have leapt out of that too-hot pot and gone forth into the world and searched and searched until it found a better place to live."

"In a more temperate climate," Trevor offered.

God, he was frustrating. Tersely, I replied, "I don't know what climate the frog would enjoy, Trevor. That's for the frog to decide. For now, I just need you to promise me that you'll agree to divorce if our relationship deteriorates beyond hope of repair."

"I, Trevor, promise you, Olivia, that if one or both of us becomes a total asshole and makes the other one as miserable as a moldering fleshpot, that we will maturely face and acknowledge that fact and file for divorce in a timely manner."

"A cooperative, respectful, fair-minded divorce."

"Yes."

Finally! "Thank you. That's a big weight off my mind." *I shouldn't have needed to work so hard for that*, I thought.

"No problem. Glad to oblige. Now, moving on, I've got some bad news."

"What is it?"

"We didn't get the apartment. I went to the broker's office first thing this morning to drop off the deposit check, and it was already taken. We missed it."

"Oh, that's too bad." It took me a moment to absorb the news, and when I did, I was crushed. Without realizing it, I'd already started living there in my mind, enjoying the big sunny windows, no street noise, and my very own laundry closet.

"We're back to square one," Trevor said. "I'll see if I can line up a few more showings. This time, if we find something we like, we've got to move fast. So keep your eye on your text messages. I'll be sending links."

"Got it."

"And, Olly? I do love you, you know. We're not going to get divorced."

"I wish we could go for a walk or something."

"We will, when you get back. So find the damn killer, okay? God, I hate killers. They keep taking you away from me."

"I'll find him, Trevor. Merritt and I will find him for sure. And if there are two bad guys, we'll find them both. Probably in the next few days."

"And don't let that cranky old bag make you feel bad. Stand up for yourself."

"Will do."

"Goddamn it," he muttered for no reason that I could discern.

"So true," I said, just to be supportive. And because I wanted us to be on the same side whenever possible against all the things that might divide us, now and forever.

CHAPTER THIRTY-TWO

What to Do?

The day had blossomed into something beautiful, befitting the long holiday weekend that officially ushered in summer. I supposed millions of Americans were enjoying it. Those of us trapped at the Muddy River Ranch certainly weren't. There was as yet no news about the hunt for the Laffertys, and no word from Sheriff Casey about when we might be allowed to leave. The day was dragging on like a terrible movie that refused to end, and the mood had slipped from fearful to irritable.

It wasn't possible to sit around the pool, much less swim in it, as the water was still discolored by Eve Exeter's blood. (I wondered if I'd ever be able to swim, not only in that particular pool at this particular time, but in any pool anywhere in the world ever again.) So most of the guests had congregated in the air-conditioned living room. Two onerous gongs of the grandfather clock informed us it was two p.m.

"They can't keep us here forever," Bree groused. "Is this even legal?"

"I'm sure Sheriff Casey will get back to us soon," Fitz said sensibly. "He seemed very eager to apprehend the Laffertys, and I suppose once he does he'll let us know next steps. We just need to hang on awhile longer."

"He's treating us like suspects. It's insulting," Barbara said.

"We *are* suspects," said Merritt. "Any one of us could have done it."

"Ridiculous. As if one of us would want to kill Eve."

A strained silence met this remark. That someone might have wanted to kill Eve Exeter wasn't completely out of the question.

Fitz broke the tension with a jarringly upbeat suggestion. "There's nothing we can do to help the situation at this point, so why don't we just carry on with the reunion activities?"

"If you're proposing that we play charades like nothing happened, you're out of your mind," Bree replied. "Someone was just murdered, Fitz. All I care about at the moment is getting myself and my child away from this bloody muddy ranch as quickly as possible. For all we know, Dave Lafferty *didn't* pull that trigger, and the murderer is still here, waiting for his chance to knock off someone else."

Barbara piped up breathlessly, "What about that stableman? He's a suspicious-looking character. The minute I laid eyes on him, I got a bad feeling and turned my ring around."

"You did what?" Nova asked, bewildered.

"I turned my ring around so the diamond faces in." Barbara performed the operation and held out her hand for everyone to see. "See? When you do this, it looks like you're wearing just a plain gold band. Of course, in certain countries, you're better off leaving all your jewelry at home."

"You don't need to turn your ring around, Barbara," the General said dryly. "Barry has been with us for years. He is completely trustworthy. He doesn't want your diamond ring, and he didn't kill anyone."

Peter Jumper spoke from the corner of the room. I'd barely noticed him sitting on the floor there, leaning his back against the wall. The prospect of a recreational activity had breathed some life into him. "Hey, Fitz. You feel like doing some more shooting?"

"I don't see how anyone could even *think* about guns right now," Nova muttered.

Fitz turned to Peter. "I'd love to, son, but this may not be the best time for that sort of thing."

In response, Peter stretched out on the floor in a fully supine position with one hand pressed to his forehead like a fainting Victorian lady.

His mother eyed him, then the liquor cabinet.

Fitz paced a few steps before erupting with "On second thought, why not? Pete, my boy, let's you and I go out in the desert and see how many empty cans we can knock off that ledge."

Peter scrambled to his feet and the two of them eagerly left the room, leaving eight of us to fret and stare at each other: me, Merritt, the General, Nova, Bree, Barbara, Conrad Zander, and Jacob Korn.

Nova crossed her long legs. "Bree is right: We shouldn't act like nothing has happened. But Fitz was right too in one respect: We would do well to find something positive and affirming to do. I have a suggestion. I think we should form a grief and trauma support group, which I'm willing to facilitate free of charge."

The remaining men—Conrad Zander and Jacob Korn—exchanged glances, stood in unison, and quickly exited through the French doors without explanation.

Now there were just six of us: five sorority sisters and me.

Nova took a pen and notepad from a canvas tote bag that was on the rug beside her chair.

"You're serious, aren't you?" Bree said in mild awe.

"Perfectly serious," said Nova serenely. "We've experienced a severe trauma, ladies. And it's far from over. It's continuing even now, as we sit here desperately trying to cope, to find our bearings in a new and terrifying world—a world in which an innocent woman was murdered in cold blood for reasons we will never come to terms with, no matter how hard we try."

She placed small round reading glasses on the tip of her nose. "As you know, I've had a lot of experience dealing with these issues, both personally and professionally, and I'm sorry to tell you that each of us, whether we are aware of it yet or not, has been deeply scarred by this morning's violent tragedy. Most of us will need PTSD counseling at some point in the future, so we might as well start now. Studies show that early treatment can help reduce the intensity and duration of future PTSD symptoms."

I recalled that Nova's podcast and blog, *Life After Death*, centered on grief and PTSD recovery, and that both were wildly successful.

She opened her notebook and clicked her pen. I had no idea what she intended to write down.

Her notebook reminded me that I also ought to keep a record of whatever was going to be said. I slipped my hand into my pocket and surreptitiously turned on my phone's recorder. I wasn't expecting to hear a full confession, but there was always the chance that a guilty party would let a telling detail slip.

CHAPTER THIRTY-THREE

Group Therapy, Part 1

I thought we might start by sharing our fondest memories of Eve," Nova said, pen poised over the open notebook in her lap.

"Oh my god. Tell me this isn't happening." Bree took out her vape pen, tossing her lizard-skin pouch on the coffee table in a lazy, haphazard manner that conveyed haughty disgust.

"Let's rearrange the chairs, shall we?" Nova said, undeterred.

She proceeded to drag her chair over to the coffee table, and I rose to join the effort. Merritt moved her chair as well. The General and Barbara, who were seated on the couch, didn't need to do anything. We'd soon created a cozy circle where we could speak to each other more intimately. Bree continued to appear skeptical, but in the end she grudgingly changed the angle of her armchair so she could almost be considered part of the group.

"There's no right or wrong and no good or bad in this journey," Nova explained. "No set timeline either. Each of our experiences will be unique." Her manner was polished and smooth, suggesting that this was not the first time she'd delivered this speech. "The events of this morning—the tragic loss of our dear friend, and the extreme, unexpected violence that caused it—either of those things by itself would be extremely difficult to process. Together, they pose a daunting psychological challenge. What each of us needs to do right now is to practice radical acceptance of our feelings and thoughts, whatever they might be in this moment and in all the moments to come, regardless of what disparaging or critical labels we might have an urge to put on them.

"We need to extend the same radical acceptance to each other's thoughts and feelings as well. No judgment, no prejudice. That's where and how the healing begins."

"I think I need a drink," groaned Bree.

Nova looked at her sternly. "No, you don't. You need to share your feelings and let the group support you. You can get through this without resorting to self-medication, Bree. I know you can. And you should. The alcohol will only dull your feelings. So, let's start the session with you. What are your thoughts and feelings at this moment? Remember: You don't have to impress anyone or even make sense. We're all in this together, and we're here to support you wherever you are in your journey."

"I honestly have no idea what you want from me, Nova. Eve was shot in the back this morning just a few minutes' walk from where we're sitting now. Her body is lying on a slab in some coroner's office as we speak. We can't paper that over with fancy words, and we shouldn't even try."

Nova nodded knowingly. "Shock. That's what I'm hearing right now, if I may be so bold as to describe the emotion I believe you are feeling. Shock is a perfectly appropriate response to a traumatic event."

"For god's sake, Nova! I don't give a damn whether you think my feelings are appropriate! My feelings are mine. They're whatever the hell they want to be, they've never been shy about making themselves known, and they damn well don't need your approval. What my feelings want to say at this moment is that this whole group therapy thing is ridiculous. It's a dodge, a cheat, an attempt to escape the fact that a killer might still be here on this ranch, perhaps even in this room. That we honestly don't know if Eve's death was the day's last murder or its first!"

Barbara started to tremble. "Don't say that, Bree. There *can't* be any more murders!"

"Oh come on, Barbara," Bree said mockingly. "Have you seriously not considered the possibility? Anything is possible. Any fucking thing. The whole world is in chaos, and it's only getting worse. Instead of trying to neutralize our feelings with all this nicey-nice chitchat, maybe we ought to be using our fear and rage as rocket fuel to help us find that murderer and take him down like the human scum he is!"

"That's what the police are for," Nova asserted calmly.

"Oh, in *that* case," Bree drawled sarcastically. "I guess as long as someone *else* is doing it, I guess we can all just sit back, relax, and jabber on about ourselves."

Nova looked perplexed, but far from beaten. "I hear your hostility, Bree. Rage is not an unusual response to trauma. But I wonder if you aren't inappropriately displacing your understandable desire for revenge onto Barbara and me."

"Oh. My. God. Ladies! We are not safe! And this therapy nonsense will only succeed in making us soft and stupid when what we need to be is smart and tough. Now, if you don't mind, I really do need that drink." She stood up and left the room.

Silence ensued. No one knew what to say. Even Nova was at a loss for words. But not for long.

"Well. Emotions run high, as we can see. I do hope Bree will come back and join us soon. We certainly don't need any more sisters stalking off. In the meantime, we still need to deal with our grief, and the best way to do that is to dive right in. So let's try this again, with each person saying a word or two about what made Eve so special, and why they will miss her. Let's start with you, Joan."

The General cleared her throat. She didn't seem completely comfortable with the proceedings, but in deference to Nova and as a dedicated team player, she was willing to participate. "I remember meeting Eve at the beginning of freshman year. I admired her right away. She struck me as very strong, very confident—the kind of person who was bound to reach her goals and make her mark on the world. At the time I didn't see myself that way. I was shy and awkward—all arms and legs and pimply skin. I'd had a very protected life until then, and not many friends my own age. None at all, really, just my horses. Eve seemed to have already become a woman of substance. I watched her and tried to copy her mannerisms; I even tried to like the things she liked. It seems silly now. But at that age, you're so impressionable, so affected by everyone in your circle. Eve gave me an ideal to strive for. I think I can say that knowing her helped make me who I am today." The room had grown quiet, and the General glanced around self-consciously, as if surprised to discover that people were listening. "Did I go on too long?"

"Not at all, Joan," Nova assured her. "What you said was really beautiful, and such a thoughtful tribute to Eve. It reminds us how profound even the simplest relationships can be."

The General nodded humbly. She seemed to be experiencing a sort of mournful peace. I was glad that Bree had left the room so that the rest of us could profit from Nova's expertise without fear of mockery.

The therapist adjusted the position of her notebook (she still hadn't written anything down), recrossed her legs, and turned her empathic eyes to Merritt. "Aubrey, what would you like to share with the group? I suggest starting with your clearest memory of Eve."

I held my breath. Would Merritt, who I had always thought of as solitary and friendless, who had responded to any personal questions I'd asked as if they were rude impertinences, who had assured me that she couldn't care less about her old sorority sisters—was she going to be pressured into sharing tender feelings with the group? It seemed unlikely, especially since the main reason she was tolerating the group at all was that she didn't dare leave the General alone and unprotected.

"Well, let's see . . ." She appeared to be rummaging through her college memory box. "It doesn't surprise me that Eve had such an extraordinary career. As Joan said, she was extremely focused and goal-oriented. Hardworking too. Fair-minded, for the most part. Humorless, I'd have to add, but you can't hold that against someone. Dry and unimaginative, of course. Functionally incapable of operating outside a very small sphere. And quite callous on occasion. Very callous, I'd have to say. She puzzled me, frankly. I used to look at her and wonder what exactly was going on in her mind. And her heart. Or if she had a heart. But"—Merritt smiled at us brightly—"those few things aside, it's clear that she made a significant contribution to the world through her groundbreaking research and teaching. I'd say that her life, overall, must be considered an unqualified success."

There was a delicate vertical furrow in Nova's brow, right between her eyes. "As always, Aubrey, you have such an interesting approach. I like the way you haven't shied away from mentioning a few of Eve's limitations. We all have limitations, don't we? Our friends know them better than anyone, and usually forgive us for them. But I have to point out that, while you gave us a clear if one-sided description of Eve's character, you didn't talk about your *feelings* at all. May I ask what you are *feeling* about Eve right now, as you sit here? After her senseless death?"

Merritt raised one eyebrow a fraction of an inch. "My feeling is that I didn't like her much when she was alive, and I don't like her any better now that she's dead."

Nova blanched at the harsh remark.

That's what you get for trying to push Aubrey Merritt around, I wanted to tell the therapist.

Barbara piped up from the other side of the circle. "No one liked Eve but me."

With visible relief, Nova turned her attention to the woman who had spoken. "You were very close to her, Barbara. Maybe you can say something kind about Eve."

Receiving the group spotlight was all Barbara needed for the floodgates of her emotions to open. She wept copiously. We all waited in silent respect as she cried, wiped her eyes, cried some more, snorted, sniffled, and finally got herself together enough to choke out the following speech: "No one knew Eve like I did. Or loved her like I did. Not even her husband. Oh, I'm not saying Conrad didn't love her. Of course he did. But it's different . . . between women . . . we had a closer friendship. I'm not talking about anything sexual here, not at all. It's just the way girls are . . . you know, when we're close to each other, we can be very close. Eve told me all her tribulations over the years, all her secrets, and I told her mine. Marriage, for example. It wasn't easy for either of us, and we talked very honestly about that. And work. Eve discussed all her worries and fears. And her hopes. She had great hopes for her company. We told each other things we couldn't tell anyone else, even things we were ashamed of. That's how it was with Eve and me. I've lost the best friend I ever had, and I honestly don't know how I can go on."

An awkward silence met this declaration. Merritt, the General,

Nova, and I all exchanged confused glances. There had been no sign of the deep friendship Barbara described. What I'd noticed, instead, was how patronizing Eve had been to Barbara. She had dismissed virtually everything Barbara said with a sneer or a jeer. At every opportunity, she had made her dislike of Barbara crystal clear.

"I understand," Nova murmured kindly. "I'm so very sorry, Barbara. You were closer to Eve than any of us. I'm very sorry for the pain you're feeling now."

Barbara nodded weakly and in a meek voice said, "Thank you. I appreciate the group's support. I really love you guys. I really missed you all these years." As the last tears streamed from her eyes, she smeared them across her cheeks with the palms of her hands.

With a faint smile Nova capped her pen and closed her notebook. Barbara's tears seemed to have satisfied her immediate goal. While Barbara sniffled, the rest of us looked up at the ceiling and quietly waited for the ordeal to end.

CHAPTER THIRTY-FOUR

Group Therapy, Part 2

We were not to be let off so easily. Because at that moment we heard the slapping of plastic flip-flops along the clay tiles of the hallway, and a moment later Kathy Lafferty appeared in the doorway. She was dressed in a striped T-shirt and yellow Bermuda shorts. A necklace of large green beads fit snugly around her thick neck, and a little Kate Spade bag in cameo pink swung from her shoulder. Her outfit screamed, *Postmenopausal American Woman on Vacation!* but her face said something different. The clammy pallor of her skin, the drops of moisture on her upper lip, the squint of terror in her eyes—all this conveyed a state of severe negative agitation. This was a woman who had just been gut-punched by life.

Bree came in right behind her, no doubt eager to hear her news, and took the seat she had vacated earlier.

The sisters pushed and pulled their chairs closer together to make room, while I jumped up and dragged another in from the dining room. Kathy took her place among us and looked at each of us in turn. We looked back at her expectantly.

"Dave is innocent, but the cops are going to pin it on him anyway. I can't believe it. I cannot wrap my head around what's happening. She's done it again, ladies. She's ruined my life twice."

No one asked who Kathy meant by *she*.

Nova carefully replied, "Welcome to the group, Kathy. I understand that this is a very challenging time for you and Dave, and that you have been harboring difficult feelings about Eve for the last forty years. I think it would make sense for you and me to schedule a time to meet privately so you can start coming to terms with it all. Right now, the people in this room are gathered as a group to support the beginnings of a grief process that, as I explained already, will be different for each of us. We began with each sister sharing her fondest memories of Eve. Would you like to become part of the group by sharing your own fond memories?"

Kathy's face was stone. Her lips didn't move.

A burble of laughter escaped from Bree. "Seriously, you're asking her that?"

Barbara sneered, "As far as I'm concerned, Kathy and Dave were in it together."

Kathy looked across the circle at her coldly. "I can't believe you said that. But I'm not surprised. You were always sucking up to Eve. You're just an ass-kisser, Barbara. You've been an ass-kisser all your life."

"Oh yeah? Well, let me tell you something. I happen to know you were guilty as charged. I have concrete evidence that you plagiarized Eve's senior thesis and tried to pass her research off as your own." She smirked. "As if anyone in their right mind would believe that someone like you could have made such a brilliant discovery."

Aha! The story behind the grudge is finally revealed! I thought with satisfaction. But which woman was telling the truth?

Kathy was unfazed. "You're such a good liar, and you've been lying for so long you probably believe what you're saying. But you know full well you forged that so-called evidence in the hopes it would make Eve like you, which she never ever did. Why would she? Why would anyone want to be friends with a sniveling patsy like you? Face it, Barbara: You sold your soul for Eve's friendship, and you got nothing in return. Who's to say *you* weren't the one who shot her in the back? Wait—weren't you supposed to have been with her at the pool this morning?"

"I wasn't there. I overslept," Barbara said, looking at the floor.

"That's what you say. But you're a much likelier suspect than me or my husband, come to think of it."

Bree jumped in. "It could have been any of us. Including me. I hated Eve. She was mean and cheap and a killjoy and a bully. She would have taken candy from a baby with no problem. When all that stuff happened between her and Kathy at the end of senior year, I totally believed Kathy, and I still do. Because Kathy isn't a cheater, and Eve definitely was. Eve stole her work, submitted it as her own, and was awarded a prestigious fellowship as a result. And when Kathy complained, Eve accused Kathy of plagiarism, which was the very thing she herself had done! Kathy got expelled a month before graduation and had to make up the credits at a community college, while Eve went on to achieve fame and fortune thanks to Kathy's research. Kathy ended up wasting her amazing brain as an obscure middle school science teacher in upstate New York. Good god. What could possibly be more depressing than that?"

"Whaa—?" Kathy began.

"Sorry, dear. I didn't mean to suggest that teaching middle school in upstate New York is depressing."

"Yes, you did, Bree! That's exactly what you meant!" Kathy's dander was up. "Look, ladies, I know a lot of you think my career wasn't that great or important, not like Eve's or any of yours, and

I'm not saying that I wasn't bitter at first. I was. I struggled with it; I obsessed. That MIT fellowship should have been mine! I was the one who discovered that sirtuins are NAD-positive-dependent protein deacetylases! My whole life would have been different if Eve hadn't stolen my work. I might have had the career she had. I didn't give a darn about fame and fortune. It was the resources I dreamed about—all that time and money to support my research. I could have done so much with that! But, thanks to Eve, I missed my chance not just that one time, but for the rest of my life. Door after door slammed in my face after I was expelled from Sarah Lawrence for plagiarism. I barely was able to get my teaching certificate, and then I had to live with the judgment of my colleagues. For years I silently fumed. But eventually I accepted my situation. I made peace with teaching. I enjoyed working with my students. I realized that I was making a positive difference in their lives, and I tried to be the very best science teacher I could be. I did good work for thirty-five years. I'm proud of my career, and I don't need anyone to feel sorry for me!"

"Oh, my darling dear," Bree hastened to say. "I don't feel sorry for you in the least. The truth is, I envy you! You have everything I always wanted: love, family, faith, purpose. You even find time to give back to your community! Look at me. I was a bartender for years. I worked in dirty, dark holes-in-the-wall—the kinds of places where day drinkers waste their miserable lives. I shacked up with more guys than I can count, and even though I told Peter his father was a traveling British aristocrat, the truth is, I have no idea who his father was, but I know it wasn't that. And as for money? At times I was so broke I scooped dollar bills out of the servers' tip jar and stuffed them in my pocket."

Kathy's face fell. "Oh, that's awful, Bree. I'm sorry you had to go through that. But now you're a famous author!"

"I know! Isn't that strange? Who would have guessed it? Least of all me. Definitely not my mother. But let me tell you a sad little secret. When the struggle was too hard and went on too long, the victory tastes like dust."

"Whaa?" Kathy said again.

Bree looked around at the puzzled and concerned faces, and decided to come clean. "I lied. Kathy's career isn't depressing. It's me. I'm depressed. I always have been, and nothing, not even thousands of fans, has made a dent in it."

"Have you considered a combination of cognitive therapy and medication?" Nova asked, not missing a beat.

Bree delivered a foul glare to the therapist.

Kathy piped up, "I need to say one more thing before you all get the wrong impression of me. While I obviously despised Eve for what she stole from me, I am truly and sincerely sorry she's dead. She absolutely did not deserve what happened to her. No one deserves to have their life cut short in such a terrible way. So while I can't and won't deny that I felt very bitterly toward her for many, many years, I still had compassion for her as a human being. *Caritas*, the Bible calls it. Brotherly love. Only for us it's sisterly love. I really did feel a little bit of that for Eve. I feel it for each of you too. We're all flawed, ladies. Every one of us." She reflected for a moment before adding, "Some worse than others, of course."

There was a solemn pause while we all thought about that.

Nova finally broke in. "What you just said, Kathy—that was really beautiful, and very psychologically mature. You might not believe this, but I spend *years* trying to get my clients to do what you just did—to fully embody such deep and contradictory emotions while at the same time smoothly integrating them into a unified experience of self and other—"

"Oh, shut up, Nova," Bree interrupted with a sneer.

"Yes, please be quiet," the General said more gently.

Nova fell silent.

"I'll take it from here," Merritt said. She had been quiet during the discussion, and now she went straight into the thick of what was, for her, the crucial point. "As Bree said earlier, each person in this room is a suspect. Some of us hated Eve for reasons we've discussed; others, perhaps, hated her for reasons unknown. Either way, I don't think any of us is wholly convinced that Dave Lafferty was her killer. I think we are all aware that the real killer may still be among us; perhaps she is here right now. If so, I wish to convey a message to that person. You will be discovered. You will be prosecuted. If you come forward now, you will have an easier time. So I ask you sincerely, for your own good, if you murdered Eve, please raise your hand."

Everyone sat still. Stiller than still. No hand went up.

Either the murderer wasn't present, or she lacked the courage to admit what she'd done.

I turned off my recorder in disappointment. For all the drama, nothing had changed. Merritt and I were still distressingly short on tangible clues in both the murder of Eve Exeter and the threat against the General's life. The therapy session had been a waste of our precious time, or so I believed.

CHAPTER THIRTY-FIVE

Not a Chipmunk

General Battersea's ankle had swelled to twice its usual size, despite periodic applications of ice packs. She admitted that it was throbbing rather painfully and that she wouldn't mind a bit of rest before dinner. So Merritt and I accompanied her to her bedroom, where Merritt recited the usual safety instructions and I performed the now-familiar ritual of checking the space for hidden intruders. As I presented the General with two Tylenol and a glass of water, Merritt plumped some pillows and stacked them at the end of the bed so the General could elevate her foot. I could tell that my boss wasn't entirely comfortable with leaving our client alone—this morning's murder had made our job of ensuring her safety even more perilous and urgent—but we couldn't very well stand around her bed watching her snooze. We had work to do.

So after we heard her lock her door from the inside, we decamped to a far table on the veranda, where we had agreed to meet Kathy Lafferty. It was late afternoon, still broiling hot, though the usually brash desert sunlight had mellowed to a soft gold.

"You didn't really think the murderer was going to confess at the group therapy session, did you?" I asked Merritt.

"I was hoping to get a reaction out of someone. A subtle tell perhaps."

"Did you?"

"Not that I noticed."

"I can't imagine any of those—" I caught myself before I said *old ladies.* "Any of your sorority sisters blasting someone in the back with a shotgun."

"There are far too many things you can't imagine, Blunt."

Kathy arrived just then, carrying a tray of three plastic glasses filled with lemonade. She set the glasses on the table. The tray was painted with butterflies.

I thanked her, marveling at her thoughtfulness under the circumstances. Some women will serve lemonade no matter what befalls them. The drink was perfect for a hot day: sweet, sour, and icy cold.

"Tell me exactly what happened from the time you and Dave left the barbecue until you were taken into custody this morning," Merritt said. "Take your time."

Kathy nervously fingered the fat green beads around her neck as she decided where to begin. True to form, she started in the nicest place possible, with a compliment for our host. "Joan was so kind last night, trying to convince us to stay for the rest of the weekend after what happened at the barbecue. Dave and I truly appreciated her support and understanding. But the two of us talked about it after she left our room, and we realized there really wasn't a way for us to make things feel right. We're not that good at pretending, I guess. And Dave was still very angry, just as angry as I was, maybe even more so because his instinct is to come to my defense. *Serve and protect,* you know. That was his motto for years in the police force, the words he lived his life by, and it's just very hard for him to see someone get away with a crime like the one Eve did to me, even if it was years ago. So we decided we'd head out early this morning, drive to Phoenix, which was the next place on our list and which we were both excited to see. I left a note for Joan on the table in the foyer. Do you know if she got it?"

"She didn't mention it to me."

"Oh, well, it was just a little thank-you note, saying how grateful Dave and I were for her thoughtful invitation and how much we'd enjoyed seeing her and Fitz and this beautiful ranch. And how we hoped that the weekend would continue to be just as wonderful as I know she wanted it to be with all the planning she and Fitz put into it."

"That's lovely," Merritt said, obviously thoroughly bored. "Did you happen to hear any gunshots while you were doing that?"

"Yes, I heard something that could have been a gunshot. I could barely hear it. It came from far away."

"You should have heard it clearly. The guesthouse isn't that far from the pool."

"Dave and I weren't staying in the guesthouse. We were staying in our camper, which was parked in the lot past the guesthouse."

"Approximately what time did you hear it?"

"I'm not sure. Maybe a few minutes before we left. I never dreamed anyone was getting killed. I figured it was just someone target shooting or something like that. I honestly didn't think too much about it. I just wanted to get on the road."

"Was Dave with you?"

"Of course."

"The whole time?"

"Yes, yes, yes. The police asked me that a hundred times. You can ask me a hundred more times if you want, and my answer will be the same. Yes. My husband was with me *the entire time*."

"After the brouhaha last night, how did he seem to you?"

"He was upset. We both were. We felt bad about ruining the party, but we were still mad, both of us. We hadn't talked about that part of my life in years, and when it all came back, it came rushing back, if you know what I mean. All the pent-up feelings."

"You must have known Eve would be at the reunion."

"It crossed my mind that she might be here, but I wasn't going to let that stop me from coming. She'd prevented me from doing what I wanted once already, and she wasn't going to do it again. And, to be honest, I really believed the whole issue was well behind me. I had no idea I'd react to seeing her the way I did."

"You and Dave were both angry and upset last night. Did you talk to each other about your feelings?"

"I really don't think that's any of your business. What my husband and I say to each other in our private moments is private. If you're wondering whether we plotted Eve's murder, the answer is no."

"All right, fair enough. You left the ranch. What happened then?"

"We had breakfast in Pecos like we planned, and we got on the highway to drive up to Phoenix, and the next thing we knew, we were getting pulled over and told we needed to come back to the police station for questioning. We got a police escort back to Pecos, and they split us up at the station. I spent hours answering their questions, over and over again, and they finally let me go. But they wouldn't let me drive the camper. I had to have an officer take me here in a squad car. I was almost afraid to come back to the ranch, knowing what you all were probably thinking about me and Dave, but I had nowhere else to go. I need to stay close to Pecos while Dave is in custody. They haven't charged him yet. But apparently they can keep him for up to seventy-two hours until they have to release him."

"I'm not surprised Casey is keeping him. Dave checks the boxes for motive, means, and opportunity. He threatened Eve publicly; he knew where the shotguns were stored and how to use one."

"But that's *all* Casey has," Kathy protested. "He doesn't have any physical evidence. That's what they're looking for now. They already applied for a search warrant, and I know they'll start tearing the camper apart the minute it's approved. The alibi I provided means nothing to them. They're convinced I'm lying to protect my husband. They kept calling me *a good wife*. But I'm not lying, and I wish *someone* would believe me!"

She lowered her voice and said in an almost accusatory voice, "I know something else, too. I heard one of the cops at the station say that, when the call came in that there had been a murder at the Muddy River Ranch, he thought for sure the victim was going to be Joan Battersea. He was surprised to find out it was someone else. When I asked him why he thought that, he said there'd been a report of a death threat sent to the ranch. To Joan."

Merritt was quiet. Her fingers were tented before her mouth as if to keep words from escaping.

Kathy's eyes flashed. "Is it true, Aubrey? Did Joan receive a death threat? If she did, you need to tell me. That information could make a lot of difference to Dave."

Merritt nodded slowly. "Yes, it's true. I came to the reunion because Fitz asked me to. He wanted someone to watch over Joan. And right now I'm wondering the same thing you are—whether Eve's death was a case of mistaken identity."

"Then you have to help us, because you know Dave didn't do it!" Kathy said furiously.

"I *don't* know that, Kathy. I don't know anything for sure yet."

"Then find out, for god's sake! Quickly! You're a famous detective, right? Picture in the paper and everything, right? I don't know about all the stuff you've done, but I heard this weekend, some of the girls talking, saying how famous you are and what an amazing career you've had. Well, you know who else had a great career? My husband. He went out every day and put his life on the line in one of the most stressful and dangerous jobs there is. Now someone has to take care of him. Sure, he gets angry sometimes and does things he shouldn't. But he never hurt anyone, not intentionally, and he never would. He knows the difference. That little performance last night? That was just to scare Eve. That's all it was. And now look where he is! He has a heart condition, you know. Atrial fibrillation. He takes meds twice a day to control it, but it can easily flare up. I'm really worried that the stress of all this might kill him. Someone needs to fix this situation right away, and it has to be you, Aubrey, because you're the only one who can. I'm not asking you. I'm begging."

"I'll do my best, Kathy. I can't say I'll be able to prove Dave innocent, but I promise I'll do my very best to uncover the truth."

"If you're as good as people say you are, I have nothing to fear. But you've got to move fast. Sheriff Casey is a terrible cop. The things he said to me to try to break me down were awful; I won't repeat them, but you can guess. He lied to me too, to get me to turn on my husband. He said they found blood on Dave's shirt, which I know for a fact cannot possibly be true. He's hungry for an arrest, and I honestly think he'd do anything to get it. There's no telling what will be in that RV when it comes out of the police garage. You understand what I'm saying, right?"

"I do."

Kathy glowered and pursed her lips. It looked like she wanted to say more but was holding back. Finally she stood up and put the lemonade glasses back on the tray. Without a goodbye, she marched the tray into the house. I watched her go, impressed. She had seemed so nice and sweet at first—*a sweet little chipmunk*, Bree had called her. But there was more to Kathy Lafferty than met the eye.

Merritt turned to me, her face pale and drawn. "I need you to do something right away. We know the Laffertys left the ranch at seven twenty-four. You say you're certain the gun went off at about seven fifteen. That means Dave would have had nine minutes to make it from the pool through the cabana to the parking lot on foot, and from the parking lot to the front gate by car. I want you to retrace his route. See how long it takes. I don't think nine minutes is enough time."

CHAPTER THIRTY-SIX

Seduction, Bribery, and a Slow Jog

The forensic team had left, taking their paraphernalia with them. Only the yellow police tape remained, sagging in some places, broken in others. The area looked vacant and forlorn, like the setting of a departed circus.

To my surprise, Conrad Zander was seated just outside the police tape in one of the many molded plastic chairs that had been set around the tables last night and stacked in a nearby corner when the party broke up. Merritt and I had interviewed him at around noon, and now it was almost five. Had he been there all afternoon? The way he was so motionless, staring fixedly at the spot where his wife had been brutally executed, was strange and troubling.

He turned slightly on hearing my approach. "Come and sit down, Olivia." He lifted another of the plastic chairs over the police tape and set it beside his own.

I remained standing, unsure what to do. I needed to get on with the task of timing Dave Lafferty's alleged escape, but Zander was obviously in a mood to talk, and I didn't want to miss an opportunity to learn something.

He favored me with a wistful smile. "You have lovely hair."

"Excuse me?"

"Your hair. It's a lovely color. I've always been attracted to brunettes."

I stared at him, too astonished to reply.

"I know I'm not supposed to say those kinds of things anymore, but I really don't see what's wrong with complimenting a pretty girl. I'm from a different generation, I guess."

"Did you ever stop to consider that your compliments might not be welcome?"

"No. I never thought that. And I don't believe it. I think Miss Olivia Blunt is secretly flattered to have someone notice her."

There was an insult in there somewhere, maybe more than one, but I didn't have the energy to unpack them. "I'm not flattered, Mr. Zander. I'm here to do a job, not to waste my time flattering *you* by pretending your compliment means something to me."

"Well, well. You are aptly named, I see."

"Just now you crossed the police tape to remove this chair from the crime scene. Did you remove anything else today, or tamper with any evidence?"

"Please, my dear. You can't be serious. The crime scene has been fully processed. Frankly, it might have yielded more clues if you hadn't blundered all over it, splashing water everywhere."

"I was trying to save your wife's life," I said.

"You clearly failed."

"I know I did. But at least I tried. And for your information, I wasn't the only person splashing water outside the pool this morning." A red warning light flashed in my head. DON'T BE CRUEL, it said. I didn't listen to it. The widower might as well know the awful truth about his wife's last moments on this earth—how she died in fear and desperation. He'd probably hear about it anyway.

"There was a good-sized puddle of water outside the pool. There." I pointed to the place. "I assume it came from your wife—either before she was shot, when she saw her killer approaching and was trying to lift herself out of the pool to get away, or after she was shot, when she bravely used what little strength she still possessed to try to crawl out of the pool to safety."

"Ah! Is *that* the mysterious evidence Aubrey was talking about that is going to lead her straight to the killer?"

Just to bother him, and because he deserved it for responding so coldly to the thought of his wife in agony, I decided to carry on with Merritt's as-yet-unexplained deception. "No investigator worth her salt would call a puddle *evidence*, Mr. Zander. *Real* evidence, *good* evidence—like the kind we have—is more direct and conclusive, and can stand up in a court of law."

He gestured to the empty chair beside him. "Sit down and let's talk."

I hesitated. The riddle of the spider and the fly came to mind.

He looked up at me with mild eyes and a disarmingly friendly smile. "I have some information for you. About my wife. Maybe we could trade secrets."

That settled it. I needed to hear what he had to say. I sat down. "What about your wife?"

"First, tell me about Aubrey. What evidence does she have? Whom does it implicate? One of the sorority sisters? Fitz? Maybe that ranch hand who's always lurking about: He's a suspicious-looking character."

"If my boss wouldn't tell you, why would I?"

"Because you and I made a pact. Your information for mine."

"Excuse me, but we did no such thing."

"It was implied. Obviously."

"By you maybe. But I didn't agree. This is no time for games, Mr. Zander. If you have information that would be useful to the investigation, you need to tell someone immediately. If not me, then Aubrey Merritt or Sheriff Casey."

He chuckled condescendingly. "You're a tough negotiator, Olivia. So let me sweeten the pot. The Sloan School of Management is a very prestigious institution. Our students graduate with jobs already lined up, most of them at starting salaries over two hundred thousand dollars. I think that's a little better than what you're doing here with this backwater apprenticeship. Aubrey doesn't respect you; that's clear to see. You have no real future with her. I could change your life with my connections, get you on the fast track."

"You're trying to bribe me!" I blurted in surprise. That had never happened to me before. I suppose I'd never had anything worth being bribed over before. And I still didn't, funnily enough, because the information Zander wanted didn't actually exist.

Zander clucked his disapproval. "Not really, Olivia. I'm offering to give you information that will help with the investigation. But I need something in return. Put yourself in my place. If it was *your* spouse who'd been murdered, would you be okay with being left in the dark? I don't think so. You'd want to know what was going on, if the cops were making progress. But you'd soon find that they won't tell you a thing, so you'd have no idea if they were handling the situation properly. What I'm suggesting is a very simple partnership that will benefit us both: You pass on the information *you* have to me; I'll pass on the information *I* have to you, and, as a bonus, I'll make sure there's a place for you in Sloan's incoming class. Or if there's something else you'd like that I can do for you, I'll do my best to make it happen."

He leaned back and casually ran his fingers through his wavy salt-and-pepper hair. He was preening, I realized. Congratulating himself on my assumed capitulation.

"I have a one-word tip to leave you with, Mr. Zander."

"What's that?"

"Tweezers. Tweezers will get that big tuft of gray hair out of your ear canal."

His expression turned stony. He slid me a look of utter contempt, stood up, and sauntered back toward the hacienda.

As I watched him retreat, I took a few calming breaths and muttered, "What an asshole."

Getting on with my job, I went to the place at the far end of the pool where the spent cartridge had been found, and prepared to retrace what would have been Dave Lafferty's escape route if he was the murderer. I figured he would have wanted to get away as quickly as possible, so he would have been moving pretty fast. However, he was over sixty and carrying about a hundred extra pounds, so his idea of fast was probably close to my slow jog.

I took out my phone, turned on the stopwatch, and off I jogged—through the cabana, up the path to the paddock, along the side of the stable, and up another path that snaked past the guesthouse to the parking lot. Once there, I jumped into our rented SUV and drove to the front gate of the ranch at about the speed I'd seen the Laffertys' RV moving on the CCTV footage. Just past the camera, I pulled over and turned off the stopwatch.

Fourteen minutes. Five minutes more than what it should have been. Which in my opinion made it very unlikely that Dave was the murderer, unless he was physically fit enough to have shaved more than 30 percent off my time. Given his age, weight, and heart condition, I was willing to bet that he couldn't have done that.

I drove back to the parking lot and sprinted to the hacienda, eager to share my results with Merritt.

CHAPTER THIRTY-SEVEN

Like a Comet

Dinner was underway in the dining room. Minus the high-end caterers, the cooking had fallen to Jenny-Lou and Alma, working with whatever Jenny-Lou had brought from the supermarket that morning. The result was a make-your-own-tacos buffet, the various dishes arranged on the sideboard. Jenny-Lou was acting the busy hostess, needlessly explaining how we might combine the available ingredients, and bossily suggesting where people should sit. The guests mostly ignored her. News that there was still plenty of beer and wine left over from the barbecue engendered some enthusiasm, but it was short-lived. The morning's murder, and the subsequent grim uncertainty of our situation, made sustained enjoyment impossible.

I took Merritt aside and reported my activities. I did not spare Conrad Zander, whom I described as dishonest, manipulative, misogynistic, narcissistic, and odious.

"I don't doubt that he's everything you say he is," Merritt replied mildly, "but a detective can't afford to let strong emotion overpower reason. You must learn to keep your personal feelings separate from your professional judgment."

"My professional judgment is that he's afraid of you."

"Ah, very good. The little trap I laid is making him squirm."

"That suggests guilt, doesn't it?"

"Not necessarily. Grand individuals like Conrad are often quite thin-skinned. They can't tolerate any whiff of threat to their status. They need to be in control at all times, if only to keep such threats at bay. I'm not at all surprised that Conrad deeply resents being pushed to the sidelines of the investigation, first by Sheriff Casey, then by me." Merritt smiled at me amusedly. "And even by you."

I proceeded to report the results of my escape reenactment. It had taken me fourteen minutes to get from the crime scene to the front gate, I explained. Since only nine minutes separated the gunshot from the sighting of the Laffertys' RV leaving the ranch, Dave Lafferty was very likely *not* the person who shot Eve Exeter.

"Excellent, Blunt. I'm very glad to have that information. But it won't be enough to convince Sheriff Casey he's got the wrong man. We need to give Casey a better suspect—the *right* one—along with enough evidence to convict that person."

Merritt and I joined the others at a long pine refectory table. A vast chandelier made of what looked like twisted elk horns drenched the room in too-bright light. Some poor animal—maybe a cougar or mountain lion or one of those cross-eyed javelinas—had sacrificed its life and furry hide to provide a wall decoration that I could not help but find disturbing. The silverware was unnecessarily large—everything in this part of the world was cast on a grand scale, it seemed—and the stoneware plates were as heavy as bricks.

There were eleven of us, including Merritt and me: the General, Fitz, Jenny-Lou, Kathy Lafferty, Bree Jumper, Nova Olsen, Barbara and Jacob Korn, and Conrad Zander. Missing were Eve Exeter, because she was dead, and Dave Lafferty, because he was being held as a suspect in her murder. I looked around . . . someone else was missing . . . Who was it? . . . Oh yes, Peter Jumper. His absence came as no surprise, as one didn't expect him to behave in the usual way. And where was the ranch manager, Barry? Probably back at the stable or having dinner in the kitchen with Alma, I supposed.

The group conversation centered on the question of when we would be allowed to leave the ranch. I would have loved to jump on a plane to NYC, but the murder had heightened the threat level considerably, and Merritt was more determined than ever to protect our client. In any case, flights out of Santa Fe were not plentiful at the last minute, even if Sheriff Casey would have let us go. No one was quite sure whether he had legal jurisdiction to keep us here against our will, but everyone was staying, at least for tonight, either because they hadn't been able to change their flights or because they didn't want to run afoul of the lawman. And I suppose some people were curious to find out how events would unfold. All eyes were on Merritt, of course, who was expected to do something miraculous in keeping with her reputation. But as far as I could tell, she was no further along than I was in figuring out what was going on at the Muddy River Ranch.

Peter arrived and helped himself at the buffet. He skulked about with a full plate, looking for a place to sit, and ended up claiming the empty seat next to me.

I tried to engage him in small talk as we chomped on our tacos, but he was so unresponsive that I fleetingly wondered if he might be deaf. Finally, in frustration, I ditched polite social norms and posed the only question actually worth discussing.

"Do you happen to know who killed Eve Exeter?" I asked.

That got his attention. He sat up a little straighter and for the first time looked me in the eye. "It wasn't my mom, in case you're wondering."

I wasn't, but maybe I should have been. "What makes you so sure?"

"There are a lot of things wrong with her, but she wouldn't kill anyone."

"Do you know where she was at seven fifteen this morning?"

"In bed, asleep."

"You know that for a fact?"

"No. We have separate rooms. But nothing can get her out of bed before ten a.m., and it's usually noon or one o'clock before she actually starts doing anything."

"What if, say, she really, really wanted to kill her nemesis?"

"Nemesis?"

"Enemy. Or, like, someone she really hated."

"Nah, that's not her thing. She hates everyone a little, but she doesn't hate anyone very much."

I tried to puzzle that one through.

He explained, sort of. "And she's really opposed to violence, especially against animals. She doesn't even swat mosquitos, tries to wave them out the door instead. I remember once when I was a kid she totally flipped out—I mean, in a *major* way—when I told her I'd been hunting gators in the swamp with my friend's dad's .22."

"Can't say I blame her."

His eyes flicked away. I was boring him.

I wasn't ready to lose him yet, so I raised the conversational ante. "What about you, Peter? Did you kill Eve Exeter?"

"Why would I shoot some old scientist lady I don't even know?"

Since he hadn't denied it outright, I tried a few motives on for size. "Well, you do like guns and violence, and maybe you meant to kill General Battersea and got Dr. Exeter by mistake." I didn't expect him to confess, but I did watch his face for signs of tension or duplicity.

"Why would I want to kill some old Army lady I don't even know?"

"Because she's part of the military industrial complex?" I suggested.

He shook his head, baffled.

"Because she tried to put an end to sexual harassment in the military?"

He grimaced as if he'd smelled an unpleasant odor.

"Because she's opposed to men being men?"

He tilted his head and squinted at me. "What?"

"Never mind." I turned back to my large plate. "Good tacos, huh?"

"They're all right," he said dully.

Conrad Zander was seated on the other side of the table and two people down. This positioning had allowed me not to have to look at him if I didn't want to. Now I heard snatches of a conversation he was having with Fitz and Merritt about a course he'd just finished teaching at the Sloan School of Management. I leaned in, interested in spite of myself. They were discussing entrepreneurship.

"So what's the secret?" Fitz was asking Zander. "Take the tech boom, for example. A lot of men our age made fortunes in the eighties, but many more tried their best to ride the tech wave to riches and couldn't. What was the difference, as you see it? What made some men superstars while others failed?"

I felt a vibration in my pocket, took out my silenced phone, and glanced at the screen. It was Trevor, sending a link, but I didn't want to miss a word of the conversation at the table. I quickly texted: I'll get back to you soon.

With a lofty smile, Zander answered Fitz's question. "As I explain to my graduate students, throughout history the successful entrepreneur has exhibited four specific abilities: the ability to perceive emerging opportunities where others see only chaos, the brains to accurately calculate risk, the confidence to make quick decisions, and the courage to act in the moment. Of these four abilities, the first is the rarest and most crucial. You see, Fitz, truly great opportunities are like celestial comets: They pass by rarely, perhaps only a few times in a person's lifetime, and quickly disappear. The superior man sees that comet and correctly perceives its value. He immediately pushes all else aside, grabs hold of it, and rides it to the stars. An inferior man may see the comet too. But he's never quite sure what he's looking at. He hems and haws, distrusts his senses, bogs himself down with procedures, and ends up missing the moment. Later, he gazes at the superior man's castle and whines, 'Why didn't *I* think of that?'"

"What a fascinating description," Merritt said. "You've clearly thought a lot about it. I can't help wondering, do you see yourself as that kind of bold, visionary businessman?"

"Well," he demurred, "no one wants to extol their own virtues, especially in the absence of real-world success. So let's just say, I think my company will answer that question for me in due course."

"Lifespan is going to be big, is that what you're saying?" asked Fitz.

Zander leaned in and whispered conspiratorially, "Frankly, my friends, *big* might be an understatement. The worldwide supplement market is worth about two hundred fifty billion dollars a year and keeps growing. As long as the products are unregulated by the FDA, there's little barrier to entry. And the demand is unquenchable."

"You mean people really buy that stuff?" asked Fitz.

"Absolutely. I probably don't need to remind you that humans have been searching for the secrets of longevity ever since Ponce de León arrived in Florida hoping to discover the Fountain of Youth. And the quest for immortality goes much further back in history than that, all the way to Herodotus, who thought he'd discovered the 'Water of Life' in the land of the Macrobians. Apparently, it smelled like violets, and the people who drank it lived to be one hundred and twenty years old." He leaned back and chortled at the joke.

"Violets," Fitz mused, his forehead scrunched in perplexity.

"That's why our logo is a purple violet. For Herodotus's violet-scented Water of Life," said Zander smugly. "My point is this: Society's current obsession with antiaging supplements is no passing fad but the latest expression of a permanent preoccupation of the human race. In other words, the supplement market is virtually unlimited."

"I assume your product has more validity than violet-scented water. It's backed by science, is it not?" asked Merritt sternly.

"Yes, of course. Actually, our product is based on Eve's undergraduate research into sirtuins. Imagine, she'd been sitting on that gold mine for decades without realizing it. Then one day it dawned on her that a dietary supplement that enhanced the action of the sirtuins found naturally in the body could theoretically extend human health span and life span. It was that simple. But could it be done? She put together a working group of her most brilliant graduate students, and in a few weeks they showed her exactly how such a substance could be produced synthetically and how its effects could be tested on mice. She named it Sirt-X.

"I met Eve as she was concluding her preliminary research. She confessed to me that, as a research scientist, she wasn't sure what to do next. I saw the potential immediately, of course. It was clear to me that a wonder supplement like Sirt-X, discovered via legitimate scientific research in a laboratory of a world-class institution such as MIT, could hardly fail. Eve and I married, Lifespan was born, and the rest is history."

CHAPTER THIRTY-EIGHT

Nighttime Visitors

General Battersea opened the drawer of her bedside table, removed a handgun, and placed it on the Navajo blanket covering her sturdy four-poster bed. One part of me was glad she had lethal protection; another part of me couldn't believe how many damn guns there were in this house.

This gun was clearly intended to be a woman's discreet companion. Smaller than Dave Lafferty's service revolver, it was fitted with a fancy mother-of-pearl handle. Merritt and I watched in silence as the General loaded it with silver bullets she took out of a carved wooden box on her dresser. Sighing, she placed the loaded pistol in the drawer of her night table.

"I've slept with a loaded gun nearby before, but I never thought I'd have to do it in my own house," she said glumly.

Merritt ignored this pointless, self-pitying remark and proceeded to what was important. "Sheriff Casey has agreed to station a police officer outside your door all night, but the officer hasn't arrived yet. Until he gets here, under no circumstances should you open the door to anyone but me or Blunt. Don't go anywhere alone. If you need a glass of milk or slice of cake like you did last night, text Blunt to get it for you. She's staying in the room directly overhead, and she'll stay awake until the sentry arrives."

That was the first I'd heard of that. I was irritated but not surprised. It was just like Merritt to schedule my time without telling me.

Just then a slight movement on the bed snagged my attention. I stared curiously at the Navajo blanket; nothing moved. As I was about to look away, one of the stripes wavered. I thought perhaps I was blurry-eyed from what was turning out to be one of the longest and most stressful days of my life. Then it happened again. I kept my eye trained on the spot, and after four or five seconds, the blanket quivered. I stared at the spot until I'd satisfied myself that I wasn't seeing things: A small bump really was moving ever so slowly under the tightly woven wool covering.

"Boss," I said softly.

She was talking to the General and didn't hear me.

"Boss," I repeated in a louder voice.

Both women looked at me impatiently.

"I think there's something in the bed."

The two women came closer. "Where?"

"There." As if it had heard its name, the little bump stopped moving and stayed completely still. Most people don't give lumpy blankets a second thought, but the bed of a retired brigadier general was no ordinary bed. General Battersea's blanket was stretched as tightly as plastic wrap over a plate of leftovers—except for the now stationary, small but obvious bump.

The General shrugged. She didn't see a problem. Even Merritt, who expected danger at every turn, was unimpressed by the bump.

One of her silver eyebrows rose a few centimeters, indicating that she found my behavior both doubtful and annoying.

I smiled awkwardly. "I'll take a quick look, if you don't mind."

Before either woman could object, I yanked the blanket and sheet out of their tight tuck under the mattress and swept the covers off the bed. I then screamed and staggered back several paces.

Merritt caught me under the arms before I fell. "Blunt, for goodness' sake, what is it now? Oh, oh dear . . ."

There was frozen silence in the room as the three of us watched a scorpion make haste toward the pillows stacked at the head of the bed.

"A giant hairy scorpion," the General said softly. "But what is it doing here?" Bless her innocent trusting heart, the woman was actually bewildered.

"Someone put it there, Joan," Merritt said tensely. "To kill you."

"That's ridiculous. The sting of a scorpion doesn't kill people. It just makes them very sick. Maybe a child could die from its bite, or an elderly person with health issues, and I suppose some people are allergic to the venom. But I'm not allergic. I was bitten by one years ago, in my thirties. The pain was excruciating, and I did get very sick. Fitz drove me to the emergency room, and a doctor admitted me to the hospital just to keep an eye on me. I had a severe rash, but nothing came of it. Eventually the pain subsided and the swelling went down. I was sent home in a few days, feeling perfectly fine."

"You're older now than you were then," Merritt pointed out.

"Of course. But I'm not . . . *elderly*." She spoke the word as if it were a crude slur.

"I think the question we need to be asking right now is who put it in your bed."

"It could have come in by itself. They sneak into houses fairly often, though it's rare that they make it up to the second floor. But once in a while one does. They're very good climbers. They like to climb up draperies, and if you leave bedclothes pooled on the floor, they can climb up and into your bed."

Merritt and I glanced at each other, both of us recalling the formerly tight tuck of the General's blankets—snug around the mattress, with perfect military corners, crisp as a folded American flag, not one tiny bit of it dripping onto the floor.

"They don't want to harm us," the General continued, trying to make light of the situation. "They just want to be left alone. When you grow up in the desert, you learn not to be afraid of them."

Not be afraid? That was a tall order. I was definitely afraid. I was afraid that if I lost sight of that scorpion for a second, it would grow huge wings and fly up at the speed of sound to attack me in the face. Honestly, I was more than afraid; I was close to panic. But I promised myself I wouldn't let myself get that far. I absolutely would not. I'd already lost my head once today over a corpse. And there had been too many occasions in the past when Merritt had had to prop me up physically and lean me on things as if I were a broken bicycle with no kickstand, and a few times she'd had to talk me down from hysteria. A minute ago she had saved me from falling backward over my own feet. I was determined that this misplaced puce arachnid would not rattle me to my core the way a rattlesnake would have.

For one thing, scorpions were much smaller than rattlesnakes, much too small to wrap themselves around your core and squeeze the breath out of you until you died. This particular scorpion was no longer than my middle finger. Also, it appeared to be disoriented, veering diagonally this way and that, with jerky lateral movements that were only making its journey up the mattress longer and more hazardous. Maybe it was traumatized at having found itself on a field of stretched white cotton with electric light blazing down upon it, just like an escaping inmate making a desperate run across a prison yard at night, only to be suddenly illuminated by a thousand-watt floodlight from a sentry tower. Nowhere to run, nowhere to hide. Bullets about to rain down.

The General, meanwhile, was taking charge. "What we usually do, you see, is we pick it up with pincers and drop it into a lidded glass jar. We don't kill it; we never do that. We let it loose outside, and it runs off and hides under a rock or in a bush or somewhere. I'll go get the pincers and the jar right now. And if Fitz isn't busy, I'll ask him to come help. He usually does the honors."

The General headed for the door and Merritt followed quickly, determined not to let our client out of her sight, especially after what might have been an attempt on her life.

"Keep an eye on that scorpion, Olivia," the General called over her shoulder. "Stay a safe distance but do see where it goes. We don't want it to wander off and get lost in the house somewhere!"

That was how it came to pass that I was left alone in a big house in the desert to babysit a scorpion. My little charge was still making its drunken way up the mattress to the stack of pillows at the headboard. I was very worried about what it might do when it got to the pillows. Maybe it would burrow among them and hide, forcing me to pick the pillows off the bed to find it, knowing that any one could have a poisonous creature clinging to the other side. Or maybe it would vanish into the pile and quickly descend the hidden north end of the mattress until it found the pine leg of the bed, which it would slide down like a fireman's pole, flatten itself to the width of a dime, and then slither into a crack in the floorboards or, if it was unequipped with that evolutionary trick, it might simply scuttle behind the dresser, and, when the General returned with Fitz and Merritt in tow, I would have to admit that I'd lost track of the eight-legged Houdini, that it could be anywhere, and then, because of me and my ineptitude, the General's bedroom would have to be closed and sealed and declared off-limits until a professional exterminator wearing a hazmat suit arrived to spray the area with noxious carcinogenic chemicals or maybe smoke the little demon out with a cluster bomb of anti-pest toxins.

These scenarios rattled through my brain in a matter of seconds, and by the time I returned to objective observation, the scorpion had made significant progress toward its likely goals of safety and possible freedom. The solution hit me suddenly. I would prevent it from hiding by removing the camouflage.

In a burst of courage, I flung one pillow after another off the bed, and, in rapid succession, four more scorpions were revealed. Stung by the sudden wind and bright lights, each in turn started to writhe and bend and squirm, until all four were crawling in different directions; all, it seemed, bent on escape.

This time I didn't scream. Primordial terror had paralyzed my vocal cords. I stepped backward very slowly, one tiny step at a time, and when I was far enough away that I felt released from the arachnids' demonic spell, I turned and fled from the room.

CHAPTER THIRTY-NINE

The Cleanup

I nearly fell down the stairs in my frantic haste to tell Merritt and General Battersea what I'd found. The General immediately turned to her husband for help. Fitz appealed to Jenny-Lou, who called upon Barry, who laid the problem before Alma, who set about resolving the situation with wordless efficiency. She wrestled a pair of salad tongs out of a crammed silverware drawer, used a footstool to take a large glass pitcher out of a high cabinet, and tucked a roll of Saran Wrap under her arm.

In a rather solemn progression, six of us (me, Merritt, the General, Fitz, Jenny-Lou, Barry) followed the short, wide-hipped woman up the staircase into the General's bedroom, where we held our collective breath as she coolly inspected the bed.

Everyone saw the same thing, but for some reason we waited for Alma to speak.

"No scorpions," she said in a flat tone that implied she'd heard Easterners tell tall tales before.

All eyes turned toward me. My cheeks grew warm in the glare of so much hostile doubt.

"There really were five scorpions on the bed. I promise. One was walking up the middle of the mattress, and there were four more at the top of the bed, hidden by the pillows."

All eyes turned toward said pillows, now strewn disrespectfully across the floor.

In the heavy silence that ensued, I blathered on. "They've got to be here somewhere. They can't have gone very far. They're probably hiding behind the dresser or something. Under the bed."

Jenny-Lou let out a shriek. "There's one!"

Sure enough, a spiny, lobster-clawed thing with a curling tail was scampering over the floorboards, traveling much faster than I would have thought possible given the shortness of its too-many legs.

"Quick! Someone get it!" Jenny-Lou screeched.

It fled under the dresser.

Barry and Fitz picked up the dresser and moved it a few feet into the room. Two scorpions who'd been hiding underneath attempted to dart away. In no time, Alma had one clamped in the grip of the salad tongs. She dropped it into the glass pitcher with an unexpectedly wicked smirk. After that, everyone joined the search, and successive cries of *Here! Over here!* pierced the air. Each time, Alma nimbly sprang to the spot and nabbed the escaping arachnid with her tongs, usually on the first or second try. The search continued until every inch of the room had been examined—the drawers of the dresser, the inside of the closet, and the bathroom, including inside the toilet tank (a favorite place, I learned, because of the damp darkness)—and we were satisfied there were no more.

Alma covered the top of the pitcher with Saran Wrap and counted the inhabitants. "*Cinco.*" She nodded at me, and I was vindicated.

A long sigh emerged from the circle of spectators. Many left the room, believing the horror was over. But it wasn't.

A fun fact about scorpions is that they live peaceably with their brethren as long as everyone keeps their distance. If they get into each other's space, they fight to the death. Now, inside the glass pitcher, nature took its terrible, inevitable course. The scorpions started crawling and writhing all over each other in ever-increasing fury. One after another would appear on top of the pile and then be quickly buried. There was no way to know who was winning or losing, but it hardly mattered, as within minutes they all lay dying. You could see the exoskeletons over their lungs heaving as they gasped their last breaths. The inside of the pitcher was smeared with milky spent venom. It reminded me of the last act of *Hamlet*, when all the players lay pierced by swords and dying or dead across the blood-puddled stage. I actually felt a little sorry for the slain warriors. Fighting for your life in a frenzied killing mob was an awful way to die.

Alma took the bodies out to the trash, then trundled up the stairs again with a stack of fresh bed linens under her arm. I followed along and helped her make up the General's bed with clean sheets because that's how I was raised. One of the rarely discussed problems of losing your mother when you were ten is that your Inner Mother's Voice, the one you carry around with you for the rest of your life, only said things to me that mothers of her generation tended to say to daughters ten years old and younger. Things like *do your homework, clean your room, put yourself in the other person's shoes,* and *always be helpful.* So it was that I had grown into an adult who was generally conscientious, mostly considerate, and often quick to be of service. This wasn't to my credit at all. It was simply my way of keeping my mother's voice alive in my head. I sometimes wondered what other comments my Inner Mother's Voice would make if my mother had lived longer. Maybe *pay off your credit card balance in full every month, eat plenty of fruits and vegetables,* and *do not scoff in the face of opportunity.*

When the bed was made and the room tidied up, Alma and I returned to the kitchen, where the group was discussing the crisis. After a few rounds of fruitless speculation, the General announced that it was time for bed. The danger was over; there was nothing more to worry about; we could all relax as she was perfectly safe.

This, of course, was an insane remark.

One scorpion might have been an innocent explorer; five were a murder attempt.

CHAPTER FORTY

The Fog of War

"This changes things," Merritt said grimly.

It was close to midnight, and we were alone in her room, having just come from bidding our client good night for a second time. Merritt had given strict instructions to the uniformed officer Sheriff Casey had agreed to post outside the General's door. His name was Officer Tucker. He was young and unimposing, with clear, milky skin and mild gray eyes. Officer Tucker had stoutly assured the elderly lady detective that he understood sentry duties perfectly well and would do his job to the best of his abilities, just as he always did.

"You realize that I'm staying down the hall from here, don't you?" Merritt pointed down the long corridor lit by sconces of coral-colored glass.

"Yes, ma'am."

"So if I happened to come out here in the middle of the night, I wouldn't find you dozing."

"No, ma'am."

I forgave Merritt for her overbearing tone as I understood that her own near failure to protect the General's life was bound to make her especially tough on anyone in a position to do the same.

Now in her bedroom with the door closed, she settled herself into the armchair's deep cushions, shook off her gold Pedro García sandals, and rested her bare feet (no pedicure) on the ottoman. She looked tired and frazzled. The Southwestern sun had put some unwanted color in her cheeks despite the broad-brimmed straw hat she'd worn outside, and her eyes were bloodshot from the dry air.

"This is a dangerous time," she told me. "We find ourselves in the fog of war, and it's more important than ever that we keep our heads. We need to come at this problem again from the beginning, reexamine everything we think we know, and carefully consider what our next steps should be." One of her eyebrows arched in what looked like a dubious dare. "How would you evaluate the situation, Blunt?"

It was not unusual for her to ask for my thoughts on a case. On one hand, she wanted to give me an opportunity to hone my detection skills under her supervision. On another, she wanted to judge me—my mental speed and accuracy, knee-jerk prejudices, excessive empathy, inappropriate guilt, irrelevant opinions, unacknowledged blind spots, irrationality, lack of rigor, emotionality, gullibility, naiveté, impulsivity, and so on—so she could measure how distant I was from investigative prowess, and thus gauge just how much responsibility she could afford to give me. There was also another, and much better, reason she sometimes asked for my opinion. That was in the pressing moments when she was stumped and needed to bat around ideas, any ideas, for the purpose of creative problem-solving. I hoped this was one of those times.

I obviously had to say something, but there was not a single helpful idea in my brain, so I resorted to the pretender's tactic of stating the obvious with great intensity. "The situation is deteriorating. Yesterday we had one crime to solve, and now we have three: one death threat, one successful murder, and one attempted murder. To make matters worse, the killer is at large, possibly right under our noses, and there's no guarantee his spree is over. General Battersea and possibly others are in imminent grave danger. We need to work very quickly to solve these crimes before another tragedy occurs. The clock is ticking."

That was literally as well as figuratively true, because the grandfather clock on the landing was at that moment striking the twelve chimes of midnight. It gonged slowly, ceremoniously, measuring each second of precious time that was being lost. As long as it was filling the air with its ponderous notes, I could barely hear myself think. *Hurry up, doddering old clock! Stop wasting time!* I thought impatiently as I waited for it to end.

"Hmm. You call what happened tonight a murder attempt. Are you sure?" Merritt asked coolly when silence was restored.

I was shocked that she was even asking the question. "Are you kidding? Five scorpions? What else could it be?"

"It was, probably. But . . ." Furrows creased her brow. "Why scorpions? There are easier and more reliable ways of ending a person's life."

"Oh, I definitely disagree, boss. Scorpions are a brilliant way of killing someone. Imagine—if the General had died from the venom, it could be argued that she hadn't been murdered at all. She was just unlucky. Because, technically, the scorpions could have killed her all by themselves, without human involvement. In the absence of an obvious suspect, that explanation could be good enough for the police to justify not investigating."

"Come now," she said with a smirk. "Who would possibly believe that five scorpions just happened to crawl into the same bed on the same night?"

"Lots of people, that's who. You're not on social media, so you have no idea what the world is like these days. People will believe anything. The freakier the better. This is just the kind of story that would immediately go viral. 'Five Scorpions Discovered in New Mexico Woman's Bed!' That post would rack up a thousand likes and hundreds of comments in under an hour from readers declaring five scorpions was nothing, they'd seen *ten* scorpions in a bed, and crazier stuff than that. The story could go through several evolutions, getting weirder and weirder as time went on. I can see the headlines now:

Deadly Scorpions Conspire to Murder New Mexico Woman in Her Bed!

Robot Scorpions Attack!

Nest of Deranged Scorpions Attempt Murder After UFO Seen Hovering over New Mexico Desert!

Woman Miraculously Survives Deadly Robot Scorpion Attack by Drinking Own Urine!

"Then, even if the real perpetrator stepped forward and confessed, no one would believe him because they liked their version of the story so much better."

Merritt rolled her eyes. She was chronically unimpressed by the masses, whom she treated with bemused mockery that slid to outright contempt without much provocation. Even so, she seemed slyly pleased by my outburst, presumably because it confirmed her deeply held belief that social media was, as she put it, "the rot at the core of modern society."

"By the way, did you happen to notice what kind of scorpions they were?" she asked.

"Big. Ugly."

"I mean, what breed. Or species, if that's the right word."

"I have no idea." To me, all scorpions were the same. Grotesque alien creatures dating from the godless prehistory of the earth.

Merritt frowned her disapproval. I think that in some childish, boomer part of her psyche she believed that I really did have all knowledge at my digital fingertips, or ought to, since that was in part what she was paying me for.

"I'll look it up," I said dutifully.

"Yes, you will," she agreed bossily. "Find out as much as you can about that particular variety. Habitat and habits and . . . whatever seems pertinent." She fluttered one hand in the air, indicating her disdain for both arachnids and the basic fact-finding that was my lowly purview.

The only chair in the room was the one Merritt presently occupied, so all this time I had been standing. I could have sat on the bed, of course. But in my view a bed was personal space, and sitting on someone's bed without an invitation was a boundary violation. At this point in the conversation, though, I was tired. Not just of trying to be rational, but also of being vertical.

I decided it would be okay on this one occasion to perch one butt cheek on a person's mattress without permission. The minute my rear touched the mattress, I was absolutely positive that something living squirmed beneath me, and I flew off the bed like I'd been launched from a slingshot.

"Blunt! What on earth is the matter?" Merritt cried out in alarm.

I clenched my jaw to keep from shouting expletives. Then I took a long, hard look at the faux Navajo blanket that covered the bed. Smooth. No lumps. No motion. I waited an extra beat. Still no motion.

"It was nothing. I'm fine."

I sat quickly on the bed again—it didn't move this time—whipped out my phone, and buried my flaming red face in it.

"What are you doing now?" she asked in perplexity.

"Research. Scorpions of the American Southwest."

"Not now, Blunt. Later. On your own time."

I put my phone away.

CHAPTER FORTY-ONE

The Human Stain

Now then, let's assume, for the purposes of argument, that what happened tonight *was* attempted murder. That gives credence to scenario number two—that Eve's murder was a case of mistaken identity. Someone, most likely but not necessarily the threatener, knowing Joan's morning routine, arrived at the pool at the correct time, fatally shot the person he believed to be his target, and when he realized he'd been wrong, returned this evening to correct his mistake." Merritt raised her eyebrows, inviting me to comment.

"That sounds about right," I said.

"Does it? I'm not so sure. It's decidedly brazen to commit one murder in the morning and attempt another the very same day, with police on the premises and an official investigation into the first crime underway. If that really is what happened, then our killer is very bold, possibly desperate. Only a person with a burning motive would take such a risk. But who desires Joan's death to such a degree? That's what I don't understand. We're rather short on motive here."

"What about Jenny-Lou?" I suggested. "She might want the

General gone so she can marry Fitz. Or Fitz might want to kill his wife so he can marry Jenny-Lou and they can have the ranch to themselves. They could be in it together."

"Ah, yes. Love and greed. Two classic motives," Merritt said approvingly. "But there may be others we're not aware of." She tented her fingers before her face and tapped them against each other. "I wonder . . . might there be something in Joan's background, something she did recently or years ago, that could have ignited such hatred in another person?"

"Probably. I mean, like Fitz said, she has enemies around the world, and I'm sure there are people who hate her in the armed forces in this country too—soldiers she sanctioned or disciplined or discharged dishonorably."

"I agree. Take a deep dive into her background. Look for news stories, public scandals—anything that might make her a target."

I pulled up my Notes app and tapped in the two assignments I'd been given: *(1) scorpion research* and *(2) deep dive re General.* It was after midnight and I hadn't slept in what felt like days, so I sincerely hoped my boss wouldn't be adding to the list.

"You know, Blunt, I believe we've missed something obvious. There's one suspect who could have committed all three crimes. Joan herself."

"No way, that's crazy," I retorted. "I really can't see General Battersea sending herself a death threat, murdering her sorority sister, and planting scorpions in her own bed."

As soon as I said it, I knew that Merritt would likely scold me for excessive trust and sympathy. She saw these as my chief flaws, the most likely obstacles to my success as a solo investigator. She had once mocked me by saying that if a crocodile told me a good enough sob story, I'd agree to put my head in its mouth. That, of course, was not true. There was no force in this world or the next that could ever persuade me to put my head in a crocodile's mouth. I had tetchily countered with the following argument: that it was cruel and unnecessary to portray someone as an idiot, as she had just done me, and, furthermore, that she was wrong on the merits. There was no reason why empathy, excessive or not, couldn't make an investigator *more* successful rather than *less.* And I intended to prove this to her as time went on.

My tone had been brash and defiant, but that was a cover-up. Part of me took every word coming from Aubrey Merritt's mouth as the absolute truth. Yet I also needed to keep my head up any way I could in our unequal relationship, lest I be crushed by the weight of her legendary achievements and supposedly greater intellect.

To my relief, Merritt didn't reprise any of her usual criticisms. She probably figured there wasn't enough time.

"Joan is a human being like everyone else," she said. "Which is to say, she's an unstable mixture of good and bad impulses and irrational beliefs based on personal experiences she fundamentally misremembers. That is human nature, Blunt. That is what we fight against."

"Human nature? But human nature is a lot of things. It isn't only evil."

"It isn't *only* evil. However, it is the only thing in this world that *is* evil. It's from human nature that evil springs. If we are human, we have the capacity for evil."

"I'm sorry. I just don't see it. Not General Battersea. She wouldn't have done those things."

"It is not our job to consider the likelihood of whether Joan walked down the dark path, or to condemn her if she did. It is our job to understand and respect that, in her human complexity, she very well might have."

"But she's your *friend,* boss. You like her. I know you do. I saw you two chatting and laughing together. You were having a nice time; you were happy—don't try to deny it. So you must know in your heart that she could never have plotted and lied and murdered someone."

"I enjoy Joan's company. She's a strong individual with clear, sensible thoughts and a determined will. But I can't say I know what she is or is not capable of. She has inner demons, Blunt. You can sense them in people sometimes; they're like the chill you feel when clouds pass across the sun. I sensed them in her."

"What kind of inner demons?"

"Who knows? Joan had a whole life no one is privy to—successive decades of disappointments and successes. A life of violence done *to* her and, possibly, violence done *by* her. She's had thoughts and feelings she's never shared with anyone, not even Fitz, out of shame perhaps, or from fear of truly knowing herself. I won't belittle my friend by assuming she's exempt from the human struggle, or by needing her to be."

"Oh, in that case," I said a little sullenly. As usual, Merritt had out-philosophized me. If the General was going to be a prime suspect, then that's how it would be. It was Merritt's call. But I felt discouraged nonetheless. Because how was a person to live in this world if they couldn't trust *their own friend*?

She assessed me critically. "You look tired."

"It's been a long day."

"All right, we'll end our discussion here, and meet again for breakfast at seven a.m. on the veranda. Don't be late. And don't forget about the scorpions."

If only I could, I thought wearily as I left the room.

The grandfather clock gonged once as I emerged from Merritt's bedroom. The work my boss had piled on me would take a few hours to complete. I really needed to go to my room and buckle down if I hoped to get any sleep that night, but as often happened when I found myself in a stressful situation, I suddenly realized I was very hungry. Dinner had been a long time ago. There might be ice cream in the freezer. Or some of that SDT cake with the brown and blue icing florets left over from last night. Or both.

The house was quiet. Fitz's door was closed. I had no idea where Jenny-Lou was, or whether Sheriff Casey was making her stay at the ranch like the rest of us, or allowing her to come and go as she pleased since she hadn't been here at the time of the murder.

I padded along the hushed, pinkly lit hallway in my bare feet. I had taken my sneakers off in Merritt's room and tied the laces together, and now they were hanging around my neck, still slightly damp from the morning's plunge. I should have removed them this morning and left them to dry out on my windowsill, but things had been so hectic that I didn't think of it, so I had been walking around all day in wet sneakers. All day my feet had been cold and clammy, and now the woven rug under my bare toes felt blissfully soft and dry.

Up ahead, Officer Tucker was hunched over his phone in a folding metal chair outside the General's door. His earbuds looked like ugly white earrings. Music was jangling out of them, loud enough for me to hear.

Shoeless as I was, earphoned as he was, and absorbed in his screen, I was able to get right beside him without him noticing. I slowly passed my hand between his face and the screen. He jolted upright, whirled his head, and stared up at me with wild eyes.

"Oh, it's just you," he said, yanking out the earbuds.

"You sound disappointed when what you should be is relieved that I'm not a murderer who just slit your throat."

He nodded, eyes averted. That was all the agreement I was going to get.

“Has anyone been by here in the last half hour?”

“No.”

“Did General Battersea try to bribe you into getting her a mug of warm milk?”

“No.”

“Have you seen or heard anything suspicious?”

He screwed up his face as if he were wrangling a difficult idea into submission. “Maybe.” Then fell into silence.

“You can tell me now,” I said.

“Some people are talking downstairs in the living room. I can only hear one of them. I can’t hear what she’s saying, but she sounds upset.”

“Okay. I’ll check it out. By the way, just to be clear, the earphones are a bad idea. The phone too.”

“Yeah, okay.” He made a show of putting them away. I wondered if he would take them out again the minute I was gone.

CHAPTER FORTY-TWO

Bree and Peter

Bree Jumper was in the living room, her back to me, alone. Nevertheless, she was speaking. *Murmuring* would be a better word. I scanned the room carefully, in case her interlocutor was hiding. I saw no one. Bree was talking to herself.

"I've tried everything, I've done everything. What else could I have done? It wasn't easy; I did my best. With no help from anyone. But it wasn't enough, I failed, and now . . . oh my god . . . what am I supposed to do now?"

"Bree," I said gently, not wanting to startle her out of what sounded like a trance of despair. When she didn't respond, I said her name a little louder. "Bree?"

She looked over her shoulder. "Olivia! Sweet Olivia. You're just the person I want to talk to. Come have a seat next to me."

She patted the couch cushion beside her. I smiled politely, opted for the chair across from her, and lowered myself into it warily. The situation—by which I supposed I meant Bree herself—seemed unstable and possibly dangerous.

Bree was dressed in a loose silk robe of vivid, extravagantly swirling greens and yellows, decorated along the hem and edges of the voluminous fan sleeves with a multitude of identical toucans that looked exactly like the iconic bird on the Froot Loops box. There was a pen and a leather notebook on the coffee table. She saw me glance at it.

"This is all so interesting, isn't it? To think you and Aubrey get to do this all the time. The rest of us just get to read about it."

"You mean, investigate crimes?"

"What else?" She winked. "I thought I might capture some bits of it on paper while I was here. Sheriff Dutch Casey, for example. What a wonderful character! So delightfully large and stubborn! And I don't want to forget certain details. The coffee situation this morning, for example. You'd think coffee would be the last thing on a person's mind after a corpse was found floating in the pool. And yet, what was everyone demanding? Not justice. Not the immediate apprehension of the murderer. No, they were clamoring for caffeine! Which turned out to be fortuitous because the lack of caffeine made everyone irritable and . . . oh . . ." She smiled wickedly. "Let's just say, *things were said.*"

I had no idea what she was talking about. "What kinds of things?"

"You didn't hear? No, I suppose you didn't. Joan and that woman, Jenny-Lou, had a bitter argument about the little dog's balls. I mean his toy balls, obviously. Not his testicles. I doubt he has them anymore, poor thing. Lopped off when he was just a tiny pup. It happens to them all these days—so inhumane. How would *you* like it, I always say to the supposed animal lovers who swear by it. It takes away the pups' character, makes the poor little things as limp and docile as fuzzy rugs. Not even dogs anymore, just fur balls that eat and poop. I personally prefer a man with testosterone, and I'm willing to take the bad with the good."

There was certainly a lot to unpack in Bree's free-floating associations, but I didn't have time for that. I zeroed in on the essential point.

"What was the argument about?"

"Well, Joan was angry. She sprained her ankle on one of those balls, and it was Jenny-Lou's job to keep them off the stairs and other places where people can fall and hurt themselves. It's a wonder Joan wasn't killed! But I detected an extra, underlying edge in their conversation, and we all know why. Two women sharing one man? Never a good thing. I don't see how Joan puts up with that floozy constantly mooning over Fitz. I adore him—everyone does—but why does he allow it? Keep Miss Jenny at the gallery if he must have her hanging around, I say. He has to know it bothers Joan."

"She doesn't seem to mind."

"What do you expect after thirty years of marriage? A scene? Hysterics? Too late for that. No, Fitz and Joan settled into their groove years ago, and they seem to have made peace with it. He lets her do her thing; she lets him do his. I could almost admire it, except so often these arrangements are one-sided. That's what I don't like. I would sleep better at night if I knew that all this time Joan had had a handsome lover in the wings. That would even things out."

I tried to picture the General with a handsome lover and couldn't. Maybe I just lacked imagination. "Would you ever ask her if she had a lover?"

"Absolutely not. Joan is so straight and narrow, so by the book and onward marching."

"So you think she would never have had an affair?"

"Oh, no. I didn't say that. Only that she'd be deeply offended if I asked."

I tried to puzzle that one out.

Bree shuddered. "This is why I only married once, Olivia. I realized that I simply couldn't make all those trade-offs and side deals. There isn't a woman I know who hasn't given more in marriage than she's received. Not one out of a hundred are happy, in my opinion. They smile and smile and enjoy whatever advantages they think they get from the arrangement. When being alone would be so much healthier and more enjoyable for them if only they had the courage to try it."

"I just got married," I confessed awkwardly.

"Oh, my. Isn't that wonderful. I wish you eons of married bliss."

"I don't think so, Bree. But that's okay. Everyone has their own opinion, and you're entitled to yours."

She took her vape pen out of her beaded lizard purse and said thoughtfully, "You intrigue me, Olivia. I'm thinking that I may have a small part in my next book for a sweet ingenue, a detective's assistant, who manages to look like a fish out of water and yet is so easy to talk to that she gets the inside scoop in half the time a trained psychologist could do it. Now, who could that be, I wonder?"

"Hell if I know," I said, embarrassed. An *ingenue*? No one had ever called me that before. And *sweet*? That was a new one too.

"How exactly do you do it? You manage to convey such empathy; I feel like pouring out my heart to you. But there's more to you than tea and sympathy, isn't there? When will you show *that* side of yourself to the world, I wonder?" At this she emitted a nasty chuckle.

I remained silent, began to plan my escape.

"It's the eyes, I think." She peered into mine. "Do you mind if I look into your eyes for a moment?"

"You're already doing it," I said, becoming acutely uncomfortable, not least because hers were bloodshot and glassy.

"You don't like that, do you? You prefer to observe rather than be observed. We might have a bit in common there, Miss Blunt. A detective and a writer—we're not that different, you and I."

Except that one of us deals with reality, and the other just makes stuff up, I might have said.

As the conversation in its present form appeared to be a fast train to nowhere, I decided to switch tracks and try to extract from it whatever benefit I could.

"Did you hear the gunshot this morning?" I asked.

"I was asleep. Dead to the world. Maybe a bit too much tequila. But we can never have too much tequila, can we?"

No comment, I thought.

"What does Peter think of all this?" I said.

"You'll have to ask him yourself. But don't expect an answer. My son is a human black box. Has been since he was twelve years old. I stopped trying to penetrate that child's mind years ago. I've learned that if I wish to preserve my sanity, I'll stop even trying to understand him. Detachment is what is called for. At least that's what they told me at Parents of Children Anonymous. The three *C*'s. I didn't Cause it, I can't Change it, and I can't Control it."

"By *it*, you mean your son?"

"No, I mean his behavior."

"Is it that bad?"

"Why do you suppose I brought him along to the reunion? It obviously wasn't for his sparkling conversation. No, I brought him with me because if I left him home alone, a biker gang would be crashing in the living room when I got back, and automatic weapons would be strewn across my imported Tibetan carpet along with a lot of dirty underwear."

"That's awful," I said.

"It is. Karma is hounding me, Olivia, and I'm not even sure what I did."

I changed the subject. "You must have been older when you had him."

"I was forty-five. It happens. Don't believe all the nonsense you young women are being told nowadays about old, worn-out eggs. Eggs are eggs. They want sperm, and they find a way to get it."

"Has Peter ever been violent?" I asked casually. I was trying to make the question seem benign, but it wasn't, under the circumstances, and we both knew it.

Bree sighed despondently. "My son loves violence. Guns, bombs, suits of armor, torture chambers, firing squads. His favorite sporting event is Monster Jam. Do you know what that is? That's when big trucks with great big tractor wheels rear up on their back tires and try to destroy each other like enraged dinosaurs. He loves stock car racing, too, when the highlight of the day is race cars flipping over and over, bursting into flames, and the drivers being incinerated before your eyes. Think of something, anything, that would horrify a normal person, and Peter will snap himself out of his stupor and run straight toward it excitedly."

"But has he ever *been* violent, as in actually hurting someone?"

"If so, I'm not aware of it. But I don't rule out the possibility. When you're on a road that leads to Rome, eventually you arrive."

"You think he could do something really bad?"

"That's my fear. You see these things on the television. Young men going crazy with guns. It keeps me up at night."

I gulped. "You don't think he could ever . . . ?" I couldn't bring myself to say it.

"I don't know what to think. That's my problem, Olivia. I don't know what to think! I used to spend hours on the phone with Nova. It really pays to have a sorority sister who's a therapist. She coached me night after night and never sent a bill. She had a similar experience with her son, you see. Finally she convinced him to join the military and he did but was injured at boot camp and came home with an addiction to the painkillers they gave him. You can imagine the rest: addiction, depression, treatment, more addiction, more depression, and finally suicide. It nearly broke her, but somehow she came through victorious, like a phoenix rising from the ashes. You see how she is now. Take note: That's one strong woman there. Stronger than I could ever be."

"And Peter?"

"I've tried everything. School counselors, psychiatrists, Ritalin, Xanax, Prozac, Klonopin. We even went on a South Pacific island retreat to do psychedelic mushrooms so that we—meaning him—could transcend our personal egos and become attuned to the music of the spheres. I found the experience exhilarating, life-changing. You may not believe this, Olivia, but I really did hear the music of the spheres! *And* I witnessed the terrifying majesty of the universe!" Leaning toward me, she whispered, "The universe is not what you think it is. It's stranger and wilder and more enormous than anyone can imagine. It far exceeds what the human mind can comprehend." She straightened her posture. "That experience had tremendous therapeutic benefits for me. I still have a small dependence on alcohol, but in all other respects I came home a changed woman. Unfortunately, Peter showed no interest in the psychedelics. The only things that thrilled him were the island's horrible creatures. In just a few days he learned everything there is to know about poisonous snakes, tarantulas, and . . ."

She stopped abruptly, her face a mask of horror.

"And what?"

"Scorpions. Poisonous scorpions." She touched her forehead, reached for her glass. A beat of silence, then: "Oh my god, Olivia. Oh my god."

"Do you think he could have . . . ?" This was a conversation of broken sentences.

"I don't know. That's the agony of it. I just don't know what that boy could do! I keep wondering: Is it mental illness or testosterone? Should I have set stricter limits and punished him when he transgressed? Or showered him with love and understanding? Sent him to a monastery in Bhutan? To a dude ranch in Montana? Is he an ordinary confused adolescent or, god forbid, the actual spawn of Satan? Motherhood is wretched, Olivia. Don't let anyone tell you otherwise. I'd think twice before I ventured into those waters if I were you."

"That's really none of your—"

But she wasn't listening. She swirled the wine at the bottom of her glass and said portentously, "Be very careful, young one. Dreams die."

My father once told me never to argue with a drunk person. You just end up going around in circles, and they're not listening anyway. I should have heeded his advice, but I was annoyed by Bree's negative attitude toward life, and replied with more heat than the situation warranted. "You don't know anything about me, and you don't know what my fate will be. It's stupid of you to pretend you do. You're just bitter, that's all, and I'm sorry for that. If you just looked at the present, at where you are right now, you'd realize you have plenty of reasons to be happy. You're very healthy, it appears, and very successful in your work, and you have old friends and a son who probably isn't nearly as bad as you say. Actually, I stalked him on the internet, and it's clear from his socials that he likes to make things and fix things. Like, by welding them. Which is very skillful and creative work. You should be proud of him for that."

She shrugged a little guiltily. "You're right, Olivia. But it's different when you're my age. You look back and see so many mistakes—yours and other people's. The things you did and didn't do, and the things you let be done to you. The people you loved and lost out of selfishness, and the people you believed loved you but really didn't.

When you get old, the past is always nipping at you—usually in the form of regret."

"Then look to the future," I scolded without mercy.

She rolled her eyes. "From the mouths of babes."

A single echoing gong reached my ears—the grandfather clock striking one thirty a.m.

"By the way, what are you doing up at this hour?" Bree asked. "I have an excuse: I'm drinking. What's yours?"

"I'm looking for ice cream."

She smiled. "There's mint chip in the freezer. I saw it there this morning when I was getting frozen waffles."

"You want some?"

"Oh no. I never eat dessert. Got to cut back on calories where I can. But you go and get some for yourself. I think some of that cake from last night is on the counter, too, if you're interested."

I thanked her for the tip and was about to leave, when she grabbed my hand. "Olivia, honey. You're not going to tell Aubrey, are you?"

"You mean, about Peter and the scorpions?"

She nodded. The worry in her eyes was a question mark.

"I really ought to, don't you think?"

"Yes, but you don't *have* to. It could be our little secret."

"Hmm. I don't think so, Bree. That information is pertinent to the case. Merritt and I will need to ask him about it when we speak to him."

"If he did put those silly things in Joan's bed, it was just a boyish prank. I'm sure he didn't mean to hurt anyone."

"Probably not." I smiled tepidly as I pulled my hand away.

CHAPTER FORTY-THREE

A Little Revenge

The ice cream was frozen so hard that scooping it out was no easy task. The spoon actually bent under the pressure. Nevertheless, I persisted and was soon able to triumphantly carry a big clay-fired stoneware bowl of mint chip and chocolate cake up to my bedroom on the third floor, checking up on Officer Tucker (no phone visible) along the way.

After inspecting the Navajo blanket for lumps, and shaking out the pillowcases, I sat cross-legged on the bed, savored the cake and ice cream, and thought about the sad, weird, scary relationship Bree Jumper had with her son. It was hard to know what was going on there. Peter was definitely a strange guy, but his mother wasn't exactly Miss Mental Health. Was Peter so juvenile and disturbed that he'd planted the scorpions in the General's bed? I could sort of see him doing it. If he did, had he meant it as a prank, as his mother suggested? Or had he actually been trying to kill the General? If so, why? Was it some kind of disturbed guy thing, such as needing something to brag about to his psycho buddies in the gun-loving, survivalist chat room? Or could he have had a more personal motive?

While the front of my brain was occupied with those thorny questions, something entirely different was happening in the back of my brain. A single synapse was sparking—an idea bubbling up from my semiconscious mind. When I turned my attention to it, it coyly dimmed its glow.

I put the bowl aside, lay down on the bed, closed my eyes, and pretended I was going to sleep. The strategy worked. That sneaky synapse fired fully when it thought I was ignoring it. It didn't give me much before sputtering out. Just a single name: Nova Olsen.

Nova: Bree Jumper's sorority sister. Who happened to be a therapist. Who gave free advice over the phone. Who also had a difficult son. According to Bree, Nova's son had died by suicide several years after a boot camp injury drove him out of military service.

The last part repeated itself: *An injury drove him out of military service.*

Forget Peter Jumper. My suspicions immediately clustered around the therapist. I recalled from my initial visit to her website that she described herself as having a "fresh approach" to coping with grief, loss, and PTSD. I opened my laptop, pulled up her website, and skimmed the titles of her blog posts.

Most of them were conventional:

Traumatic Grief and You

The Traumatized Heart

Life After Loss

Suicide Survivor: A Grief Like No Other

But these stood out as "fresh":

The Upside of Anger

Symbolic Revenge: A Little Goes a Long Way

Does Anybody Really Know What Fair Is?

Even the Score (If Only in Your Mind)

How to Forgive the Unforgivable (It's Not What You Think)

A Healing Rx for Those Who Can't Forgive

Restoring Karmic Balance as a Precursor to Total Healing

I clicked on one title that especially interested me: "Symbolic Revenge: A Little Goes a Long Way." The entry was brief, less than five hundred words. But it put forth a truly radical idea, definitely a "fresh approach." It said that in a traumatic death there were many victims: first, the actual victim; then all the people close to the victim who felt powerless, vulnerable, and adrift in a world that no longer made sense to them. They were spiritually and psychologically wounded. Spiritual leaders advised them to forgive the unforgivable, which was impossible because the unforgivable is, by definition, unforgivable. They were told that their failure to attain this unattainable goal would keep them in an eternal limbo of unexpressed rage.

The answer, wrote Nova Olsen, PhD, was to express a little bit of one's justified rage by enacting a little bit of relatively harmless revenge, just enough revenge to prove to oneself that one did indeed wish for revenge, that one was fully capable of enacting revenge, and that it was only one's mercy and inherent nobility that held one back from exacting the full price that the perpetrator owed for his heinous deed. Only after traumatically bereaved individuals had proven to themselves that they were not just victims of the perpetrator, but also were the powerful, merciful overlord of the perpetrator, could they truly let go of their rage and move on to the work of healing.

How a bereaved individual carried out this therapeutic act of "symbolic revenge" depended on the opportunities and resources available and their personal determination. If the individual had experienced a minor offense, the revenge act might be as simple as spitting in the evildoer's food or drink. Or keying the evildoer's car. If the offense had been major, a certain amount of planning and creativity was required. Dr. Olsen advised keeping the size of the revenge act proportional to the size of the offense that had engendered it. As a general rule, she wrote, acts of relatively harmless (aka symbolic) revenge needed to be both bold enough to satisfy the bereaved individual's psychological need, and minor enough (1) to keep the individual anonymous, thus avoiding public censure and the danger of reciprocal revenge; and (2) to demonstrate that the evil in the bereaved individual was noble and restrained compared to the brazen immorality of the evildoer.

I blinked a few times in confusion. Dr. Olsen's method for dealing with violent trauma was clearly unusual. I found it rather difficult to understand. Even after reading the blog post a second time to be sure I had the gist, I thought I must have missed something. The juvenile act of spitting in someone's food or drink would enhance the healing process? It certainly would be a revolutionary breakthrough if it worked. On the other hand, it would make eating and drinking a lot less enjoyable for many people.

Information about Nova's son was easy to find. His name was Owen. He had grown up in Santa Cruz, attended Santa Cruz High School and Piedmont College, where he'd been a member of an a cappella singing group called the Warbling Wonks and the Copernicus Society for amateur astronomers. Too soon after college graduation came his obituary. The family encouraged donations to the Opioid Crisis Foundation. A bit more sleuthing revealed that Owen Olsen had been a recruit at Fort Sill in Oklahoma. A visit to that website yielded nothing at first, but when I eventually stumbled upon a page that listed past base commanders, I saw the name Brigadier General Joan Battersea. The dates indicated that the General had been in charge at Fort Sill when Owen Olsen was in basic training there.

I slammed my laptop shut, and, after poking around the inside of my duffel to make sure no creature had made a home in it, I pulled out a clean T-shirt and put it on, then pushed my feet into my now-dry, faintly pink sneakers. The whole time I was thinking excitedly, *Wait until Merritt hears this!*

Once again I passed Officer Tucker in the hall. He was pouring steaming coffee from a thermos into a paper cup.

"Has anyone been by?"

"Just you. Three times."

"Right. Anything suspicious?"

"The people in the living room left. They were stumbling around like they were drunk."

"How about General Battersea? Any changes there?"

"Nope. Still snoring."

"Thank you, Officer Tucker. Stick with it. The sun will rise in"—I checked my phone—"about four hours."

I was about to knock on Merritt's door, when I started to doubt myself. Was my theory about Nova Olsen sound and reasonable? Or was it, to use one of Merritt's favorite words, *far-fetched*? It couldn't be any more far-fetched than Nova's theory itself, could it? But was it important enough to get my boss out of bed in the middle of the night?

Merritt didn't like theories, as a general rule. *A theory proves nothing,* she liked to say whenever I would speculate, even though she often speculated rather wildly herself. The only thing that really impressed her was evidence.

I had to admit that Nova's crackpot blog entries were evidence of nothing. She could have written them for many reasons (money, fame) without believing a word of what she said. Hypocrisy was rampant among people who professed to have all the answers. Look at yogis, politicians, teachers, and parents. No, Nova's posts alone didn't prove anything.

I needed hard, physical evidence to convince Merritt of my theory. But where would I get it? How could I prove that Nova Olsen had planted the death threat in the General's mailbox as symbolic revenge for her son's tragic death?

I thought back to the first time I'd met Nova, in the parking lot. She had just parked her red Toyota Camry with Texas license plates. Those plates jumped out at me now. Texas? Nova was from California. The car must be a rental. She must have picked it up at the airport when she flew in from San Francisco, just as Merritt and I had picked up our SUV. Nova said she'd arrived at the Santa Fe airport that morning. In which case, she couldn't possibly have left the death threat in the General's mailbox. But what if she *hadn't* arrived that day, but several days before?

We knew that Nova had access to the invitation. That was Means. My theory gave her Motive. If I could prove that she'd been in Santa Fe or Pecos or within driving distance of the ranch on Tuesday, the day the threat was delivered, instead of Friday, when she claimed she'd arrived, I would have nailed down Opportunity. Nova would be catapulted to the top of the suspect list in the first crime. And possibly in the others.

If only I could find out what day she'd rented the car . . .

I hurried back along the corridor as quietly as possible so as not to wake anyone. Officer Tucker held up four fingers as I passed him.

On the first floor I noticed that the lights were still on in the living room. Officer Tucker had reported that "the people" (by which

I assumed he meant self-talking Bree) in the living room had left. I looked in to see if someone else had gone in and turned the lights on. The room appeared to be empty, until I noticed a pair of feet sticking over the arm of the couch. Bare feet. Bree's feet. I knew they were hers from the lime-green toenail polish. I tiptoed into the room and peeked over the back of the couch to make sure she wasn't dead—not an unlikely possibility in this house. She was stretched across the cushions, sleeping peacefully, a small wet spot on the pillow under her cheek from saliva that had drooled out of her mouth. There was no Navajo blanket to put over her (where were they when you needed them?), and I was in a hurry, so I didn't go looking for one. I left her where she was to sleep or perchance to dream of Ferguntress Philliter's treacherous journey back to the Land of Sapiens. I hoped that someday Bree, too, would find her way home.

CHAPTER FORTY-FOUR

Olivia Investigates

First I needed to check that my memory was right, that Nova's car really did have Texas plates. As I hurried to the parking lot, I swept a bright beam from my phone's flashlight back and forth in a wide arc across the gravel path in case there were any snakes about. This was not phobic on my part; it was a reasonable precaution. Snakes slithered into the open at night when the air was cooler, and it was entirely possible that one or more would be enjoying a sinuous stroll under the weakly shining desert moon.

My flashlight beam soon illuminated the red Toyota Camry, parked right next to the Audi SUV Merritt and I had rented. The Camry's plates were indeed from Texas—near proof that the car was a rental. Gratified, I moved on to my next task: finding out what day the car had been rented. How was I going to do that?

It didn't take long to remember that car rental agreements show the rental date. I had stuffed ours into the pocket of the driver's side door. Other people might put theirs in the storage area between the two seats, or in the glove compartment. In any case, car rental agreements were usually kept inside the car. If I got my hands on Nova's, I would know for sure whether she'd been lying when she said she flew in from San Francisco Friday morning. Then Merritt would have to give my theory some credence. I might even hear her say the words I always longed to hear: *Good work, Blunt. Nicely done.*

The night was peaceful and very quiet. There wasn't so much as a breeze or the hoot of an owl. I used my flashlight to peer into Nova's car, and right there on the passenger seat was a folded packet emblazoned with the yellow Hertz logo. Slipped into its inside pocket would be the agreement.

As I reached to open the passenger door, a faint warning sounded in my head. What if the car was locked and the alarm went off? I drew back, thought about it. I thought long and hard and couldn't decide what to do. I shined the light into the car's interior again, and there in plain view was the Hertz packet. It was just lying there, ripe for the plucking. Nestled inside was information that would tie Nova to the threat on the General's life, and possibly to far more than that—to murder. Or, alternatively, the date on the agreement would prove Nova's innocence, and I would keep my possibly far-fetched theory to myself. What was inside that Hertz packet would either make me a hero or save me from being thought a fool.

Why would anyone bother locking their car out here in the desert anyway? I thought. *It's not like this is a high-crime area.*

I clasped the door handle. Immediately a heart-stopping scream erupted from the Camry. Then the *whoo, whoo, whoo* started, blaring at a thousand decibels through the still night air.

My heart raced. What to do? I doubted I could run back to the main house and up two flights of stairs to my room fast enough to pretend I'd been sleeping when the alarm went off. Besides, Officer Tucker had seen me go downstairs. I looked around wildly. It was almost already too late to run anywhere. Lights inside the house were flicking on. A few seconds later the floodlight that illuminated the back door and gravel path came on, and the next thing I knew a flashlight beam was wavering toward me. Behind it was a large dim figure. Blinded as I was, I couldn't see the person, but I recognized the voice.

"Put your hands in the air!" Officer Tucker had to yell to be heard over the blaring alarm.

I complied.

He shone the light directly in my face. Squinting, I turned away from the glare.

"What are you doing out here?" he bellowed.

"I needed to get something out of my car." I hollered back, pointing to the SUV. "I brushed against this red car by accident, and . . . this happened! I swear I barely touched it. Alarms are so sensitive these days!"

Officer Tucker strolled over to the car and swept his flashlight beam across the trunk, the hood, and all around the interior, including the front and back seats, the floor, and the dashboard. It was obvious that the Camry had not been tampered with.

The second-floor window directly above the back door lit up. That was Merritt's room. I cringed, realizing I would have to explain this somehow.

Fitz's light was on as well. The bedroom at the front of the house was dark. That was the General's room. The fact that she was sleeping through this fiasco was the only good thing I could think of at the moment.

Now from the path on the other side of the parking lot, Nova herself emerged clutching a terry cloth robe around her thin body. "Is that my rental car?" she screeched. "The red Camry?"

"I believe it is, ma'am," roared Officer Tucker.

She had the key fob in her hand and beeped it. The alarm was silenced. In the sudden quiet she asked, "What happened? Was someone trying to break in?"

"It was just me. I'm sorry. I was getting something out of my car and I brushed against yours by accident," I said.

She glanced at my empty hands. "Did you find what you were looking for?"

I had to think fast. "I came out to get my sunglasses, but they weren't there. I must have left them in the house."

Sunglasses, Olivia? Really? It's the middle of the night! Not for the first time, I wished I were a better liar.

Officer Tucker and Nova gave me quizzical looks, but didn't say anything.

"I'm glad that's all it was." Nova cinched her robe, and padded back in the direction of the guesthouse.

Officer Tucker and I returned to the hacienda. I was really hoping I'd be able to slip up to my room without meeting anyone, particularly my boss. But when I got to the second floor, I saw a trapezoid of light spilling across the Navajo-themed rug outside her open door, and I heard the following words spoken in a neutral but firm tone: "Blunt, come here, please."

I did as I was told.

She stood in the doorway, arms crossed. "Was that you? Did you set off the car alarm?"

My lips stuck themselves together, and my mouth made a strange shape. It was odd. I didn't feel entirely in control of my face.

She stepped aside. "Perhaps you'd better come in."

CHAPTER FORTY-FIVE

A Good Idea Poorly Executed

There was really no point in trying to wriggle out of the car alarm fiasco.

"It's me. Hi. I'm the problem. It's me," I said. Most of the world's population would have loved the Taylor Swift quote, but Merritt probably didn't even know the pop star existed.

"Have a seat. Explain." Her tone was neutral, bordering on friendly. She was pretending to have an open mind, but we both knew it was an act. She was just offering me as much rope as I needed to thoroughly hang myself. I decided to go in a different direction.

"Before we get to the car alarm, I have a theory I'd like to discuss with you."

"Oh, dear," she said.

"I think I know who sent the death threat. And who might have done the other crimes as well." I told Merritt everything: the injury Nova's son, Owen, had sustained in boot camp; his subsequent addiction and death; and Nova's unusual theory that bereaved individuals could heal from traumatic loss by practicing a new technique she'd invented called symbolic revenge. I kept the best part for last. "You know where Owen was serving when he was injured?" I didn't wait for an answer. "Fort Sill, under the direction of Brigadier General Joan Battersea."

Merritt squinted at me skeptically. "You're suggesting that Nova left the death threat for Joan as a way of exacting revenge for her son's death?"

I nodded excitedly.

"But Joan wasn't responsible for Owen's death."

"Not directly. But Owen's shoulder injury occurred while he was at boot camp, and there could easily have been some kind of Army negligence involved. Then, to make matters worse, a military doctor prescribed a drug that he must have known was habit-forming. The result was tragic and predictable. Nova could easily have followed the chain of events backward to what happened at Fort Sill. And where did the buck stop at Fort Sill at the time Owen was there? It stopped with none other than Joan Battersea, who unknowingly tempted fate by sending Nova an invitation to spend a weekend at her ranch."

Merritt didn't say anything, but from the look on her face I could guess what she was thinking: *far-fetched.* Or something worse.

"I'm not saying it's *rational,*" I persisted. "But people who send death threats aren't exactly known for clear thinking."

Merritt was frowning. "Do you believe all that stuff about symbolic revenge?"

I shrugged. "Yes, no, maybe. It's way too deep for me and, anyway, who cares? The important thing is that if Nova was angry about Owen's death, it would make perverted sense to take it out on the General."

"Okay. Let's play it out. Nova writes a death threat on the reunion invitation in red Sharpie and leaves it in Joan's mailbox, hoping Joan will be terrified by it. How do you go from there to Eve's murder and the scorpions?"

"Well, what if simply delivering the threat isn't enough for Nova? She wants to see the General squirm and sweat and look upset. Maybe even tell her sorority sisters about the threat and admit to the unrelenting fear she's feeling. At which point Nova would show extreme sympathy while privately basking in evil glee.

"But . . . does Nova get that satisfaction? No. The General, being herself, refuses to bend under the pressure. She looks perfectly fine and doesn't mention the death threat at all.

"So what does Nova do then? Her strategy of symbolic revenge has failed to provide relief. Maybe her theory is wrong: Symbolic revenge isn't enough. Only real revenge, blood revenge, will bring the closure she needs."

"That's quite a story." Merritt was still frowning, but it was a thoughtful frown. "It does seem a bit far-fetched, like most of your ideas, but I'll keep an open mind. Now, please explain what any of this has to do with setting off a car alarm at three in the morning."

"Certainly. I'd be happy to." I explained that Nova's car rental agreement would show the date she rented the car, and that would tell us whether Nova had been in New Mexico at the time the threat was delivered to the ranch.

"Excellent idea, Blunt. Very resourceful."

I beamed. "Thank you."

"And the car alarm?"

"It went off when I tried to open the car door."

"Are you aware that most parked vehicles are locked and alarmed?"

"I am."

"And yet you . . . ? Why?"

I shrugged helplessly. I had no idea why I'd thought that breaking into a suspect's car in the middle of the night was a good idea.

It had seemed perfectly reasonable at the time. Now, of course, it did not seem that way.

As I didn't, or couldn't, explain my behavior, Merritt did it for me. "I'll tell you why. Swept up in the excitement of having a good idea, you allowed yourself to be driven by impulse instead of reason. You desperately wanted the payoff that you imagined would be waiting for you on the other side of that car door, and you were too impatient to find a less risky way to get it."

I wisely kept my mouth shut.

"Your good idea was poorly executed. Not only did you fail to meet your objective, you may have alerted the suspect to your intentions and given her time to hide the evidence."

I nodded very slightly to show that I had heard and understood.

"What did you tell Officer Tucker when he questioned you?"

"I said I bumped into Nova's car by accident."

"Did he ask what you were doing out there in the first place?"

"I said I was looking for my sunglasses in our SUV."

"Sunglasses," Merritt repeated in a dry tone, glancing toward the pitch-black windowpane. She didn't need to say more.

CHAPTER FORTY-SIX

All About Scorpions

It was almost four a.m. when I got to my room. I still had to do the scorpion research Merritt had requested, and as I was expected to give her my report at seven a.m., I gave up hope of sleep. I'd never worked through an entire night before, not even in college, when a glut of cheap ADHD drugs on the Queens College campus had made the practice commonplace. So I was jittery with fatigue when I arrived in the kitchen the next morning, my brain stuffed with more information about scorpions than anyone could possibly want.

Alma was making scrambled eggs and bacon and with a bean, corn, and pepper side dish. Not a bad breakfast for day two of a forced house arrest. I would have offered to help if I hadn't been an entire minute late for my meeting with Merritt. As I knew from long experience, my boss and tardiness did not mix, and she counted tardiness by the minute. But even my desire to avoid yet another round of reproach could not stop me from dallying in the kitchen until a fresh pot of coffee finished brewing. I poured myself the biggest cup I could find, splashed and spooned in a lot of cream and sugar, and hurried out to our designated meeting place on the veranda. On the way, I passed Jacob Korn sitting alone in the dining room, engrossed in something on his laptop. I offered a quiet "Good morning, Mr. Korn," and he glanced up at me briefly, silently, his eyes magnified and blurred by the smeared lenses of his glasses. I got the feeling he couldn't remember my name. It was also possible he'd never learned it in the first place and had no idea who I was.

Merritt was at the table at the far end of the veranda, near a hedge of white-blossomed chokecherry bushes. She was wearing a cool, crisp, button-down shirt, her eyes shielded by her sunglasses. Her bright silver hair was held back by a floral headband. On most people this would have been a fashion faux pas; on her it was chic, very late fifties, but in a good way. I wouldn't have been surprised if the next day a few of the sisters didn't show up wearing floral headbands that would look stupid on them.

She asked me about the scorpions.

I took a swig of coffee and proceeded to enumerate the many similarities and differences between and among the three most common scorpion varieties of the American Southwest: the giant hairy scorpion (its actual name), the stripe-tailed scorpion (just what it sounded like), and the bark scorpion (nothing to do with dogs).

Merritt cut me off mid-sentence. "Please, Blunt. I don't need the entire Wikipedia page."

Cutting to the chase, I explained that the scorpions in the General's bed belonged to the first group: the giant hairy, which was the largest and least lethal of the three varieties. The General herself had correctly identified the first one she saw; at the time I'd thought the term was merely descriptive.

"Scorpion stings usually aren't fatal," I said. "They hurt a whole lot—some describe the pain as excruciating—and the pain and swelling can last for hours. But, according to one reputable online source, in the United States only four people in eleven years have died from scorpion stings, and that was from the bark scorpion. The sting of the giant hairy is the mildest of them all."

Perplexed, Merritt tapped her fingers on the patio table. "So it's possible that what we witnessed was not a murder attempt."

"I wouldn't go that far. A scorpion can sting several times, and there's no telling what five might do. Let's say, hypothetically, that each scorpion stung the General three times; that would be fifteen stings. Definitely not a walk in the park. Now, I wasn't able to find any information indicating that the venom of the giant hairy would be fatal at fifteen times the usual dose. I assume the subject hasn't been medically studied yet. In any case, there's going to be a lot of poison circulating in the victim's body. And if the victim happened to be allergic—"

"Joan isn't allergic. She said that last night."

"True. But she also said that Fitz had to drive her to the hospital in Pecos, and the doctors insisted on keeping her overnight for observation. Scorpion stings usually don't require hospital admittance. Most people do fine at home with cold compresses and OTC pain relievers. So maybe that single sting wasn't as benign as General Battersea suggested. We know how much she likes to downplay threats."

Merritt nodded thoughtfully. "How would someone go about finding them?"

"It's surprisingly easy. Scorpions hide most of the day under rocks and plants and in crevices. They come out at night to hunt. Their exoskeletons glow bright green under UV light, making them easy to find in the dark. Our scorpion catcher would have needed five things: a flashlight to light his way in the dark; a black light to make the scorpions' exoskeletons glow—you can get a basic black light at Amazon for under twenty bucks; something to pick them up with, such as a long-handled wrench or salad tongs like Alma used; and enough containers to put them in. You can't put them all in the same container or they'll kill each other, as we saw last night. So our scorpion catcher would have needed five containers—those plastic Tupperware things with the snap-on lids would do the trick. Then he'd need a backpack or something to carry them in."

"How long would it take to find that many?"

"I have no idea. They don't congregate in groups, so I guess it would depend on the average size of an individual's territory and how closely packed they are in the environment. It's common knowledge that they like dark, cool places—the nooks and crannies of rock formations, for example, or the cracks in concrete or stucco. I suppose if you knew where to look, you could find five in under an hour. But that's just a guess."

"The person who found, captured, transported, and released the scorpions in Joan's bed had very specific attributes," Merritt said. "In addition to knowing how to find them, he had to be able to handle them without the irrational squeamishness that incapacitates many people such as yourself. That suggests someone familiar with the desert, probably someone who had hunted arachnids before."

I mentioned Peter Jumper. "He loves scorpions. You saw how he behaved at the barbecue. Apparently, he was introduced to them on psilocybin vacation in the South Pacific with his mother. Bree worries about him constantly, seems to think he's capable of violence. Bree says he hasn't done anything really bad yet. But she's waiting. She apparently believes he might."

"Peter Jumper." Merritt rolled the name on her tongue as if she were tasting it. Then grimaced as if she didn't like the flavor.

"Honestly, boss, I think anyone else could have done it too. I was able to learn everything an aspiring scorpion catcher would need to know in fifteen minutes, just by reading what was on the internet."

Merritt looked out across the desert. I knew she was thinking, trying to fit pieces of the puzzle together. After a while she turned to me with a dejected sigh. "Something's wrong, Blunt. The mind that executed this assault on General Battersea is a type of criminal mind I haven't met before. And the assault has almost nothing in common with yesterday's murder. A nest of scorpions is a cowardly and likely ineffective method of attack. A gunshot is bold and almost certainly fatal. I'm beginning to think we're dealing with two very different criminals here, yet it seems likely that the crimes are related. Which leaves me no choice but to posit the existence of a criminal partnership."

A sober silence followed this remark. I had the queasy feeling that, once again, the case was spinning out of control, and all I could do was hang on until the whirling stopped and the path forward revealed itself. I sipped my coffee but it was lukewarm now.

Merritt continued her logical reasoning. "We know that the creatures weren't in Joan's bed Friday night, and we can assume they weren't put there during the day yesterday, when they would have been sequestered in their rocks and crevices, which means that they must have been put in her bed yesterday evening, between about an hour after sunset and ten o'clock when Joan retired for the night."

I checked my weather app. "Sunset was at eight eleven p.m."

"So who was missing for at least an hour between eight and ten p.m.? Conversely, who do we know was present?"

Whereas Friday night had been an upbeat time of silly games and funny stories, last night couldn't have been more different. The atmosphere had been tense and chaotic. There was an argument, I recalled, between Kathy Lafferty and Jacob Korn about Sheriff Casey's handling of the investigation. Kathy insisted that Casey was trying to frame her husband; Korn said the evidence against her husband was obvious and undeniable. Kathy became livid and incoherent; Korn remained coolly adamant. They almost came to blows.

"Sorry, boss," I said. "People were restless, coming and going all the time, and I wasn't paying a lot of attention. Anyone could have snuck off for an hour without being noticed. The only two we can exclude from the suspect list with any degree of certainty are Nova and Bree. They were out on the veranda most of the night drinking margaritas. They've been hanging out together all weekend, sometimes with Kathy but most of the time it's just the two of them."

Just then, Nova herself came out on the veranda carrying a tray with her breakfast on it. She paused and glanced around, clearly looking for a place to sit.

Leaning toward me, Merritt spoke in a low voice. "The information you tried to get last night from Nova's car rental agreement can perhaps be more easily obtained from her luggage tag. Not the personal ID affixed to her suitcase, but the long white tab the airline uses to identify the flight number and destination."

I nodded.

"Her suitcase will be in her room, likely with the tag still attached. If she ripped it off, you might find it in the wastebasket. Go now. I'll keep her occupied until you return."

Donning her huge sunglasses, she called out happily, like a girl hailing her BFF across a cafeteria, "Nova, over here! Come sit with me."

As I slipped away I brushed past a smiling Nova and heard Merritt say, "You and I haven't had a real chat yet, just the two of us." The coziness in her voice sounded completely authentic.

CHAPTER FORTY-SEVEN

Bingo

I hurried away feeling hopeful and excited. Merritt was taking my theory seriously, which meant it wasn't so far-fetched, and with her smart suggestion about the luggage tag, we just might be on the verge of a breakthrough.

The guesthouse, a one-story adobe building with a flat roof, looked like a Pueblo revivalist roadside motel. The rooms were in a straight row facing east. Each had a single window in which a rustic plaid curtain hung, and a heavy weathered wooden door that looked like it might have been hand hewn from the timbers of the Alamo.

The door handles were hunks of twisted wrought iron, without visible locks or keyholes. Fitz and the General must have decided that keys weren't needed here, any more than they were needed in the bedrooms of the main house, since the people staying in these rooms would be family and friends. There was probably a simple button lock or something like that on the inside to ensure a guest's privacy when the room was occupied.

Which room was Nova's? I studied the building carefully. The curtains in two of the rooms were open to let in morning light; the others were drawn. As it was still early, I supposed the people in the darkened rooms were sleeping. When Conrad Zander came out of one door and headed toward the hacienda, I could make a pretty good guess which room was Nova's. I glanced up and down the concrete walkway that skirted the guesthouse. As far as I could tell, no one was observing me, so I opened the door and slipped inside.

It was bright and cheerful, though the walls were thin: I could hear the murmur of voices in the adjoining room. The shawl Nova had been wearing the night before was draped over a chair, and her suitcase was on the rack at the end of the bed. The white airline tag was attached to the handle, just as Merritt had said it would be. The information it provided was clear and concise: May 19. United Airlines flight 1430, San Francisco to Denver. United Airlines flight 4684, Denver to Santa Fe.

May 19 was Monday. One day before the threat was delivered. My fingers tingled with excitement. I couldn't believe my good luck. So far the case had been maddeningly short on physical evidence. We had acquired only one clue: a series of faint footprints. Now we had a second clue, and it was a big one. I snapped a photo of it and texted it to Merritt with the triumphant caption She lied!

I slipped my phone into my pocket and was about to leave, when the voices in the next room got louder. A man and a woman were arguing. Jacob and Barbara Korn, I surmised, through process of elimination. I put my ear to the wall and heard a male voice:

"Yeah, you're right. I never liked her. She was a cold bitch who thought she was better than everyone else."

"She was intelligent and cultured and she made you feel inferior because anyone who's had any success in this world makes you feel inferior."

"She thought she was better than you, too, Babs, only you were too busy sucking up to her to see it."

"How dare you say that! She was my friend."

"A friend who treated you like shit for forty years. And you kept doing her bidding."

"I don't have anything to be ashamed of. I wasn't the one who shot her."

"What are you saying? That *I* did it? Oh, come on! I was up at the hacienda when it happened. I told the sheriff he could check the CCTV if he needed proof. I said I went up there to get the hell away from my wife. He understood exactly what I meant. We even laughed about it."

"You're horrible."

"You can't stand that I have an alibi and you don't. No one knows for sure where *you* were when it happened."

"I was right here. I overslept!"

"I don't believe you. I saw you set your alarm."

"I set it, but I forgot to take my phone off silent."

"Sure, sure. You forgot to take your phone off silent. That's a nice story. You think the sheriff's going to buy it? I don't. He'll be coming for you pretty soon, Babs, as soon as he gets done with the ex-cop. You're the next obvious suspect. You're the only one who knew Joan wasn't going to be there so Eve would be alone. Hell, maybe you went to the pool as planned, just to take a swim, and you two gals had a nasty catfight. She told you what she really thought of you, so you shot her. I can see it happening clear as day. I might even tell the sheriff that."

"You wouldn't."

"Don't tempt me."

"You know I could never do anything like that."

"Do I? Don't forget that I've seen the other side of you, the side no one knows about."

"I hate you right now, Jacob. I think I may have always hated you."

"Yeah, there it is. That's the side I'm talking about."

Oh my god, I thought. Had my ears deceived me? Had I really just heard a married couple accuse each other of murder? How could they stay together? How could they even be in the same room? Just listening to their vitriol through a wall was enough to make me nauseated. Bree had described the General and Fitz as having "found their marital groove." Was this a marital groove too? The groove where you spent every waking hour loathing the other person and accusing them of terrible things?

As a detective I should have eavesdropped longer, in case they spilled some juicy clue, but as a human being I just couldn't take any more. The couple were still hurling contemptuous remarks at each other as I tiptoed out of the room, shutting the door softly behind me.

CHAPTER FORTY-EIGHT

Why Be Good?

Nova and Merritt were still on the veranda when I returned. Their tense postures told me that the friendly chat had taken a turn for the worse. I figured Merritt had seen the photo of the luggage tag and had wasted no time in confronting Nova.

As I took my seat at the table, Nova abruptly stopped talking and glared at me. "You," she said icily. "You broke into my room."

"The door wasn't locked," I replied, as if my behavior were the door's fault.

"You had no right—"

Merritt cut her off. "I instructed my assistant to search your room, so if you need to be angry at someone, be angry at me. Though you're in no position to be angry at anyone but yourself. Now, let me repeat my question. Why did you lie to us about the date you arrived in Santa Fe? Was it to deliver a death threat to Joan?"

"You call it a death threat, but that's not what it was. I had no intention of hurting her."

"Not physically. You wanted to hurt her emotionally, the way you were hurt when your son returned from boot camp dishonorably discharged with a prescription for opioids in his pocket."

"Yes, I was hurt and angry. What happened to my son was wrong. He never harassed that girl. She was a serial accuser with borderline personality disorder, and she threatened him with a knife because *he* refused to sleep with *her*. It was bad enough that he broke his shoulder trying to escape her clutches, but then he was charged with sexual harassment and theft—for items she planted in his locker!—and dishonorably discharged. Those discharge papers were signed by Brigadier General Joan Battersea. Owen tried to deal with the injustice done to him—he sought counseling; he tried his best to reintegrate into society—but deep down I think he knew that the stain on his character would never be erased, and after a while he stopped fighting for himself. The drugs made it easy for him to give up. He felt good when he was high—and only then. His death is a story that's been repeated across this country tens of thousands of times."

"Joan was your sorority sister. You could have called, explained, urged her to reconsider."

"Don't think I didn't try. I called and couldn't get through. I wrote and didn't get a response. I even drove to the camp to try to talk to her, but they stopped me at the gate. She must have been aware that I was trying to reach her, and she ought to have known why. I believe she was deliberately avoiding me. What kind of sister is that?"

Merritt frowned. "That doesn't sound like Joan."

"Doesn't it? You heard what she said at the barbecue: In war, there are winners and losers. No shades of gray, no extenuating circumstances, no false convictions. I believe that in her mind Owen had got what he deserved. She wasn't going to waste her time indulging his crying mother, especially one she had a personal relationship with, lest she be accused of doing favors for her friends. These issues were so politicized back then—still are, I assume. She'd paid a heavy price for pushing forward her initiatives on sexual harassment in the military, and no one could have admired her strength of character more than me. But years of fighting for what's right wear a person down. What starts as idealism turns into rigidity. I believe that our beloved Joan of Arc had come to the point in her life when she no longer was capable of asking herself whether she'd made a mistake."

Merritt's eyes were narrowed by skepticism, but they shone with the hard light of reason. "What about you, Nova? What's your excuse? With all your professional training and your years of experience in matters of the heart, how could you possibly have believed that a death threat would be any kind of remedy for your suffering?"

"It *was* a remedy," Nova insisted. "You see, I'd arrived at the point in my grieving process where I was able to accept that the justice I was seeking wasn't going to come—not ever, not for Owen or for me. All I could hope for was to feel better any way I could. You have to understand how angry I was, Aubrey, and for how many years. I needed to discharge my anger, to try to cleanse myself, and punching pillows in a therapy session or journaling in a notebook didn't help me at all. Hurting Joan in a small way—*that* gave me some relief. It made me feel that there was justice after all—justice that I was meting out because I can. I'm not proud of what I did, but I'm not ashamed either. What person hasn't been grievously wronged by this world? Who isn't owed more in compensation than they will ever receive? Why should the wounded work so hard to be good when the people who inflict the injuries go on being bad?"

Merritt was shaking her head sadly. "You've fallen, my friend. I'm sorry for that. The question is, how far?"

"What's that supposed to mean?"

"Where were you at seven fifteen yesterday morning?"

"You can't seriously think I killed Eve."

"I'm just asking where you were when she was shot."

"I was in my room. Asleep. I didn't wake up until the police knocked on my door and told me there had been a murder."

Merritt stared at her, expressionless.

Nova stayed silent, chewed her lip, and the standoff stretched out, getting more and more uncomfortable. I fought an urge to blurt out an irrelevant remark just to break the tension. Finally, Nova cracked.

"I have to ask, Aubrey . . ." She paused, as if she'd come to a doorway and couldn't decide whether to pass through. "What are you going to do?"

"What do you think?"

The therapist shrugged, feigning indifference. "Scrawling a few words on a card isn't illegal."

"You know it is. If you're a first offender with a clean record and you show remorse, you'll probably get off with probation and community service."

The therapist blanched. "So you intend to report me to the police?"

"Not if you report yourself first. To Joan. We'll let her decide if the authorities should be involved. But you have to do it now, this morning. Before I change my mind."

"Aubrey, really . . . I can't possibly explain to Joan . . . you know how she is . . . she would never understand . . ."

Turning to me, Merritt said in a hard voice, "Dial the sheriff, Blunt."

I whipped out my phone and started to google the Pecos police department to get the phone number.

As I was waiting for the website to load, Nova spoke up. "Okay.

Fine. You can put your phone away, Olivia. I'll tell Joan what I did. And why. And I'll tell her I'm sorry. Which I am."

"Sorry for what you did, or sorry you got caught?" Merritt asked.

Nova ignored the question. "I've agreed to tell her, Aubrey. You have my word. But please, let me do it in my own time, in my own way."

"You have until noon," Merritt said.

Nova Olsen glared again. Her lips set in a tight line, she got up and walked away.

"Do you think she'll really do it?" I asked when she was out of earshot.

"It depends on who she's more afraid of: me or Joan."

"Probably you," I said.

"I hope so."

CHAPTER FORTY-NINE

A Gauntlet Is Thrown

Our conversation with Nova Olsen left me with contradictory emotions. The fact that she'd admitted her crime was gratifying, but her confession had also stirred up a vague anxiety. Before coming to the Muddy River Ranch, I never would have imagined that a flock of former sorority girls in their sixties would turn out to be such a twisted and disturbing group. Now, after witnessing all the pain, regrets, and stale resentments packed underneath their superficially pleasant exteriors, I couldn't help feeling discouraged and a bit confused. Wisdom was supposed to come with age, but what I was seeing were battle scars.

My mood rose when Merritt removed her sunglasses and favored me with a rare smile. "You did good work there, Blunt."

"Thank you," I said, flushing with pride.

Her approval was deeply satisfying. So often in the past I (and Merritt too!) had questioned whether I had the temperament to succeed in investigative work. Along with her, I'd worried that my skin was too thin, my stomach too sensitive, my heart too soft, and my brain too slow. Now I had identified the author of the death threat using my own deductive and research skills, with only one small (if loud) misstep along the way and a single suggestion from my boss. This was a true accomplishment, one that Merritt was graciously recognizing, and for the first time in my nearly yearlong, often difficult apprenticeship, I felt a spark of confidence in myself and my prospects.

I should have known that feeling would be short-lived.

Merritt continued, "Thanks in part to your good work, I expect to be done here by the end of the day."

My brow furrowed. "Wait a minute. We figured out who left the death threat, but we still don't know who murdered Eve Exeter and who put the scorpions in the General's bed."

"True. But if I'm not mistaken, only one more question needs to be answered, and if the answer is what I suspect it will be, the entire sequence of events will fall seamlessly into place."

I was dumbfounded. "How on earth?"

"I won't make it easy for you, Blunt. If you want to be a detective yourself someday, you need to take every opportunity to improve your rudimentary detection skills. I suggest you try applying your nascent reasoning power and spotty psychological acuity to everything you've learned thus far. Think, Blunt. Think very hard."

"I am thinking hard! And I don't see how fingering Nova brings us any closer to solving the other two crimes. In fact, as far as the scorpions go, I saw Nova drinking tequila with Bree here on the veranda last night, so she was probably drunk as a skunk and could hardly have gone out hunting for them. So how do you get from this one breakthrough to almost solving everything?" I scowled as an old suspicion returned to me. "Unless you have more information than I do."

"I assure you, I don't."

I scowled even more. "You must. There's no way—"

Merritt's vivid eyes glinted like blue steel. "I'm losing patience with you, Blunt. Someday I won't be here. What will happen to the agency then? Could you solve even one case by yourself? Or would you walk around half-blind and half-deaf, waiting for the criminal to grab you and confess?"

My blood ran cold. *Someday I won't be here.* I'd never heard her talk like that.

She stood up and threw her napkin on the table with force. "As I've explained to you time and time again, all detection comes down to three basic techniques: observation, logic, and psychology. I will add, though I shouldn't have to, that observation involves noting what is *not* present as well as what is. And it need not be limited to the visual realm. A good investigator observes with her ears as well as her eyes. Your ears, Blunt. You have two, one on each side of your head. Solve these cases, my young friend. Solve them before noon today."

I asked almost piteously, "What if I can't?"

"Then you're fired." With that she stalked off, leaving me alone.

CHAPTER FIFTY

Olivia's Dark Hour

What? Fired?

She couldn't be serious. But I knew she was. Which made her the most obnoxious, mean-spirited, entitled, and incompetent boss any assistant could possibly have. The games she played were so trite, so old-school, so absurdly unhelpful, so . . . *bossy.* But what else would you expect from a fancy-pants sorority girl? Dozens of snobbish delusions of grandeur were probably choking her overeducated mind. Was she so out of touch with today's world that she actually believed that her melodramatic ultimatum constituted fitting boss behavior? Or was she pathetically attempting to relive her long-ago sorority glory days by hazing me as if I were some pimple-faced, knock-kneed freshman rush? Who knew? Who cared? Sure, she might be famous and brilliant and almost always right. But that didn't give her permission to be cruel and oh so superior. Truly great people treated others with kindness and respect. My father, whom I adored, had taught me that, and no one would ever convince me otherwise.

Aubrey Merritt had grievously misjudged me. Threats held no water for me. It didn't matter whether they came from the pope, a mob boss, or a nationally renowned private investigator—I was completely unfazed. Just to prove it, I decided I would do *absolutely nothing* to solve the two remaining mysteries. Why should I? I'd already done more than my fair share of eye-straining, backbreaking detective work while she pleasantly whiled away the hours drinking peach iced tea and chatting with her old-lady friends (whom she didn't even like and glibly suspected of murder!). In fact, I'd been working so hard that I hadn't had a wink of sleep in over twenty-seven hours.

Emotionally and physically exhausted, I dragged myself back into the house and traipsed upstairs to take a nap. I lay down on top of the twin bed, too tired to check for scorpions and rattlesnakes first. The instant I closed my eyes, I realized that sleep would be impossible to achieve. While my body was overweary and my heart felt bruised, my brain was lit up and doing somersaults, thanks to too many cups of coffee, adrenaline, the paradoxical effects of too little sleep, and the taunting gauntlet Merritt had tossed at my feet, which I had absolutely no intention of picking up.

I decided to skip the nap and take a stroll outside, have myself a lonely little think. I had just descended the stairs to the first floor when, out of habit, I checked the grandfather clock in the hall. It said 7:16. Up ahead, I noticed the edge of Angel's orange ball under the hall table. I picked it up, intending to return it to Jenny-Lou when I saw her. At the door of the kitchen, I thought, *Wait. That can't be right.* Confused, I retraced my steps and examined the clock-face again. There was nothing unusual about it, except that its hands were indicating a completely erroneous time. I lowered my gaze to the glass door, behind which the heavy brass pendulum was housed. It hung motionless.

Strange. The clock was stopped at 7:16—the exact time I'd noticed as I raced past it yesterday morning after hearing the gunshot. That time, minus the minute it likely took me to run down the stairs, was the evidence upon which the very specific murder time of 7:15 a.m. was based.

A dreadful thought occurred to me. Had the clock been stopped when I ran past it? If so, the actual time of the murder would be *after* 7:16, perhaps many minutes after, which meant that the murder window would also need to shift to later in the morning.

My testimony regarding the time of the murder gave Dave Lafferty barely enough time (in my opinion, given his age and size, actually *not* enough time) to shoot Eve Exeter, race through the cabana, run uphill to the parking lot, jump into his RV with his wife, and drive past the CCTV camera at the front gate by 7:24. If the gunshot had actually happened *after* 7:16, then there was even less time for the ex-cop to make that trip, and a far stronger argument that he could *not* have been the killer. Yet Sheriff Casey was using my testimony as a cornerstone of the case he was building against Dave Lafferty!

I felt shaky and started to sweat. A man could go to jail due to a possible mistake I'd made.

I needed to rectify the situation immediately. I sat on the bottom step of the staircase, placed the orange ball beside me, pulled out my phone, and navigated through all the necessary screens until I got the Pecos police department on the line. Sheriff Casey, I was told, was not in the office. There was no telling when he would be back.

I hunched over and rested my forehead on crossed arms, hiding my face from the world. The fact that I could have been so doltish as to quote the time of a nonworking clock absolutely sickened me. I felt even sicker when I realized that Merritt was bound to hear about it.

What had she said? *Observation involves noting what is* not *present as well as what is. A good investigator observes with her* ears *as well as her eyes.* It was clear to me now that she'd been referring to the non-chiming of the grandfather clock, which I had not noticed not hearing.

Jenny-Lou came down the corridor at that moment. The feisty spaniel, Angel, ran alongside her, yapping joyously.

She pulled an exaggerated sad face when she saw me. "Now what's got *you* looking so bothered?" The way she said it suggested that a lot of other people were also looking bothered, which was likely true.

I pointed to the grandfather clock and said morosely, "It stopped."

Angel trotted over, sat on his haunches, and stared first at me, then at the ball, then back at me. His button-black eyes sparkled with excitement. I really didn't feel like playing fetch, but he was so eager that I reluctantly summoned the strength to roll the ball down the hall. He raced after it, pounced on it delightedly, trotted back, and dropped it at my feet, his tail wagging at top speed. So I did it again.

Jenny-Lou was studying the clock. "Now, how did that happen? I swear, antique clocks have minds of their own. Too much time on their hands. Ha ha! But you really don't need to take it so hard, Olivia. I can get it going again in no time."

She opened the glass door, behind which hung the stationary pendulum. As she bent over and ran her hand across the clock's inner floor, I rolled the ball to Angel a third time. This time, when he brought it back, I dropped it in my pocket. Enough of that. Angel glared at me, so I extended my palm for him to sniff.

Jenny-Lou stood up straight, a puzzled look on her face. "Why, that's funny. The key's not there. It's been in that exact spot for years. Never moved. And now it's plumb gone! I wonder who took it." Hands on hips, she frowned as she considered the answer.

My palm didn't interest Angel, but my sneakers did. He started sniffing them with a lot of interest. Top, sides, all around. He probably smelled blood from the pool water on them.

"I bet it was Fitz," Jenny-Lou concluded. "He's always fussing over this clock, and he's getting forgetful. He must have put the key in his pocket by accident. I'll go and get it from him, so don't you worry, Olivia! We'll have this old clock working again in no time."

She scooped up the spaniel and tucked him in the crook of her arm. Summarily denied more whiffs of bloody sneaker, Angel squirmed in objection.

After Jenny-Lou had gone off in search of Fitz, I pondered the meaning of the missing key. An interesting possibility occurred to me. What if Fitz hadn't innocently pocketed the key? What if someone had stolen it? Stealing a clock key made no sense. You couldn't sell it or do much else with it. But what if you weren't interested in the key itself but in what it could do, and what its absence would prevent others from doing?

Maybe the person who took the key wanted to make sure that the clock was not reset before the right people had noticed the very specific time at which the clock had ceased functioning.

If that was the case, I hadn't made a mistake at all! Someone had come along, stopped the pendulum, set the grandfather clock's hands to precisely seven sixteen, and pocketed the key.

I tried to remember the last time I'd heard the clock's slow, heavy gongs. It was early this morning, I recalled, when a single chime prompted Bree to ask what I was doing up at that hour. That was at one thirty a.m.

Who could have done it? Only someone who was in the house

between one thirty a.m. and whatever time this morning Merritt had noticed the unusual silence.

But that wasn't the only condition. The guilty party also needed to know that the time of 7:16 was significant, which reduced the list of suspects to individuals who were privy to the details of the investigation. That list was pretty short: myself, Merritt, Sheriff Casey, Deputy Roundtree, and any other members of the police force they had shared information with. But Merritt and I obviously didn't do it, Casey and Roundtree weren't here (unless they'd snuck in), and the only cop present in the house last night was Officer Tucker, and why would he want to interfere with the investigation?

I recalled Officer Tucker informing me that two people had been chattering in the living room, when in fact Bree had been the only chattering person I'd seen there. Later, he said he'd heard people leave the living room—clumsily, perhaps drunk—when in fact Bree hadn't gone anywhere but was passed out on the couch. So . . . had someone else been in the hallway at that time? Was the clumsiness Officer Tucker described actually the sound of that mystery person opening and closing the grandfather clock's pendulum case?

Or had the culprit carried out his plan much later, when everyone was asleep?

I sat there on the stairway's bottom step—cranky, bitter, overtired, with every intention of quitting my stupid job before I was fired—while my energized brain burned ever brighter and cartwheeled ever faster from one fact to the next. Shotguns, orange balls, shoe prints, black lights, and nighttime texts. People hating people. Four scenarios. Venn diagrams: three circles overlapping, one small area common to all three. The parade of possible connections seemed endless and unstoppable. In the background, suspects whirled.

I have no idea how long I was there, eyes closed, rocking slightly, hugging myself tightly so as not to fly apart from the force of so much thinking. I probably should have had one of those corkboards you see in movies with different-colored threads jetting out this way and that between different-colored pins. That was how crazed I felt. At long last my brain's pace slowed. A shadow shifted, a small piece wobbled, a bigger piece slid smoothly into its perfect slot, and the next thing I knew, there was a mad scurry and scrambling of many pieces, and with a big sudden *whoosh* the picture was complete.

My eyes snapped open and I said out loud, firmly, "Oh my god, she's right."

CHAPTER FIFTY-ONE

A Private Triumph

Merritt was in the living room talking to Fitz and the General. She looked up when I walked in. Was she just a little bit glad to see me? A little sorry for her harsh words? I hoped so.

"Can I talk to you for a minute?" I said.

She followed me out of the room. I wanted to make sure we could talk at length without being interrupted or overheard, so I persuaded her to stroll with me past the stables down to the Pecos River.

The trek was longer than I thought it would be. The sun blazed down on us from a sky of eye-squinting blue, and there wasn't so much as a puff of breeze. It was just after ten a.m., so it was not as hot as it would be in a few hours, but it was still pretty hot. I could see that Merritt was not enjoying the hike. She wasn't dressed for it either. Her Pedro García sandals were soon covered in red dirt, as were the hems of her loose white linen pants.

The river was disappointing. Brownish water a few inches deep flowed sluggishly across brownish pebbles along the riverbed and around brownish rocks of various sizes. Had the water looked a little cleaner and been a little deeper, we might have enjoyed some relief from the heat by wading in and splashing it on our sweating faces. As it was, we stood side by side on the riverbank as I tried to remember what had made me think this was a good idea. There was no place to sit unless on the ground, no shade to shelter under, and nowhere else to go, unless we wanted to slosh through the muddy water and head into yonder foothills of scrub brush and cacti (which I, for one, did not).

Then, out of the silence, came a metallic hissing. It sounded like the rapid clicking of a hundred mini castanets.

It couldn't be . . . except it was. The rattlesnake was coiled on a flat rock, its raised head swaying and dipping, as if it was scouting the air for a sniff of who or what had disturbed its nap. It was way too close to us—close enough that I could see the diamond pattern on its oily-looking skin, the filmy black dot that was its eye, and the tiny tip of a yellow fang protruding from its upper lip.

If I were alone, I would have been utterly hysterical. But my phobia paled in light of the fact that Merritt's ankle was within easy striking distance of the reptile's venom-filled fangs.

"Boss," I said softly. "Please step behind me slowly, then turn around and very slowly go back the way we came."

"So soon? We just got here." She wiped beads of sweat off her forehead.

"There's a rattlesnake about three feet off your left foot," I said calmly. "If you turn your head ninety degrees, you'll see it."

She did so. "It's a diamondback." Her whisper trembled with fear.

"Uh-huh. You go. I'll follow."

She moved diagonally backward a foot or two, until my body shielded her from immediate danger, and then she turned and walked quietly away from the river.

I was just about to do the same, when the snake dipped its head and slithered off the rock in a motion that looked like smoothly falling water. It proceeded to flow across the packed red dirt in a sinewy S pattern, seeming to travel both forward and sideways simultaneously, and its speed was unexpectedly fast. It was gliding straight toward me. Suddenly I was back at the Bronx Zoo, and Mr. Driscoll was teaching science to our third-grade class before we entered the World of Reptiles: He was rhapsodizing about evolution as always, how it had bestowed upon snakes a remarkable ability to sense vibration, and what to do if we ever encountered one in the wild. *Stay absolutely still.*

So I stayed absolutely still. I didn't breathe. I was a veritable pillar of stone as the snake passed by me in gentle, undulating curves, within inches of my feet.

CHAPTER FIFTY-TWO

Eighty-Five Percent Certainty

Merritt seemed not to have noticed the incredibly courageous way I had shielded her from danger. She, too, had been scared in the moment, had allowed me to protect her, but now she was acting like nothing out of the ordinary had happened. It was very disappointing, as I would have liked a pat on the back, but I was used to not getting much in the way of approval from her. So I metaphorically patted my own back.

You handled that encounter unbelievably well, I told myself. Not decompensating had been my first accomplishment. But to have then tamped down my own terror enough to put my boss's safety first, and then to have stoically endured such a close brush with my nemesis—that went well beyond what I'd believed myself capable of. I took a long moment to feel the pride.

"Well? What did you want to say to me?" Merritt asked. Sweat stains had appeared under the arms of her sleeveless camp shirt. Her usually paper-white skin was salmon pink; she was literally cooking in the Southwestern sun.

"I think I know who planted the scorpions in General Battersea's bed."

"You're sure?"

"I think so."

"What makes you young people believe that *I think so* is a satisfactory answer to a question?" she huffed. "It's a perfectly useless reply. It can do nothing but engender confusion, which in turn leads to errors. In the future, when I ask you a question, an honest *yes* or *no* will suffice."

"I'd like to be more definite, but I'm just not totally, completely sure."

"Is your solution logical? Psychologically sound? Supported by evidence? Does it fit within the known or assumed parameters of the criminal act's time and space?"

"Mostly, I guess. Sort of."

"Blunt," she said with harsh impatience. "Be clear. Can you or can you not identify the person who put the scorpions in Joan Battersea's bed?"

"I can say who it was with eighty-five percent certainty."

"Then you do *not* know, and you do *not* have a solution to the crime."

"I was hoping we could discuss it."

"A great detective refrains from consulting others so as not to be contaminated by their inferior thoughts."

"But we work together. We're a team. Aren't we?"

"We're a team *for now.* Someday we won't be a team, and before that happens you need to learn how to handle cases on your own. Alone. With no one to turn to for help."

"Why do you keep saying things like that? *Someday I won't be here* and *Someday we won't be a team.* Are you trying to tell me something?"

"I'm stating an obvious fact. Don't start hoping for my early retirement."

"Of course I wouldn't hope for that!" I said with heat in my voice. Gosh, why did old people always have to be so touchy about getting old? I mean, it's not like they hadn't seen it coming.

"What about the other matter?" Merritt asked. "The murder of Eve Exeter. How are you doing on that?"

"Not well."

"Uh-huh. Another vague response. I *could* interpret it to mean that you've made some progress, but it was disappointing. Perhaps that's what you're hoping I'll think. But the truth is different, isn't it? The truth that you are trying to camouflage with your mealy-mouthed reply is that you have made no progress whatsoever."

"That is correct."

Merritt checked her wristwatch as we arrived at the house. "It's eleven o'clock. You have one more hour to report back to me with the complete solutions to the remaining two crimes, or—"

"Yes, I heard you the first time. But I don't believe you. You have too much invested in me to let me go."

"Really? Is that so? Do you think you are irreplaceable?"

I sidestepped that question as a new idea crossed my mind. It was quite radical and surprising. Until that moment I wouldn't have imagined such a thing was possible. *What if Merritt was pressuring me to solve the cases because she couldn't?*

"Do *you* know the solutions?" I blurted.

"Of course I do. They're easier than you think. Honestly, Blunt, I wouldn't have given you this task if it was difficult."

CHAPTER FIFTY-THREE

The Sisters Convene, Part 1

Fitz hurried over as we entered the house, saying he had important news to share. Apparently the police had discovered incriminating evidence and had formally charged Dave Lafferty with the murder of Eve Exeter. Dave would be arraigned at the Santa Fe courthouse the next morning. Sheriff Casey was coming to the ranch this afternoon to update us on the status of the investigation and, presumably, to let us all go home.

This was bad news for Merritt and me (and the Laffertys, of course). If everyone left the ranch as early as tomorrow or possibly even tonight, our investigation would end. And with alternative suspects scattered to their home states, Sheriff Casey would have even less incentive to look beyond the ex-cop.

Merritt immediately called for an emergency meeting of the Sigma Delta Tau sorority sisters. It was to be a private and exclusive meeting, only for the sisters (and me). It was to be held in Fitz's Den of Guns, presumably because that room was at the far end of the hacienda, where we would have more privacy.

The women trickled in one by one. General Battersea, Barbara Korn, Nova Olsen, Bree Jumper, Kathy Lafferty. We were seven altogether, if you included Merritt and me. We all squeezed around the copper-topped coffee table. Merritt took charge. She explained what was happening.

"I knew it!" Kathy burst out. "He's got Dave, and he's not going to look at anyone else! What are you going to do to save my husband, Aubrey? You have to do something!"

"I intend to," Merritt replied coolly. "But first, I wanted us to come together as a group, because there are certain issues—certain things that people in this group have done—that need to be aired and resolved within the family, so to speak. I'm hoping we can put these issues to rest quickly, before the sheriff arrives, and agree among ourselves not to discuss them with anyone outside this group ever again. If we can do that, I'll be free to focus on the most important job—unmasking Eve's true killer—without worrying that lesser crimes will become distractions."

She looked sternly at each woman in turn. "This discussion will not be easy. But if we stick together, tell the truth, and assume both blame and praise as required, we might be able to transcend personal resentments, and keep each other safe from unwarranted police scrutiny."

The women's assent was immediate and unanimous, no doubt helped along by the fact that Kathy was softly weeping and murmuring, *"He's innocent, he's innocent . . ."*

"I'll start at the beginning," Merritt said. "Early last week, someone put a death threat in the mailbox at the gate to this ranch. It was scrawled on an invitation to our Sigma Delta Tau reunion—the same one we all received in the mail—and it said, 'She who lives by the sword shall die . . .'"

The women gasped in shock and disbelief.

"I naturally suspected that the person who wrote and delivered the threat was one of us—or should I say, one of you . . ."

Sharp objections rose from the assembly.

"And it *was* one of you."

"Oh my god!" Barbara sputtered. "You mean someone in this room sent Joan a death threat? I don't believe it!"

Merritt's eyes traveled slowly to the therapist. "Would you like to say anything, Nova?"

Nova sighed in resignation. There was no escaping Merritt's steely gaze. "It was me. I did it," she announced to the group.

"You? But why?" Barbara asked. "Why would you do something like that?"

Nova shook her head wearily. "I can't explain right now. It's too much, and you wouldn't understand . . ."

Merritt said, "Nova was harboring a terrible grudge against Joan ever since her son died. Isn't that right, Nova?"

"A *grudge?* You call it a *grudge?*" Nova said. "That's totally unfair. My anger is based in facts about the way my son was treated by the military." She glowered at Merritt. "I don't need to defend myself to you, Aubrey. In my opinion, you would benefit from several years of therapy yourself. Even in college I could see that you were far too categorical in your thinking—everything so black and white—right and wrong—good and bad—all the usual reductionist dichotomies—and you obviously haven't changed since then."

I couldn't believe my ears! From the moment I met Aubrey Merritt, I'd been a little afraid of her. Her reputation, intellect, expertise, even her wealth and fashion sense, had all conspired to make her something of an icon in my mind. Now here was someone bossing her right back—telling her she needed to go to therapy, of all things! And I couldn't disagree. Something was definitely going on with

Aubrey Merritt. Threatening to fire me if I didn't solve two crimes in one hour was extreme, even by her standards.

"But what difference does any of this make?" Nova was saying. "The issue has been dealt with. I confessed to Joan as I promised I would. Didn't I, Joan?"

The General nodded. "She did confess, Aubrey. Please don't be too hard on her. The pain of having lost a child is enough of a burden for anyone. I remember the young man: Private Owen Olsen. Olsen is Nova's married name, so I never put it together that he was her son. And I was never told that she'd tried to contact me. My staff must have assumed she just wanted to harass me for what had happened to him. I had no knowledge of the medical treatment he'd received, or the prescription for painkillers, or of what happened to him after he left the base. I only heard the story today from Nova, and my heart is broken for her.

"As I explained to Nova, and I'll tell you all now as well, I truly do not think the Army made a mistake. There was strong evidence that Private Olsen had sexually assaulted that young woman. Sexual crimes are an epidemic in the military, as I expect you're all aware. Most of the time they aren't prosecuted because evidence is lacking or the victim withdraws her complaint. We can only guess at how many incidents go unreported because the victims fear retribution and don't trust that the system will protect them. Private Olsen's accuser was one of the rare ones who came forward and presented strong evidence. The young man was tried in a military tribunal and the verdict, I believe, was just. I admit there may have been something of a show-trial atmosphere in that case, but that doesn't change the seriousness of the crime or the fairness of the punishment. I offered to share the trial transcript, but Nova said—"

"I said I don't want to see it. I don't want to talk about it either. My son is dead, and I don't see the point of rehashing everything."

"Of course. Excuse me. It's obviously a sensitive subject." The General looked around the circle at our sad and somber faces. "Suffice it to say that I understand Nova's pain, and I've forgiven her for what she did. I'm aware that she was trying to hurt me, but, as anyone who knows me has heard me say a hundred times, a person in the public eye can't afford to have thin skin. Unfortunately, my career afforded me many opportunities to rise above personal attacks. I learned that the best way to cope was simply to remind myself that the haters—that's what the young people call them—are to be pitied, not feared."

Barbara turned toward Nova and asked curiously, "Did you really hate Joan that much?"

"I hated everyone who had anything to do with my son's addiction, and I hated myself for not being able to save him."

"Oh, Nova. Dear friend. I'm so sorry. Did you try therapy?" Barbara innocently inquired.

Nova shook her head miserably.

"*Physician, heal thyself,*" Bree murmured.

Merritt summarized icily, "So instead of confronting your own pain and loss, you concocted a harebrained, bogus psychological theory that would allow you to harm another person and feel righteous about it."

Nova stiffened but said nothing.

The General charged into the breach. "Aubrey, please. No harm was done. Nova confessed and I forgave her. Let's move past this now."

The phone in my pocket vibrated. I figured it was Trevor sending another link. I felt horrible not replying, but I couldn't exactly whip out my phone and start texting at a time like this. I'd get back to him the minute this meeting was over. The vibrations went on a little longer, then stopped.

"I wouldn't say *no harm was done,*" Merritt asserted. Again, she addressed the therapist. "Your death threat may not have caused immediate harm, but your vindictiveness set a whole chain of events into motion. I heard from my assistant that you pressured Kathy to confront Eve about that long-ago crime. Apparently your persuasion was quite forceful. You essentially bullied her into doing something of profound personal importance to her for which she was neither fully committed nor adequately prepared."

"Bullied her? That's ridiculous," Nova countered. "I urged her to confront Eve because I believed it would have a positive impact on her mental health. I still think I was right. The unresolved conflict between those two was the elephant at the party, and it needed to be named and dealt with."

"*Oh, it was dealt with all right,*" Bree said under her breath.

Kathy spoke up. "What I did wasn't Nova's fault. *I* made the choice to confront Eve, and I take responsibility for it. Looking back, I do think it was unwise. I should have picked a different time and place, somewhere private, just the two of us, and I should have planned what I wanted to say. Instead, I got confused and hysterical and made a scene and got everyone upset. I especially ruined the weekend for Dave and me because afterward we felt we had to leave the ranch, and we were really enjoying the reunion up until then. I truly regret not keeping my emotions in check. If only I'd stopped to sort out what was really in my heart, and what I truly wanted to say, and rehearsed a little . . . or, honestly, I could have just written it all in a letter—"

"It wouldn't have made a stick of difference," Bree interrupted. "Eve's alleged brilliance was the core of her identity. Never in a million years would she have tolerated any suggestion that someone else—particularly you, my dear—was the brains behind her work, especially when it was true. You were dead meat from the moment you opened your mouth. From before that, actually."

"That doesn't mean she deserved what happened to her," said Kathy piously.

"Of course not. But the fact that she was murdered doesn't mean we need to set a golden halo around her head and beat our chests in atonement for our presumed misdeeds, just to expiate our survivor's guilt. You were horribly wronged, kiddo, and you said so, and you got mad as hell and stomped your little feet, and threw a perfectly good, very large glass of sangria in her face. You confronted your dragon with your tiny sword, and dragged the buried treasure of precious truth into the light. It was a good show, which I thoroughly enjoyed. I say to you, *Brava! Brava!* Next time, FYI, you can get the same effect with ice water."

"There won't be a next time. I don't plan on throwing a drink at anyone ever again," Kathy said contritely, but there was a pink glow of pleasure in her cheeks.

Barbara broke in impatiently, "Ladies, what are we doing? All this talk about elephants and sangria! Have you all forgotten that yesterday one of our sisters was murdered right under our noses? Each one of us has a responsibility to her, whether we liked her or not. Why aren't we talking about *that*?"

CHAPTER FIFTY-FOUR

The Sisters Convene, Part 2

Barbara's right," Merritt said. "It's time to move on to the next topic: the apparent murder attempt against Joan. If you don't mind, I'm going to step back and let my assistant, Olivia Blunt, take it from here."

What?

Five surprised and doubtful faces swiveled toward me. My mind went blank. I felt dizzy.

"Miss Blunt?" Merritt prodded with a mocking semi-smile.

I had no choice but to go for it. I told myself that, if I failed, it would be Merritt's mistake, not mine. She was pushing me onto the stage, knowing I was only 85 percent sure!

I tried to appear confident. "I think Mrs. Merritt is referring to the scorpions that someone put in General Battersea's bed. Five giant hairy ones. I'm not being flip. That particular species is actually called the giant hairy scorpion or sometimes the giant desert hairy scorpion." I was overexplaining as I scurried around my brain trying to collect my scattered thoughts. Smiling woodenly, I stumbled along. "It looked like it could have been a murder attempt. Which made sense, given the death threat General Battersea received earlier in the week. So Mrs. Merritt and I asked ourselves, Did someone try to murder General Battersea by planting scorpions in her bed? If so, who? And why?"

The women were staring at me in such puzzlement that I wondered if I'd accidentally been speaking the wrong language. But no, it wasn't that. They were simply waiting for me to say even more.

"Kathy, I give you a lot of credit here. The scorpions were a very creative idea! I mean, it looked like it *could* have been a murder attempt, but was it really? Probably not. Because they probably wouldn't have killed General Battersea even if they had stung her, unless they stung her very many times, or she was allergic, which you erroneously—in my opinion—assumed she wasn't. But the situation probably wouldn't have got that far anyway, because any normal person would definitely have noticed five of those horrible things in their bed before they stretched out between the sheets. So, again, it *looked* like a murder attempt but it *wasn't* a murder attempt. What an elegant solution! You managed to suggest that a murderer was still out there, trying hard to end the General's life, which gave credence to the idea that the General was the intended victim in the pool shooting too. In which case, Eve's death was a case of mistaken identity, and your husband was off the hook."

The sisters pondered that for a few moments. Finally Bree turned to Kathy. "Sweet Jesus. How did you get your hands on that many scorpions? Weren't you afraid to pick them up?"

"Oh, they don't scare me," Kathy explained with bashful pride. "I was a science teacher, remember? I used to adore reptiles and arachnids. I did a whole unit on them every year. The people from the zoo would come to the classroom and put on demonstrations. They let the kids touch the snakes and whatnot. And then they'd make the room dark and turn on a black light and all the scorpion exoskeletons would glow vivid green and the kids would all be screaming and jumping up and down with excitement. It was a very valuable educational experience for them." She smiled fondly at the memory.

"For you, too, apparently," Bree said dryly.

I continued. "But that's not all you did. There was also the matter of the stopped clock."

Kathy looked surprised. "Oh, you figured that out?"

"At first you had me stumped. I knew that the person who tampered with the clock had to fulfill two criteria. First, they had to have been in the house between one thirty a.m., which is the last time I heard the clock chime, and about nine o'clock this morning. Second, they somehow knew the significance of seven sixteen. For those of you who don't know, that is the time I saw on the grandfather clock shortly after the murder—a fact that put the murder at the very precise time of seven fifteen. I gave that information to Sheriff Casey and Deputy Roundtree when I spoke to them yesterday morning, and later I informed Mrs. Merritt. But they were the only people I told, and only Mrs. Merritt was in the house last night. As I didn't suspect my boss, I was left with a perplexing question: Who else could have done it?

"Then I remembered you saying that the cops grilled you for hours at the police station. Apparently, they tried to get you to rat on your husband by insisting they already had enough evidence to charge him in the murder. I'm sure they would have informed you that they had video of your RV speeding through the front gate at seven twenty-four. But the only way they could make that evidence meaningful is if they also told you that someone had noticed the time of seven sixteen on the grandfather clock soon after the gunshot.

Thus, you, Kathy Lafferty, most likely knew not only the time I'd quoted to the sheriff, but also its implications for your husband's guilt.

"You would have realized pretty quickly, I think, that the case against Dave would rest on the question of whether he could have got himself from the pool to the front gate in nine minutes—a very unlikely, but perhaps not impossible, feat for a man his age. It occurred to you that, if you could find a way of throwing the timing of the gunshot into question, you could weaken the prosecutor's key argument. Specifically, you needed to give Dave *less* time to make his hypothetical escape."

I smiled at the retired teacher. "Honestly, Kathy, I'm impressed. You were desperate to save your husband from a false accusation, so you set about dismantling the case against him any way you could."

Murmurs of approval rose from the sisters.

Kathy didn't register the compliment. Her face was slack, fearful. "Are you going to tell Sheriff Casey what I did? Because if he hears that I tampered with evidence or did anything to endanger Joan—"

Merritt broke in. "I see no reason to involve the police. Unless Joan wants to press charges against you for the scorpion fiasco."

The General blustered, "Press charges? Of course not! What would I press charges for? 'No harm, no foul' is what I always say. No, best to keep all this in the sisterhood. We do better when we stick together! Isn't that right, ladies?"

There was a lot of nodding and echoes of *That's right!*

Kathy turned to the General. "I'm really sorry, Joan. The giant hairys really aren't that dangerous. I would never have put them in your bed if I thought—"

"Of course you wouldn't have. That goes without saying. You were just trying to help your husband. No one can fault you for that." The General gave one of her big guffaws—slightly higher pitched than usual, betraying faint nervousness. "I'm just glad Olivia noticed that bump moving under the blanket when she did!"

Just then there was a knock on the door, and Jenny-Lou poked her head into the room. "Sorry to disturb your meeting, ladies. I just want to let you know that Sheriff Casey arrived and wants to see everyone in the living room right away. He has an announcement to make."

CHAPTER FIFTY-FIVE

Turf War

The bandy-legged man strutted in front of the long windows, stomach straining against his leather belt, sweat stains under his arms.

The sweep of clay-colored earth behind him appeared desolate, vaguely menacing. It was high noon. The scorching sun had driven the desert creatures into hiding. Even the snakes and scorpions had slithered under rocks or scuttled into shadowed nooks to protect their skins from the burning rays.

Inside the hacienda, the air conditioner was blasting. An unnatural chill prickled my skin. My mouth was dry and my hands were shaking, because, in addition to feeling weirdly cold, I had no idea if I was about to be fired. I had held up pretty well when Merritt put me on the spot just now at the sorority meeting. My hunch that Kathy Lafferty was behind both the scorpions and the stopped clock had turned out to be correct. I had even understood her motivation correctly, and the meeting had ended on a gratifying note of peace and unity. If you added that victory to my previous correct identification of the death threat sender, I was doing pretty well and ought to have been in good shape job-wise.

But Merritt was not one to give partial credit. There was still a final task in front of me. I needed to solve the murder of Eve Exeter pronto, and the sad truth was, I didn't have a clue. The fact that Merritt had described the solution as easy only increased my frustration.

The deadline she'd given me had just passed. She hadn't pressed me for the last answer, and now with Sheriff Casey on the scene, it looked like she wasn't going to. There was still time, but probably not much. Only luck would save me now. I quietly murmured her oft-repeated advice: *"Be a person upon whom nothing is lost."*

A few people were already present, waiting for the lawman's announcement. Barry and Alma seemed to be wondering what, if anything, would be required of them. Peter Jumper leaned his spindly frame against the back wall, making it easier to slip away when he felt like it. Jenny-Lou occupied one end of the couch, Angel on her lap. The black-and-white spaniel stared at me fixedly, the dark pebbles that were his eyes bearing an eager look. Playing fetch with him on a couple of occasions apparently had been enough to grant me Favored Human status. As more people arrived, chairs were brought in from the dining room. Merritt and I took our places at the front of the room. I was on one side of her; Kathy Lafferty was on the other.

When everyone had settled down, Sheriff Casey said, "I called this meeting to thank you for your cooperation over the last twenty-four hours, and to bring you up to speed on the status of the investigation. This morning David Lafferty was officially charged with the murder of Dr. Exeter."

Kathy immediately objected. Putting a restraining hand on her leg, Merritt whispered something to her. Kathy calmed down, but I could see it wouldn't last.

Sheriff Casey pretended not to have noticed the brief commotion. "As far as next steps go, you're free to leave the ranch now if you choose to, but I have to ask that you remain in the area for a little longer. The district attorney will be interviewing each of you at the police station in Pecos. The interviews will start later this afternoon and ought to be finished by the end of day tomorrow. Once you've spoken to the DA, you'll be able to return to your homes."

"We already told you what we know," Bree pointed out.

"The DA will have specific questions for each of you as he builds his case against the defendant."

Again, Kathy started speaking in a desperate, high-pitched voice, and I heard Merritt say to her, "Let me handle this."

Merritt approached the sheriff and said a few words to him. He nodded, and the two of them moved offstage, into the kitchen, with Nathan Roundtree and me following.

"I have information I believe is pertinent to the case," Merritt told the sheriff.

Casey squinted, sizing her up. "Are you that famous private investigator I keep hearing about?"

"I'm well-known in some circles."

"Solve all your cases, apparently."

"So far."

"And you've got information about this case?"

"I do."

The lawman shrugged, dubious but intrigued. "I suppose I can spare a minute to hear what you have to say."

Merritt nodded at me, and I immediately produced the only physical evidence we had: photos of damp shoe prints in the cabana.

I then grabbed notepaper and a broken pencil from a utility drawer and sketched a rudimentary map showing the pool, cabana, stable, parking lot, and the route to the front entrance. I kept the distances between locations roughly to scale and added a few bullet points.

- *Gunshot: 7:15.*
- *Video of Laffertys' RV: 7:24.*
- *Time elapsed: Nine minutes.*
- *Escape route reenactment: Fourteen minutes.*
- *Mr. Lafferty: over sixty years old, significantly overweight, atrial fibrillation.*
- *Conclusion: Mr. Lafferty could not have been the murderer.*

Sheriff Casey frowned and pressed his lips together. "That's all very interesting. But why would Lafferty have gone through the cabana? Going through the gate would have cut off two sides of a triangle and got him to his RV a lot faster. He wouldn't have had any trouble getting off the ranch in nine minutes if he went that way."

I blinked slowly. Had I not been clear enough? Once again, I showed him my photo of the footprints. "These footprints indicate that the killer escaped through the cabana."

"I didn't see any footprints."

"They were probably dry by the time you and your forensic team arrived. And maybe you didn't go into the cabana right away. But here . . . see . . . ?" I pointed at one of the prints. "This picture was taken minutes after the murder. The outline is very faint, but it's definitely a footprint. There was a trail stretching from the front door to the back. The back door leads to a dirt path that skirts the stables, passes the guesthouse, and dumps you in the parking lot. Like I showed you."

Casey shook his head. "My people didn't find any footprints."

"We did, as you can clearly see. I'll send you these photos so you can add them to your file."

"Don't bother. I couldn't use them as evidence. There's no telling when they were taken, or even where they were taken."

"There's a time stamp right there!" I pointed at it, feeling desperate.

"Doesn't matter. Where physical evidence is concerned, I stick to what my forensic people tell me. They're professionals and they're very good at what they do."

I stared at him in consternation. He seemed to be misunderstanding everything. How could I convince him? "Let's just say then, for the sake of argument, that Dave Lafferty *did* take the shorter route to the parking lot. In that case, how do you explain these photos?"

"Honey, I don't even know there *were* footprints. I know that's what you're trying to convince me of, and you've got some fuzzy pictures there on your phone, but I didn't see any footprints where you say they were. I didn't see any at all, matter of fact. Neither did my people. As far as I'm concerned, there weren't any."

I felt dizzy all of a sudden, as if the ground had been yanked out from under me. Could he *do* that? Just ignore our evidence? Was that even legal? I looked at Merritt helplessly.

She took over. "You brought Mr. Lafferty to the police station for questioning this morning, but you didn't formally charge him with murder until late this afternoon. You must have found something in the interim, some kind of conclusive evidence. What was it? Did you get prints off the cartridge?"

"Sadly, no. The cartridge was clean. But we found gunshot residue on clothing in the suspect's camper, and his fingerprints were on the gun case." Casey swelled with confidence. He clearly believed himself to be on solid ground.

Merritt's eyes flashed. "Are you not aware that many of the guests,

Mr. Lafferty among them, were engaged in recreational shooting the day before the murder? You'll find gunshot residue on the clothing of five or six other people on this ranch as well. And those same folks would have been opening and closing the gun cabinet all afternoon."

Casey's color rose. "What are you trying to say?"

"That your evidence is useless. It won't stand up in a court of law."

The cop glared at her but didn't speak.

I wanted to cheer. Casey had kneecapped my argument; now Merritt had demolished his! I waited eagerly to see what would happen next.

Merritt changed her tone to one of gentle cooperation. "You and I have the same goal, Sheriff. We both want to bring a killer to justice. I would like to ask you for a small favor now, if I might. The possibility exists that Mr. Lafferty is innocent of this charge and the real murderer is in the other room. If you would give me a little time to ask a few questions of the people gathered there, there's a good chance that I'll be able to expose that person and prove their guilt."

"That's a pretty big claim you're making there," the lawman drawled.

"A half hour, that's all I ask. Thirty minutes. If I come up short, no harm done. You'll still have Mr. Lafferty in custody."

Sheriff Casey exchanged glances with Deputy Roundtree, whose eager expression clearly showed where he stood: He wanted to see the renowned detective in action.

Casey hitched his thumbs in his leather belt and shrugged his big shoulders. "All right. Lead the way, Mrs. Merritt. Let's see what you can do."

CHAPTER FIFTY-SIX

The Hard Part

The people in the living room were talking in low tones among themselves, no doubt impatient at the delay. They looked up expectantly as we entered, and then confusedly as Merritt instead of Casey took the floor.

She didn't waste time with introductions. "As some of you are aware, the Muddy River Ranch saw some troubling incidents over the last few days, but there was only one serious crime: the murder of our Sigma Delta Tau sister Eve Exeter. Before I say anything more about it, I'd like us all to observe a moment of silence to honor her."

The room grew quiet. I scanned the assembled group. The murderer was here, if Merritt was to be believed. But who was it? Most heads were solemnly bowed, except for Conrad Zander's. He was gazing straight at me with an undisguised lecherous smirk. Ugh. I pointedly ignored him and proceeded to the next person who was showing no respect for the dead: Peter Jumper. Mouth agape, he was staring at the plaster ceiling as if it were a fascinating new invention. Not for the first time, I wondered what was up with him. Barbara Korn's expression was undeniably sad. Her husband, Jacob, was not by her side but across the room, hunched over his phone, shoulders curved down like the two sides of an emoji frown. Fitz and the General were sitting close together. They looked bewildered and miserable. Poor souls, they couldn't get their heads around what their weekend had wrought.

When enough time had passed, Merritt raised her head and announced, "I believe I have identified Eve's killer, and I'd like to share that information with you now."

Everyone sat up a little straighter and gave the detective their full attention—the innocent with hope and curiosity; the guilty party, whoever it was, most likely with fear and dread.

She looked smart in her white linen, even though the hems of the pants were sullied by red dirt from our near-fatal trek to the river and the delicate Pedro García sandals would never be what they once were. At some point between then and now, she had taken the time to brush her bright silvery hair smoothly off her forehead, cool her previously flushed complexion down to its usual alabaster white, and apply her favorite fiery red lipstick. I had often marveled at her ability to exactly calibrate her social presence: She could command a room effortlessly whenever she wanted to; or she could fade into obscurity, becoming just another harmless old lady whose value to society had long since passed. Now, of course, she was assuming her full magnetic power. She stood straight, and her vivid dark blue gaze was level and direct. It seemed to travel slightly over the heads of her audience.

"Eve's murder has been an unusual and perplexing case for me. On one hand, it was devilishly challenging; on the other, absurdly simple. The first challenge came from the fact that it wasn't immediately clear who the killer's intended target was. The death threat Joan received earlier this week raised the possibility that *she* was the intended victim and Eve's death was an unfortunate mistake.

"As you can imagine, lack of clarity about what is, perhaps, the most fundamental aspect of a murder investigation creates numerous complications. In this case, my assistant and I had no choice but to embark on two investigations simultaneously—one into the murder of Eve Exeter, another into the possible attempted murder of Joan Battersea.

"The second challenge we encountered was an alarming paucity of evidence. Usually a killer leaves behind some trace of himself, or makes some small mistake. After Eve's death, although my assistant and I combed the crime scene diligently not long after the murder took place, we were able to find only one clue: a trail of damp footprints that were almost dry by the time we discovered them, and thus yielded no identifiable tread marks. Even the shoe size could not be reliably determined. With nothing more to go on than these ghostly traces, all we could say for sure about the killer was that he had passed through the cabana when his shoes were wet—presumably from a puddle of water the victim had splashed onto the side of the pool either as she tried to escape or as she suffered and died.

"Despite this inauspicious beginning, my assistant and I set about diligently doing our work. Over the course of numerous interviews, we uncovered the expected complement of grudges, secrets, jealousies, resentments, regrets, and general unhappiness, until finally, through some rather imaginative investigative work, Miss Blunt was able to identify the author of the death threat."

I couldn't believe my ears. Merritt was giving me public credit for my contribution! I inwardly smiled at the way *far-fetched* had morphed into *imaginative.* Maybe she was finally willing to recognize the value of my unique approach to crime solving (if that's what it was).

A few audience members nodded at me with respect and gratitude, and I smiled with suitable modesty. The warm, fuzzy feelings in my heart were really lovely to experience, but I was quickly jolted back to reality. Merritt's earlier promise to fire me hadn't been rescinded. The fact remained that I had missed the deadline to solve the last of the three crimes, and it was too late to rectify that situation now, even if I could have (which I couldn't), because Merritt was in the process, apparently, of doing it herself. Now I felt foolish for having so greedily gobbled up the crumb of recognition she'd tossed in my direction, as it might actually have been her sly way of helping to ease me out the door.

I listened as she explained to the audience that she had nothing further to say about the death threat. The matter had been privately discussed and adjudicated, and the concerned parties had agreed to move on.

"With the confusion stemming from that lesser crime behind us," she continued, "it was reasonable to assume that Dr. Exeter had indeed been the killer's intended target. Therefore, Miss Blunt and I proceeded along that investigative path. We were naturally aware that Sheriff Casey had taken the Laffertys into police custody, and that Kathy had been questioned and released. She reported to us that Dave was the primary suspect, that search warrants were being obtained, and that he would very likely be charged with the crime. The die was cast, it seemed.

"That was a low point for me, as I suddenly had to change my priority from proactively finding Eve's killer to reactively checking the sheriff's evidence against Dave Lafferty. That is not the kind of effort I enjoy. I would much rather follow my own instincts than look over other people's shoulders. The point became moot, however, when we were all blindsided by a wholly unexpected event: what appeared to be the attempted murder of Joan via scorpion attack. Now Miss Blunt and I were thrown back on our heels once more, needing to readjust our priorities and proceed along multiple paths at once.

"Fortune smiled then, as it does sometimes in the most subtle and beguiling ways, often when one is stumbling in the thickest clouds of doubt. Shortly after rising this morning, I realized that I wasn't hearing the periodic chiming of the grandfather clock—a rhythm I had apparently internalized. I could recall hearing the clock at midnight when Miss Blunt and I were talking in my room. In fact, the gongs had rung out so loudly that we'd stayed quiet through all twelve strikes. I recalled hearing it again not long after that, when Miss Blunt left my room—a single strike that would have been either twelve thirty or one a.m. But now in the morning the grandfather clock was silent, and when I went to investigate, I saw that the pendulum was motionless.

"That was it. That was the key that turned the lock. I won't lead you through the circuitous thought process that followed that seemingly mundane observation. Suffice it to say that I was soon able to identify the culprit in the apparent attempt on Joan's life. I was greatly relieved. The separate crimes that had confused the investigation had at last been cleared away, leaving me free to focus my attention on the one question that remained: Who shot Eve Exeter as she swam alone in the pool shortly after seven a.m. yesterday?"

Merritt smiled at her listeners. "Do you remember when I told you that the case was both extremely difficult and absurdly easy? Well, I explained the hard part. Now I come to what was easy."

CHAPTER FIFTY-SEVEN

The Easy Part

The case broke open for me with one simple realization: I'd been approaching the problem from the wrong angle. Following usual investigative practices, I'd been digging into possible motives and searching for evidence when simple opportunity was all I needed. Whoever shot Dr. Exeter at that time, at that place, would have to have known, not only that she would be there, but also that she would be alone.

"Who fit that category? Well, anyone at the barbecue could have overheard Joan, Eve, and Barbara discussing their plan to meet at the pool the next morning. Even the people who weren't present could have been told by others who were. But who knew that Joan had sprained her ankle and canceled? Only Eve, because Joan told her via text; and Barbara, because Eve texted her and Barbara replied to the text, so we know she read it.

"The change of plans happened after midnight, so it's reasonable to assume that the news of Joan's cancellation would not have traveled beyond Eve and Barbara. Unless, of course, either one or both of the women mentioned it to their husbands.

"The suspect list was now quite short. Only three individuals could have fatally shot Eve: Barbara Korn, Jacob Korn, and Conrad Zander."

In the lull that followed, people turned in their seats and craned their necks to glimpse the three suspects. Each wore a different expression. Barbara looked startled and upset; Jacob appeared scornful; Conrad Zander wore his usual supercilious smile.

"I ruled out Barbara fairly quickly," Merritt said.

"I should hope so!" Barbara exclaimed. "Everyone knows I would never hurt Eve. I adored her! She was the only true friend I ever had."

Merritt sighed. She disliked having to take time out of her presentation to educate the uninformed. "That's not why I crossed you off the suspect list, Barbara. Strong feelings—whether of hate or love—actually *increase* the likelihood that their bearer will engage in a violent act. And frankly, considering the deplorable way Eve treated you, I had no trouble imagining you lashing out in a moment of unbridled rage."

"Then why did you cross me off the list?"

"Your gun-handling skills are abysmal. That's what my assistant told me after observing you at the shooting range. Apparently you couldn't hold the barrel straight in front of you and were too discombobulated to pull the trigger. Now, while there is anecdotal evidence suggesting that in rare instances intense anger can improve a shooter's skills, I judged that your deficits in that department were too great to overcome."

Barbara appeared perplexed, as if she couldn't decide whether to be relieved or offended.

Merritt paced in front of the sun-bright windows, her manner determined and her voice crisp. "You, Mr. Korn, were next on my list."

"I have an alibi. I was here at the house. Check the CCTV camera if you don't believe me."

"I did. And there was indeed footage of you entering the hacienda through the side door at six fifty-two a.m. But your behavior was rather odd. Before you opened the door, you stopped and tilted up your head to stare fixedly at the camera for four seconds. Now, four seconds may not sound like a lot, but it is a very long time to gaze into the blank lens of an overhead camera. Unless you wanted to make very sure that the camera recorded you entering the house at that particular time, and that your identity would not be mistaken."

"Hey, I'm a tech guy. I like cameras. I wanted to see what kind it was."

"Uh-huh. What kind is it?" asked Merritt.

Jacob scowled.

Merritt went on to her next point. "Another thing I found odd was your reason for going to the hacienda so early in the morning: You said you needed a quiet place to catch up on work. Yet if you'd simply waited for your wife to go to the pool as she intended, you could have stayed in the room and had all the privacy you needed."

"I didn't want to wake her," Jacob said.

"Exactly. You didn't want to wake her. Despite having woken her many times in the past when she overslept, as apparently she has a tendency to do."

"This is different. We're on vacation."

"True again. This is indeed a special time. And as you knew how eager your wife was to enjoy every possible moment with her friends, I would think that yesterday morning would have been the one instance when you would have been sure to remind her of her plan. Yet you left her sleeping alone in the room at precisely the time she should have been awake and getting ready."

"This is a ridiculous conversation. Why are we even talking about this?"

"And why, Mr. Korn, when you said you needed a quiet place to work, would you have set up your laptop on the dining room table, which was likely to become noisy as guests arrived for breakfast? Certainly the den or the veranda would have afforded you more privacy."

"Oh, come on. You're reading way too much into everything."

"True. Each detail is minor and can be explained away. But taken together, they formed a pattern: You wanted to be seen."

Jacob started to protest, but Merritt barreled on. "I suspect you did something else too. I think you silenced your wife's phone so her alarm wouldn't go off. You knew that after several unaccustomed glasses of sangria and the jet lag she was still complaining of, silencing her alarm was all you needed to do to prevent her from showing up at the pool. And who would ever know you'd done it? Keeping a phone on silent mode is a mistake anyone can make. You figured Barbara would blame herself. And she did."

"Oh no, no way." He waved off the accusation. "That's pure speculation. There's no way you can prove that."

"I didn't need to prove it. I only needed to create a theory of how the crime might have unfolded, and follow that path where it led."

"Theory of what? A theory that I shot my wife's friend? You know I couldn't have done it. My alibi is solid. I was here at the hacienda the entire time."

"Never fear, Mr. Korn. I know you didn't murder Eve. You were just an accessory. Your job was to keep Barbara away from the pool, and you did your job quite well. You silenced her phone, and then, knowing what would soon happen, you went about the business of giving yourself an airtight alibi. I'm afraid you tried a little too hard, though. The extra effort you put into being noticed raised my suspicions right away."

CHAPTER FIFTY-EIGHT

Dead End

"Who is left among the three? Only you, Conrad."

Raising his chin, Conrad Zander said with suave pomposity, "What an absurd creature you turned into, Aubrey. A world-famous detective—is that what you call yourself? I confess I don't see it. No, what I'm seeing is just another old woman, years past her prime, trying to convince the world she's important."

Whoa! No one—and I do mean *no one*—had ever spoken to my boss so disrespectfully before, at least not that I'd witnessed. I wanted to punch Conrad Zander in his smug face, and I just might have done it, too, had not Merritt carried on as smoothly as ever, without so much as a blink or wobble.

"For my own sake, for the pleasure I take in my work, I wish you'd been a worthier opponent," she said. "You see, Conrad, the great, gaping blind spot of a narcissist is that he overestimates his own abilities while underestimating the abilities of others. Trapped inside the cage of delusion, he is forever incapable of perceiving reality clearly. That is not a smart way to be, my friend. It leads inevitably to mistakes."

Merritt's incisive clapback infuriated the businessman, though not for the reason I expected. "Mistakes? What mistakes? There were no mistakes! Other than a couple of faded footprints, which you admitted were no use to you."

"Ah, you sound so pleased with yourself! You really believe you pulled off the perfect murder, don't you? Is that why you kept loitering at the crime scene? Did you enjoy watching the forensic team do their work and walk away empty-handed? And did you keep your vigil after they were gone, not to mourn your dear wife, but to admire your spotless handiwork? I think so. The lack of crime scene evidence was your ace in the hole, or so you thought. You were depending on it to keep you safe if the case against Dave Lafferty fell through."

The businessman should have looked anxious or angry; instead, he was positively gloating. "Correct me if I'm wrong, my dear Aubrey, but I do believe you're acknowledging that there is no conclusive evidence linking me to the crime scene."

"That's unfortunately true, for now. But before you start congratulating yourself, let me say that I've never encountered a perfect murder, not in thirty years as a private investigator. Something always shows. The killer always makes a mistake. I doubt that you're the one exception to this rule. Keep in mind that I've been investigating your wife's murder for less than two days and have already identified you and your coconspirator. A full police investigation—one that takes as much time as it needs—is bound to uncover evidence that will prove your guilt."

"Ridiculous," he sneered. Then, to put a finer point on it, he added, "Preposterous, utterly farcical."

Merritt let all the words roll off her. "And while there may be no physical evidence yet, there's plenty of circumstantial evidence that will warrant further questioning by the police. Indeed, you made one mistake after another, Conrad. And the first was the most glaring: You didn't ask for my help. Imagine it if you can: A man's wife has been brutally murdered, there's a highly regarded detective standing right next to him, yet he doesn't immediately seek her advice.

"At first I chalked it up to garden-variety misogyny; then I noticed that you didn't approach Sheriff Casey either. Ninety-nine out of a hundred people would have been demanding action and accountability; you slunk away. And when I finally cornered you at the pool, you immediately placed the blame on Mr. Lafferty and ardently insisted on his guilt, despite the glaringly obvious problems with that theory.

"Your behavior troubled me enough that I laid a very simple trap for you: I told you there was clear evidence pointing to a different killer, that I was on the verge of discovering who this person was. An innocent person would have been grateful, eager to help. But your narcissism wouldn't let you do that. The mere suggestion that your crime wasn't perfect rankled, and you became argumentative.

"First you needed to take me down a peg, so you asserted that a supposedly higher authority than me, the forensic team, had informed you that the killer didn't leave a trace—something they never would have said. Then you tried to bully me into revealing my evidence. When I refused, you all but demanded it in your domineering way, and I refused again. At that point you changed your strategy. You decided to feed me a reason to exclude you as a suspect. You said you were raised as a Quaker and lived by the Quaker ethic of nonviolence. You wouldn't touch a gun, you said."

Merritt shook her head in mock disappointment. "Your cleverness brought you far in life, so naturally you relied on it to take you through this crisis too. But it's possible to be too clever—an error no intelligent person would make.

"If only you'd had enough sense to retreat at that point. But you simply couldn't accept that an old woman like me was refusing to do your bidding. So you tried to create a back channel into my investigation through my assistant. Here again your arrogance did you no favors. The decades you spent harassing your female students apparently implanted in your brain the pathetic assumption that no young woman could resist your advances. Miss Blunt, not far off in age from your usual prey, would be an easy mark, you thought. You behaved with her just as you had with me. When your first attempt at manipulation failed, you changed your strategy. You tried to drag her into a partnership. When that attempt also failed, you tried to buy her fealty by promising her admission to your elite university."

Merritt gave a sad, knowing smile. "As the proverb says, 'There's no fool like an old fool,' and an elderly narcissist is the biggest fool of all."

Conrad Zander folded his arms across his chest and coldly addressed his accuser. "Be careful, my dear, or you'll find yourself faced with a defamation lawsuit."

Bree waved her arm in the air like an excited student. "Aubrey, what about motive? Can you tell us why he did it?"

"I cannot," Merritt said simply. "I have no idea what his motive was. Or why Mr. Korn agreed to follow him down the dark path. But the law does not require motive to convict a man of murder."

Bree turned a perplexed face to the businessman. "You must have had a reason, Conrad. If you did shoot Eve, I mean."

"I don't have to listen to any more of this," Conrad Zander said, but he made no attempt to leave.

There was a small commotion in the back of the room. Barbara stood up. In a baggy cotton dress, her hair a mess, she looked haggard and unkempt. She addressed the room in a soft, mournful voice. "I think I know why he did it. Why Jacob did it too. It was because of the IPO. That was it, wasn't it?" She looked from one man to the other for confirmation, as if they would give it. "Conrad? Jacob? Wasn't that the reason?"

When neither man responded, she looked at Merritt. "I'm sure that was it."

Merritt asked her to explain.

What Barbara said boiled down to this: Negative product reviews for Sirt-X had started cropping up on a Reddit discussion board. Customers were complaining of rashes that varied in intensity from mild to severe. Eve had been quite concerned and had told Barbara all about it. She suspected that Sirt-X was triggering an immune response, and she wanted to do more testing. Unfortunately, the kind of testing she wanted—double-blind, placebo controlled—was extremely expensive and time-consuming, and would indefinitely delay the long-awaited IPO presently scheduled for October. Conrad had vehemently opposed the idea of further testing. He was ready and eager for the big payday they'd all been working for. But Eve was adamant. She refused to go forward until the safety issues were addressed.

I found myself grinning with delight. There was the missing motive, spelled out for us with a capital *M*!

"You're sure about this?" Merritt asked her.

"I heard Jacob and Conrad discussing the situation on a few occasions; the last time was about a week ago. They were really angry and frustrated, saying what an idiot Eve was being. Jacob said this was a hell of a time for her to grow a conscience."

Jacob broke in, "You're dreaming, Babs. I never said that. I didn't even know about the damn reviews."

"You definitely did, Jacob. I told you about them myself, after I'd talked to Eve. I heard you and Conrad discussing them. Conrad wanted you to use your tech skills to make them go away."

"Shows how little you know. You can't make things on the internet *go away.* Once they're there, they stay forever."

"I know that. But you can do other things. Like, you can flood the search results, or put them in different priorities—things like that. That's your specialty at work. If anyone would know how to bury negative reviews, it's you."

"As usual, you have no idea what you're talking about. I'm a Cross-Platform Integration Systems Research and Development Manager, which has nothing to do with *flooding* search results, whatever the hell *that* means."

The couple glared at each other across the room. I wondered if we would soon have a double murder on our hands.

On a personal note, I was relieved. I had researched Lifespan from every angle I could think of, just as I'd examined many of the entities connected to the reunion guests. I'd found no red flags, nothing to raise alarm. If Barbara was right, and Jacob had buried the negative reviews, then that would explain why I'd missed them.

Merritt turned to the businessman. "What do you say, Conrad? Did you murder your wife to keep your company's IPO on track?"

"Oh, come on, Aubrey. You're not really going to take Barbara seriously, are you? The idea that I would shoot my wife over a business decision is utterly laughable. I'm getting tired of this charade now. You're not a brilliant detective, and you should stop pretending you are. It's undignified in a woman your age. Until and unless you can produce concrete evidence of my guilt—which you just admitted you don't have—I must insist that you stop playing this silly game. Your behavior is unconscionable and irresponsible. I think I may have to file a complaint against you with your professional organization."

That's when I knew for sure Conrad Zander really was the killer. It was the snidely delighted way he kept coming back to the question of evidence and Merritt's lack thereof—as if he was basking in the beautiful perfection of his crime. Sadly, though, my gut feeling didn't help anything. As Merritt had drilled into me a dozen times, feelings don't solve crimes. Only evidence can do that.

Means, opportunity, motive. Conrad Zander had all three. Yet there he sat, dripping with smug complacency, believing he couldn't be caught, and possibly being right.

It was a detective's nightmare.

CHAPTER FIFTY-NINE

Hail Mary

All this time the people in the room had been quiet and engrossed, moving their heads back and forth like spectators at a tennis match, as they watched Merritt and Conrad Zander spar. Now, in the wake of the businessman's insulting speech, they started to murmur and stir. Fitz grunted, the General whispered something to Barbara, and Nova Olsen slipped her notebook into her capacious purse. Everyone seemed to have wordlessly agreed that the show was over and Conrad Zander had won.

I saw Sheriff Casey raise his palms to Merritt in a gesture that said, *That's it? That's all you've got?*

He had a point. Opportunity pointed directly at Zander, but by itself it couldn't prove the case. Zander's postmurder behavior had been odd and reprehensible, but not a compelling argument for his guilt. The business conflict Barbara had described was a plausible motive for murder, but even that was not enough.

The hard fact was, Merritt hadn't closed the deal. She had no evidence.

I blamed it on the lack of time. The murder was less than thirty-six hours old; as recently as this morning, we'd still been thinking the General might have been the intended target. The arrest of Dave Lafferty had added pressure to the situation. Then, minutes ago, Sheriff Casey had announced that his net was tightening around Dave and everyone could go home soon, thus forcing Merritt's hand. She'd had no choice but to go forward with what she had—which was good, but insufficient. Soon Conrad Zander and the other guests would scatter to different states, and Sheriff Casey would probably revert to his original suspect. While Aubrey Merritt experienced the first failure of her storied career.

She stood silent, lips pursed, eyes sharply intelligent as usual, but squinting, as if she was searching for clues she might have missed. She didn't seem embarrassed or defeated or diminished in any way, as I would have been. But she must have realized she was all but beat.

I could think of several developments that would help the situation: (1) the cops getting Jacob Korn to squeal (but why would he do that when it would only implicate himself?); (2) Barbara remembering something else she'd seen or heard and coughing up a gem of a clue; (3) forensics lifting a print off the shotgun after all; or (4) a new witness who could place Zander at the pool around the time of the murder. But these were all Hail Marys. Just a rookie's long-shot hope that a little miracle would turn a probable loss into a sudden win.

Damn it, my phone was vibrating again! I was sure it was Trevor. I really didn't want him to feel frustrated or worried, but there honestly could not have been a worse time for us to talk. I couldn't possibly discuss apartments with him when every second that passed was bringing Merritt and me closer to professional ruin. Right now

I needed to focus all my energy on detecting. I gritted my teeth until the vibrating stopped.

People were standing up and starting to leave the room. Peter Jumper slipped out the door, and Jenny-Lou set Angel down on the ground to roam where he would. Liberated from his mistress's embrace, the spaniel sat perkily on his haunches, and stared at me intently from across the room. Did he know I still had the orange ball in my pocket? For me at that moment his behavior was annoying, so I moved a foot or two to my left, which brought me in line with Conrad Zander, still ensconced in his throne-like wingback chair in the middle of the room. Was he really going to get away with murder? Was there truly no way to pin the crime on him? In near-hopeless desperation, I closed my eyes, turned inward, and let my thoughts unspool. Once again I glimpsed the killer's fleeing shadow and saw that faint trail of footprints—the only physical evidence we had—and then, like a sudden gift, the answer appeared.

I reached into my pocket and took out the ball. When I held it up so Angel could see it clearly, his tail started to thump. I was glad for all the bocce I'd played with my dad at the park near our house, because I was pretty good at rolling balls to precise locations. I took careful aim and rolled it across the rug. It came to rest about three inches from Zander's feet. Angel happily trotted over and clamped it in his jaw. Then something else got his attention. He dropped the ball and sniffed one of Zander's canvas boat shoes. And kept sniffing. Top, sides, all around the shoe. Zander jerked his foot to shove the dog away. The spaniel fell back a foot or two, then doggedly returned and resumed his important business.

Angel was really intrigued by what he was smelling on Conrad Zander's shoes.

CHAPTER SIXTY

Dusk and Peace

The blood was invisible to the naked eye. First, because it was very faint, having come from the blood-tinged pool water the wounded Eve Exeter had splashed onto the concrete as she tried to escape the shooter. Second, because Zander's canvas boat shoes were a dark gray color that hid stains. But those things were no hindrance to Angel, upon whom Evolution, ever wise and generous, had bestowed an olfactory superpower.

As the spaniel was reveling in his discovery, I approached Merritt and whispered what I thought was going on. She glanced over at Conrad Zander, who was shuffling his feet about in an ineffective effort to avoid the canine's nose. I couldn't tell if he understood what was happening. Merritt spoke privately to Sheriff Casey and, as everyone was leaving the living room, no doubt disappointed by the great detective's failure to solve the case, the lawman asked Zander to remain.

Zander was taken to the police station in Pecos for questioning. When the blue glow of luminol revealed traces of blood on his shoes, he was put in a cell, the same one Dave Lafferty was released from. Merritt and I were confident that DNA analysis would identify the blood as Eve Exeter's.

Zander's arrest caused a stir among the guests. People couldn't stop talking about it, but as afternoon shifted to evening, and the muted colors of dusk softened the air, an atmosphere of quiet calm suffused the household. Everyone was kinder and spoke in gentler tones. Nova Olsen and the General murmured together as if they were indeed old friends. Appreciated from the shaded comfort of the veranda, the desert seemed a more benign and tranquil place, and the sunset streaks of pink and orange in the western sky looked especially glorious.

This was what Merritt and I worked for—not money or fame, but the deeply felt peace and harmony of a world restored to order. The fact that those moments were fleeting didn't diminish their power.

The appearance of Jacob Korn would have ruined the mood, so I was glad when he kept to his room. It was unclear what, if anything, would happen to him. Manipulating Google searches to bury negative product reviews was not a crime, as far as I knew. Neither was silencing your partner's phone, staring at a CCTV camera for four seconds, or working on your laptop in a dining room. Our best hope was that Zander had texted Korn in the hours before the murder, asking him to keep Barbara away from the pool, and that Korn had replied in the affirmative. Of course, if Zander really was the criminal mastermind he believed himself to be, he would have avoided using any of his electronic devices, but I wasn't ruling it out. One of the more astonishing things I'd learned in the course of my apprenticeship was that even the most cunning villains couldn't seem to stay off their phones.

Jacob did suffer a more immediate penalty. At dinner, Barbara announced that she'd informed her husband that she was filing for divorce. Tearing up a little, she admitted, "I should have done this a long time ago." Her sorority sisters offered enthusiastic support. Everyone agreed that she was making the right choice, that after a brief, bumpy transition, life would open up for her, confidence and energy would return, and she would be happier than ever before.

Merritt and I graciously accepted the warm congratulations offered to us, but we knew that luck had played a bigger role than we could be comfortable with. First Merritt had zeroed in on opportunity, then Barbara's unexpected story had established motive, and then my last-minute gambit had provided evidence. Without those last two serendipitous developments, the murder of Eve Exeter would not have been solved in the short time allotted. Merritt privately bemoaned how close we had come to failure. A full case review when we were back at the office was called for, she said. I maintained that we'd actually done an amazing job in an unusually complicated situation that had forced us to solve two minor crimes even as we tackled a brutal killing. If our final act had been a bit improvisational, I argued, that was to our credit too.

"Self-congratulations is unwarranted in this instance, Blunt, just as it is in all situations. Excessive self-regard is the enemy of good detective work."

"I was only saying—"

"Don't. The truth is that we were saved by an aggrieved wife and a playful spaniel. I don't ever want to come that close to failure again."

"Still . . . when you consider that there were actually three crimes all mixed up with each other! And the time was so short!"

"A detective must work within the given parameters of each case, however unfavorable they might be. Our clients don't want to hear excuses."

I muttered a few crusty words under my breath.

Merritt sailed on. "Certain aspects of the case haven't been explained to my satisfaction. If the rashes Sirt-X users experienced really were mild and rare, why was Eve so keen to embark on lengthy human trials that would have delayed the IPO indefinitely and possibly bankrupted the company? The legal case against Conrad can proceed without an answer to that question. Nevertheless, as an investigator, I'd like to know. I'm sure you'd like to know as well, Blunt, or you ought to. Every case has something new to teach us about human psychology. Not even I can afford to let a lesson go to waste."

"How can we find out?"

"Barbara's our best bet. She was close to Eve for years. I suspect she knows more than she has said so far."

So after dinner that night, we took Barbara aside and spent a long time listening to her stories. It was an oddly pleasant experience. There was a new lightness to her, almost a giddiness. Her eyes and smile had a sparkle that hadn't been there before. Eve's murder had done her the priceless favor of revealing the true depth of her husband's depravity, and after decades of feeling lost in the dismal swamp of her marriage, she had finally stepped out of the mire onto firm, sunny ground. Since there was no question anymore about her being loyal to Jacob or Conrad Zander—or even Eve, for that matter—she answered all our questions gladly and with plenty of detail.

CHAPTER SIXTY-ONE

Trevor Has Something to Say

My phone vibrated as we were leaving Barbara. I saw Trevor's name on my screen and nearly cried. I had forgotten to text him back all day! I motioned to Merritt that I was going to take the call. She went on without me and I headed upstairs to my room, holding the phone to my ear.

"Olly, what's going on? You didn't reply to my texts! Have you looked at that link yet?" He sounded irritated.

"I'm sorry, Trevor. I'll do it now. You sent three links, right?"

"I sent the same link three times."

"It's been so busy here—just one thing after another. But at least I've got good news! Merritt solved the case a few hours ago. I did a pretty good job of assisting, I thought." I added that last part with a sort of bashful pride, hoping he might want to take a moment to applaud.

"A few hours ago? You could have looked at the apartment then!" He was definitely irritated.

"I'm really sorry. But it was super hectic around here. And, frankly, kind of exciting, too, and a little terrifying, actually, if you count being in the same room as a person who killed his wife terrifying."

"Well, will you open the link now, please?"

"Sure. I'll take a look and get back to you right away," I said in a chipper-sounding voice.

"I need your answer in the next five minutes. I think this apartment is perfect. If you agree, I'll call the broker's office tonight and leave a message that we want to take it, and I'll be at their office first thing in the morning to drop off the deposit check. We can't miss this one, Olivia. We need a July first move-in date, and the websites aren't even listing July apartments anymore. They've moved on to August, September, and into the fall."

"Okay. I'll do it right now. But, Trevor, if this place doesn't work out, that's no big deal, right? We can just stay where we are."

"No, we can't. Our apartment isn't ours after July first. It's already been rented to someone else."

I had known that, sort of.

"You don't seem to get what's going on here, Olivia. We have a deadline, and the New York rental market is a jungle. When I've gone to these showings, there's, like, a line of people waiting to get in to see the places. If you like what you see, you have to be ready to pounce. Frankly, the whole thing is stressing me out, and if you really want to know, I don't like doing it alone, especially since this move was mostly your idea. You're the one who was constantly moaning that our place is too small."

"You sound kind of mad."

"I am! How can I not be? I spent the last two days scouring websites and trekking all over New York, and just when I find a place I think is really great—that is actually within our budget and may be the last July apartment left in the entire city—and all I want is for you to give it one minute of your time so I can grab it before someone else does, you go all Dr. Watson on me."

"I really hate it when you make fun of what I do."

"Fine. I'm sorry. But I am frustrated. I sent you three texts today, and you didn't reply to any one of them. It feels like I'm doing all the work, and you couldn't care less!"

"Of course I care. I care a lot! But if I happened to be a little preoccupied today, maybe it was because PEOPLE WERE BEING MURDERED HERE!"

"They're always being murdered where you are, Olivia. When are the people around you *not* being murdered?"

I had no answer for that.

"I'll call you back in five minutes," I said.

The apartment looked fine. It wasn't amazing and it didn't have a laundry closet or big windows, but it did have a tiny dishwasher and a southern exposure with only partially obstructed views. The floors were parquet, which I hated, but they would be mostly covered with rugs, and the whole place was freshly painted. The paint color was stark white, which I personally found kind of blinding, but at least the rooms looked fresh and clean. Best of all, there was a small window at the end of the narrow galley kitchen where I could grow my herbs.

I texted Trevor. It's beautiful and perfect. You're awesome and I love you. Thank you for finding this beautiful home for us (and for putting up with me).

I sat there cross-legged on my bed, staring at my phone. He was probably leaving a message on the broker's voicemail and maybe then he'd just go to bed. He probably wouldn't get back to me until the morning. But I kept staring at my phone anyway. Then, magically, the screen lit up. I eagerly read his message.

Good night, Sherlock. Sweet dreams.

I thought, *I really, really, really ought to let the Sherlock thing go.* In the scheme of things, it wasn't important at all. But I'd already told him I didn't appreciate *Watson,* so what made him think I'd be okay with *Sherlock*?

Before I could stop myself, I texted: I'm not sure how I feel about you calling me Sherlock. It makes this sound like it's a game and it isn't. There are real dead bodies here, real dead people. People crying and scared they might be next. I know you mean well and it is kind of cute, I guess, to call me Sherlock, and I don't want to overreact, but I'm just not feeling the Sherlock vibe right now. And, to be clear, I won't ever be feeling it. Okay with you?

Absolutely. You know I love you and if Sherlock isn't working for you I hereby strike it from my vocabulary forever.

You don't have to go that far.

True. I will only go as far as needed. Good night, Olly. Watch out for flying bullets. (Can I say that?)

That's less of a joke than you might think.

You're scaring me now.

I wanted to text back, *You should be scared.* But I truly didn't want him to worry.

It was never easy to explain to people what I did for a living. I always got weird reactions, as if folks just couldn't believe that anyone could be a detective in real life. My husband was a case in point: Even he couldn't resist the stray joke or two. The only person who took my job at face value, and simply respected it, was my mother-in-law, Zuzanna, who waited eagerly for each case to be concluded and then debriefed me like a pro.

Good night, Trevor. I love you, I texted. I considered saying *I miss you,* but that wouldn't have been true, and I always tried to be truthful where emotions were concerned. Saying *I love you* was easy because it was true, even now when I was a little bit annoyed (mostly with myself). But I didn't miss him at that moment. I was actually kind of glad we were at opposite ends of the country.

Back at you, Olly. Sleep well.

I was relieved that he didn't parrot *I love you,* because both of us saying it would have been too gooey under the circumstances. *Back at you* was exactly right.

I padded down the hallway to a little lavatory with weathered wood walls and an overhead pull light. As I was washing my hands, I noticed a speck lodged under a fingernail, and flicked it out. It looked like dirt but it was weird dirt: dark and globular. Then, in a quick flush, the blood drained out of my head. I realized it wasn't dirt at all. It was a tiny dried pellet of Eve Exeter's blood. It had been decomposing under my fingernail all this time, and now it was swirling down the drain. Feeling dizzy and gutted, I sat down on the toilet seat and stared at my hands. They were shaking. They looked clean, but who was to say there hadn't been other tiny pellets of dried blood under other fingernails? Maybe I'd been shedding them all day. Maybe I'd rubbed my nose and unwittingly inhaled particles of the dead woman's body.

What am I doing with my life? I wondered. *Is this really what I want?* Would it be so awful to work at a regular boring job—the kind where dead people's blood doesn't worm its way under your fingernails, and you have time left over at the end of the day to pick out curtains and new plates? To daydream and grow herbs and make pasta Bolognese? If I had a normal job, I would get a puppy and take it for long walks . . .

I slipped into bed dreaming of puppies, completely forgetting about snakes. (I think, after seeing the killer hauled away, I may have fallen prey to the wishful delusion that all the snakes had slunk away too.) I closed my eyes and reassured myself that everything was okay now. Trevor and I had had a fight, not our first, and had come through it pretty well. Knock on wood, we would have a nice apartment in July. I allowed myself to feel happy. And grateful. Trevor had done an amazing job. The apartment was bigger than the one we had, and that was the main thing we (or I) had wanted. More importantly, I was going to do better at responding to texts, no matter what was going on around me. Because normal life keeps rolling along, even while bullets are flying and people are dying, and if I was going to continue in this line of work, I would have to find a way to do justice to both.

CHAPTER SIXTY-TWO

Holiday Postmortem

The next morning, amid a lot of hugging and promises to stay in touch, the remaining guests left the ranch. Kathy and Dave drove off in their RV. Nova gave Barbara, Bree, and Peter a ride to the airport in her rented car. Jacob Korn hired an Uber. No one offered to host another Sigma Delta Tau reunion; one had been more than enough. As our flight didn't depart from Santa Fe until early evening, Merritt and I stayed behind to spend a quiet Memorial Day with our hosts.

"It all began back in college," Merritt said, "when Eve stole Kathy's discovery about the role sirtuins play in the aging process."

"You must be joking. What could that old villainy possibly have to do with Eve being murdered by her husband forty years later?" Fitz said.

A fat brown cigar was pinched between the first two fingers of his hand. He hadn't lit it. He seemed to just like holding it that way, with his pinkie (the one with the big turquoise ring) standing tall.

"Sweetheart, please let Aubrey get a bit more of the story out before you interrupt," the General said.

"All right, all right," he grumbled. "But we don't need to start so far back, do we? I just want to know why he did it. Don't try and tell me it was the damn IPO. That's a damn stupid reason to shoot your wife."

Merritt smiled indulgently and took a sip of her iced tea. We'd just had lunch, and the plates were still on the table. It felt pleasant to linger on the shaded veranda, with the desert stretching out and the red hills in the distance. There was nowhere to go and no more work to be done. It was a holiday, and the whole point of it was simply to spend time with friends.

"I'm sorry, Fitz." Merritt dabbed her lips with a napkin. "But we *do* need to start that far back, if we want to understand why the murder happened."

"Carry on, Aubrey," the General said. She probably didn't mean it to sound like a military order, but it did.

"As we know, Eve was awarded a prestigious fellowship based on that stolen work and, after earning her doctorate at MIT, was asked to join the faculty. For the next three decades, she enjoyed virtually unlimited access to resources—money, time, laboratory space—to support her supposedly groundbreaking research into the biochemical mechanisms of aging. But despite all the support she was getting at MIT, her research never amounted to anything. Eventually the scientific world stopped watching her every move, and her status at the university was eclipsed by ever-younger colleagues who couldn't care less about her early promise. It seemed that her glory days were far behind her—until she got the idea of creating a sirtuin supplement. Which she did. Sirt-X changed everything for her. It made her a contender again in the scientific community, and raised her long-dormant hope that she could indeed make a worthwhile contribution to the world."

"Amazing. Did Barbara tell you this?" Fitz asked.

"She revealed quite a bit. I think she was glad to unburden herself. I'm filling in the gaps, of course, but I'm probably not far off."

"Those two had an odd relationship," he observed.

"Apparently they were quite close over the years, despite what we saw this weekend. While Eve publicly disdained Barbara's fawning hero worship, she apparently made good use of it privately, even to the point of using Barbara as a close confidante."

"And how does Conrad fit in?"

"Eve met him shortly after her discovery of Sirt-X. He was having his own problems in academia. His teacher ratings were subpar, and his record of publications was skimpy. A rumor that he was a sexual predator followed him persistently, increasing in volume from one semester to the next, with, as yet, no specific charges being filed, perhaps because his ambitious victims feared—correctly, I believe—that bringing a harassment case against a faculty member would slow their job offers to a trickle. Although he was something of an academic failure, he was a shrewd entrepreneur. He immediately recognized the huge market potential of Eve's new supplement.

"Eve and Conrad quickly understood what they could do for each other. Eve had the surefire product that would make Conrad's fortune and prop up his flagging reputation. Conrad had the expertise to take Eve's brainchild into the real, cash-producing world. In partnership—perhaps only in partnership—they could each reach the pinnacle of their careers. They married within months of meeting; shortly after that, Lifespan, Inc., was born. Under Conrad's direction, Sirt-X was manufactured in a third-rate facility in Thailand. Advertised widely and available for purchase on the company website, sales grew faster than predicted. In time, a public stock offering was scheduled. Their fortunes and the fortunes of others—notably IT expert Jacob Korn, an early investor—were about to be made.

"But all along Eve had had a secret psychic vulnerability: guilt. A part of her was aware that she had stolen her sorority sister's work, that her position and reputation had not been fairly earned. Over the years she'd worked hard to push this knowledge into the recesses of her mind, and she'd had some success. But in her private moments, she was haunted by the fear that the scaffolding of her life would crumble if her work was ever scrutinized.

"Karma came in the form of negative product reviews. When more and more customers on a Reddit discussion board reported unexplained rashes after using Sirt-X, her anxiety spiked and didn't subside. She complained to Barbara that she was experiencing agitation, intrusive thoughts, insomnia. That when she did sleep, she had frightening dreams of falling from great heights. She was terrified that, if Sirt-X was examined too closely, she would be questioned and doubted. Like a child she would be called upon to 'show her work,' and the world would finally discover she was a fraud."

"So sad. And all because of a mistake she made forty years ago," remarked the General.

"A mistake she never bothered rectifying," Merritt said sternly. "I suspect something changed in her when she saw those customer complaints. Was there a moral reckoning? Did she crave redemption? Perhaps it could be earned by doing honest science at last. If she pulled Sirt-X off the market until its safety was proven, she just might experience the true self-respect that had always eluded her.

"So, to her husband's shock and horror, and the dismay of her colleagues at Lifespan, she called for an immediate stop in production until further testing could be done. She wanted human trials this time—double-blind and placebo controlled.

"Conrad knew that a sudden stop in production would spook potential investors. The IPO he'd been working toward for years—the one that would make him rich and rehabilitate his professional reputation—would fall apart. He also knew that the kind of trials his wife was proposing were outrageously time-consuming and costly. They were well beyond the capabilities of a start-up such as Lifespan, and they probably always would be. What's more, he believed that additional product research was completely unnecessary. Supplement manufacturers were under no obligation to reach FDA standards of safety and efficacy. It was widely understood that consumers proceeded at their own risk.

"Basically, what his wife was demanding would effectively kill their fledgling company just when it was on the verge of great success. She was a research scientist; she couldn't be expected to know these things. But he was a businessman, and he couldn't possibly allow her to have her way when the wealth and glory he felt entitled to were so close at hand.

"At the same time, Conrad understood the danger posed by the Reddit discussion board. Those unexplained rashes heralded a potential avalanche of future lawsuits, and that, too, would drive investors away. The obvious solution was to quash public complaints until after he and his cronies had cashed in.

"It was at this point, I think, that Conrad would have approached Jacob. He probably offered him a hefty sum in return for his services, and Jacob agreed to take care of the problem.

"The Reddit discussion board was soon flooded with fake rave reviews about Sirt-X. Having shrunk to a small percentage of the total, the negative reviews could be rejected as the rantings of a few neurotic hypochondriacs. Next the whole thread dropped precipitously in search results across platforms, replaced by studies that referred not to Sirt-X, but to a plethora of academic research papers on sirtuins, which by that time had attracted a lot of interest from the biomedical community. A casual Googler of Sirt-X would thus learn only that sirtuins were an extensively studied, naturally occurring protein that played an important role in the health of the human body, that the normal aging process depleted them, and that oral supplementation was being studied as a way of keeping their numbers up.

"Conrad was satisfied that Jacob's digital manipulations were enough to dispel the immediate risk to the IPO, but Eve was increasingly adamant about the need to stop production immediately and return to the testing stage. Thus far, no amount of persuasion had been able to deter her. When the couple arrived at the Muddy River Ranch for the Sigma Delta Tau reunion, Conrad was privately grappling with the question of how to handle his stubborn, irrational wife.

"I doubt he was contemplating murder at that point. Then something unexpected happened. Hotheaded Dave Lafferty stormed the barbecue wearing his holstered revolver and threatening Eve's life. This gave Conrad pause. What if the ex-cop carried out his threat? That would be an answer to his predicament! But of course that wasn't likely to happen, not with so many people milling around.

"Then fortune smiled again. At around midnight on Friday, Eve casually informed him that Joan had sprained her ankle and would not be joining Eve and Barbara at the pool at seven a.m. as planned.

"Conrad was steeped in entrepreneurial theory. For years he had lectured his students about the importance of recognizing opportunities, taking calculated risks, and making quick decisions. Do you remember, Fitz, at dinner on Saturday night, how reverently he talked about the successful entrepreneur's special talent for capitalizing on opportunities that others overlooked? He said that a great opportunity was like a comet shooting across the sky. You had to know its value when you saw it, and then you had to grab it quickly, before it disappeared.

"I believe that when Joan texted Eve to cancel her morning swim, just such a comet appeared in Conrad's mental sky, and all the stars fell into line behind it. First, the skeet shooting the day before had put a potential murder weapon in the hands of many guests, who also would have left fingerprints on the gun case and ammunition box. Second, the pool was located a good distance from the hacienda and guesthouse; it was hidden from view; and it was unlikely to be used at that hour of the morning. Third, a swimmer was vulnerable to attack. With her head in the water, she wouldn't be likely to see or hear a person approaching and would not be able to escape quickly if she did. If birdshot from a single-barreled shotgun did not kill her immediately, she could be pushed under the surface until she succumbed, with the water muffling her screams. Finally, the pool was the perfect depository for the murder weapon. Cleansed of fingerprints and DNA, the shotgun would implicate many while identifying no one. The murderer had only to walk away.

"Here was the perfect opportunity to protect his company from his wife's catastrophic demands, collect his well-deserved fortune as planned, and rehabilitate his reputation. All that was needed to make the plan foolproof was to keep Barbara away from the pool. So Conrad called on Jacob Korn again."

"And the rest is history," said Fitz. He struck a wooden match on the sole of his boot and held the flame to the end of his cigar. He puffed, waved the match out, and said, "Jacob silenced Barbara's phone so her alarm wouldn't go off, then came up to the hacienda to establish an alibi, in case the plan went south and he ended up needing one."

There was silence on the veranda as we all thought about what had happened. The single gunshot, a few seconds of thrashing, and a woman dead. It was quick, sad, and terrifying. It made me want to run home, put on baggy sweatpants, curl up on the couch beside Trevor, and watch something stupid on TV.

The General leaned back and gazed at Merritt. "Oh, Aubrey. I had no idea when I invited you that things would turn out like this."

"Do we ever know how things will turn out?"

"If you hadn't come, I don't know what would have happened."

Fitz snorted. "I do. Dave Lafferty would be facing trial for murder. And Conrad and Jacob would be back in Boston preparing to cash in when Lifespan went public."

"And Barbara would still be miserable in her marriage," said the General.

"And we wouldn't know who sent the death threat," I added, tooting my own horn a little bit.

"Eve would still be dead, though," Merritt said with deep regret. "You know, I've often thought what a privilege it is to solve murders. I'm always so grateful and humbled when justice is served. But I do wish there was a way to prevent them from happening in the first place. I wouldn't mind being out of a job."

Fitz chortled. "You want to change human nature, is that it? Ha! Good luck!"

The General agreed. "I'm afraid you'll never run out of work, my friend."

"Like an undertaker," Merritt said dryly.

"Or a soldier," the General added matter-of-factly.

"Or an artist," said Fitz with a faint smile. A puff of smoke swirled around his head and disappeared into a vast sky of unbroken blue.

Acknowledgments

My first thanks goes to my wonderful former agent, the late Esmond Harmsworth, to whom this book is dedicated. Everyone needs someone in their corner, and he was always in mine, no matter how many genres I wrote in and how many pseudonyms I acquired. It is very unlikely that I would have a career without him.

I am also grateful to the terrific people at Berkley. Tom Colgan and Carly James's smart, sensitive editing brought out the best in Olivia's story. Copy editor Angelina Krahn caught a dozen mistakes that had slipped by me. Loren Jaggers, Jessica Plummer, and Anna Venckus tirelessly ensure that Olivia's story reaches the widest possible audience, and a whole flock of dedicated professionals—designers, production specialists, salespeople, and others—worked behind the scenes to bring this book to life. A special shout-out goes to Emma Ladji, whose audiobook narration perfectly captures Olivia's spirit and all the nuances of the text.

The good people at Aevitas Creative Management are doing tremendous work in bringing Aubrey and Olivia to foreign markets, and in arranging media sales in this country too. Thank you to Kayla Grogan, Allison Warren, Ruby Rechler, Erin Files, Mags Chmielarczk, Kate Mack, and Lily Stephens. I am thrilled to be working with agent Chris Bucci, who gives me excellent creative feedback and valuable guidance on what might come next.

My family and friends are my treasures. Robert, Ben, and Ellen Sophia know how important they are to me and how grateful I am for their support. Carol and Kurt Harrington's good company brightens any day, and on several occasions they generously gave me an inspiring place to work. Holly Robinson is a spirited, unswerving companion on this journey of a lifetime. Len Rosen's wise heart is a gift to all who know him. And Hank Phillippi Ryan remains an inspiration in writing and in life.

Like all writers, I am indebted to bookstore owners, librarians, and reviewers who proudly support and promote the richness and vibrancy of our country's literary culture.